LIAR CITY

ALLIE THERIN

carina
press®

Recycling programs for this product may not exist in your area.

ISBN-13: 978-1-335-62194-8

Liar City

For questions and comments about the quality of this book, please contact us at CustomerService@Harlequin.com.

Carina Press
22 Adelaide St. West, 41st Floor
Toronto, Ontario M5H 4E3, Canada
www.CarinaPress.com

Printed in U.S.A.

For a moment in time on 4th Street.

LIAR CITY

Chapter One

The question everyone asks, of course, is what do we know about the empath mutation? We know the correlating empathic abilities threaten our privacy and the sanctity of our minds. We know the empaths cannot be allowed to freely use this empathy, because no amount of so-called pacifism gives them the right to use their abilities to discover emotions we do not consent to share. But there is a far more important question they ought to be asking: what don't *we know about the empaths?*

  —C. Stone, confidential funding memo to the Empath Initiative

Reece supposed if he'd been a *look on the bright side* kind of empath, he might have had a platitude ready, something pithy about how insomnia's single perk was being awake no matter what time someone called.

But platitudes and perks and so-called *bright sides* were for people who could still lie to themselves, and no one had been able to lie to Reece since March. So when his chirpy ringtone shattered the silence of the diner, he instead jerked in surprise and dropped his cup, which crashed to the Formica table and sent orange juice flooding right off the edge onto his jeans.

He cursed and scrambled out of the booth. Under the hard stare of the lone waitress, he snatched the phone up in gloved hands and fumbled to silence it. Ducking his head so he wouldn't have to meet her suspicious eyes, he squinted at the screen.

Unknown caller.

"Great," he muttered. This was obviously going to be good news, an unknown caller at four a.m. on a Tuesday. He put the phone to his ear. "Who is this?"

"We've never been properly introduced."

The man on the other side of the phone had a deep voice and a sugar-sweet Southern accent, and that was the extent of what Reece could read. Even before March, he'd despised how electronics stripped a voice, replacing a symphony with a cheap music box. Now it grated on him to no end to have to flounder blindly with a stranger. "How did you get this number?"

"Seattle's only got two empaths. I'd wager everyone has your number."

Reece narrowed his eyes. "Not my new one. And that wasn't an answer."

His thigh was already growing cold and sticky. He balanced the phone in the crook of his neck as he grabbed a cheap napkin from the dispenser and scrubbed at his jeans. The napkin shredded against the fabric without soaking up any juice.

There was a noise in the caller's background, a rushing sound, as the man said, "Maybe Detective St. James gave it to me."

Please. Jamey would eat her own badge first. "Maybe you be straight with me or I hang up."

"Aren't you awful prickly for an empath?"

"I don't like phone calls." Were those cars Reece was hearing? A highway, perhaps?

The deep drawl rolled through the phone like a lazy river. "I'm Evan Grayson."

The hairs on the back of Reece's neck rose. He knew that

name from somewhere, like the echo of a dream that had vanished in the daylight. "Should I care?"

"You—"

"More importantly: are you driving right now?"

There was a pause.

"I knew it," said Reece. "You shouldn't talk on the phone when you're behind the wheel. It's dangerous for you and everyone else on the road."

"That's not more important than my name."

"Yes it is. Cell phones cause one out of every four car crashes in the US."

"You've got no idea who I am," Grayson said, "and the empath priorities of a Care Bear."

"Just doing my part to keep the streets safer. Somebody should and it's obviously not going to be you." Reece sat back down on the dry side of the booth. He was still being watched by the waitress, but then, she'd had eyes on him since he came in. More specifically, she'd had eyes on his gloves, and it wasn't the stare of someone wanting a phone number from the short, skinny guy covered in juice. He lowered his voice. "So, Evan Grayson, what do you want?"

"Are you sitting down?"

"Dancing, actually. I can't contain my joy that I'm party to your four a.m. reckless endangerment—"

"Tell me you're sitting."

Sittin'. Reece glanced out the droplet-streaked window at the dark street beyond, where a liquor store's neon signs illuminated the flecks of sleet in the falling rain. Even stripped by the phone, the out-of-place accent was a shot of unexpected warmth against the freezing November night, and Reece's defenses were apparently cold traitors because he found himself answering instead of hanging up. "Yes, I'm sitting."

"There's been a murder."

Reece fumbled the phone. He seized it in both hands before it could fall. He clutched it too tightly, clenching his teeth.

Grayson's voice floated up from the speaker, tinny and distant. "Did you drop your phone?"

Reece put it back to his ear. "No," he lied.

"Now you know why you needed to sit. I'm used to empath pacifism. Most of y'all don't even like that word."

Reece took a hard breath. Blew it out. He couldn't make out a single emotion in that drawl and had no idea if he was being mocked. "So why tell me about it?" he said tightly, trying to shove away encroaching thoughts of human cruelty, of pain and suffering beyond his help.

"Because this murder is gonna be the biggest case of Detective St. James' career and she's got nothing."

Reece's stomach dropped. "Nothing?"

"No leads. No theories. No clues. The city's not gonna take her failure well. You might know what an unhappy press is like."

He swallowed hard. He knew exactly how unforgiving the press could be, and the thought that the news might drag Jamey through that same mud—but no, she wasn't a fool who ran her mouth like him, and there was no better person to solve a major crime. "If there's something to find, she'll find it."

"Unless finding it would take an ability she doesn't have. An ability only a handful of folks with delicate ears have. Pretty sure you know where I'm going with this."

"What I *know*," Reece said, free hand balling into a gloved fist, "is that Jamey would call me if she needed an empath."

"For a petty theft? Sure. Grand larceny, even, assuming no one got scratched. But the way I hear it, Detective St. James would take a bullet before she called her precious baby brother to a homicide."

Reece tightened his jaw. "I would help her with anything."

"That's why I called. She's at the Orca's Gate Marina."

And Grayson hung up.

Reece stared at his phone in disbelief, then slapped it down on the table with a huff. He didn't know Evan Grayson from the president. He could be a bully wanting to ridicule the empath aversion to violence. He could be another anti-empathy activist who'd dreamed up a new conspiracy. He could be simply *lying*; thanks to the phone, Reece wouldn't know.

He bit at one gloved thumb and worried it between his teeth. He'd noticed Jamey's car was gone at three a.m. when he'd given up on falling back asleep and gotten off her couch for a drive. But he hadn't thought anything of it. Jamey didn't need much sleep and sometimes she was out at night. It didn't mean she was on a case. It didn't mean Grayson was telling the truth. And it certainly didn't mean his sister could use his help.

He found himself dialing her number anyway.

Four rings, then voicemail. He dropped his phone to the table again and buried his face in his hands, his pulse too loud in his ears. Was he really considering going to the scene of a—

He cut off the thought before the word formed, but he was already on his feet. If there was even a chance Jamey needed him, he would be there.

As he approached the register at the end of the bar counter, the waitress came over with dragging steps and stopped a few feet away. She pointed at his hands. "You never took off your gloves."

His fingers automatically flexed inside the stiff material. "Of course I didn't—"

"I thought you were just cold when you came in. But you're an empath, aren't you?"

Great, another place to cross off his list of insomnia haunts. "I'm also a Pisces, but no one ever asks about that." Under her relentless stare, he reached for his wallet, pointing back to the booth with his other hand. "If you have a rag, I can—"

She recoiled. "How did you know I was pissed about having to clean up?"

"There's juice everywhere, anyone would be—"

"Are you reading my mind?"

"Emotions aren't—"

"I thought the gloves keep us safe from empathy!"

Reece bit his lip, then said, "They do."

He knew it would be a lie before he said it. And sure enough, the sound rang sour in his ears, like hearing himself sing off-key.

The gloves did block his empathy, that part was true, but it would take only a second to yank them off and get bare hands on her bare skin. Only a second for the touch of his hands to shred every mask and expose her true emotions to him, clear as words on a page, whether she wanted to share them or not.

And she was still safe. He'd never read her without consent. No empath would. It was a lie to say the *gloves* kept people safe because what kept people safe was the empaths themselves.

But he wanted to drive the fear from her eyes, so he chose the lie she and the rest of the public needed to believe.

No one knows the gloves can't stop you from hearing those lies now—

Reece quickly shoved the thought away. He put half of his meager cash on the counter, enough to cover the juice, tax, tip and extra for the cleanup. "Sorry about the mess." At least it wasn't another lie.

He pulled his hood over his dark hair as he pushed out the doors of the diner, the bell jingling too brightly behind him as he darted through the sleet to his car.

It was closing on five a.m. by the time Reece arrived at the marina north of the city, and his clothes were still damp with rain and juice despite blasting the heat the entire drive. He slowed his car as he approached the turn-in, his pulse speeding up. There was a police perimeter set up at the entrance, and what looked like most of the force in the parking lot beyond, whirling red and blue lights bright against the night's tenacious darkness. Mixed in with the cruisers was an ambulance, a black Explorer—and the unmarked navy blue Charger the Seattle Police Department had given Jamey.

Reece gritted his teeth. He'd wanted Grayson to be wrong.

He pulled up to the barricade and an officer in a puffy coat tapped on the driver's window, which was luckily the one that still worked. The previous owner had not been kind to the car, but that's why it had been in Reece's budget. He managed to roll the window halfway down with only a grunt of effort.

The officer shone his flashlight into the car, making Reece's eyes water. "This is a crime scene. You should be in bed, kid."

Cold rain peppered Reece's face as he held up his consultant ID card, a recent gift from the SPD's public relations front man, Liam Lee.

Your big mouth might make me less work if the press knows you're officially part of the team, Liam had said, when he'd created the card for him.

Your big sister is worth putting up with her wreck of a brother, more like, but Reece would grudgingly admit the card came in useful.

"Oh!" The officer glanced at the card, but he was more interested in the gloves. "You're the detective's brother. I've heard about you. Did she call you in?"

"Why else would I have come?" Reece said, because *no* was the wrong answer.

The officer jerked his head toward the chaos beyond. "Go on in. I'll tell her you're here."

Reece drove down to the lot and parked his Smart car next to Jamey's navy blue Charger. He killed the engine but sat in the car, fingers clenched tight around the steering wheel. The tiny space seemed claustrophobic and overheated as he tried to pretend his rapid breaths weren't loud enough to drown out the rain dotting his roof.

This Grayson guy had been right about where Jamey was. Based on the slew of officers on scene, he was likely also right about why. And as much as Reece wanted to turn around and drive anywhere else, Grayson might also be right about Jamey needing his help.

He stared at the whirling red and blue lights as he tried to slow his breathing. The police would let him help, even on a case like this. *Especially* on a case like this. No matter how much buzz the empathy bans were getting, they weren't in place yet, and most law enforcement were still happy to exploit empathy if it got the results they wanted.

A shock of freezing wet air swirled in as the driver's door of his Smart car was yanked open.

"What are you doing here?"

Jamey had found him, her tall figure bundled in a thick coat and a hat tugged over her dark curls. There were stress lines at the corners of her deep brown eyes, but the sight of her was still steadying enough to slow Reece's heart to something close to normal.

He tried for a smile and managed a grimace. "Possibly having a panic attack?"

She huffed and moved to shield his open door from the worst of the rain. "You don't want to be here."

"I really don't."

"How did you find this place?" She wrinkled her nose. "And why do you smell like oranges?"

Ugh, her nose was too good. "I got a call that you needed my help."

She frowned. "Who?"

"Some guy with this outrageous Southern accent. Said his name was Evan Grayson."

Jamey blanched.

Reece's heartbeat promptly rocketed right back up. "Funny," he said, gaze locked on the fear on her face, "he seemed to think I should know his name too. Who—"

"Out of the car." Reece started to twist out of his seat, but Jamey, as always, was faster. She grabbed him by the arm and extracted him with one easy tug. "Let's go."

"Go where?" he asked, as she steered him through the rain and the parking lot, past a barrier set up around a Ford Transit with a smashed headlight and toward a plastic tent stamped *Property of Seattle Police Department.*

"Somewhere I can keep an eye on you."

"Who's Evan Grayson?"

Jamey shook her head. "Not right now," she said. "This is a homicide scene and you're three seconds from a panic attack. We're not talking about Grayson too."

"But how could Grayson make it worse?"

"Not *now.* You're already a mess."

"When am I ever anything else?" he muttered bitterly.

"Stop," she said. "I know better than anyone that your compassion's a strength."

She tugged his arm. He sighed and tried to make his legs move faster.

The tent was at the end of the parking lot, right before the edge of the tarmac and a sharp drop-off to the ocean beyond. Past the tent was an arched sign that read *Orca's Gate Marina,* adorned with a smiling killer whale that seemed inappropriately cheerful, given the circumstances. Beneath the sign, a well-lit wooden ramp led to a collection of pristine yachts and private sailboats moored at the docks.

When they reached the tent, Jamey abruptly paused, one hand on the plastic flap. "Put your hands in your pockets."

Hide his gloves? He drew back. "Since when do I embarrass you?"

She gave him a funny look. "Since never?"

He folded his arms over his chest, but that had been unfair of him. She'd looked out for him his whole life. Whatever her reason, it would never be shame.

The icy rain dampened his hair as she bent to his eye level. "I know what you think—that if you show you're willing to hide, it will make people more nervous about empaths," she said. "But just this once. Trust me."

He sighed. "You know I do."

She was studying his face. "You were sleeping when I left. I guess that didn't last much longer."

"I look that bad, huh?"

"Don't be a jerk," she said. "I do notice your insomnia."

"Yeah, well, nightmares will do that to you."

"They'll stop soon." Her promise was twisted into discordance and he cringed. Her shoulders dropped an inch. "Sorry," she said. "I wish I really believed that. You used to sleep like a baby."

He blew out a breath. "You used to be able to lie to me. A lot's changed."

She gestured pointedly around the marina. "I would like to have changed you running mindlessly toward anywhere there are people in pain or you think you can help. This is the last place you should be right now."

There was a strained edge to her voice, a tense set to her shoulders. He tried for a lighter tone, even if only for a moment. "Careful with that concern. People will wonder which one of us is the empath."

She made a face. "No they won't. The touchy-feely shtick is your thing, just like I don't call you for a spot at the gym."

"I don't even know what that means."

"Exactly."

As she pushed the plastic tent flap aside, he jammed his hands deep in the pockets of his hoodie and said, "Grayson's name put fear on your face."

She hesitated. "It was—"

"Don't tell me it was my imagination. I'm an empath. It's never my imagination." He kept his gaze on her. "Nothing scares you. Why does Grayson?"

He watched subtle emotions dance across her face as she tried to decide what to tell him. Finally, she said, "Because I think this is his kind of crime."

The hairs on the back of Reece's neck rose. "You're afraid Grayson might be behind this?"

"No." She ducked into the tent, her words barely reaching his ears. "I'm afraid he might show up."

Chapter Two

...while acknowledging SB 1437 would impose the strictest limits on empathy yet, bill sponsor Senator Hathaway said, "We simply cannot have empaths in government jobs. If one can know another's emotions, it would be too easy to manipulate them, and we have only the empaths' word for it that they would never. Our citizens must be able to trust that their elected officials operate with autonomy."

When asked for her response to critics who point out the bill will impact even nonpolitical agencies, Hathaway replied, "To those who call the act fearmongering or overreach, I say it is only the start of the protections we need."

—excerpt from the Emerald City Tribune,
"Proposed bill would limit empath involvement in government, politics"

Inside the police tent, a space heater ran on a generator, and while it didn't make things warm, it was better than outside. More than a dozen officers were packed into the tent, mostly clustered around a folding table set with cardboard carafes of coffee. Two officers were hunched over a second folding table, concentrating on a laptop.

Several heads turned in Reece and Jamey's direction as they entered, but most saw Jamey and went right back to their business. The few interested looks that persisted were on her, not Reece, and people being interested in Jamey certainly wasn't new.

She pulled Reece against the plastic wall at the far side of the tent, officers shifting to give them a patch of space. "Stay here and keep a low profile until—"

"Low profile?" Reece matched her whisper. "If you need an empath's help—"

"We can't have it." And before Reece could ask why the hell not, she said, "I'm getting you out of Seattle."

Reece's eyes widened. "I think you better tell me who Evan Grayson—"

But she touched a finger to her lips, so he clamped his mouth shut. A moment later, he heard the voice too.

"—of course, of course." A sleepy-eyed police officer, probably in his early thirties like Jamey, was pushing out from the crowd, a phone glued to the side of his face. His gaze zeroed in on Jamey. "Detective St. James would be happy to go back to the yacht—"

"Little busy here, Taylor," said Jamey.

"—and I'm sure she can answer your questions," Officer Taylor said into the phone. "I'm looking for her right now." Taylor covered the phone with one hand and mouthed *please*. "I'll drive the kid home," he whispered, jerking his head toward Reece. "How'd he wander into this mess?"

"I'm *twenty-six*," Reece said. "She's just tall."

"He's my brother," said Jamey.

Taylor's gaze darted between Jamey's light brown skin and Reece's paleness. "Half brother," Reece clarified, like he usually had to.

Taylor jammed his hand tighter over the phone's speaker. "Your *empath* half brother?" he hissed at Jamey. *"Here?* I am all for it, but if Parson finds out, aren't you gonna get sacked?"

"What?" Reece said sharply.

"I'm trying to get him out of here," Jamey said, ignoring Reece. "If it was up to me, I'd hide all the empaths in the Pacific Northwest."

"What a mess," Taylor bit out. "You know the FBI prick is already asking about the senator's anti-empathy bill? And he's trying to get Stensby to stop working on the list of pulp mills you wanted—"

"No, we *need* that," she said. "The van's tires reeked of sulfur."

"I believe you," Taylor said quietly, "but that prick doesn't because the rest of us can't smell it."

"Maybe the rest of you should—smell harder," Reece interjected, with a quick glance at Jamey. She was usually so careful about hiding things like that. If this case was bad enough to have her slipping up—

Maybe he wouldn't think about that.

There was conflict in Jamey's eyes as she looked from Reece to the wooden ramp that led to the moored yachts. "Fine, I'll talk to Agent Nolan, but quick," she said to Taylor. "*Please* stay with Reece."

"I don't need a babysitter!" Reece snapped, as Taylor flashed her a thumbs-up.

But she'd already disappeared.

Reece sighed. He looked over at his new companion, who was now thumbing through the phone. He opened his mouth, but before he could ask Taylor why Reece showing up could get Jamey fired, his own phone vibrated in his pocket.

With a frown, Reece pulled it out.

Stay where your sister tells you

Don't wander off

Goose bumps broke out over his skin. Like with the call, there was no phone number to see, but it had to be Grayson—Reece could count on one hand the number of people with his new number and have fingers left over.

But why would Grayson send a text like that? Reece was here to help Jamey. Where would he possibly wander off to at a *crime scene*?

He jammed the phone back into his pocket. He glanced at Taylor again, at his open, guileless face. High time *someone* gave him some information tonight. "So." He bit his lip. "Some case, huh?"

"No kidding," Taylor agreed. "Stensby wanted to call you and Jamey shut him down. I thought we weren't going to even talk about bringing an empath here, but I guess the case is crazy enough to make her risk it."

Reece coughed awkwardly. "Guess so."

"Stensby said Jamey won't call you at all anymore if anyone is so much as bruised. The last few months, the rule's been no violence, or else no empath consultant."

Reece tried to shrug it off. "It's been complicated." *Hey, I'm not even lying.*

"Ah." Taylor nodded knowingly. "Girlfriend." At Reece's scoff, he shrugged. "Boyfriend?"

"There's no one," said Reece. "Who wants an empath around?"

"I do," said Taylor, which wasn't a lie and which Reece found reassuring right up until Taylor added, "And none of the officers are going to rat you out for showing up. A senator murdered on a billionaire CEO's yacht—this story's going to be big enough. Can you imagine what the press would say if they knew we'd added an empath to this horror show?"

Horror show. Cold sweat broke out on Reece's brow. He curled his fists tightly in his pocket and tried to focus on

Jamey. Grayson had said she needed his help. The dead didn't have feelings; they wouldn't need an empath for those already lost. "Any leads?"

"Just the witness we can't reach."

"Can't reach?"

Pity softened Taylor's eyes. "Hard to talk when you're catatonic."

Oh.

"The theory is he actually saw the killer. But there's no reaching him, unless—" Sudden hope lit Taylor's face. "Is that why you're here?"

Don't wander off, Grayson's text had said.

But this wasn't *wandering off*. Grayson didn't know about the witness—or maybe the witness was how Reece could help. And whoever Grayson was, he didn't get to tell Reece what to do.

Reece adopted the most casual voice he had. "Remind me: where was the witness?"

It was easy enough to ask Taylor to grab him a cup of coffee, then slip out of the tent without anyone noticing. Reece pulled his hood up again against the rain and tried to dodge the worst of the ice-edged puddles as he scurried across the dark parking lot to the ambulance tucked in among the cruisers.

He knocked on the vehicle's door, and an EMT with a blue uniform and bloodshot eyes poked her head out. He held up his hands, making the gloves obvious. "Can I see the witness?"

Relief crossed her face, and she moved to let him enter, warmth washing over him as he climbed the two steps up into the cramped ambulance interior.

His gaze went straight to the middle-aged man on the gurney, propped in a sitting position and wired to unfamiliar machines. The man was staring blankly into space, a small spot of red blooming on the gauze beneath his nose. At least the poor man didn't seem to be in any pain.

"He's still catatonic?" Reece asked, as he pulled his damp hood back.

The EMT nodded. "I thought there was no way we were getting an empath on scene. Who called you in?"

"Detective St. James is my sister." Not actually an answer, but it was good enough to smooth the concern from the EMT's face. He gestured at the man. "Do we know his name?"

"Vincent Braker, marine mechanic who services motors in the dry dock here at the marina. His time card puts him off-shift at eleven. We think he hit the bar down the street then came back for his car."

"People shouldn't do that," Reece said, before he could stop himself. "Drunk driving kills thousands every year."

She shot him an unimpressed look. "Is this really the time?"

He winced. "Sorry." He gestured at himself with gloved hands. "Empath. Sometimes my feelings just kind of come out of my mouth before I can stop them."

"Aren't you guys supposed to be all sweetness and rainbows and pacifism?"

"*Pacifist* and *polite* aren't actually synonyms," he said weakly. "And I'm really sorry he's hurt. What happened to him?"

The EMT ran a finger down her chart. "Well, his blood alcohol level was .07, so that part of the story checks out."

The EMT's forehead was wrinkled, like she was worried about more than Braker's drinking. "What part doesn't check out?" he asked.

She hesitated. "Nothing."

Lie. "It's a little more than nothing, isn't it?"

The EMT startled, her gaze going to his gloves again, and he could have kicked himself. People were jumpy enough with what they knew empaths could do. No one needed to know an empath was walking around capable of *more*.

But then the EMT relaxed. "Of course I can tell *you*. Detective St. James was the one to ask for the tests. She said to keep it private, but if she knew you were coming, she must have intended you to know."

"She must have," Reece said, a little weakly.

"His catecholamines are way above normal." His confusion must have shown on his face, because she clarified, "Adrenal hormones. He's got blood work like I'd expect from the Hulk—well, if the Hulk was catatonic."

Why would Jamey have wanted to test a catatonic man's adrenal hormones? Reece took a seat on the bench opposite Braker and stuck the tip of his gloved thumb between his teeth. "If he's catatonic, what makes everyone think he's a witness?"

"He's the one on the 911 call." He glanced at her, confused again, but she nodded. "On the call, he says he thought he heard screaming, then suddenly starts screaming himself and the call is cut. We were first response and found him curled in a ball on the dock." She gestured at the gurney. "Already gone."

Reece's chest twisted.

"I don't know much about empaths." She snorted. "Guess no one really does, though, right? That's why you have to wear those gloves, why Stone Solutions has all those ads." She mimicked a man's deep voice. *"Stone Solutions, Defending American Minds."*

"I've seen the commercials," Reece said flatly.

"I guess you would have," the EMT said awkwardly. "All I meant was, can you help him?"

"In theory," Reece said.

He hadn't done a read of his own on anyone since March,

since the one he emphatically *did not think about*. But empathy might be able to help now, and he'd do it if it could save Braker.

Except getting through Braker's catatonic state would take surgical precision, the kind Reece had never learned. And since March his empathy felt about as controlled as an angry bear on a fraying leash. "Maybe we should call a stronger empath. Cora Falcon, at the Seattle Veterans Medical Complex, is—"

"We tried her already. She's not answering her phone."

He frowned. That was unlike Cora. "Did you try the hospital? She works first shift, maybe she got there early."

"We tried that too. I know it'd be controversial, getting an empath involved in this murder, but—" The EMT let out a frustrated huff. "Nothing we try helps."

Reece couldn't care about controversy, not when more red was blooming on the gauze beneath Braker's nose. "Why haven't you moved him to the ER?"

"We were about to and then we got the orders."

"Orders?"

"Staff already on-site can care for him but no new doctors." She gestured at Braker again. "And no hospital."

That didn't make sense. "Who could give an order like that? *Why* would you give an order like that?"

"I have no idea," she admitted.

Reece was in no state to use empathy—hadn't been in months. But Braker was in a worse state that he was. "He can't consent to my read," Reece pointed out, but he was already moving to sit on the edge of Braker's gurney. "And evidence obtained with empathy is inadmissible in court. The defense might move for everything he says to be thrown out because an empath woke him up."

"I don't care about legal hypotheticals," she said impatiently. "I care about his life."

Reece did too. He stared at the man's blank eyes, his too-slow blinks. "I don't know if I can help him."

"No reason not to try, though, right? Procedural and privacy issues aside, they said in basic that empathy itself is safe as snuggles."

Reece huffed a half laugh at the ridiculous metaphor. "It is. Empathy can't hurt anyone."

Lie.

He stilled.

Lie?

Reece touched gloved fingers to his lips. How? Lies were *intentional*; the speaker had to believe they were lying. He'd been telling the truth.

"See?" she said. "If it can't hurt, you should try."

"I, uh. Right." He tried to push his confusion to the side. There was a catatonic man who needed help, and there was no part of Reece that actually believed empathy could hurt anyone. "I—"

In his pocket, his phone vibrated again.

Oh no. No, Reece wasn't going to look at that—except he'd snuck away to the ambulance, and his stupid guilty empath conscience was already pulling the phone out of his pocket.

Another text, from an unknown number, and this one made Reece's heart stutter.

Don't touch the witness

Chapter Three

Austin; Phoenix; Los Angeles; San Francisco. Four crime scenes; four dead empaths. Four stories skipped by all news outlets; four police reports redacted to the point of uselessness.

This is some bullshit.

—Detective Briony St. James' personal notes

The wooden dock shifted under Jamey's feet as she strode quickly past rows of rain-slick moored yachts pearlescent against the blackness of the choppy sea.

Reece was right; she rarely felt fear and she wasn't a fan of it now. But she could appreciate the way it put the world in knife-sharp focus. She'd need that focus if even half the rumors about Evan Grayson were true.

If he really was the Dead Man.

Half the force would argue the Dead Man was fake, nothing more than another empathy conspiracy theory. Jamey couldn't blame them. Who believed in shadow agents, rumored to appear anytime crimes involved empaths? It sounded ridiculous.

Except Jamey had followed the rumors since their first whispers, a couple years ago. And now the senator behind the toughest anti-empathy bill ever drafted was dead, and who was on Reece's phone within hours? It didn't matter that Jamey had kept her suspicions out of tonight's reports and run distractions. Grayson was real and Grayson knew about Senator Hathaway's murder and Grayson had *called her brother*.

Ten to one he was already on his way to Seattle, and she had to get Reece out of here.

The yacht with the bodies, *The Bulwark*, loomed up ahead but a man she didn't recognize was coming straight toward her, in his late thirties, perhaps, with brown hair, pale skin, and narrowed eyes. "Detective! A word."

His voice was obnoxiously loud in the thin, cold air. She reluctantly stopped on the dock. "What kind of word, Officer…"

"Agent," he snapped. "Special Agent Nolan. We have a crisis."

"Triple homicide, yes," she agreed. "It's terrible."

"Terrible doesn't cover it, St. James. This isn't some random hobo. This is Senator Hannah Hathaway, dead from fuck knows what, on Cedrick Stone's yacht, in the town where American Minds Intact is headquartered. And not one single hippie at this crime scene seems able to put down the weed long enough to grasp what that means."

Random hobo? She'd definitely found Taylor's FBI prick. "What does weed have to do with anything?"

"I have to assume you and everyone else is smoking it. Why else would you take an officer off the highest-profile murder investigation in years to compile a list of pulp mills?"

The mud caked into the Ford Transit's tires had reeked of sulfur and wet wood, and she didn't have time to waste before following that lead. "I have a sensitive nose. I thought I smelled something."

"What, are you fucking pregnant or something? We have IDs on the two thugs murdered with the senator. They were obviously hired to kill Hathaway and they weren't from any pulp mills. It's a hit, we should be looking for the money trail."

Two bodies had been found with Hathaway. One of them had been a former wrestler and notorious muscle-for-hire with a long rap sheet. His neck had strangulation marks, deep enough to be made by an offensive lineman—but narrow and small, the right size to match a petite sixty-five-year-old senator who would have struggled to carry a full bag of groceries.

Jamey had a hard time believing the answers were going to be as straightforward as a hired hit.

"Who's *we*?" she said, instead of voicing her other thoughts. "The *highest-profile* murder investigation in years should mean FBI agents swarming this yacht like flies, ready for a big jurisdiction fight. Where are the rest of you?"

A muscle in Nolan's jaw twitched. "I don't know."

"You don't *know*?"

"I'm here from DC for a cruise. I know Lieutenant Parson, I got suckered into this because he called me personally. The FBI has a Seattle office; I was told more agents were on their way, but..." He gestured around the yacht.

Rare unease shivered down Jamey's spine. "But they're not here."

"That's not the only problem," Nolan said, his lip curling. "Now there's the security footage."

The marina itself normally ran security cameras throughout the parking lot. Those cameras had been shut off just after midnight, and the marina's staff were clueless as to how it had happened.

But the gas station across the street had a camera that caught the edge of the marina's exit. She'd watched the night's footage twice herself: a partial view, the edges of the bumper and body molding as a red car with wide tires came barreling out of the exit so fast it had fishtailed.

Then, twenty minutes later, thin and bald tires under a green bumper, driving out of the marina at a leisurely pace.

They'd already put out an APB on the second car, which was thought to be Vincent Braker's green Hyundai—although obviously their catatonic witness wasn't the one behind the wheel.

Forensics was still working to identify the make and model of the red car as soon as possible. The driver could be another witness—or in serious trouble.

"What happened to the security footage?"

"You tell me, Detective," he said, lip still curled. "Because all of a sudden, every file we got from the gas station is gone."

"Gone?"

"Technical issues," Nolan said, making air quotes around the words. "Your officers are still trying to recover the files. How hard can it be?"

Files vanishing before they could identify the car or the driver.

How very convenient that FBI agents would fail to show and technical issues block their investigation right when Evan Grayson got involved.

"The mayor called again," Nolan said. "American Minds Intact found out about the murder, and now we have the loudest opponents of empathy in the damn country claiming the senator was killed because of her anti-empathy agenda."

Jamey barely managed not to wince.

"This case is a shit show," he said. "I'd almost expect the Dead Man to show up, if I believed in ghosts."

He strode past her, continuing up the dock toward the tent and the parking lot, disappearing at the top of the ramp.

Ghosts.

Jamey had a folder in her desk at headquarters, kept in the locked lower drawer. It was full of cases she'd been collecting over the past two years. The most recent one was from the summer, another multiple homicide but with an empath among its victims. She'd requested records directly from San Francisco PD. The report had been barely two pages long, with no photos of the crime scene available and the empath's cause of death listed as drugs.

As if anyone who knew an empath would believe that.

There had been no arrests associated with those murders, and despite the shock of multiple deaths, it hadn't made national or even local news. It'd made the anti-empathy blogs, though, gleeful speculation that the mythical Dead Man had appeared to quiet the press and bring everyone to justice.

There were rumors about what Grayson considered justice too, and it didn't involve due process.

Reece needed to be long gone before Grayson got here.

Reece stared at the text on his phone, mind churning.

Don't touch the witness

How the hell did Grayson know what he was doing?

Before he could come up with an answer, his phone went off again.

Get out of there

Run

Reece shot to his feet, nearly dropping his phone with fumbling hands. The EMT was staring at him like he'd lost his mind, which might not be far from the truth. He looked helplessly toward the ambulance door. "I, um, I have to—"

The EMT's expression crumpled. "You're not leaving, are you? Look at him, he needs you."

There was more blood on the gauze under Braker's nose now. "Mr. Braker," the EMT said, pleading eyes on Reece. "We've got someone here to help you."

Was Reece really going to abandon this man to his catatonia because of some texts? Because of some inexplicable lies? No string of words mattered as much as this man's life.

Reece jammed his phone back in his pocket and perched on the edge of the gurney. He shoved down all of his nerves about the read; Braker hadn't given any signs of pain, but even if he did, Reece would take it in and deal with it.

It wouldn't be like March.

"Can you hear me at all, Mr. Braker?" The catatonic man wouldn't see them, but Reece held up his gloved hands anyway. "I'm an empath."

Braker jerked upright and screamed.

Shock sent Reece tumbling off the gurney and crashing to the floor. *"Help him."*

But the EMT was already in motion, elbow-deep in one of the overhead bins.

Reece rolled onto hands and knees and looked up just in time to see her grab a syringe. He flinched, covering his face as she went for Braker's neck.

The screaming stopped.

"Figures the empath isn't a fan of needles." The EMT was loud in the sudden silence. "You can look now."

Reece reluctantly peeked through his fingers. Braker was slumped on the gurney, eyes closed, chest slowly rising and falling. "What did you do?"

"Sedative," she said. "What did *you* do?"

There was a suspicion in her voice that hadn't been there a moment ago. Reece shook his head. "Nothing. I don't understand—"

The ambulance door swung open without a knock or a

warning, revealing a tall man with a hard mouth and wide eyes. "I thought I heard screaming—" His gaze landed on Reece and outrage blossomed. "Who the hell let this kid in here?"

"I did, Agent Nolan," the EMT said. "He's an empath."

"Empath?" Nolan's gaze darted to the gloves, then to Reece's face. "How did you find this scene?"

Reece cleared his throat. "It's complicated."

"Oh, it's not complicated," the EMT said, perky and helpful. "He's Detective St. James' brother."

That was the wrong thing to say, Reece instantly knew. Nolan's confusion hardened into anger. "Brother." He moved closer to Reece. "And is there a reason Detective St. James didn't tell the FBI she's got an empath brother?"

Shit. "Why should she?" he said defensively. "She's also got a ficus and too many shoes and I bet she didn't mention those either."

Nolan's lips pressed flat. "Putting aside that I found her brother, not her ficus, cozying up to our only witness, it's because the murder victim is Senator Hathaway."

Shit shit *shit.* Every empath in the country knew who that was, because Senator Hathaway had put forward the harshest anti-empathy bill ever drafted. Cora had railed against it yesterday because it would ban empaths from government work and she'd have to leave the veterans' hospital.

No wonder Reece wasn't supposed to be here.

Nolan's eyes were still narrowed "I'd like to know what an empath thinks he's doing at the scene of Hathaway's death."

"Trying to *help,*" Reece said, ignoring Nolan's eye roll. "I don't care about her job or her agenda. I'd be sorry for anyone this happened to."

"You sorry for that guy too?" Nolan jerked his head at

Braker. "And you thought your sister and your bleeding heart gave you the right to trespass on our investigation?"

"He was going to try to bring the witness out of catatonia," said the EMT.

Nolan stilled. "Empaths can do that?" He looked between Braker and Reece, the scorn slipping from his face. "Can *you* do that?"

Reece watched Braker's chest slowly rise and fall. "I don't know."

Nolan jerked his head at Reece's hands. "You still have your gloves on. Did you actually touch him?"

"No," Reece admitted. "But—"

"But nothing," said Nolan. "We need to know what he saw. Get your hands on this guy."

Reece looked at the EMT, but despite her lingering distrust, she nodded. "He's right. You didn't actually try."

Because Braker had *screamed*. Reece hesitated.

"I need to talk to him," Nolan said, as he bent over to examine Braker's face. "He's catatonic, for crying out loud, it's not like you can make him worse—" Nolan froze. "What the hell is that?"

Reece stared, his stomach curdling.

A thin trail of blood, like a tear, was trickling out from the corner of Braker's eye.

Reece staggered up to his feet. The EMT was already at Braker's side, on her radio, but Reece could only stare, disbelieving, at Braker's face.

No.

No, bleeding eyes were things that happened in nightmares, not real life.

Reece moved toward Braker but Nolan grabbed him by the hood, yanking him back. "What's happening to him?" Nolan demanded. "Was it something you did?"

"How could it be?" Reece snapped. "An empath couldn't hurt him if we wanted to!"

Lie.

Reece drew in a sharp breath. "Empathy can't hurt him." *Lie.* "I can't hurt him." *Lie.* His hand went to his mouth.

How was he lying? What the hell part of him could possibly believe that wasn't the truth?

The EMT was shining a light in Braker's eyes and muttering quick words into her headset, calling for backup. Nolan still had Reece's hood in his fist. "If you didn't do it," he said tightly, "can you fix it?"

Reece's gaze stayed fixed on Braker's bleeding eyes. Maybe Reece was the problem. Maybe part of him thought his empathy wasn't controlled enough for catatonia—that he was still too fractured since March.

And if his empathy could somehow hurt this poor man—

He rapidly shook his head *no*. "And don't ask me to try."

Nolan dropped Reece's hood, his hand going to the small of his own back, where Jamey kept her handcuffs. "Listen, kid—"

The EMT shoved between them, scrambling for something in the cabinets. Reece seized his chance. He darted for the stairs and leaped for the door.

If empathy could hurt Braker, Reece was going to put his out of reach.

As Jamey was running up the dock, Taylor was coming down, paper cup in hand. She skidded to a stop. "Who screamed?"

Taylor blinked. "I didn't hear anything."

She strained her ears but the screaming had stopped. There was nothing to hear but officers in the parking lot and the soft lapping of waves against yachts. Taylor was looking at her questioningly. Taylor—and only Taylor. "Where's Reece?"

"I was coming to ask you that." Taylor held up the paper cup. "I got his coffee."

"Coffee." Jamey took a breath through her nose. "Did he ask you to get that for him?"

"Yeah, he did," said Taylor. "And then he disappeared. I looked everywhere, but he's not in the tent, he's not in the parking lot—"

"Tell me you didn't tell him about the witness."

Taylor's eyebrows drew together. "He didn't already know?"

Jamey scrambled past him. Taylor chased at her heels, coffee cup still in his hand. "Jamey—"

Distantly, she heard the ambulance door smack the side of vehicle, sneakers on concrete, and then, most tellingly, the soft purr of a fuel-efficient engine.

And as she crested the top of the ramp and looked to the marina exit, there was nothing left to see but a pair of vanishing Smart car taillights.

And the turn signal. Of course.

She was nearly to her own car when Nolan came tumbling down from the ambulance. "Detective!"

She spun on her heel and met Nolan head-on. "What happened?"

"Your *empath brother*—" He stressed the words. "—fled a crime scene. The EMT says he told Braker he was an empath and our only witness started screaming bloody murder. No pun intended."

Jamey looked to the marina entrance where Reece's car had just disappeared. "He ran from someone who was screaming?"

"No," Nolan said pointedly. "He stuck around until Braker started bleeding from the goddamn *eyeballs*."

Shit.

"He's two seconds away from an arrest," said Nolan.

Jamey tried to push down her concerns enough to deal with

Nolan. "For what? You said he got close. Did he actually touch the witness?"

"Just because there was no contact—"

"No contact means no empathy, no Fifth Amendment violation, and forget assault or battery—empaths are incapable of even self-defense," Jamey said. "All flight, no fight."

Behind her, Taylor was sipping from the coffee as his gaze went back and forth between them.

"Don't worry," said Nolan. "I've got a bone to pick with you too. Did it slip your mind to tell me that one of Seattle's two empaths happens to be your brother?"

"Reece can't help with violent crime."

She turned away but Nolan got back in front of her. "Why the fuck not? Maybe you're sweating your DA throwing a fit, but the empathy laws can be interpreted a little more loosely than you might be used to. Your brother just pulls the witness out from catatonia, then leaves. He doesn't read the witness's emotions, we don't write it down, our evidence stays nice and admissible, see?"

"This isn't about trials and fruit of the poisonous tree," she said, because maybe Nolan was cavalier about bending the law, but she wasn't, and that wasn't the problem anyway. "We have to keep the empaths away from this investigation."

Nolan went a deep shade of red. "You don't have the authority to make that call."

"And *you* don't have the authority to force Reece to use empathy. He's still a person and he's still got rights, no matter how much Senator Hathaway wanted to change that."

Nolan went even deeper red. "So you'd rather let a murderer run loose in Seattle than inconvenience your brother?" His lip curled. "Don't be surprised when the press quotes me saying you're a disgrace to the force."

On Jamey's priority list, her own reputation fell somewhere

below finding jeans with a decent inseam. She'd lost her chance to catch up to Reece by car, so she turned away from Nolan and quickened her steps toward the tent.

Taylor scrambled after her. "For the record," she told him, as she slowed enough he could catch up beside her, "Reece won't touch caffeine." Between the empathy and the anxiety, he said his blood pressure didn't need any help rising. She plucked the half-full coffee out of Taylor' hands and took a long sip. "And you owe me one for losing him."

"Worth it to see you go head-to-head with Agent Jackass."

"Great, because I need a favor." She passed him back the cup. "Off the record." Taylor paused, tilting his head. "Can you get a fake driver's license made in a couple hours?" she said. "A good one?"

"You thinking of doing undercover work?"

"Not for me."

"But then—oh!" he said, understanding flashing on his face. "You thinking of hiding Reece from the empath controversy on this case? Probably a good idea; the press would lose their shit if we had an empath working Hathaway's murder. And, well." He coughed. "Considering what happened the last time Reece talked to the press…"

Ugh, even Taylor knew about that. But while having Reece on the case would be a public relations nightmare in more ways than one, having him on Evan Grayson's radar was worse. "There's a lot to hide him from."

"I'll see what I can do," Taylor promised.

Speaking of the press. Jamey stopped just outside the tent, pulling out her phone and turning to shield the screen as she sent a text. It wasn't strictly against the rules for an SPD detective to date their public relations manager, but it didn't mean they were advertising it to the force.

Did you mean it when you said your dad's charter was mine anytime?

Liam probably wouldn't be able to reply yet—they had a dead senator, his phone was probably ringing off the hook with reporters and politicians and conspiracy theorists—

But his answer came almost instantly.

Always

And despite her worries, Jamey felt the tiniest pang of hope. Maybe she really could put Reece out of Grayson's reach.

A second text came in from Liam: please tell me Reece isn't working this case.

Over my dead body, she sent back.

That would take approximately three SWAT teams, so good enough for me

She snorted. She'd call him in a minute. She sent Reece a text he'd see when he parked, and checked for flights from Seattle to Juneau. There was still a seat on an eleven-thirty direct. Perfect.

She heard the rumble of engines as she bought the ticket, and her gaze went back to the marina's entrance just in time to see the first local news van pull up.

"Circus is starting," Taylor said.

"And there goes Nolan." She pointed to the FBI agent, who was trudging up toward the barrier. "How long 'til he tells them I'm a disgrace to the force?"

Taylor snorted. "Guy's a prick. The same people who freak out over empathy and privacy don't think twice about letting their phones and internet browsers record every detail of their lives. Everyone sane knows empaths can't hurt anyone."

Jamey's gaze stole down to the marina, to the bobbing yacht with its bloody bodies. "Right," she said slowly. "What you said."

Chapter Four

Name: John Doe
Source of referral: self (walk-in)
Presenting concerns: nightmares
Assessment:
[This section intentionally left blank]
                    —*Seattle Veterans Medical Complex patient records,*
                            filed by empath therapist Cora Falcon

Call Liam the instant you park, asshole.

Reece huffed at his sister's text, but it'd be a lie to say he didn't deserve the insult. He would know.

Whether he deserved the missed call and waiting text from the unknown number—well. He cut the Smart car's engine but reached for the radio, turning it up until the bass was thumping loud enough to drown out any thoughts he might have about that.

He ran a thumb over the phone like a worry stone as his gaze stole out the windshield. The dawn was breaking behind him, illuminating the boardwalk across Alaskan Way. At this hour, and this temperature, the touristy space was deserted save for a pair of hardy seagulls, and beyond the wooden rails, the choppy ocean was as gray as the lightening sky. He focused on the water, on the colorless waves that were so reassuringly not red.

The radio crackled as the music faded. *"—breaking news sending shocks through Seattle this morning, with Washington Senator Hannah Hathaway found dead overnight at a local marina. Law enforcement has not yet released a statement, but the senator's death is reportedly part of a multiple homicide—"*

He turned the key with a violent twist, plunging the car into abrupt silence. He wasn't calling Liam, not yet.

He was calling Cora.

He chewed on his thumb as the phone rang. He and Cora were the only two empaths in Seattle, and that kind of solidarity would have made them friends regardless. But Cora was one of the kindest people Reece had ever met, a therapist who worked with veterans with PTSD. And after March, and the months of violent nightmares that made him sick, he'd finally reached out to her for help.

But it was as the EMT had said: the other empath wasn't answering her phone. It rang and rang until her voicemail picked up. *"Hi, you've reached Cora Falcon. I'm so sorry I missed you! Leave a message and I'll call you back."*

"Hey, it's Reece." He bit his lip. "Sorry to bother you. After yesterday I'm probably the last person you want to hear from."

There was a very good chance she'd never forgive him for coming in. After all, reading him had been so terrible it had made her *faint*. He could only hope she was too kind for grudges.

He cleared his throat. "Anyway, the nightmares I told you about—the eyes—something happened this morning that makes me think—well. Just call me? When you can?"

He hung up, stomach still roiling. It wasn't like he could tell her about the strange lies he'd heard himself say this morning. He couldn't tell her he was hearing lies at all. That was too big a secret to ask her to keep.

But what part of him could possibly believe he was telling a lie when he said *empathy can't hurt him*?

No, don't think about that. Think about something else, anything else.

He quickly glanced at his phone screen, where Grayson's unread text was still waiting. Grayson, who had put fear on his fearless sister's face.

Okay, maybe he should think about anything else *except* Grayson.

Reece stared at the icon a moment longer. He could ignore it. He *should* ignore it.

But ignoring people hurts their feelings, a little voice in his head said.

Oh, come on. This was different. Completely different. Surely his prickling conscience didn't apply here?

"Dammit," he said out loud, and opened the text.

Just four words from Grayson: We need to talk.

Four short and thoroughly ominous words.

"Sure we can talk," Reece muttered. "We can talk about you respecting the rules of the road, right after you tell me who the fuck you are."

With a sigh, he called Liam, because if he was dealing with his sister's tetchy boyfriend at least he wouldn't have to deal with his thoughts about Grayson.

The phone rang so many times he almost gave up, but then—"Liam Lee, SPD public relations, can you hold?"

Even through the phone Reece could hear how frazzled he was. "Jamey told me to call. But never mind, you sound busy—"

"Reece? Hold on." There was a moment of silence, then Liam was back. "Jamey bought you a ticket to Juneau."

"*What?*"

"My dad runs a float plane charter up there. I'm seeing if he can meet you at the airport."

A last-second ticket to Juneau? Reece didn't want to think about how much that had cost Jamey. And then a float plane? "Look, I get that Jamey doesn't want me on the case, and I guess you probably don't either—"

Liam snorted.

"Oh come on," said Reece. "That last time wasn't that bad—"

"Which last time?" Liam said flatly, and Reece could practically hear the air quotes around *last*. "When you ran your mouth around reporters about empathy and mind control?"

"Well—"

"Or did you mean when you gave local news those perfect sound bites about empaths' plan for world domination?"

"I—"

"Or was it when you told the press that the SPD keeps you around for more than your sexual flexibility? That went over so well. I didn't have any apologizing to do to the mayor after that quote went public."

Reece flushed. Liam was never, ever going to let that one go. "I'd try to explain myself, but I see you're already familiar with sarcasm."

Reece would grudgingly admit Liam was great for Jamey. Both were loyal, caring, and annoyingly smart. They were biracial in different ways and they *got* each other, got what it was like navigating a world built for people who were only one thing. It didn't take an empath to see the two of them were falling wildly in love.

But Jamey was a package deal with a high-strung empath half brother one R-rated movie away from another nervous breakdown, because she refused to abandon Reece when they were all that was left of their family. Liam's carefully worded press releases were always kinder to Reece than his big mouth deserved, but not one of Jamey's boyfriends had stuck around when they realized the extent of the weird-ass empath shit she dealt with because of him. Why would the SPD's long-suffering PR manager?

Beyond that, they never told anyone that Jamey had quirks of her own. They didn't know why, and Reece was an anxious, fragile wreck who could not handle the thought of his sister subjected to the same scrutiny as empaths. So Liam only knew his girlfriend had sensitive hearing. A sensitive sense of smell. What was he going to do if he ever found out the rest?

Reece cleared his throat. "I just think banishing me to Alaska seems extreme."

"Does it," Liam said dryly. "I'm preparing my battle plan and resigning myself to even more overtime then I already face."

"But I haven't done anything today to make your life difficult!" *Lie.* Reece winced.

Liam put salt in the wound as he said, "Did you show up at the crime scene this morning?"

"Well—"

"Did you, an *empath*, show up at our most notorious *anti-*empathy senator's murder scene when her body was found on Cedrick Stone's yacht?"

"Just because the boat she was found on belongs to some rich guy—"

"Oh my God. You don't know who Cedrick Stone is. You wear his product *every day*."

Reece glanced down at himself. "He's a…sweatshirt mogul?"

"Cedrick *Stone*," said Liam. "From *Stone Solutions*."

Oh.

Reece looked at one gloved hand and flexed his suddenly

prickling fingers. "Right," he said, with a lightness he didn't feel. "That guy."

Because yes, he did know who that was. He'd seen him on TV, promising that his newest product was *eight percent more effective at blocking empathy* or some other blathering. Reece didn't listen, just wore whatever pair of government-mandated gloves the Empath Initiative agency gave him. The gloves were stiff and hot but they did their job and kept him from accidentally reading a stranger when buying groceries and he'd never given any thought to their creator.

"Right. That guy." Liam's imitation of Reece was scarily accurate and not particularly flattering. "Look, people are going to blame empaths for Senator Hathaway's death and it could get ugly. Come meet us at the department; you can lay low until your flight to Juneau, and then hopefully I can get you off the grid."

"Why? You want a witness-free way to drown me in the sea?"

"Funny," Liam said flatly. "It's for Jamey. She wants you to be safe and I want her to be happy, so get over here already."

Reece turned the key in the ignition, ready to get in one last righteous dig, then hang up on Liam and drive off in a satisfied huff. "You know I don't talk on the phone while driving. So if you want me to leave, why are you busting my ass about what I say to the press—"

Shit. He tried the key again, and again got nothing but a quiet clicking noise as the engine refused to turn over.

"You're right, how inconsiderate of me," Liam said. "I should be more *flexible*."

The line went dead. Reece decided not to think too closely on which one of them might be better at righteous digs and dramatic hang ups.

He sat back in his seat with a sigh. Well, this was what he

got for driving on an old, unreliable battery in a cold snap. He could call Liam back, but Liam was frazzled and Jamey was worried, and Reece could handle it himself just fine.

He got out of the car and went to get his portable charger out of the back. He'd have a few minutes to wait while his car charged—maybe enough time to figure out who Evan Grayson was.

Chapter Five

Your jack-o'-lantern might be frowning or smiling this year—but did YOU choose which emotion to carve? Or could it have been EMPATHIC INFLUENCE? Read the story that will change how you see Halloween—forever!

—Gretel Macy, *blogging for* Eyes on Empaths

Once Reece had the battery in the passenger footwell jumped and the Smart car idling, he opened the hatch at the back of the car again. But as he lifted the carpeting and panel over the engine, his gaze landed on something small and black affixed to the underside of the panel.

"Again?" He dislodged the Empath Initiative tracker with a hard yank and tossed it over his shoulder. "Have fun tracking that," he muttered. For all of the clamor about empathy and privacy, empaths sure didn't get any privacy themselves.

A couple minutes later, with the charger carefully secured back in the hatch, he sat back in the driver's seat to let the car idle and charge the battery.

He picked up his phone. He wasn't good at doing anything with it besides making calls. The gloves got in the way, and he never took them off in public, even on a freezing morning with only a few hardy souls trudging around the waterfront. He didn't want to make anyone nervous, and he'd learned the hard way that nothing good came of not wearing gloves around others.

But even Reece could put *Evan Grayson empaths* into a search engine.

The first few hits were all from *Eyes on Empaths*. Of *course* they were; *Eyes on Empaths* was, as its bold banner claimed, "The Number One Empath-Awareness Blog in the Pacific Northwest." Reece was far more familiar with it than he wanted to be, because it was run by Gretel Macy, the daughter of Beau Macy, founder of the country's biggest conspiracy theorist organization, American Minds Intact. *Eyes on Empaths* knew more than the press most of the time because it had a direct pipeline to all the lies and sensationalist trash AMI pushed, and the worst part was Gretel herself *wasn't* a liar. She was worse: a true believer with unshakable faith in her own bias.

He frowned, and then clicked the first link anyway.

It took him to a blog post about Senator Hathaway's death—damn, Gretel had gotten that story up fast. It was full of ludicrous rambling trying to connect Senator Hathaway's death with October's stupid feature story about empaths influencing what people carved on their jack-o'-lanterns. Reece rolled his eyes, and left a pointed comment.

Hello empaths don't have mind-control powers and if we did, we wouldn't waste them on pumpkins.

He left a few more choice words and then went back to the search results, and the next hit took him to a page on the Dead Man.

The hairs on Reece's neck rose.

Why had he been taken to a blog page on the *Dead Man*? Evan Grayson was real; the Dead Man was fake, just a scary fairy tale invented to keep empaths in line. A supposed shadow agent operating outside the law, one who showed up anytime empaths thought about stepping out of line, protecting the public in secret from the so-called dangers of empathy.

The whispers said darker things too, about bodies and violence wherever the Dead Man went. But Reece tried not to hear those, and they were bullshit anyway. All of it was. The Dead Man had been dreamed up by fearmongers who thought empaths might use their powers for harm. He was nothing but myth.

Reece had always believed that.

He stared at his phone.

Possible Dead Man sighting in San Francisco!

Most say the Dead Man is only an urban legend, but our savvy readers know better. Eyes on Empaths *has ALWAYS believed the man known as the Dead Man, one Evan Grayson, is out there engaging in heroic anti-empathy work to protect the innocent.*

And now, at a crime scene in San Francisco involving a dead empath, a witness saw a tall civilian ordering reporters away. And the witness heard an officer refer to the man as—AGENT GRAYSON.

Are YOU ready to believe?

And as fear began a slow creep up his spine, the phone in Reece's hand began to ring.

Unknown caller.

Even an empath conscience wasn't enough to make him answer that. He scrambled out of his car, leaving the engine running as he held the phone at a distance like a poisonous snake and ran for the boardwalk across the street.

Jamey better be getting him a new phone with that ticket to Juneau, because this one was going in the sea.

As he darted across the street, he nearly collided with a fleece-clad jogger coming down the sidewalk at a fast clip. Reece threw himself sideways with a painful wrench, nearly falling as he just managed to avoid making contact.

"Watch it!" the jogger snapped.

"Sorry, sorry." Reece tried to get his feet back under him as he straightened up on the sidewalk.

But the man had stopped running, eyes on his smart watch. Then his gaze fell on Reece's hands and the man paled.

Oh no.

"Someone just sent me a text. They know my name." Beneath his fleece hat, the man's eyes were wide and full of terror. "They want me to tell the empath that if his phone goes in the ocean, everything I own will follow."

Reece sucked in a breath.

The man's eyes went impossibly wider. "Now it says if the empath doesn't answer their next call, they'll start with my Audi."

It was only a car, but Reece couldn't bear the man's genuine panic. "Get out of here," Reece said to him. "Don't be collateral damage for someone who knows how to threaten an empath."

The man didn't need telling twice. He took off at a sprint, leaving Reece alone on the sidewalk, staring at the phone in his hand.

On cue, it began to ring again. Reece took a deep breath, and this time, he answered.

"I know what you are now."

"I gave you my name," said the Dead Man. "I'm not trying to—"

"You're a *dick*."

There was a pause. "You sure you know what I am?"

"You're supposed to be a bogeyman, dreamed up to scare empaths onto the straight and narrow," Reece snapped. "Except the Dead Man's actually just a dick with an accent, bullying the rest of the world to get what he wants."

Grayson's drawl was lazy in his ear. "That man's possessions were never in danger."

"Bullshit. I've heard lots of rumors about you and not one ever said you make empty threats."

"Because I don't," Grayson said simply. "I meant there was never a chance the threat wouldn't work on you."

That got under Reece's skin like a splinter. "Leave innocent people alone. If you want something from me, come get it from *me*."

"I don't need an invitation, Care Bear."

Reece stiffened. "You're on your way to Seattle?" But he already knew the answer, because that was the deep rumbling of an engine in the background.

"Where else would anyone want to be in November?" Grayson said dryly. "I hear it never stops raining and never warms up. Sounds like paradise."

The Dead Man was coming here. Alaska suddenly wasn't far enough. "Are you coming because of Senator Hathaway?"

"Did you think I was coming because of someone else?"

Could the Dead Man somehow know Reece heard lies? But that was impossible; no one else knew but Jamey, and she was safer than a bank vault.

He leaned on the railing, the metal cold against his body as he stared at the gray ocean stretching out to green trees and houses across the bay. He was as uncomfortably adrift in their conversation as an empty skiff on the water, unable to anchor a single emotion onto Grayson's deep voice. He *hated* phones. "I don't know what to think when the world's only empath hunter calls."

"I'm not an *empath hunter*," said Grayson. "I'm a specialist."

"Oh yeah?" Reece said, scoffing. "And what, exactly, do you specialize in, pacifism or privacy violations?"

"And here I thought y'all were more complicated than sound bites from either side."

Reece clenched his teeth. "Specialist. Hunter. Whatever. Mr. Dead Man—"

"Mr. Dead Man?"

"Sorry, is it *Dr.* Dead Man? Did you go to six years of zombie school? What do you want?"

"You didn't answer my call."

"I was driving."

"I know. I got your auto-response." Grayson read it out. *"I don't use my phone behind the wheel and neither should you.* Hashtag *drive like an empath.* Are you capable of communication without sass?"

Reece wrapped a hand around the rail, the cold blocked by the glove. "You're driving right now. I can hear your engine. Sounds big. Upgraded. Like it eats too much gas while its distracted driver endangers the road."

"We don't all of us drive like empaths. And I'm parking, so you can stop fretting."

Yeah, right. The Dead Man was on his phone and on his way. Reece wasn't going to stop *frettin'* anytime soon. "You still haven't said what you *want.*"

"Let's start with you telling Detective St. James to cancel the trip to Alaska."

Reece's heart leaped into his throat.

"That's where she was planning to hide you, isn't it? Good plan. Would have given someone trouble trying to track you off Mr. Lee's float plane, if it was available."

If it was available? What the hell was that supposed to mean? "Do you always talk in riddles?" he snapped, trying to shake off the fear skittering up his spine.

"Do you always ask so many questions?" Grayson cut his engine. His low voice dropped just a little lower. "Tell me you didn't try to read the witness in the ambulance."

"You're the one who sent me to help him in the first place!" Reece snapped.

"No."

"Yes, you—"

"I told you not to touch the witness. I told you to run."

Reece threw up his free hand. "Then why did you say Jamey needed—"

"I said she was investigating a homicide and had no leads, because I knew you'd go straight to her."

Goose bumps broke out on Reece's skin. "You *lied* to me."

"Nothing I said was untrue."

"Dead men tell no tales? Just bald-faced lies?"

"It wasn't a lie." A car door opened in Grayson's background. "Your sister was my best bet. I assumed you'd tell her my name and she'd immediately come up with a workable plan to get you out of town. And she tried, but you didn't listen."

"It was a misunderstanding." *Lie.* Reece winced.

"That right?" Grayson's voice was so unsettlingly emotionless. "Mr. Davies, there's a dead senator in your town. I've got a job to do, and I can't have an empath running around, trying to help people and getting into trouble or worse. If you're not gonna stay where your sister wants you to, then I can take you somewhere you can't *misunderstand* your way out."

Reece's fingers tightened on the guardrail. "You're not as scary as you think you are," he said, the sour notes of the lie loud in the thin morning air.

"This isn't me trying to scare you, sugar. When that happens, you'll know." The car door slammed shut. "I believe Detective St. James is waiting for you at police headquarters. If I were you, I wouldn't go."

"You can't possibly think I'm going to listen to *you*."

"You already showed me you won't," said Grayson. "So I already know I'll be saying *I told you so*."

The line went dead. Reece glared at the phone, only to see it shaking in his trembling hand. He set his jaw and looked at the ocean again, tempted to prove Grayson wrong and pitch the phone into the waves like a baseball.

But the jogger's frightened eyes instantly sprang back to mind, so he shoved it in his pocket with a curse instead.

Unreadable, other empaths said, when rumors were whispered about the Dead Man. *Immovable.*

Merciless.

Well, he hadn't said he was coming because of Reece and more importantly, he wasn't here yet. Reece spun on his heel and crossed back to his still-running car, calculating a driving route that would take exactly the thirty minutes he needed to finish safely charging his battery and end up at police headquarters.

"Agent Nolan?" The rapping came again on the window of the Explorer. "Sir?"

Special Agent Damian Nolan darkened the screen of his tablet before lowering the window to reveal an officer with a panicked expression. "What?"

"Did you see the truck that just arrived on scene?"

"I'm not traffic control, I'm *busy*," said Nolan. "Get rid of them."

"Sir, it's the driver. We were told—"

He cut her off. "Don't tell me about the problem, tell me when it's solved."

The officer pressed her lips flat, then nodded once and disappeared.

Nolan looked back to the FBI's empath database and the file on Reece Davies, then tossed the tablet to the passenger seat. His concentration had been broken, but it didn't matter: the file was as useless as the empath himself. Just a sob story of an absent father, a dead mother, and a broke twentysomething who'd never finished college and slept on his sister's couch. Didn't even use his empathy enough to make the file interesting, only sporadic consulting for the SPD on nonviolent crime.

Definitely no record of making catatonic men scream.

Nolan scrubbed a hand over his face. If he could leave in the next thirty minutes, he might still be able to make the final boarding call for his cruise—

His phone rang, Agent Ramos' name and number on the caller ID. "Tell me you're on your way."

"I wish," she said.

He let out a hard sigh. "What's keeping everyone?"

"Orders."

Nolan groaned. "*Whose* orders? I'm not even supposed to be here. Where's the official FBI response?"

"I don't know." Ramos made a frustrated sound. "It's— weird."

Something in the tone of her voice raised the hairs on his neck. "Weird how?"

In the background, he heard her close a door. "You asked about Seattle's other empath, the one who works with the soldiers at the veterans' hospital?"

"Cora Falcon." He sat up straighter. "Did you find her? Can we get an off-the-record read of the witness?"

"We're not allowed to call her."

"What? We have a *dead senator*. If we want an empath and no questions, we can have a goddamn empath and no questions. If not Falcon, there's an empath who consults for the Bureau in Chicago—"

"No dice. Empaths have been forbidden from the crime scene and the witness."

Wait, *what*? Yes, using empaths for anything law-enforcement-related was a gray area, making judges testy, defense attorneys froth at the mouth, and the little whiners themselves too opinionated about their reads only being used for "good." But a full empath ban from a location? That was the kind of thing Hathaway had wanted to pass, but it wasn't law yet. "By whose order?"

"Someone higher than me." She lowered her voice. "But I bet you it's the same person keeping us off the scene."

Nolan huffed again. "Well, I'm already here, but what the hell am I supposed to do alone? All I've got is a catatonic witness I can't even get near, because some special doctors showed up and they won't talk to anyone."

"Special," she repeated meaningfully. "I'll call if I learn anything new."

Nolan hung up with a frown. Who could forbid that empaths even set foot on a scene of this importance? His irritation with Davies kicked up another notch. If the little whiner had kept it together, they could have had answers already.

He stepped down from his SUV to the parking lot. But as he glanced across the lot, he paused. The ambulance with Braker had vanished, and in its place was a black truck. Not one of the Northwest's mud-stained beaters either, but a giant cowboy wet dream with a gleaming four-door cab and a racing exhaust.

Nolan crossed the lot, only to find the truck was empty. His frown deepened.

He made his way down the wooden ramp and onto the dock, which shifted under his weight as he walked toward Stone's yacht. The SPD had already amassed a list of angry yacht-owners threatening to file suits over being kept away from their property that morning. He'd have to make sure the situation was handled with tact; the SPD couldn't be trusted to get anything right.

Case in point: as he approached Stone's yacht, *The Bulwark*, an unusually fit man was emerging from the ladder of an open hatch on the aft deck, a fringe of blondish-brownish hair visible under his winter hat, his tall frame and broad shoulders covered by a stylish shearling coat that was definitely not police-issue.

How the hell had the SPD missed a civilian climbing onto Stone's yacht? Nolan broke into a run. "Sir!"

The man looked up, younger than Nolan had expected, maybe twenty-five or twenty-six.

"Sir," Nolan called again, masking his anger with curt politeness. Stone wasn't the only millionaire to keep his yacht here, and this stranger could have walked straight off a glossy poster in a swooning teenage girl's room. Pretty boys and empaths; this place really was a circus. "I'm afraid you're trespassing on a crime scene. I'll have an officer escort—"

"Special Agent Damian Nolan?"

Nolan paused. The Texas drawl was a surprise, out of place against the gray skies and freezing rain. He reflexively touched his gun through his jacket. "How do you know my name?"

"You can keep that Glock where it is. My name's Evan Grayson."

Nolan's blood went cold. "Agent Grayson." He stood, frozen in place on the dock, as Grayson shut the hatch. "I didn't know—" *you were real* "—you were coming."

"I'm getting a lot of that this morning."

Agent Grayson. The so-called Dead Man.

Nolan had had a partner once who had believed in the Dead Man. *Don't mess with the empaths*, he'd warned Nolan. *Not worth using them for reads, because if you fuck it up, that's when the Dead Man shows up.*

Nolan had scoffed. He had better things to do than believe in urban legends—except this particular urban legend was standing right in front of him.

Grayson had a paper bag in hand, making no attempt to hide what he was doing as he placed it inside his coat. Hazel-brown eyes sized up Nolan but nothing in Grayson's expression changed. "There weren't supposed to be any FBI agents at the scene."

"FBI should be all over this case," Nolan said. "What are *you* doing here? Because of Senator Hathaway's anti-empathy agenda?"

"I'm here for lots of reasons." Despite how the ship bobbed in the rough water, Grayson's footing never wavered. He nodded at the hatch he'd just closed. "Y'all didn't search the engine room."

"Stone's lawyer was too fast. She threw up every roadblock in the book and a few I think she made up. The SPD's Detective St. James is working on her." Nolan gestured at Grayson's coat. "But I guess that didn't stop you."

"Mr. Stone is my coworker, in a sense. This isn't search and seizure, it's just stealing." Grayson didn't offer an explanation for the paper bag, only stepped toward the door at the back of the yacht.

No fears, his ex-partner had said about Grayson. *And no limits. The scariest thing you've ever heard of, Agent Grayson's worse. Don't get mixed up with empaths. It's not worth it.*

His ex-partner had been an idiot. Grayson was a kid with a bad reputation. Another freak for the circus. Nolan stepped up onto the boat.

The yacht's entertaining area was still stained with blood, the fancy spread of food and drink still overturned on the floor. The scene had been cataloged and the bodies moved to the morgue, but the yacht remained smeared with the battle scars of the early-morning hours' inexplicable violence.

Grayson didn't avert his eyes as he gracefully stepped over the stains on the floor. Maybe a man with a moniker like *the Dead Man* wasn't going to be put off by a little blood. Or a lot of blood.

The bodies had been taken to the morgue, but Nolan had his own personal pictures, the ones he always took at bad scenes in case they could later spark a new thought. Maybe he could offer them in exchange for some goddamn answers.

"If you're looking for the bodies—" Nolan started.

"I was sent the forensic photographer's photos. They were enough." Grayson nodded toward the bloodiest part of the couch, where Hathaway's body had lain, although his gaze stayed on Nolan. "What's your theory on cause of death?"

"The MEs are saying the three victims died of drug overdose, strangulation, and traumatic brain injury, respectively." Nolan counted the deaths off on his fingers.

"I asked for *your* theory."

Nolan hesitated. "There were two dead men found with Hathaway," he said, more slowly. "Big ones. Bad ones, with rap sheets and records. Muscle for hire and expensive as hell, because they do time instead of cut deals."

"They were known for keeping secrets?" said Grayson.

Nolan nodded. "One had the deepest strangulation marks I've ever seen—but small, like a petite woman would leave. The other man had four types of cutlery in him, including a shrimp fork through his skull. That takes strength too—but he died second. And the senator herself, well."

Nolan looked at the couch again, where Hathaway's body had been. "The MEs' preliminary report was theorizing drugs. All I saw was blood."

"Are there any more bodies?"

Nolan huffed. "We found *three.* How many more do you want?"

"Just answer the question, Agent Nolan."

Watch your tone, Nolan was tempted to say. Ghoulish nickname or not, Grayson was pushing his luck with that attitude. "No," Nolan said curtly. "We had divers do a search around the yacht."

Frankly, Nolan had questions of his own. "I heard empaths

have been banned from the case. You're—well, you know."
He gestured uselessly, hoping it conveyed *weirdo freak Dead
Man*. "Do you know anything about the ban?"

"Of course."

There was a soft chime. Grayson looked down at his phone.
His expression didn't change as he stared at the screen. And
then, without explanation or closure, Grayson strode back out
onto the aft deck.

Nolan chased after him, climbing down the yacht stairs
after Grayson, who'd jumped gracefully down to the dock.
Grayson was already walking over the dock, toward the marina, and while Nolan was almost as tall as Grayson, he had to
walk at a near-run to keep pace. "I've been with the Bureau a
long time and never heard of an order like that. Who gave it?"

"I did," Grayson said, as he strode up the ramp.

Nolan's lips pressed into a thin line. "Wasn't that hasty?" he
bit out, tailing at Grayson's heels as they crossed the tarmac.
"We have a catatonic witness who might know the identity of
the murderer. Maybe we could use an empath to reach him."

"No."

"It's a gray area," Nolan protested. "We just use the empath to bring the witness out of the catatonia, we don't let
the empath elicit any testimony and we won't have a Fifth
Amendment problem. We get answers and a quick win, and
we've got a dead fucking senator so I want a win. Look, Agent
Grayson—"

Grayson came to an abrupt stop at the black truck. "I heard
an empath already went into the ambulance with that witness.
I heard you went in after him."

"We didn't know about the empath ban yet," Nolan protested. "No one saw the harm."

"Pretty sure Detective St. James told you not to use empaths."

"St. James is hardly a neutral party," Nolan said derisively. "People have blind spots when it comes to their little brothers."

"Some folks," Grayson said enigmatically. He leaned against the passenger door of the truck. "What happened in the ambulance with Mr. Davies and the witness?"

Nolan huffed. Why was Grayson wasting time with these questions? "There was an EMT—"

"I want to hear how much you know."

A shiver of unease crawled over Nolan. Why would Grayson care how much an FBI agent knew? "Nothing happened," he said, because if Grayson wasn't giving answers, neither was he.

"Agent Nolan," said Grayson, his neutral gaze never wavering, still casually leaning on the door of his truck. "I just got some news that's gonna complicate this mess even further. What that means is I don't have time for you to leave stuff out."

This uppity kid who thought he had the right to do whatever he wanted—he was nothing but a rumor with a scary name. In fact, how did Nolan know he really was the Dead Man? Why would the Dead Man be this young? Look like *this*? Grayson might not have been Agent Grayson at all, just a civilian fucking around where they shouldn't.

He stepped forward, into Grayson's personal space. "Are you calling me a liar?"

"Should I be?" Grayson said, without flinching.

Nolan jabbed Grayson in the chest. "Watch your tone," he snapped. "How do I know you're who you say are? You have a badge of some kind?"

"I don't answer to any agencies."

"So you have no proof and maybe you're the liar," said Nolan, reaching for his cuffs. "And maybe I arrest you for interfering with a crime scene and evidence tampering—"

Grayson reversed their positions so fast Nolan's head spun.

The air left his lungs in a painful burst as he hit the passenger door hard enough to dent the metal.

"The people of Seattle do not have time for this." Grayson's voice and expression remained as unruffled as if they were having a banal conversation about weather. "Every second you waste could mean someone else's life. What happened in the ambulance?"

He had Nolan against the truck with one hand in the center of his chest, pinned to the passenger door like a lab specimen to the dissection table. They were nearly the same size but Nolan *couldn't move.* His heart pounded as he tried to answer. "The empath refused to do the read. And then he ran."

"Anything else?"

"Just—the *eyes.*"

"The eyes," Grayson repeated. "Talk. *Fast.*"

Chapter Six

Reporter:...in continuing coverage of the tragic death of Senator Hathaway, no official statement yet from the police. Cedrick Stone, CEO of Stone Solutions, makers of the famous anti-empathy gloves, has promised his company's resources are at the disposal of those searching for Hathaway's killer, while American Minds Intact president Beau Macy spoke with us this morning to give his organization's position on this shocking crime.

Macy: AMI has been there since the beginning. We're as old as the Empath Initiative; as old as the oldest empaths. And we know that this gruesome death of the most staunchly anti-empathy senator is no coincidence.

Reporter: You believe Senator Hathaway was targeted by the pro-empathy movement?

Macy: Maybe the movement. Maybe more than that.

Reporter: But you can't think the empaths are behind this. Privacy issues are one thing, but empaths are pacifists, completely averse to violence.

Macy: So they themselves keep telling us. Convenient how that works, isn't it?

Reporter: That's...something to think about.

Five minutes at HQ, and Jamey had somehow gotten roped into dealing with Cedrick Stone's lawyer.

"Mr. Stone is saddened by this tragedy," said the lawyer on the other end of the phone. "He's distraught at the whole situation. He's mourning a dear friend and a valued colleague today."

Jamey leaned back in her chair at her desk at headquarters, phone balanced in the crook of her neck, and twirled a freshly sharpened pencil in her free hand. "Uh-huh."

"Mr. Stone will prepare a statement," the lawyer continued. "He will stay strong for the community. He will be a beacon of hope for those in grief."

On the other side of the bullpen, officers Stensby and Kosler were whispering about Hathaway's anti-empathy bill. Jamey spun the pencil again, eyeing the *Job Safety and Health Law* poster tacked to the bulletin board. "Uh-huh."

"Mr. Stone is not going to comment on these deaths," said the lawyer. "Mr. Stone is not going to share anything with the police unless you have a warrant."

"You think someone will take up the bill in Hathaway's place?" Kosler muttered.

"Of course," Stensby said under his breath, *"she's basically a martyr for the anti-empathy cause now."*

"Mr. Stone—"

Jamey threw the pencil like a dart into the center of the "o" in *Job*. "Mr. Stone should know we found three bodies on his yacht. One of them was the senator, one went by the street name the Torturer, and the third still had a shrimp fork between his eyes."

There was a small intake of breath on the other end of the phone.

"I don't care who Stone thinks he is," said Jamey. "I'll get my warrants. I'm giving your client a small window to do the right thing."

There was a pause on the other end of the phone. "Let me call you back," the lawyer said.

"You have fifteen minutes." Jamey hung up just as Taylor walked up to her desk.

"Bad news," he said. "Those samples you wanted, for the mud on the Ford Transit's tires. They're lost."

"Lost?"

Taylor spread his hands. "Apparently? Lab refused to give details—they just said we're not getting test results for this case. *Any* test results."

No results. That meant the dirt and the bloodwork she'd asked for—gone.

"For what it's worth, I did get this." Taylor handed over an excellent fake driver's license with Reece's picture and the name Connor Kendrick.

She tightened her hand around the license. "I owe you."

He shook his head. "I got to do the famous Detective St. James a favor," he said, clapping her shoulder with a grin. "I'm the envy of half the force right now."

She slipped the fake license into her pocket. Now all she needed was Reece, who should have been at the station at least twenty minutes ago.

She was about to call Reece, obnoxious auto-responses be damned, when Lieutenant Parson crossed the bullpen, heading her way. She got to her feet. "Lieutenant," she started to say.

He jerked his head. "With me." She followed him down the short hall into his modest office across from Liam's. He sank into his chair behind the desk. "Get the door?"

She shut it behind her but remained standing.

He looked at her from under bushy gray eyebrows. "You're working on the Hathaway case."

"We need to find that red car," said Jamey. "The driver could be another witness, or in danger—"

Parson cut her off. "The search is off. We have to stand down."

Stand down? "I thought we needed to do everything possible to solve this case."

"We need to keep up that appearance."

"Appearance?"

"For PR's sake, we need to make it look like we're still working this case to the last officer," said Parson. "But I've been told to pull everyone back."

Officers pulled back. Just as her samples went missing. Jamey frowned. "Who's getting in our way? The FBI?"

"No," Parson said brusquely. "Higher."

Ah. Of course.

"I'm only telling a select group," said Parson. "I know you have a personal stake in this case, so you especially have to step back."

"Sir—"

He held up a hand and cut her off. "Get out there and flash your badge. Shake things up, talk to the press, talk to the lawyers—"

"But don't actually solve the multiple homicide in my city." Oh, this really was some bullshit. She was going to get Reece safely out of town, and then Evan Grayson was going to have a lot to answer for.

"It wasn't my decision," said Parson, "but we're going to respect it, *and* we're going to keep it quiet. Let everyone else think everything is business as usual—well, as far as anything about this case is usual. You got me?"

"Sure," she said, glad Reece wasn't around to hear her lie.

As Jamey left Parson's office, she heard Liam's voice from the elevators.

"Jamey!" As handsome as always, Liam wore his familiar sweater vest and tie combination, his hurried movements
sending his glasses sliding down his nose. A few quick steps
brought her to meet him halfway across the bullpen.

"You look stressed," she said, as soon as they were close
enough that Liam would hear a whisper.

They were the same height, their eyes level as Liam shoved
his glasses back into place and read from his phone. "*I don't use
my phone behind the wheel and neither should you.* Hashtag *drive
like an empath.*" He waved the phone in the air. "What is that
supposed to mean?"

"That Reece doesn't think it's safe to answer the phone or
check texts while driving," she said. "And that he refuses to
do it."

For a man who was perfectly polished in front of a camera, Liam sure could swear creatively in private. "But this is
an emergency!"

"And if you figure out how to make him care, let me
know," Jamey said, with feeling.

Liam's face puckered up like he'd sucked on a lemon.
"Come with me?"

She followed him through the bullpen as he led her not
to his interior office but to the closest window. He pointed
through the rain-streaked glass to Fifth Avenue one story
below, to the sea of plastic ponchos dotted by fuzzy microphones. A crowd of reporters gathering right outside HQ's
front doors.

"There has to be a way to stop Reece before he walks
through that circus." Liam put a hand on the window. "I sent
him three texts."

"I'm sure he'll read them in time," Jamey said weakly.
Reece would've heard that lie too.

Liam looked around the bullpen, then moved closer. In a
quieter voice, he said, "I have more bad news. My dad's plane

is in the shop. He flew in a storm in the Tongass Narrows two days ago and one of the floats busted against the dock."

Shit.

"My dad's asking around, calling his contacts, but I can't promise someone else can keep a secret."

"I'll figure something out," she said, although what that would be, she had no idea. "Thanks for trying; I know Reece makes your job tougher."

"Yeah, but he's your *brother*." Liam shrugged. "You eat kimchi for me, I put up with Reece's big mouth for you."

"I *like* kimchi," she pointed out. "I like it spicier than you."

His lips quirked up at the corner. "Reece isn't that bad. No matter what his mouth says, his heart's always in the right place—"

Liam's phone went off. He glanced down and his expression went very still. "I take it back." He was still staring at his phone. "He's the worst."

"What's wrong—" Jamey was interrupted as the phone on her desk across the pen began to ring. "Stone's lawyer," she said to Liam.

He nodded, already turning toward the door. "You solve a murder. I'm going to get your brother and *personally* escort him past those reporters. Possibly gagged."

"His heart's in the right place," Jamey reminded him.

"It's not his heart that he can't keep shut," he called over his shoulder.

Reece stared through his rain-streaked windshield at the crowd amassed in front of the Seattle Police Department headquarters.

He'd been so pleased with himself for finding a tiny slice of curb to fit his car into, noticing parking options were slim for an early Tuesday morning, even by downtown standards.

Then he'd seen the reporters like a human moat between him and Jamey.

He was still sitting in his car at the curb, frozen like a deer in headlights, when someone slapped their palm against the driver's window, making him nearly jump out of his seat.

He jerked his head to see Liam, his expression even more vexed than usual. "Window down," the other man said testily.

A ticked-off Liam was still an improvement over a reporter. With a grunt of effort, Reece rolled down his window enough to talk. "I just got here. Why are you already mad at me?"

"If I call, you answer."

"It isn't safe to use a phone while driving."

"I don't care if you're navigating an eighteen-wheeler through a field of china and kittens! You know what's even less safe?" Liam pointed down the street to the crowd. "You, bringing your big mouth here, in front of all of them."

"Probably is less safe," Reece agreed. "I'm a very good driver."

Liam's eye twitched. "Then next time," he said, with the kind of dangerous sweetness that meant nothing good, "drive *away* before you comment on *Eyes on Empaths*."

Oh. Crap. "How did you—"

"You use your real name on all your social media!"

"Well, yeah," said Reece. "I'm not going to *lie*."

Liam made a deeply frustrated noise and held up his phone. "You wrote that if empaths had mind-control power, you wouldn't waste it on pumpkins, you'd be brainwashing the President."

Reece winced, but his conscience made him add, "I may have also mentioned hypnotizing Congress—"

"Oh, I know," Liam said, eye twitching again. "And I thought you couldn't possibly have written something that inflammatory during the murder investigation of an anti-empathy senator, not fifteen minutes after I told you to keep a lid on it. But oh yes. You did." He leaned down. "Gretel Macy wrote a fresh article for her *Eyes on Empaths* blog, chock-full of new theories based completely on your comment, and she emailed it directly to me with a request for a statement."

Reece groaned. "Oh, come on. It's just a blog—"

"—run by the daughter of the AMI *president*. She bumps shoulders with all the big names in this city and most of the anti-empathy crowd reads her blog. You just gave them months of ammo."

"But all the other commenters on the blog were saying empaths are behind Hathaway's death! That's so unfair, Hathaway may have hated us, but we wouldn't—no empath would *ever*—" Reece cut the words off, not even wanting to say it.

Liam sighed, but his eyes had softened. "Not everyone thinks empaths are behind this. No matter how difficult *some* empaths make our lives."

He glanced at the crowd of reporters, then back to the window. "Let's just thank the stars that Gretel Macy isn't a real reporter and no actual news stations are picking up her articles. My main concern right now is getting you past all those cameras without you saying something that's going to ruin my career."

"I can keep my mouth shut." *Lie.* Reece raised his eyes heavenward.

"No, you can't," said Liam, and of course *that* wasn't a lie.

"Can't you just make a statement or something, and then the reporters will go away?" Reece said, with more whine than intended.

"I was waiting until my heartburn medication kicks in, like I do when I have to call about my student loans." Something soft hit Reece in the face. "Put that on."

"What—"

Something hard followed. "And these."

"But—"

"Do you have a hat?"

Reece pulled the soft thing off his head and held it up: a navy blazer a size too big. "Is this *yours*?"

Liam pointed. "Those are too."

Reece looked down to see a pair of plastic glasses frames in his lap. He picked them up and found them heavier than expected. He put them on and made a face. "I can't see."

"It's two blocks; you'll live." Liam pursed his lips for a moment, then said, "Any chance you'll take off the gloves?"

Reece rolled his eyes. He pulled off the glasses and tossed the lot on the passenger seat. "No."

"Reece—"

"I'm not taking off my gloves. I'm not wearing a disguise and I won't use fake names online. Empaths scare people, and if I show them I'm willing to hide what I am, I'll make their fear worse."

Several expressions crossed Liam's face, from distress to grudging respect before finally settling on resignation. "*Fine.* But not one word out of you. I mean it, Reece."

"Why are you so tense?" Reece complained, as he climbed out of the car.

"I thought you needed touch for the paranormal shit."

Reece stiffened, but Liam was shutting Reece's door, apparently unconcerned that an empath had picked up on his emotions. "I didn't read you," Reece said anyway. "Anyone could see you're on edge. There's no point stressing; the press always hates me."

"This time is different." Liam grabbed Reece's sleeve and pulled him into a walk. "This isn't actually about my career, all right? The city is tense and no one likes empaths this morning. So please, for once just shut your mouth, and keep it shut until I get you into HQ."

The closer they got, the bigger the press of reporters seemed, and despite his bravado Reece's stomach began to hurt from nerves. He tried to keep his eyes on Liam's shoes, which were really too nice for such a gross winter day.

But when they reached the building and the first reporter turned in his direction, he froze in place.

"It's the empath! Mr. Davies! Davies!"

Like a coordinated wave, the reporters whirled on them.

"Mr. Davies, can you confirm you're here to consult on Senator Hathaway's death—"

"What can you tell us about this murder—"

"What do you think Hathaway would say if she knew you were on this case—"

"Ladies and gentlemen." Liam's PR voice was perfectly calm, like they weren't facing down a hostile crowd of microphones and cameras. "The SPD's empath consultant will not be working—or *commenting*—on this case. He's here for other reasons. The SPD will release a statement shortly."

A chill suddenly broke over Reece's skin. He glanced over his shoulder, not sure what he was looking for.

"Mr. Davies." A reporter used Reece's moment of hesitation to force her way between Reece and Liam and jam a microphone in Reece's face. "Empaths claim they can't tolerate violence. Can you tell us how you're involved in the investigation of such a brutal triple homicide?"

Reece's stomach lurched. "I—"

A different reporter elbowed his way in. "This crime is shocking to even the most hardened among us—"

"If an empath can consult on such a gruesome murder," said a third, "are they lying about their violence aversion—"

More reporters pushed forward, surrounding him, and he couldn't see Liam anymore.

"Have you heard AMI's allegations that empaths are involved—"

"What do you say to people calling for your removal from the case—"

A new voice spoke from somewhere to Reece's left. "No questions."

The deep drawl wasn't loud, but it cut through the chaos like a blade, drawing all of Reece's attention, twisting through his ears, down his throat and into his stomach.

His knees promptly buckled out from under him and he tumbled to the ground, catching himself on hands and knees just in time to vomit all over the pavement.

Gasps of disgust broke out above his head. The press of reporters immediately lessoned as all of them scrambled backward, away from Reece. He screwed his eyes shut as his stomach roiled and his heart pounded in his throat.

Steps echoed nearby, and Reece opened his eyes to see gigantic black boots appear on the sidewalk by his hands. He lifted his head as the newcomer crouched, filling Reece's sight with his completely expressionless face.

"I did warn you," said the Dead Man.

Chapter Seven

In the earliest days of the empath emergence, no one had any idea how to protect the non-empaths from the empaths' abilities. Then EI came along, then the gloves, and now things like SB 1437. But there's never been an empathy defense quite like Agent Grayson.

—*classified internal memo at the Empath Initiative*

At the sound of Grayson's voice, Reece gagged again, turning his face into his shoulder as his body shook with dry heaves. For the first time he could ever remember, he wished for the filter of electronics, for the phone they'd spoken through before that had stripped out whatever it was that was making him sick.

"Well, that wasn't expected." Grayson said it in the same flat tone he'd said everything else, leaving Reece with no idea what that meant. Grayson straightened and turned to a pair of officers. "Get rid of the press."

A clamor of protest rose from the reporters. "You can't make us leave," someone snapped.

"They can if I order it," Grayson said, as neutral as if he were remarking on the gray skies.

Reece's stomach turned over again, but this time, he didn't retch. Grayson was moving farther away, Reece realized, the distance making him quieter and lessoning the impact of his voice. The angry crowd was also being drawn away, Reece momentarily forgotten in their outrage at Grayson.

Reece swallowed down his gorge and pushed himself onto his knees with shaky arms.

"Reece!" Liam was scrambling forward.

"I didn't do this to make your life difficult," Reece croaked, and then coughed.

"Shut up." But there was no bite in Liam's voice. He crouched and grabbed Reece by the wrist, over the glove, and pulled Reece to his feet.

As the two of them pushed through the glass doors into police headquarters, Jamey was rushing their way. She reached for Reece's arm as the door swung shut and the crowd's noise quieted. "Where did Grayson go?" she said, as she held on to him, looking into his eyes like she was assessing him for a concussion.

She was squeezing his arm too tight, stressed enough to forget her strength, but it was grounding. "He was right next to me. Jamey—"

She winced. "You figured out who he is?"

Reece nodded grimly.

Her mouth tightened, as she glanced out the glass doors to the still-packed sidewalk beyond. She shook her head. "I don't see him anymore. But I don't believe he's gone."

"*That* was the Dead Man?" Reece and Jamey's surprise must have shown on their faces, because Liam added, "Gretel Macy sent me her *Eyes on Empaths* article. That is not what I would have expected a guy called the Dead Man to look like."

To his serious credit, Liam hadn't run away screaming. Instead, he was still here, discussing the Dead Man while hovering at Jamey's side like a helicopter. "What do we do?" he said to Jamey. "Do we get Reece out of here?"

"No." Reece said it quietly, but firmly. "I don't want anyone getting hurt for me."

"I'm going to deal with Grayson," Jamey said to Liam. "Will you wait for me?"

Liam nodded. "Whatever you need," he said. "I trust you."

Not a lie, Reece vaguely realized, and then Jamey was pulling him deeper into the station.

She took him past security and into one of the small rooms where they interviewed witnesses, closing the door behind them. Reece dropped into one of the plastic chairs while she remained standing at the glass door, staring through the blinds. His mouth still tasted like vomit. With her nose, poor Jamey could probably smell it.

"I'm sorry," he said.

She shook her head. "Not your fault."

Not a lie, but that just meant *she* believed it, not that it was objectively true. He watched his sister watch the police station outside their room. "Grayson wanted me to tell you to cancel the trip to Alaska."

She glanced at him. "You talked to him again?"

"The dick threatened to have some jogger's car thrown in the ocean if I didn't."

"The car? But not the jogger?"

"So what?"

"It's a threat that's effective on an empath, but without any violence. Not what I expected from the Dead Man, that's all." Jamey pulled something from her pocket and tossed it on the table. "Alaska's not an option anymore anyway; Liam's dad's plane is busted. All I have is this."

Reece picked the driver's license up. "My detective sister got me a fake ID. Normal people would make some kind of joke about missed opportunities for underage drinking."

She scoffed. "Us. *Normal*."

Reece pocketed the license. "But if not Alaska, then where? What are we going to do now? Grayson's already here."

"He is," she said, tenser than usual. "Did he tell you what he wants?"

Reece shrugged helplessly. "He's not really an explanations kind of guy."

"You would know. Because apparently now you get personal calls from the Dead Man." She turned back to the blinds, her jacket moving enough to reveal her holster.

Reece quickly averted his eyes from the gun. He was enough of a mess as it was. "What if he knows, Jamey? What if he knows I hear lies?"

"That's not why he's here." Before he could ask how she could say that with such certainty, she twitched, and he knew she was hearing something he wasn't. "Speak of the devil." She frowned. "The unexpectedly handsome devil."

Reece followed her gaze out through the blinds. Grayson was cutting a line through the station, the tallest one in the room but moving with graceful strength just like Jamey did. Heads turned as he passed, and Reece could plainly see the emotions play out on their faces: curiosity, envy, suspicion. Attraction.

But from Grayson himself, he got nothing, not one single emotion. It gave Reece the creeps. "Who's afraid of the big, bad Dead Man?" he muttered.

"You are," said Jamey.

That wasn't a lie either.

"There's nothing I can do, Damian."

Agent Nolan sat back against the driver's seat of his Explorer, mouth in a tight line. This was the third time Assistant Director Jacobs had given him this useless response.

The marina was empty now, devoid of both press and police after Grayson had cleared the scene. Grayson, who had listened to Nolan spill everything he'd seen in the ambulance and then let him go without a backward glance, driving off without threats or a *don't tell anyone* warning.

And now Nolan knew why. "He assaulted me."

"You said he pushed you against his truck. Did you assume he was some useless piece of teen girl eye candy and pick a fight, only to get your ass handed to you? You wouldn't be the first."

Nolan wasn't admitting anything. No one had witnessed the altercation. He could say Grayson had attacked him un-provoked and it'd be his word against Grayson's in a hearing. "I want to file a complaint."

"Agent Grayson operates outside our jurisdiction."

"He's under someone's jurisdiction."

"I don't think he is," said Jacobs. "He's associated with the Empath Initiative, but he doesn't answer to them."

Nolan scoffed. "So he's—what? A rogue agent? A vigi-lante? *Batman?*"

"He's a weapon."

That made Nolan scoff again. "Against what? *Empaths?* I don't like that mind-raping thing they can do, but Jim, have you ever met an empath?"

"I've worked with the one here in DC. I know where you're going with this."

Nolan went on anyway. "I met another one this morning. Complete crybaby. I could have held my foot over a spider and made him putty in my hands. No one needs an anti-empathy weapon. And even if we did, Grayson's too dangerous."

"He *is* dangerous," Jacobs agreed. "He's also unique, so you're going to have to drop this and move on, from both your beef with Grayson and this case. The FBI isn't getting involved in either."

Nolan set his jaw.

"You're supposed to be on vacation anyway," Jacobs said. "Book another cruise."

"Sir—"

"I don't want to hear from you for two weeks."

Nolan continued to hold the phone long after Jacobs hung up, anger simmering. Grayson didn't even have a file with the FBI, nothing but his name, his Dead Man alias, and the word *classified*. Probably barely old enough to train at Quantico but had the gall to imply that *Nolan* was the one interfering with the investigation and endangering people.

Ugh, Nolan needed some air.

But as he was about to leave the SUV, his phone rang again, an unfamiliar number with the Seattle area code. "This is Nolan."

"Special Agent Damian Nolan." The man's smooth voice sounded vaguely familiar. "I'm glad I was able to reach you. I'm wondering if I might have a moment of your time."

"And who are you?"

"The owner of the yacht you're investigating, of course," the man said wryly. "My name is Cedrick Stone."

Reece bit his lip as Grayson stepped up to the glass door. Unlike the business clothes Jamey usually wore on duty, Grayson wore jeans and a sweater, although they gave him an *I don't need a suit to run this show* look rather than Reece's *I got dressed off the floor* chic. Grayson's gaze was on Jamey as he held up a water bottle in one hand and knocked at the door with the other.

She stepped back, folding her arms over her chest. He opened the door but didn't step into the room, only holding the water bottle out to Jamey. "For the empath."

At the sound of Grayson's voice, Reece's stomach gave a warning lurch, but thankfully he didn't vomit again.

Jamey didn't take the water. "Is it poisoned?"

Grayson took it back and twisted the top, and Reece heard the seal break. Grayson held the bottle back out to Jamey. "Unless you need me to drink from it first?" he said dryly, making Reece's stomach protest again.

With narrowed eyes, she took the water bottle and turned just enough to set it on the table in front of Reece, not taking her eyes off Grayson.

Reece eyed the bottle. Loath as he was to accept anything from Grayson, the sight of the water made him again taste the bile on his tongue, and he found himself reaching for the drink.

"Are you coming in?" Jamey said.

Grayson nodded at Reece. "When he's ready."

"Ready for what?" he muttered, between welcome cold gulps of water. "More projectile vomiting?"

"You won't throw up again. You'll get used to me. Like riding a bike."

"Or living next to a landfill." Reece set the bottle down, the plastic crackling under his gloved hand. "Are you saying empaths always throw up the first time they meet you?"

"Some empaths. Not all of them."

"But if you knew it could happen, why didn't you approach me slowly in the first place?" Reece demanded.

"Because I didn't expect vomiting from *you.*"

Grayson's eyes and face were blank as stone. Reece still had no idea what any of it meant. "Yeah, well, next time be more careful," he said irritably. "You just made me puke in front of a million cameras."

"Closer to a dozen, but if you're well enough to exaggerate you're well enough for me to come in."

Grayson stepped into the room, shutting the door behind him. Reece's stomach twisted over on itself, but Grayson was right: he was adjusting to the other man's presence and the nausea was subsiding.

Reece still could barely stand the sight. "What's *wrong* with you? Your eyes—and your face—"

Jamey cleared her throat. "There's actually nothing wrong with his face. I mean. I'm just saying."

Reece gave her a withering look.

"Did you think the Dead Man was just going to be a cute nickname?" Grayson said.

"I didn't think the Dead Man was going to be real at all," Reece shot back.

"Haven't you heard?" Grayson said. "I'm just a story; a bogeyman dreamed up to scare empaths onto the straight and narrow."

Reece startled. The sarcasm should have turned to a lie's discord in his ears; should have soured the sugar-sweet accent. But Grayson's drawl had stayed melodic as ever. "That's not right."

"Your words. Not mine."

"I know, I just—" Reece snapped his mouth shut as the puzzle pieces abruptly slotted into place.

Whatever it was about Grayson that stopped Reece from picking up emotions when looking at him, he likewise couldn't find them in Grayson's voice. Just like he couldn't see Grayson's feelings in his eyes or face, Reece hadn't heard the lie in Grayson's words because he *couldn't*.

But Grayson's gaze was still on him, so he buried his shock. If Grayson didn't know Reece could hear everyone else's lies, Reece was going to keep it that way. He scrambled for something to say. "I've just heard stories about you from other empaths. Wild stories."

Grayson tilted his head. "Like what?"

Reece's heart was starting to pound. "That if we don't keep our empathy to ourselves, you show up in the middle of the night and we disappear, leaving only a cover story behind."

"That's just a rumor," said Grayson, and Reece felt better right up until Grayson drew the blinds on the door. "I can show up any time of day."

Reece drew back.

Jamey drew her gun.

Reece world's tunneled to the weapon. *"Jamey."*

Jamey's hands never wavered as she aimed between Grayson's eyes. "It wasn't Reece."

Grayson could not have seemed less concerned to be staring down the barrel of her gun. "You've guessed."

Reece barely heard their voices over his own heartbeat thundering in his ears. "Jamey—"

"I suspected." She cocked the gun. "You showing up confirms it."

Cold sweat broke out on Reece's forehead as phantom pain spread through his chest, the way a bullet might tear through flesh, pierce an organ, shatter bone. *"Jamey."* His voice cracked on her name.

Grayson still didn't seem alarmed. "You're not gonna use that, Detective."

"You think I won't shoot you?"

"Oh, I think you'd kill me fast as I can blink," he drawled. "But not in front of your empath brother."

In the small room's sudden silence, Reece's fast breaths were loud and grating. His chest was on fire, his vision blurred around the edges, seeing nothing but the weapon, cocked and ready—

With a huff, Jamey holstered her gun.

Reece slumped to the table, air leaving him in a great rush.

Grayson leaned casually against the wall with the air of a man accustomed to being threatened at gunpoint. "Appreciated, I'm sure."

Reece buried his face in his hands, gloves cool against his sweaty skin. Jamey's hand came to rest in his hair, her apology for pulling out the gun, even if she'd done it to protect him.

When he looked up, he found Grayson's neutral gaze on them. "What?" he snapped at the blank hazel eyes. "The great specialist has never seen an empath have a panic attack?"

Grayson looked to Jamey. "You should get him a paper bag."

"He recycles them."

"Fair enough," Grayson muttered. "Did you tell anyone your suspicions?"

"So they can get the torches and pitchforks ready? Of course not. You showing up is all the bad I can handle."

"I've never said the reason I'm here has anything to do with your brother."

"You've never said it doesn't either," Reece muttered.

Grayson's attention shifted back to Reece. "You're very suspicious."

"You didn't give me the truth," said Reece. "And that's something I don't easily forgive and forget."

Jamey's hand moved to the back of Reece's neck and squeezed warningly. He got her message loud and clear: *shut up.* "I know why he's here." Her narrowed eyes were on Grayson. "It isn't for you."

"No?" Grayson made it a question.

"No," Jamey repeated, firmly. "Because even if you won't believe me when I say Reece is incapable of harming anyone, you better believe me when I say I can alibi him."

Reece could not have heard right. "You can *what?*"

"We were still up together at midnight," said Jamey. "And he was asleep on the couch when I got the call."

Grayson folded his arms, looking perfectly at ease discussing hypothetical guilt for an unthinkable crime. "He could have gone out and come back."

Jamey shook her head. "Do the math for the travel time from our house. Not a chance."

"Average ninety-six miles an hour on the highway—"

"My car's top speed is ninety," Reece interrupted. "Now will one of you fill me in?"

"No," Grayson said, just as Jamey said, "Yes."

Grayson looked at Jamey. "An empath shouldn't hear it."

"He deserves to know."

"Would you want to know," said Grayson, "if you were him?"

That made Jamey pause. Reece's stomach sank. "Tell me," he said anyway, even if he wasn't sure he meant it.

Jamey crouched in front of Reece's chair, their eyes almost level. "You're not going to like it."

Compared to Grayson's blank pages, Reece could read novels in Jamey's subtle expressions. "Stop wondering if you're going to break me and just spit it out."

She bit her lip but took him at his word. "Senator Hathaway was killed by an empath."

Chapter Eight

From: Stone, Cedrick <s.stone@stonesolutionscorp.com>
To: Owens, Jason <j.owens@stonesolutionscorp.com>; Whitman, Vanessa <v.whitman@stonesolutionscorp.com>
Subject: White paper

Doctors, your latest white paper, "Emotional Influence and the Endocrine System," did us proud. An entire generation of empaths, yet I feel so many still do not grasp that emotions are not just about how we feel, but can effect what we're physically capable of in a given moment.

I appreciate your sound judgment in selecting which findings to share with the public. I'm having copies sent to Hannah ASAP.

It took Reece several seconds to process what Jamey had said. When he finally did, his mouth fell open. "That's impossible."

Jamey held up her hands placatingly. "Reece—"

"That doesn't even make sense!"

"Nothing about this case makes sense," she said. "Senator Hathaway's cause of death wasn't drugs—she was pumped full of the hormones that fuel emotions until her heart burst."

Reece fought back a shudder. "But since when are empaths capable of that?"

It was Grayson who said, "We've had one generation of

empaths. You think you're the be-all, end-all of what your kind is capable of?"

Reece winced. "I might believe some empaths have powers others don't," he said carefully. "But so what? Empaths can't—we can't—" He swallowed. "The idea that an empath could hurt someone, it's—"

Ludicrous, he was going to say. But he was thrown back to the ambulance and the words from his own lips.

Empathy can't hurt him. I can't hurt him.

He'd heard those as lies. Which meant some part of Reece had believed he was lying—

He stood so fast he knocked his chair over.

No. No, those lies had been a fluke. Yes, he had violent nightmares, and yes, he had an ability no empath should have, but no matter his strange nightmares and abilities and lies, he couldn't hurt anyone. No empath could.

"*This* is why I need an alibi?" he snapped at Grayson. "Because you think an empath did it—and you think that empath could be me?"

"Was it?" Grayson asked neutrally.

"*No!*" Reece threaded both gloved hands in his hair. "No," he said again, bitterly. "Of course not."

Jamey got to her feet too, more slowly, her gaze fixed on Grayson. "Are you and I going to have a problem, Agent Grayson?"

Reece tensed, but Grayson only pushed off the wall, calm as ever. "No, Detective. If I thought he'd done this, we wouldn't be standing here chitchatting." He put his hands on the table, bringing him eye level with Reece. "I didn't plan to tell you," he said. "I was gonna let you keep your innocence. But you wanted the truth, and there it is: some empaths can use their abilities to kill."

Reece didn't want to hear this. He dropped back into his seat, not trusting his shaky limbs. "But how?"

"All you need to know is I'm gonna stop them," said Grayson. "That's what I do and that's why I'm here. But I've also got to do something with you."

"Go ahead." Jamey's hand was back on her holster so fast Reece hadn't seen it move. "I might even let you try."

Grayson raised his head at that, but Reece spoke first. "Wait, why *are* we *chitchattin'*? You said you had somewhere you could take me—why am I not already there?"

Grayson glanced back at him, then pushed off the table and turned to Jamey. "Another body was found an hour ago."

Reece stiffened. "Great," Jamey said flatly. "Someone who drives a red car with wide tires, by any chance?"

Grayson nodded once. "Red i8. Dr. Jason Owens, formerly director of Research and Development at Stone Solutions."

"And the same empath who killed Hathaway also killed Owens?" she asked.

"We're betting on it," said Grayson.

Reece squeezed his eyes shut, throat tightening. He'd never heard of Jason Owens, but the thought that there was another empath out there committing these acts hurt his stomach more than Grayson's voice.

Jamey rested her hand on the back of his neck again, a comfort until she said, "First good news I've heard all day."

"*Jamey!*"

They both ignored his outrage. "You knew him?" said Grayson to Jamey.

"Dr. Owens and I met. Once." Jamey folded her arms. "How come no one's told the SPD about his murder?"

"Stone Solutions has an internal investigations and enforcement team," said Grayson. "They keep things quiet."

"Silent, apparently," said Jamey. "But what's more mess at Stone Solutions have to do with Reece?"

"Another complication," said Grayson. "Your brother is complicating everything and I don't have time for it. We have four bodies already and the empath is probably just getting warmed up."

"Oh boy," Jamey muttered. "Well, I'm in."

"I work alone."

"My city, my case," said Jamey. "If you want sympathy while you whine about it, try the empath."

Grayson's gaze swept over her, where she stood at Reece's side. "Yes ma'am," he finally muttered. "But that still leaves—"

Reece cut him off. "If an empath did this, you should have an empath's help to stop them," he said, and hey, his voice only wavered a little. "I'm in too."

"Like hell you are," said Jamey. "You're going to Alaska."

"He can't," said Grayson.

"Why not?" Jamey said. "Maybe we don't have a float plane, but that was just to keep him from *you*."

"I'm not who you should be worried about—well. Not right this second, at any rate," Grayson amended, which was not particularly reassuring. "But I can't rely on Stone Solutions today and it's not easy to find another safe place for an empath."

"Oh please." Reece wiggled his gloved fingers. "What am I going to do, break out of a jail cell with the power of feelings?"

"Safe," said Grayson, a little more quietly, "doesn't always mean keeping an empath in. Sometimes it means keeping others out."

Reece made a face. "Oh, thanks, that's clear as mud." He looked at Jamey. "Do his riddles make any sense to you?"

But Jamey had stiffened, that rare flash of fear visible on

her face. "He stays with me, then. I'll figure out what to tell Lieutenant Parson."

Reece groaned. "I'm sure that will go over great."

But Grayson shook his head again. "Mr. Davies here showed up at the station and reporters wanted to know how he could stomach a homicide. He works a homicide with a cop, they're going to start asking what else empaths can stomach."

Reece winced.

"Part of my job is making sure the public believes all empaths are pacifists, today more than ever," Grayson said to Jamey. "Or are you eager to see those torches and pitchforks you mentioned?"

Jamey frowned. "What's your bright idea, then?"

Grayson spread his hands meaningfully.

Reece's eyes widened.

"Oh no," said Jamey. "Absolutely not. Over my dead body."

"There are worse things than dead bodies, Detective," Grayson said. "Worse things than Dead Men, even."

Their eyes locked over Reece's head, and he had the uncomfortable sensation they were having a second, unspoken conversation that he didn't understand.

"Do you think I'd consider taking an empath with me if I thought I had a single other option I could count on?" said Grayson. "It's temporary, until I have a better solution, but Seattle can't wait while I'm working on that."

Jamey set her jaw. "And why would Reece ever agree?"

"Because if he goes with you, he'll be stressed all day about your job and the people he's scaring. He goes with me, he only has to worry about his own safety, and he's an empath so he probably doesn't even know how. You know which one he'll pick."

Jesus. Apparently Grayson called himself a *specialist* for a reason. Reece had been naked with people who hadn't seen him that clearly.

"You want to protect your brother. That's admirable," Grayson said to Jamey. "I'm sorry your best option is the Dead Man."

There was nothing snide or smug in Grayson's tone. If anything, his apology seemed sincere.

Jamey narrowed her eyes. "Fine." She stepped closer to Grayson. "I'm not going to make a threat in front of Reece," she said. "Just remember that he's soft, but I'm not. And I'm not scared of you."

Grayson seemed to consider that. Consider her. Then he simply nodded once. "I'm sure I don't need to tell either of you how confidential the nature of our suspect is."

"You're right, you don't," said Jamey.

"I'll make sure they're expecting you at Dr. Owens' home, Detective," Grayson said. "Be careful who you talk to. Not everyone on the team knows the truth."

"Like I'm going to talk to *anybody* from Stone Solutions," she said.

Reece tensed. He glanced up at Grayson. "Are you and I also—"

"You saw more of a homicide scene than you should've already," said Grayson. "I'm not about to take you to another one so you can *wander off* again. What we *are* taking is your car."

Reece tried to pretend Grayson's brusque reassurance hadn't made his shoulders relax. "*My* car?"

"Mine's getting detail work on the passenger door."

Reece wrinkled his nose. "What, the Southern gentleman doesn't like mud splashes?"

"Something like that," Grayson said.

As he was following Grayson out the door, Jamey caught

Reece by the wrist. He could tell what she was thinking from the set of her mouth.

"I know," he said. The Dead Man could never learn Reece could hear lies. "I'll be careful."

He tried not to wince as the words soured in his ears. He hadn't realized that would be a lie.

Cedrick Stone was calling *him*?

"Mr. Stone, sir," Nolan said, trying not to sound surprised. "We've been trying to reach you all morning. I called Stone Solutions several times myself and heard you weren't available."

"Yes, my lawyer informed me Detective St. James was being quite persuasive. Despite her counsel, I find myself disinclined to leave my current location."

Nolan tried to think of how to politely say *there's talk of your arrest*. "Measures like subpoenas and warrants have been floated."

"I have larger concerns, I'm afraid," Stone said, his voice as smooth and polished as a river rock.

"What's more concerning than getting dragged before a judge over a murder investigation?"

"I'm in terrible danger."

Nolan sat up. "We can protect you. The FBI—"

"There is only one person on earth capable of the protection I need, and that would rather be like asking the proverbial fire to protect you from the frying pan."

Nolan's hand balled into a fist. "The Dead Man."

"You're quick on the uptake, I see." Stone gave a polite cough. "I've just learned that the two of you met."

Nolan's lip curled, fresh anger sharpening his voice. "And I've just learned Cowboy Batman is apparently too unique for something as petty as an assault charge."

"He is unique, unfortunately," Stone agreed. "Agent Nolan, what do you know about empaths?"

Nolan snorted before he could stop himself.

"Yes, I'm often the target of that reaction." The humor in Stone's voice had a sharp edge. "The US government doesn't quite share that sentiment, which of course has been good for business."

To put it mildly. Stone's blood-soaked yacht alone cost more than Nolan's net worth. "I know the Empath Initiative has jurisdiction over all things empath," said Nolan. "But apparently Grayson somehow supersedes even that."

"Evan and I are well acquainted, which I'm sure isn't surprising given our respective lines of work. That doesn't mean I approve of his methods. Take this morning: asking questions is one thing, but laying hands on an FBI agent was quite another."

Nolan looked out the window at the bobbing yachts. No reason to mention he'd called Grayson a liar and tried to arrest him for evidence tampering. "I appreciate your understanding."

"It was no way to treat an exceptional agent with skills like yours."

"You looked at my record?"

"Naturally," said Stone, like snooping on people was a trivial matter. "You did some very impressive undercover work two years ago. Are you still so remarkably talented?"

Stone wanted something; was flattering Nolan for a reason. "A US senator was found dead on your yacht. You're wanted for questioning by both the FBI and the SPD."

"And a smart agent like you knows I wouldn't ask you to compromise your investigation! I simply want to offer a trade."

"I'm listening." And he was, despite knowing he should be alerting the Bureau and having the call traced.

"I fully intend to come forward when I'm able to do so," Stone promised, "and I fully intend to cooperate. And at that time, I'm offering to work exclusively with you."

That had Nolan sitting up even straighter. That kind of access, the attention and leverage it would bring—"And in exchange?"

"You provide me with updates on Evan Grayson."

"Why?" Nolan said suspiciously. "You knew he and I had a run-in this morning. You must already have a source."

"I can keep up with the FBI and the police, it's true. Evan, however, is a different matter. He operates on his own terms, with complete autonomy. I believe that's dangerous. And I believe you might agree with me."

Nolan stared at the yachts, white against the gray sky and sea. "You propose this like you think I could get close to Agent Grayson."

"You can't," said Stone. "Nor would it be good for your health to try. But you can get close to Detective St. James."

Nolan frowned. "St. James? Really?"

"Her brother is an empath. Evan will have a sharp eye on him, and she, in turn, will have a sharp eye on Evan."

Nolan had already had more than enough of St. James and her whiny brother. "We didn't exactly get along this morning."

"I think an agent with your experience would find that fence easy to mend," said Stone. "She's a detective, you're an FBI agent. She'll be inclined to trust you, and her empath brother will make her unlikely to trust Evan. Mr. Davies really is a glaring weakness of hers."

It was true that Nolan was a good actor, when he wanted to be. It was possible he could mend their relationship if he pretended to care what happened to Davies, and it might be worth dealing with St. James if it meant he got to exclusively question Cedrick Stone.

But this wasn't procedure. "I'm not authorized to bargain like this with a potential suspect," Nolan reluctantly pointed out, even as his mind started looking for loopholes.

"You tried to report the Dead Man, and the Bureau hung you out to dry," said Stone. "Consider if your faith would be better placed in me."

Nearly thirty minutes had passed and the red BMW i8 parked the wrong way at the curb hadn't budged.

Ollie stared at it through the diner window as Penny wandered up to his side, tying the diner apron on behind her back.

"Go tell them to leave," she said.

Ollie frowned. "You do it."

"I shouldn't even be here. I worked the night shift. Martin had the balls to call and wake me up to come in because he's too cheap to hire someone else. I need our shitty coffee." She stormed back into the kitchen.

Ollie sighed, but wiped his hands on his apron. He stepped out of the diner, the bell jingling behind him as he crossed the sidewalk to the car and knocked on the tinted driver's window. "Excuse me, but you're going to have to move your—oh."

As the window dropped it revealed the driver, a pretty young woman with light brown eyes the size of dinner plates. Her hair was bound over one shoulder in a braid, dark brown against her pink-and-red patterned shirt. "Is there a problem?" she asked.

He shook himself. Pretty or not, she couldn't park here. "This spot is reserved for customers. You haven't come in and ordered anything."

She smiled. For some reason, he shivered. "I'm afraid I'm being a news junkie," she said, and even her voice was cute and sweet. "But who can blame me today?"

He could hear her radio in the car. "*—the latest news in the* *shocking death of Senator Hannah Hathaway. In a perhaps ironic moment, the SPD's empath consultant, Reece Davies, was seen this morning in the vicinity of police headquarters—"*

"Ain't that the truth," Ollie said. "I can't believe Senator Hathaway's dead." He looked down the sidewalk, then leaned in. "Did you hear AMI say empaths are behind it?"

"Really?" She blinked up at him with long lashes. "Empaths?"

"Mmm-hmm. And I bet they're right; creepy fuckers, always trying to read your mind."

"Not hard when the mind is as complex as a picture book." She smiled her strange smile again. Must be a private joke.

"My boss says if the bill gets passed, we'll have a green light to kick empaths out of the café," said Ollie. "That'd be nice, right? Never have to let one of the little creepers stay?"

"—and while the department has not yet released its promised statement, we would hope that, considering her stance on empathy, there is no intention of using an empath to consult on the senator's death."

The pretty girl cocked her head. "Can I ask you something?"

He put a hand on the door frame and leaned forward, into the car. "Sure." He squinted as his eyes adjusted to the dim interior and then frowned. One of her hands rested on the steering wheel, displaying a wrist ringed with a mess of scabs and bruising. And her shirt wasn't pink and red; she was in pink scrubs, like a nurse, but stained all over with—

She set her other hand on top of his. The world fell away, his entire attention diverted by the softness of her skin, by the intoxicating sound of her voice as she asked, "Do you like your boss?"

"Mr. Davies was seen this morning vomiting on the steps of police headquarters—"

"Mr. Martin? He's—"

"Or do you want nothing more than to see what color his intestines are?"

"—*under speculation that the gruesomeness of the murders is proving too much for an empath to handle.*"

Rage consumed Ollie, his vision going as red as the stains on her scrubs. "I'm gonna shred his skin and rip out his guts."

"*We have no word of any suspect yet in custody, meaning the perpetrator of this monstrous multi-murder may still be at large.*"

She patted his hand and smiled. "Use something fun, like a vegetable peeler." And the i8's tires squealed as she sped away from the curb.

Chapter Nine

The public is not supposed to believe the Dead Man exists, but we at Eyes on Empaths *are NOT the public. We know the Dead Man is real and we pride ourselves on separating fact from rumor.*

Fact: He has complete autonomy when it comes to anything involving empaths

Fact: He's selfless and dedicated in his mission to protect the innocent

Rumor: His middle name is Miguel and he's really hot (but Eyes on Empaths *is hoping this is fact, for obvious reasons)*

—*Gretel Macy, blogging for* Eyes on Empaths

Grayson looked ridiculous in Reece's car.

"Is your head actually touching the roof?" Reece asked, as he climbed into the driver's seat. Jamey hated riding with him, and Grayson was even taller and more muscular. At least Reece still had enough room, since Grayson had twisted himself into an odd angle that kept his broad shoulders out of Reece's space.

Grayson only held up Liam's blazer and glasses, his face as unreadable as ever. "Whose are these?"

"What makes you think they're not mine?"

"They're nice."

Reece rolled his eyes and put the key in the ignition. "There's nothing wrong with hoodies."

Grayson used one long arm to move Liam's stuff to the admittedly spacious area behind Reece's driver's seat. "Is that really what you think?"

"I'm not taking fashion advice from someone called the *Dead Man*."

"I wouldn't believe you take fashion advice from anyone." Grayson gestured with his phone. "Is there a good reason the tracker for your car says we're next to the ocean right now?"

Reece leaned in. "If the Empath Initiative doesn't want me to find its tracker," he said, with cloying sweetness, "tell them not to put it in my engine."

"I advised them to put it in your trunk this time."

"That's where my engine is."

Grayson seemed to consider this. "Speaking of tracking." He held out his hand. "Your phone."

"Why?" Reece said suspiciously.

"So I can make sure no one can find us through it."

"Maybe I want Jamey to know where I am."

"Maybe your big sister isn't the only one who might try."

Reece grudgingly passed the phone over. As Grayson messed with it, Reece turned the key. Thumping bass filled the car, and Grayson twitched, exactly like Jamey always did.

Reece immediately reached over and turned it off. "Jamey has sensitive ears too," he said, when Grayson looked his way.

As Reece put on his turn signal and pulled the car away from the curb, Grayson eyed the duct tape on the ceiling, the sticky and discolored console full of candy wrappers, the broken glove box, and then, worryingly, the stereo.

"No country," Reece said firmly.

"Did I say something?"

Somethin'. Now that he was getting used to the creepy flat voice, Reece was annoyed to realize he did, in fact, enjoy the accent. "No music when I drive. *Only* when parked. No distractions from you, period."

"How are you not distracted by *this*?" Grayson gestured at the candy wrappers, which in fairness were overflowing from the console. "This is a car, not a piñata, even if it's about the same size, and the whole thing smells like fake fruit. I'm gonna have to crack a window and it's thirty-six degrees out there."

"You can't." Reece tried not to squirm as Grayson turned back to stare at him. "I'd let you," he promised, "but the window's stuck and I haven't had a chance to—you know, how about instead of giving me that judgy stare, you tell me where the reporters went?"

"I got rid of them."

"How?"

Grayson pointed out to the street. "Head toward the water. It's close."

Reece rolled his eyes as best he could while keeping them on the road. "Someone should add *allergic to answers* to your Dead Man file."

"You really think anyone gets to keep a file on me?"

He'd bet good money that the Hypocrite Man had a big, juicy file on Reece. "Am I going to have to lug you around in my car all day? What are you even made of, titanium?"

Grayson removed his winter hat, setting it on his lap before pulling down the passenger visor. "Since when do empaths have opinions on physical bodies?"

"You're too tall. It's throwing off the handling."

"The *handling*."

"Yes, the handling! *And* you're hurting my gas mileage. Your muscles are literally bad for the planet."

At the stoplight, Reece glanced over to find Grayson studying himself in the visor mirror. "Are you *primping*?"

Grayson cut his eyes to Reece, then back to his own reflection. "Some of us aren't averse to combing our hair."

Reece self-consciously ran a hand over his own hair before he could stop himself. Even through the glove, he could feel it sticking up oddly. Admittedly, it had been a few days since his hair had seen a comb. Or a brush. Or a shower. "So what? I'm sure you're pretty enough for both of us."

"Aw, thanks, sugar. I didn't think an empath would notice looks either."

Patronizing dick. "*Fine*. You're right; I'm a typical empath whose concept of attractiveness is mostly predicated on inner beauty, and if you have any of that, it's hidden from me by your creepy zombie vibe."

Grayson raised an eyebrow.

"No disrespect," Reece hastily added, as he drove downhill toward the water.

"We're here," was all Grayson said. "Park there, right in front of that building."

Reece started to pull into the spot, then paused.

"Yes, the curb is yellow," said Grayson. "Do it anyway."

Reece put the car in reverse. "I'll find another spot."

"Sure, sure, and the homicide investigation will just keep while you find the perfect parking space."

Reece ignored his bitching, driving on and fitting his car into a space just around the corner. "Give me a second to look for change."

Grayson gave him a very flat look before unfolding his gigantic body from the tight car with surprising grace.

"There is nothing wrong with doing your civic duty and paying for parking!" Reece called after him.

He was fishing out his wallet to count his sad amount of remaining cash when Grayson suddenly opened the driver's door. Without a word, he stuck a parking sticker to the windshield, then turned and strode off.

Reece blinked. Then he scrambled out of the car after Grayson. "I don't need the Dead Man to pay for my parking!"

"Yes, you do," said Grayson. "I've seen your bank statements."

"*How* have you—never mind, you're not going to tell me." Despite his words and long legs, Grayson had Jamey's trick of walking at a pace Reece could match. "Where are we going anyway?"

"Hathaway's office."

Reece winced. "They're going to be thrilled to see me."

The government building's lobby was instantly forgettable, with a worn blue carpet and a modest collection of couches and chairs. Two people were in the waiting area, paging through old issues of magazines, while a single security guard sat behind a desk with a high edge.

Grayson walked straight to the desk. "We're here to see Pitney Adams."

"No visitors today," the guard said in a bored tone, not looking up.

Reece put his hands on the desk's high edge and stood on his toes to peek over. The edge hid an assortment of security monitors, but it looked like the guard was actually reading a novel back there. Something with magic, judging from the cover.

Grayson folded his arms on the edge and leaned down. "It wasn't a request."

The guard finally looked up, first at Grayson, then past Grayson to Reece and Reece's gloves. His nostrils flared.

Reece refused to be cowed. Hathaway's bill wasn't law; the guard couldn't throw him out. Legally, Reece still had just as much right to be in this building as any other taxpaying citizen.

It just didn't mean anyone connected with Hathaway was going to welcome him with open arms.

The guard made a show of going back to his book. "Adams is busy."

"He's still gonna see us," said Grayson.

The guard snorted, and finally put the book down and got to his feet. He was tall enough to meet Grayson's eyes, and in an exaggerated mockery of Grayson's drawl he said, "I'm mighty sorry, son, but I'm afraid I can't."

If the taunt bothered Grayson, it was impossible to tell; his expression didn't change as he pulled out his phone. But Reece's hackles were up. "There's no need to be rude," he snapped at the guard.

The guard looked down his nose at Reece. "Let me guess: you think your boyfriend's accent is cute?"

"And you think it's an insult to call someone gay. If you have a problem with me—and you obviously do—have it with me and leave him out of it."

The guard's expression turned even more hostile. "Stay out of my head," he hissed. "I hear things about your kind, working here, and now the one person trying to put a leash on you is dead. So yes, I have a problem with you and the way you can rape people's minds."

Reece *hated* that accusation. He flinched, just as Grayson looked up from his phone and said, "We're done here."

Reece couldn't hear a single change in that flat voice, but the guard froze with his mouth half-open in response, doubt on his face for the first time.

The shrill ring of the phone on the guard's desk made Reece jump. The guard snatched it up.

"McCarthy." He listened for a moment, then blanched.

His eyes went to Grayson, and he somehow grew even paler. "Yes. Yes, I understand. Yes, sir."

The guard fumbled to put the phone back on the cradle, missing the first time with his trembling hand. "Adams will see you right away."

Reece frowned. "You seem scared all of a sudden."

Grayson met the guard's eyes. "Tell the empath you're fine."

The guard's eyes dropped to the desk. "I'm fine."

Lie. Reece opened his mouth—then snapped it shut. He'd promised Jamey he'd be careful about his abilities in front of Grayson, and the guard wasn't hurt, just scared, for no reason that Reece could guess.

The guard stumbled the ten steps to call down the elevator, and as soon as it opened, he swiped his security card on an inside panel before pressing eight for them. He immediately scurried away, eyes fixed on the floor.

Reece craned his head to look out of the closing elevator doors. It didn't look like the guard was going back to his desk.

"That was all very chivalrous," Grayson said dryly, as the elevator doors shut, "but I'm awful far from a damsel in distress."

"Yeah, yeah, big tough Dead Man. You going to explain how you made this happen?"

"Why would I?"

Jamey cut her siren and lights, sparing the residents the ruckus as she exited the I-90 floating bridge onto Mercer Island. The trees and yards were lush green against the gray skies and the stately homes lining the streets had cars in the driveways worth more than she made in a year.

Jason Owens' home was at the end of its street, by the water. Jamey parked in the driveway. Time to see if Grayson was a man of his word.

As she exited the car, a man was rushing toward her. "Excuse me, you can't—"

She held up her badge. "Detective St. James, SPD. You're supposed to be expecting me."

"Oh." The man's demeanor immediately changed to flawless respect. "Yes, of course. Agent Grayson said you were coming. Follow me."

Five minutes later, she stood in the middle of Jason Owens' study, eyeing the wall. The Stone Solutions internal investigations and enforcement team buzzed around her with the same efficiency as the SPD at a crime scene. But her attention stayed focused on the mahogany bookshelves, tasteful paintings, and thick layer of blood sprayed across all of it.

"Detective St. James?"

The newcomer had pitched her voice at an unusually soft volume, pleasantly quiet to Jamey's ears. She turned to find a beautiful woman in a white lab coat over jeans, probably also around thirty, with dark brown hair in a ponytail, umber-brown eyes behind glasses like Liam's, and a noticeable scar on her neck, the kind that might be left by a knife.

"Aisha Easterby. I'm the ME," she said, as Jamey shook her hand. "Congratulations on being the first outsider Agent Grayson has ever authorized to enter a scene like this. How did you manage it?"

"Pulled a gun on him."

Easterby blinked, then seemed to accept that. She gestured to the bloody wall. "I see you found ground zero." When Jamey cocked her head, Easterby added, "Most of the rooms are in a similar state. But we think this is where it started." She pointed to a small drop cloth a few feet away. "With the eyes."

"The eyes are—"

"Still under there."

Jesus. Jamey took another long look at the blood smeared

on the wall and along the spines of several of the books. "Did you know Dr. Owens before his death?"

Easterby's lips thinned. "Yes," she said, with no enthusiasm.

Interesting.

Easterby glanced around the room, gaze lingering on the man dusting for fingerprints. "If you have questions—"

"I do. But let's go somewhere we won't be overheard." Jamey pointed at Fingerprints. "Because it's not just him. There are four other people listening in on us from the hall."

Fingerprints squawked. The corner of Easterby's mouth turned up. "You find a spot. I'll follow you."

Jamey found a balcony off the master bedroom with a stunning view of Lake Washington and no eavesdroppers. She leaned on the railing, taking in the calm gray waters and the houses dotted in amongst the green pines on the other side of the lake. "I didn't see a red i8 parked anywhere outside."

"No. But there's a ten-year-old green Hyundai on the driveway registered to a Vincent Braker. We had already theorized the suspect stole the Hyundai from the marina; seems likely they've switched it for Dr. Owens' car here."

Great. Their suspect was driving around in a flashy sports car and they were still unstoppable.

Easterby joined her at the rail. "The other thing that's missing is Dr. Owens' phone. Laptop, tablets, all accounted for, but no phone on the body or in the house."

Odd. Maybe the perp snatched the phone with the car, but Jamey wouldn't expect an empath to care much about tech; Reece didn't like phones because he said they interfered with picking up emotions. "What's the official explanation going to be for Owens' death?"

Easterby sighed. "Drugs."

"*Drugs.*"

"It's the usual story." Easterby glanced at Jamey. "But if

you know Grayson, I'm guessing you know the real reason Jason Owens was suddenly filled with the desire to tear himself apart."

Jamey glanced at Easterby's neck. With a scar like that, so close to the jugular vein, she'd probably been lucky to escape with her life—whatever it was that this sweet, friendly doctor had needed to escape. "That depends. Are you here with Stone Solutions or are you here with Grayson?"

"My checks are signed by Cedrick Stone, but it's all an ouroboros around the empaths," said Easterby. "The government agency, the Empath Initiative, is supposedly at the top, but they bend over backward to give Grayson anything he wants, including agents on call. And for all its private company posturing, Stone Solutions gets obscene amounts of money from the Empath Initiative, because why spend corporate wealth when your company can get handouts from taxpayers? But that money is conditional on letting Grayson pull strings here too."

She added, a little wryly, "Grayson says he's the proverbial lone wolf. But if he ever does form his own team, I'll be first in line."

Jamey gestured around them. "Does everyone here know Grayson as well as you seem to?"

"No," Easterby admitted. "The rest of the team thinks we come after the cops to clean up scenes too gruesome for the public to discover. I've just met the Dead Man for—well." She touched her neck. "Reasons of my own."

Jamey's gaze darted to Easterby's scar.

"Grayson didn't do this, if that's what you're wondering," Easterby said, wryly but firmly. "I can't tell you the story—it's classified—but Grayson is the reason I survived."

Classified. Jamey wanted to know, but she didn't push. "Has anyone talked about the killer's motive?"

"No. But no one does in these cases. These killers don't

need a motive; it's sadism for sadism's sake." Easterby bit her lip. "Although…" She shook her head. "Never mind. It's uncharitable of me. I shouldn't speak ill of the dead."

"I'll do it then," Jamey said. "Good riddance to Jason Owens."

Easterby startled. "What makes you—"

"He showed up at my place a few years back and tried to convince me that my brother turning twenty-one meant he had to come to Stone Solutions for mandatory tests."

"How did that go?" said Easterby.

"I explained the actual law to him in nice small words. There may have been a strong implication that he shouldn't come back." Jamey glanced at the house behind her. "An implication pretty similar to this scene, actually. I should probably make myself a suspect."

Easterby huffed a short laugh. She leaned on the rail next to Jamey, closer this time. "So your brother is a—oh!" Her face lit. "Of course: Detective St. James with the empath brother. I've read about you guys. There's this blog everyone in the industry follows, *Eyes on Empaths*—"

"I know it." Jamey turned away.

"Wait," Easterby said, drawing Jamey back. "I just check it for news, I don't believe the trash they publish."

"You work at Stone Solutions."

"Yeah, but I *like* empaths."

"Really?" Jamey said dryly. "When you know how Owens and Hathaway were killed?"

"I'm hardly going to blame the empath," Easterby said, with feeling.

"Why not?" Jamey said, nonplussed.

Easterby winced. "I shouldn't have said that, it's all classified. Just—I like empaths. And not in a creepy, *I want to run tests on them* kind of way."

"You know the world's only empath hunter by name."

But Easterby only shook her head. "Grayson isn't an empath hunter. And he's not the enemy. Not yours, not your brother's."

"He's not our ally either."

"No," Easterby admitted. "He's definitely not that. He's—complicated."

Complicated. Jamey looked back out to the lake. The Dead Man was turning out very different than she'd expected, from his indifference to a gun in his face to his sharing information to his good looks and *yes ma'am*s. "I want copies of all your reports."

"Sure."

"And any theories for where our suspect is heading next."

"Of course."

"And I want to know if anyone sees that red i8."

"Naturally." Easterby was stealing glances at her, chewing on her lower lip and fidgeting in a way she hadn't been earlier. "So," she finally said, "would it be weird and tacky and totally inappropriate to ask for a phone number?"

"Sorry," said Jamey, "I'm seeing someone."

"Oh, not *your* number! Your brother's."

Jamey blinked.

"No one ever makes a play for him?" Easterby shook her head. "It's amazing how few people have figured out what should be obvious about empaths."

Whatever *that* meant. "You're not getting my empath brother's number. You work for an empath hunter and Stone Solutions."

"Yeah, but—"

"Deal-breaker."

"But—"

Jamey pointed at the house. "My threats look like that."

Easterby sighed. They were quiet a long moment, and then

she said, "I would have taken your number too. Just, you know.
For the record."

Jamey grudgingly smiled.

Chapter Ten

Love tabletop RPGs…but you're inviting an empath to game night? Try Dungeon-Free Dragons! All beasts, no battles: the perfect choice for the pacifist in your life!

—internet advertisement

The elevators opened into the reception area of Senator Hathaway's former office suite on the fifth floor. Reece hung back, waiting for Grayson, only to have him gesture for Reece to exit first. Reece gave him a dirty look but led the way into the lobby area, hyper-conscious of his gloves.

The reception furniture was a bit nicer than the lobby's—although still not too nice, striking the perfect balance between elegant but modest enough not to be accused of wasting taxpayer money. An enormous portrait of Hathaway dominated the area while a flat-screen TV on the wall silently played a local news station with subtitles.

Pitney Adams was waiting for them, a sour man with a pinched mouth and red eyes with heavy bags. He glanced between Grayson and Reece, his expression turning even more sour when he saw the gloves.

He turned to Grayson, unsubtly ignoring Reece. "I was told to assist an Agent Grayson?"

He started to offer his hand, then drew it back when Grayson's arms remained firmly folded over his chest. Adams finally looked at Reece, his mouth pinching farther. And this time, his hand didn't move. "And Mr. Davies, I presume?"

Reece smiled without humor. "Not even going to pretend you'll shake my hand?"

Adams' hostility deepened. "May I ask what an empath is doing here? I would hope you're not presuming to investigate the death of our nation's staunchest opponent of empathic influence."

His generic accent and formal manner of speaking reminded Reece of Liam's PR persona. But Adams' voice had an edge of genuine dislike Liam's had never had, no matter how angry Reece made him.

Reece opened his mouth, but Grayson spoke first. "He's here because he's with me. I don't think we need more explanation."

Adams' hostility flickered, momentarily replaced with unease. "I'm sorry, Agent Grayson," said Adams. "I don't believe I was told if you're FBI or...?"

"Or," said Grayson.

The unease settled on Adams' face. "How do you know who I am?" Reece quickly asked, trying to drive it away.

"You're the only empath to ever consult with the police in Seattle," said Adams, which was true until he added, "I've been informed of your work."

Lie. But before Reece could ask how he *really* knew him, Grayson said, "Or you could admit you saw him throw up on TV."

Reece looked at Grayson, then followed the other man's eyes to the TV. "Oh *no*."

Because there he was on-screen, on hands and knees on the wet sidewalk in front of police headquarters. The frame tastefully ended just above the actual puking, but a screaming caption proclaimed, *Empath police consultant Reece Davies vom-*

its on news of senator's murder. And of course the video somehow didn't capture *Grayson*, the reason Reece had thrown up
in the first place.

"Perhaps we should step into my office?" Adams said pointedly.

Reece looked around and realized that while there were
only a handful of people in the reception area, every last one
was staring at him. He flinched. "Yes, please."

Adams' office was a small space with mismatched furniture
and a view of the side of the high-rise next door. A commen-
dation from the mayor and two degrees from colleges even
Reece recognized hung right behind the desk where any guest
in the office would have to see them. The office was as tidy as
Adams' hair, but it was also near the communal kitchen and
smelled like an overfull fridge past due to be cleaned.

Adams sat behind his desk and made a hollow gesture at the
single chair for guests. Reece hovered by the wall as Grayson
shut the door, expecting Grayson to take it.

"Sit, Mr. Davies."

Or not. Maybe the Dead Man had manners. Sort of.

Reece took a seat, his eyes immediately drawn to the large
photo in a flashy frame that was prominently displayed on the
desk. It looked like a recent picture of Adams with two others,
Senator Hathaway and a suited white man who was somehow
familiar. The three of them were posed in front of dark windows, the words *Yokota's Sushi House* above their heads. Hathaway and the suited man had their arms around each other
with the platonic familiarity of longtime colleagues, and the
suited man had his other arm draped over Adams' shoulders.
Adams was holding a small blue gift bag, and while he was
smiling for the camera, his eyes were on the suited man.

Reece couldn't read a picture like he could a flesh-and-
blood person, but he could hazard a guess as to the kind of

man who schmoozed like that with a senator and her PA. He pointed to the suited man. "Who's the douchebag?"

Adams bristled in instant offense, his hand wrapping around the sleek smart watch on his wrist.

Oops.

Grayson leaned back against the wall. "That's Cedrick Stone. He's CEO of Stone Solutions."

Oh. Reece looked at the picture again. Yes, that was the smarmy face from TV, the one who promised that his products were the key to keeping American minds safe from empathy.

"He's a brilliant inventor," Adams said, and that note of sycophantic fanboyishness sure explained the prominence of the picture. He looked at Reece's gloved hands, and his lip curled. "Of course, someone like you might struggle to see that."

Someone like you. Reece narrowed his eyes. "I see he took you to a fancy restaurant on what I'm guessing was your birthday, not the kind of place a government worker gets to go on their own dime. I'd also guess that gift bag held the watch you're fondling and I bet he convinced you not to document any of it for the taxpayers, claiming it was all *between friends*, so I also see that he's the kind of man who doesn't hesitate to use his money to manipulate anyone both useful to him and sad enough to fall for—" Reece bit his lip before he could keep talking.

Too late. Adams was red-faced and reaching for his phone. "*Empathy?* In this office? The police will—"

"It wasn't." Reece held up his gloved hands. "Fully muzzled and I've had all my shots."

"But—"

"Don't you have faith in your hero's brilliant inventions? I'm not using empathy. I don't need it when you're a billboard."

Adams went a deeper shade of red. "You're exactly the reason we need Mr. Stone," he hissed. "Who knows where the world would be if we hadn't had him to counter the empath emergence?"

"You'd all be screwed," said Reece, "because these gloves are the only thing that keeps me from turning you into the next minion in my bisexual harem. If I took them off, it'd be nothing but emotional slavery for everyone from here to Tacoma."

Adams' jaw dropped. Grayson tilted his head, eyes boring into Reece.

"That was sarcasm," Reece quickly said. "Very, very sarcastic sarcasm. The gloves don't stop us from anything but accidental reads."

"All the more reason we need the safeguards of Mr. Stone's products and Hannah's bill," Adams said emphatically.

Reece sat back in the chair with a huff. "You do realize that I would never—" His eyes fell on Adams' corkboard. "Never mind. You really do think I'm two seconds away from emotionally enslaving the greater metropolitan area."

Adams drew back. "If you're reading me—"

"You're an AMI member." Reece pointed to the *American Minds Intact* propaganda neatly pinned to the board: rally posters, flyers, bumper stickers. "Believe me, I'm familiar with *that* name." It also meant Reece really needed to skip the sarcasm, because Adams was likely to take it seriously. Most *Eyes on Empaths* readers were also AMI members. "No wonder you're such a fan of Cedrick Stone."

"AMI is a valued team player in this office," Adams said haughtily. "So is Mr. Stone."

Reece's mouth started moving again. "You mean they poured money into Hathaway's campaign so she'd push the bills they want, because I bet you're not the only viper in this pit whose loyalty can bought—"

The flash of shame at his own words made Reece clamp

his teeth down on his lip, hard enough to sting. Adams got under his skin, but that was no way to talk about the dead.

He expected Adams to rage at him for his disrespect, but the other man just set his mouth in a hard line. "Mr. Stone and AMI's campaign donations are public record. This office has nothing to apologize for. What more do you want? I sent Hannah's schedule to a detective with the SPD early this morning. This is a horrible business and I should be left alone. I want a chance to mourn."

Lie. Reece only barely kept his reaction from showing on his face.

His gaze stole to the picture again, but Adams and Hathaway stood close enough together that he didn't see any apparent enmity. Maybe they weren't well acquainted? "Have you worked here long?"

"A year," Grayson answered for Adams.

"That's also public record," Adams said.

"You know what wasn't in any records?" Grayson said, neutral as always. "Where Senator Hathaway really was last night."

Adams sat back in his chair. "I beg your pardon?"

"The schedule says her last meeting was with the mayor. I'm asking where the senator went after that in her nice dress and heels. You're her PA, with access to her schedule—what's missing from it?"

Reece's stomach lurched. He hadn't known Senator Hathaway had been dressed up when she died. It made it seem more personal, somehow.

Adams' tone was as crisp as his starched shirt. "I wasn't privy to Hannah's personal life. If her schedule says her last meeting was with the mayor, then that's all I know."

Lie. "You know obstructing an investigation is a crime, don't you?" Reece said.

Adams wiped at his brow, but what he said was, "I don't know where she went after that meeting."

Lie. Reece desperately wanted to call Adams on it, but he couldn't do it in front of Grayson, not without revealing himself.

Frustrated, he looked over the desk, spotless save for a stack of printed news articles. The top article's headline had been highlighted in bright yellow and starred again with blue ink, for emphasis.

Senator Hathaway Makes Third Monthly Visit to Seattle Veterans Medical Complex.

Reece craned his neck for a better look. "When is that from?"

Adams snatched the article up. "None of your business," he said, turning it over to hide the text from view.

"It's from yesterday," said Grayson.

"Yesterday?" *Reece* had been at the SVMC yesterday, to see Cora about his nightmares. He must have missed Hathaway by just hours. That was unsettling. "Why was she at that hospital?"

"It's on the schedule I sent." Adams tapped his fingers on the back of the page. "Hannah's dad was a veteran. She's been open about his struggles and eventual suicide. She was visiting the hospital because she cared about veterans' issues."

That wasn't a lie, but there was no compassion in Adams' voice for either Hathaway's dad or the other soldiers. Reece frowned. Cora and her fiancé might have mentioned a meeting yesterday when they were bashing on Hathaway's bill, before Cora had read him and—well. Reece wasn't going to think about Cora passing out right now. "Weren't there people at that hospital fighting against Senator Hathaway's anti-empathy bill?"

"I'm sure I don't know." Another lie. Before Reece could

push, though, Adams added, "You know her bill is almost certain to pass now? After such a tragic death, other senators are fighting over who's going to take up the cause in her memory."

There was gloating in Adams' eyes, threaded through with relief. Relieved that the bill would still pass? When had that been in doubt?

Reece leaned forward. There was more Adams was hiding. Reece could almost see it, like a thread hanging loose on a sweater, and if he pulled on it, all of Adams' lies would fall away and he'd know everything Adams really felt—

Reece froze. Jesus, that kind of privacy violation—he shouldn't even be thinking about it. What was wrong with him?

He looked up, and realized Grayson was watching him. But instead of speaking, Grayson pushed off the wall and went for the door without so much as a goodbye. Reece rolled his eyes.

"Thank you for your *help*," he said to Adams, making air quotes around the word, then chased after Grayson.

"Are we actually done talking to Adams?" Reece asked, catching up to Grayson in the reception area.

"That depends."

"On?"

"You."

Reece furrowed his brow. As they waited for the elevator, he could feel all eyes on him. Grayson's stare was the weightiest of all.

"Are you planning to elaborate?" he finally said, trying to pretend the picture of him vomiting at Grayson's feet wasn't still flashing on the lobby's flat-screen TV.

"In a moment." Grayson had a pen in hand and was toying with it.

Reece's mouth opened in outrage. "Did you *steal* that from Adams' desk?"

"No," said Grayson. "I'm just borrowing it. I'm gonna leave it here."

"You're not *borrowin'* anything," Reece said. "Put that back—"

He was cut off by the ding of the elevator. As the doors opened, Grayson put his arm out like a reflex, gesturing for Reece to go in first.

Apparently you could take the boy out of the South, but not the Southern chivalry out of the boy. Man. Dead Man. Reece went in, leaning against the elevator wall as Grayson followed. "You hold elevator doors for everyone?"

"Your city took my sun. You can't have my manners too." Grayson hit a button and the elevator suddenly screeched to a halt.

Reece stumbled at the unexpected stop and only just caught himself on the elevator wall. Then Grayson jabbed the pen up over his shoulder, at the back corner of the elevator, and glass shattered.

Reece's eyes widened. "What did you just do?"

Grayson leaned against the elevator wall. "Got rid of the camera."

"You *what*?"

"I need to know if I'm going right back to Mr. Adams' office and I don't need an audience for this conversation." Grayson fixed Reece with a considering scare. "What did you learn that you don't want to tell me?"

Reece stiffened. "Nothing?" *Lie.* He tried not to wince.

"Please. I do know I'm the Dead Man, sugar. Of course there's stuff you're not gonna tell me."

Reece adopted the most guileless, wide-eyed expression he

had. "How could there be? I didn't touch him and my empathy doesn't work without touch."

Lie. He bit his lip.

Grayson's face, of course, gave nothing away. "None of your empathy works without touch, huh?"

"Nope, not at all, never has." *Lie lie lie.* Reece added some innocent blinks, for good measure.

"And how much of it works without," Grayson cleared his throat, "*sexual flexibility?*"

Reece's cheeks flushed hot. He was doomed to regret that press statement for the rest of his life. "There's this thing called sarcasm. I've discovered it doesn't always translate well in print."

"Or government offices." Grayson looked perfectly comfortable against the stopped elevator's wall, unlike the way Reece was fidgeting on his feet. "You're not adding Mr. Adams to that pack of emotional minions, but if you learned something that could help this investigation, you should share it."

Reece huffed. "Even if there *was* more I'm not telling you—and I'm not admitting anything—I'd have good reason to keep it quiet. If I tell you something you don't want to hear, you might stick me wherever it is you stash empaths who step out of line. So you think I'm going to trust you?"

"I wouldn't," said Grayson, "if I were you."

Well, *that* didn't make Reece feel better.

"But then, if I were you," Grayson added, "I also wouldn't want to take a chance that more people could die while I dragged my feet to keep myself safe."

Reece swore. "I *hate* how well you know empaths." He thought over what he'd seen and what he could say without revealing too much to the Dead Man. "Adams thinks very highly of Cedrick Stone."

Grayson waited.

Reece tried to carefully elaborate. "He's very loyal to Stone."

Grayson waited.

Reece threw up his hands in frustration and the words burst from him in a flood. "Adams is solidly middle-class but angry he isn't rich and believes there's not enough for everyone and he's not getting his fair share so he chose a safe government job but likes money and even more than that likes to feel like he's getting things other people aren't so a rich man like Stone giving him attention and presents and treating him like he's special would have bought his loyalty in a way a year working closely with Senator Hathaway never—"

Nausea tore through him. Reece scrambled for the elevator wall, swallowing down the sudden urge to vomit. He pressed his forehead against the cold metal and took deep breaths, uncomfortably aware of Grayson's blank stare.

Grayson's cool drawl broke the silence. "That's what you deduced without touch?"

Panic sent Reece's stomach lurching again, but he hadn't let on that he'd heard Adams lying. "Sorry to disappoint. But I've never claimed to be the world's most powerful empath."

"Uh-huh," said Grayson. "And this is normal, for you?"

Was it? The emotions had been right there on Adams' face, so strong Adams had been sweating. But connecting the dots like that, without any contact—

That was new, and that was supposed to be a boundary Reece never crossed without permission.

Reece made a noncommittal noise, and tried to think of something to say that might annoy Grayson enough he'd drop the subject. "How about we contrast Adams with *you*, a man who thinks he's so special that he doesn't feel the need to prove it?"

"I know you can't read anything off me," said Grayson. "So where'd you come up with that?"

Reece looked up from the elevator wall, way up, all the way to Grayson's unreadable hazel eyes. "You don't exist in a vacuum. I see how people react when you're around. Every person you meet is nervous. Well, unless they're on Team B, the people who want to bang you."

Grayson raised an eyebrow.

Reece gestured at himself. "Obviously I'm Team A."

Lie. Son of a bitch. Reece never wanted to know which traitorous cell in his clearly unhinged brain was to blame for *that*.

Grayson hit something on the elevator panel, and with a screeching protest it grumbled back to life and began to descend again.

"So we're not going back up to Adams' office?" Reece asked.

"You're not." The elevator doors opened, and Grayson again waited for Reece to exit the elevator first, like he hadn't just trapped Reece in said elevator only moments before. "Whether I go back remains to be seen."

"Oh look, riddles, what a fresh change of pace." They walked into the lobby, where a different security guard was at the desk, speaking urgently into the phone. "Do you practice being an enigma? Look at me, the mysterious Dead Man; I speak in riddles and have weird elevator manners, fear me, empaths?"

"Do you practice your sarcasm, making sure no one can take you anywhere unless they enjoy inappropriate sound bites?"

Reece made a face. "I don't actually try to—shit."

Outside the windows of the lobby, a crowd was gathering. People in coats and fleeces, pressed close to the doors, each face angrier or more fearful than the next. Poster-board signs on sticks were being passed around, with messages like *Honor Hathaway, Pass Her Bill* and *Protect American Minds From Empathy*. Behind the growing mass of people, camera crews were setting up.

Reece cringed. "They're going to freak if they see me come out of this building."

"They won't be here to see it." Grayson already had his phone out.

"What?" Reece threw up his hands. "No. Stop it, they have a right to protest, you can't use your weird powers to make them leave."

Grayson barely spared him half a glance before turning away to speak into his phone.

"Why does everything have to have so much *drama* with you?" Reece demanded. He pointed across the room, to the *Exit* sign on the other side of the elevators. "Look, we can go out those stairs instead. Problem solved."

Grayson covered the phone. "Are you done?"

Overly dramatic *and* a dick. Maybe Grayson didn't listen to anyone but Grayson, but that didn't mean Reece had to. He turned on his heel and stomped off to the stairs.

Chapter Eleven

...dozens of protesters gathered in Washington, DC, today outside of the headquarters of the new Empath Initiative. Empath rights activists argue the nascent agency, helmed by former defense contractor Charles Stone, has too much power and only views empaths as threats.

There were also several empaths on scene, thanking activists for their support but asking them to please be careful and not get hurt.

—*excerpt from a thirty-five-year-old copy of the* Emerald City Tribune,
"*New federal agency adds heat to empath debates*"

The stairs from the lobby of Hathaway's building led Reece into the adjoining parking garage. He took a deep gulp of the welcome cold air, letting it settle his still-shaky stomach.

He wove through a modest collection of Hondas, Mazdas, and Toyotas before emerging past the parking gate and onto the sidewalk. The gathering crowd at the building's front doors was a low rumble like thunder, but it hadn't yet reached around the block or to his car, which was parked at the curb up ahead.

He'd wait in the car for Grayson, but he wouldn't turn it on. He'd let it stay cold and miserable, see how that Southerner liked it.

He would totally do that. Yes, he would.

He sighed.

Aw, who was he kidding. Dead Man or no, Reece would start the heat right away, because being an empath sucked.

He'd almost reached the car when the peace was shattered.

"What were you doing in that building?"

He stumbled backward, nearly tripping over his own feet. *"You."*

Gretel Macy had come around from the side of his car. Daughter of the AMI president, the brains behind the *Eyes on Empaths* blog, and probably the truest believer in the entire anti-empathy bunch. Today she had pink lipstick, a white beanie pulled over shiny hair, and the same suspicious expression she always wore for him.

"When did you go from annoying blogger to creepy stalker?" he said. "How did you find me?"

Gretel had her phone out, and Reece would bet anything she was streaming live. "Your face is on the news and you're getting recognized. My hotline got a tip that a guy in gloves matching your description was in the same building as Senator Hathaway's office. Our network is strong, and we have our eyes—"

"—on empaths. I *know.* You say it a lot." Reece tried to temper his irritation. "It's perfectly legal for me to be in any public building, even a government one."

"Hathaway's bill would have changed that. Empaths must be stopped from influencing the emotions of our representatives. I think my viewers are too smart to buy your presence here as a coincidence."

Reece reached for Liam's advice. "No comment."

He tried to move past Gretel to his car, but she stayed stubbornly in place. "What were you really doing in a government building?"

If he rushed at her, she'd bolt in fear before letting them touch. But that was a pipe dream: he'd trade his car for whatever gas-guzzler Grayson drove before he'd deliberately scare her.

He gritted his teeth. "No comment." Liam was going to be so proud of him.

"Did you go to Senator Hathaway's office?"

"No. Comment."

"Are you trying to brainwash our politicians?"

Reece threw up his hands. "Fine, yes, you caught me. I was trying to get the First Amendment revoked with my crazy mind-control powers. Our forefathers were clearly high when they dreamed up freedom of press."

Her hand flew to her mouth.

Aw, crap. "You're going to publish that, aren't you." He rubbed a hand over his face. "*Fine*. Use your sensationalist blog to tell AMI and the rest of Seattle another ridiculous lie. My day can't get worse." *Lie*. Reece pinched the bridge of his nose and sighed.

Gretel drew her head back, affronted. "I don't print *lies*."

In a possibly ironic twist, she believed that so deeply that it wasn't a lie. "Yes, actually, you—"

"And my blog's not *sensationalist*."

"You wrote a story accusing empaths of controlling what people carve on their jack-o'-lanterns—"

"*And*," she interrupted, barreling right through his complaint, "I'm not just a figurehead. I actually do write the—"

"I know."

She paused. "What?"

"I know," he repeated. "It's the most frustrating thing about you. You're completely sincere and super smart and you work really damn hard. I bet you even do the fancy computer website crap all by yourself."

She blinked. "The coding?"

He snapped his fingers. "Right. That." She was still staring at him. "Can I get to my car now, please?"

She opened her mouth, then closed it. And then it fell open

in a gasp as Grayson appeared behind her and plucked the phone from her hand.

"Sorry, ma'am," he said, in what was almost a polite tone, as he dropped the phone to the pavement, and stepped on it. "National security."

Gretel's eyes darted up to Grayson's face, and Reece saw the storm of emotions warring inside her: outrage, curiosity, and despite everything, desire. Sheesh. Must be nice to look like Evan Grayson.

"Are you the Dead Man?" she finally asked, as guarded awe eventually won out over her other emotions.

"I'm afraid I can't comment on that."

She let out a tiny gasp. "You are," she whispered. "Oh my God. I've got to go." She hurried off, reaching into her coat pocket as she did.

Reece rolled his eyes. *"I'm afraid I can't comment on that,"* he said, imitating Grayson's deep voice and drawl. "You think you're so mysterious."

He stepped toward his car—when Grayson grabbed Reece by the wrist, over the glove, and jerked him forward and down against the hood of his own car. A second later, heavy handcuffs closed around his wrists with a snap.

"We have a problem, Mr. Davies."

Reece's spinning head hadn't caught up to his sudden cuffs. Grayson had moved so *fast*, maybe even as fast as Jamey. And he'd gotten Reece down without ever touching him anywhere but the gloves.

"Are you mad that I left?" Reece carefully stayed completely still on the hood. He *probably* wouldn't hurt Grayson if he tried to squirm away, but much better not to even take the chance. "I'm not your fanboy or sycophant like Gretel; I'm not going to blindly follow you when you're being an idiot."

"The other problem."

"What, that you put cuffs on me and didn't buy me dinner first?"

"Really?" Grayson said dryly. "You're gonna sass me right now?"

Reece could feel one hand on his gloved wrists, no other points of contact. "Are you sure you're holding me down securely enough?"

"Don't start this with me."

"You're barely touching me and these handcuffs are very loose. Don't you know if you did this to someone else, they might be able to wrench your arm and escape? Kick you in the shins? You could get hurt, Agent Grayson."

"Mr. Davies—"

"But if you were holding them down tighter, you might hurt *them*, and I don't like that either. You know what, none of this is safe for anyone involved—"

"You can cut the *innocent empath* act." Grayson leaned over Reece. He still wasn't touching him anywhere but the gloves, but the move brought him closer to Reece's ear, and for fuck's sake this was an arrest, Reece was absolutely *not* going to think about Grayson getting closer. He was Team A, dammit. "I'm not falling for it."

"What *act*?" Reece demanded. "And what problem do we—"

"I just saw in the elevator that you can use empathy without touch. Did you think I'd watch you skip out of Hathaway's building when you're hiding something like that?"

Reece's stomach plummeted. How did he know? Reece had been so careful not to let on about hearing lies.

"I don't know why you agreed to come with me when you had this secret," said Grayson. "Or why you'd admit that you picked up all those things about Adams."

What stuff about Adams? Reece hadn't said anything about

Adams' lies. "Because I want to solve this case too! People are in danger—"

"Yeah, they're in danger from *you*," Grayson said. "And my job is to protect those people from dangerous empaths, including the ones who hide what they can do."

"But I haven't hurt anyone—"

"I gave you a chance and you lied right to my face. Why would I trust that you're not lying now?"

Reece winced.

"And here your sister's a detective with the Seattle police. If she was hiding this secret too—"

Reece's heart rate spiked with anger and fear. "Leave Jamey out of this—"

He sucked in a breath, because suddenly, he was seeing memories of Adams again.

Deep bags beneath his eyes, not one night's lost sleep but weeks—
Pinched mouth twisted in triumph—
Sweat on his brow as he lies about knowing where Hathaway was—

"The bill," Reece said hoarsely.

Grayson went still.

More words burst from Reece in a rush. "Adams was gloating about it but also relieved. That's victory snatched from the fear of defeat. But if Hathaway's death meant victory for the bill—"

"—then she was gonna be its defeat," Grayson muttered. "She was gonna withdraw it?"

"Three visits to a hospital where an empath is trying to help veterans like Hathaway's dad." Reece could still see Adams' face, fingers tapping on the back of the article, no compassion for Hathaway's lost father, lying about knowing the bill opponents were there. "Maybe they got through to Hathaway."

"Adams was sweating when he said he didn't know where a dressed-up Hathaway went for her last meeting."

"He's hiding something—or covering for someone—oh no."

Reece lurched to the side. Grayson caught him by gloved wrists, keeping him from tumbling to the pavement as he gagged hard enough to hurt his chest. If he'd had an ounce of food left in him, he'd have puked it all over the sidewalk.

"That does not feel good," he said weakly, as he rested his cheek on his Smart car's hood and panted.

"Why are you sharing everything with me?" Grayson's voice was still flat, but he seemed genuinely confused. "I've got you in cuffs and you decided to use insight again?"

"Does it look like I'm *decidin'* anything right now?" Reece made a face as another wave of vertigo swamped him. "Is *insight* your fancy way of saying food poisoning?"

"Some empaths can pick up strong emotions without needing touch. We call it insight. It's not without precedent—and it's never a good thing."

Grayson wasn't talking about the lies.

Reece might have been relieved if he hadn't had to bite back a grunt as his stomach made another attempt to empty its contents. "Maybe not," he said, "but you know what's worse than all this puking? You threatening *Jamey*."

That didn't seem to be what Grayson had expected to hear. His hand was still on Reece's wrists, but there was no pressure, even though Grayson probably could have flattened him faster than Reece could say *I didn't do it*.

"How long've you been able to do this?"

Reece had to be careful, but it wasn't like he could take back his insight or whatever it was. Might as well tell the truth. "How long has it been since we left Adams' office?"

"You're really claiming this is the first time?" Grayson said skeptically.

"Why, you think I'm *lying to your face* again?"

"Are you?" Grayson said, in that unnervingly flat drawl.

Fear shot up Reece's spine, but the thought of Jamey made him clench his teeth and push his fear of Grayson back down. "This is the first time this has ever happened to me," he said tightly. "And there's a bigger problem."

"The Dead Man has you in handcuffs over the hood of your car for lying about new abilities, but sure, you think you have bigger problems."

"Yeah, I do," Reece snapped. "Because you suspected this insight thing was happening to me."

"I *am* an empath specialist—"

"Which means you just set it off in me again."

Grayson hesitated. "Well—I wasn't trying—"

"How *could* you?" Reece demanded. "Just when I thought you couldn't possibly be a bigger dick, you decide to top this morning's puking incident?"

"First of all, I didn't know you were gonna vomit at my feet—"

"It made the *news*."

"Second, this was an accident—"

"Still your fault."

"And *third*," Grayson went on, over Reece, "how do you figure this tops that?"

"You just made me stomp all over Adams' privacy!" Reece said furiously. "I don't ever want to use empathy without consent, and no one can consent to insight, whatever the hell it is."

There was a long moment of silence. And then Grayson was pulling Reece upright by gloved wrists.

"All right." There was a click, and then Grayson had taken off the handcuffs. "I believe you."

"You better," Reece muttered, as he shook out his hands. "Turn my insight off."

"I can't."

"I thought you were an *empath specialist*—"

"It's not a switch, it's a trigger. It'll stop." Grayson tucked the cuffs away on his belt. "And if it doesn't, then we'll have a much bigger problem on our hands than you accidentally reading Mr. Adams."

"Oh goody. More riddles." Reece flexed his prickling fingers, his stomach still churning. He hadn't read anyone since March—he did *not* want to do it now, and definitely not like this. "Did you have to cuff me over the hood of my own car? What is your obsession with drama—is it because you're hot? Do you just assume all the world's a stage and no one can take their horny eyes off you?"

"No," Grayson said pointedly, and Reece couldn't hear any emotions, of course, but he liked to believe he could annoy even the biggest stoic. "I can't take chances. If I miss an empath hiding something, innocent people might pay the price." To Reece's surprise, he then added, "But I was wrong about you and I owe you an apology."

Oh. That made Reece's stupid empath conscience twinge, because he *was* lying right to Grayson's face. Maybe Reece hadn't had this insight thing before today, but he sure as hell was hiding how everyone's lies were clear as bells to him.

Reece pushed his conscience aside. Yes, Grayson had given him a chance to come clean, but he'd also shown Reece how fast he could shift into full-on Dead Man mode. If Grayson decided Reece was a threat after all, he wouldn't stand a chance.

"Please," he sniped. "You didn't even think I was dangerous."

"How do you figure?"

"I may not get to the gym much—" *ever* "—but I bet you lift things that weigh almost as much as me."

"More than you," said Grayson.

"All right, more than—"

"A *lot* more than you."

"Yes, *fine*," said Reece. "But see? All those muscles and you barely touched me."

"Maybe I didn't think you were dangerous to *me*."

"Yeah, okay, but you're supposed to be this big scary empath hunter, right? Aren't you going to ruin your reputation if you're careful with us?"

Grayson seemed to hesitate. "My reputation'll survive," he said, and turned back to the car, as if that had been explanation enough.

Reece rolled his eyes. "Can I trade arrests for answers? One empath in handcuffs equals one Dead Man sharing information?"

"Sure," said Grayson. "Here's some: don't ever try to use your insight on purpose."

Reece gave him a filthy look. "You're the boundary-stomping dick who triggered it. I don't want to use it on accident."

"Care Bear." At the nickname, Reece reluctantly looked up at Grayson's vault of a face. "Don't ever try to use it on purpose."

Reece rolled his eyes. "Fine."

"And don't wander off again."

"*Fine.*"

"And don't—"

"Will you just confirm that I'm *not* under arrest?"

Grayson shrugged. "The day is young."

Reece threw up his hands.

As Grayson opened the passenger door, Reece snapped, "Don't you dare get in my car without that apology."

Grayson paused. "For manhandling you?"

"For bringing Jamey into this."

Grayson's shoulders relaxed, like he'd been ready to move

but had settled instead. "She's law enforcement. Be kind of an issue if she was helping her empath brother illegally hide extra powers."

Nerves threatened to crawl up Reece's spine again, but he ignored them. "Don't ever bring up Jamey," he said darkly. "I don't care what you do or say to me, but my sister is off-limits."

Grayson looked at him for another long minute.

Reece didn't look away. No amount of Grayson's unsettlingly expressionless face was going to make him back down.

But then Grayson seemed to find whatever he was looking for in Reece. "Fair enough," he conceded. "My apologies," he added, the very picture of perfect Southern manners.

Reece looked at him suspiciously, but as far as he could tell Grayson was being sincere. "As long as we understand each other."

"I understand you just fine." Grayson dropped into the passenger seat, shaking the entire car. "Reporters may be incoming. We'd best get moving."

Reece rolled his eyes and climbed into the car. "I thought you were going to stomp all over the First Amendment and make them leave."

"I said *may* be incoming. You want to stick around and find out?"

"Where are we even going?"

He gestured to Reece's hands on the steering wheel. "Ever wanted to see where they make those gloves you got at ten and two?"

Reece groaned.

The unknown caller on Jamey's phone could only be one person.

She stepped to a corner of the lobby of the Seattle Veterans

Medical Complex, as far from the crowd as she could manage. "Reece better be all right."

But she could hear Reece's voice in the background. "I didn't say you could use the phone in the car."

"You're driving, not me. But if you're fixing to change that—"

"Like I'd let a phone-using menace to the public behind my wheel. Just don't distract me with your conversation."

Grayson's deep drawl was back in her ear. "Your brother's a very careful driver."

"That can't surprise you," she said. "You're supposed to be an empath specialist."

"Been a while since I've been in the passenger seat."

Who was the last empath that the Dead Man had let behind the wheel? "You're better off letting him drive," said Jamey.

"Why's that?"

"Trust the voice of experience." She leaned against the hospital wall and tuned out the murmurs of all the people flowing around her, up and down the laminate hospital floors. "Where are you taking Reece next?"

"Stone Solutions."

She shoved right back off the wall. "You've got five seconds—"

"Because of Dr. Owens' death," Grayson immediately clarified.

Jamey relaxed against the wall. "You better have extra eyes on him in that snake pit."

"Yes, ma'am," Grayson muttered. "Learn anything new at the scene?"

"That your lackeys need my help to find a red sports car, a fancy phone, and my brother's number."

"Your brother's number?"

There was a high-pitched yelp. "My *what*?"

"That's right," she said to Grayson. "And I don't care how nice she acts, I'm not sharing my empath brother with an ME who works for Stone Solutions."

"Dr. Easterby isn't acting—she *likes* empaths," said Grayson.

There was another yelp. "Someone who likes empaths wanted my number? A *doctor*?"

"I mean," said Grayson, "I don't think it's a kink or anything—"

"Who cares if it is?" she could hear Reece protesting. "Empath here, we don't judge."

"You judge every last person behind a wheel and find them wanting," Grayson said.

"The rules of the road apply to all drivers, even Dead ones. Now, ask Jamey if she gave the doctor my number—*Jamey*—"

"I don't believe an empath would approve of driving distracted." There was indignant sputtering in Grayson's background as he asked Jamey, "You at the hospital?"

"I'm about to question the staff about Hathaway's visit yesterday."

"Can you ask if anyone suspected Hathaway planned to withdraw her bill?"

"*Withdraw* it?" Jamey repeated. "She made her name campaigning on a platform of protecting the public from empathy."

"I have a good hunch she was weakening." Grayson lowered his voice to the barest whisper. "I assume you got other things to investigate."

She heard Reece put on his turn signal in the background in ignorance, Grayson's voice too quiet for his ears. But Grayson had known she'd be able to hear it. Interesting. What else did Grayson know about her? "I'm looking into the suspect too."

"Keep me posted." Grayson cut the call.

Jamey rolled the phone in her hand for a moment.

Keep *me* posted. Not *us*.

How long could they possibly keep the suspect's identity from Reece? It had to only be a matter of time before he put it together that there were only two empaths in Seattle, and if he wasn't pegged for the crime, the other one was.

She tucked the phone away and headed for the receptionist's desk. A pale woman with her hair in a bun lifted her head as she approached. "Can I help—"

Jamey held up her badge. "You're expecting me."

"Oh!" The woman's hands fluttered. "Yes, of course. The detective who wants to talk to anyone who met with Senator Hathaway yesterday." The woman shook her head. "Her death is so shocking."

And this woman didn't know the half of it. "I assume neither Dr. Camden nor Cora Falcon are here?"

"Well, it's as I told the police department this morning," said the receptionist. "They both put in for emergency leave around midnight."

As she told the police department—except this was the first Jamey was hearing of it. All the *actual* police had been pulled off the case, so who had the receptionist talked to? Stone Solutions? The Empath Initiative?

Frowning, Jamey leaned on the desk. "Can you find me someone to talk to?"

The receptionist pursed her lips and scanned her computer screen. "Dr. Jones might know something. I believe he's also against the anti-empathy bill. I'll page him. You can wait in his office."

Dr. Demarco Jones' office was closet-sized but cheerful, decorated with pictures of three young kids with ringlet curls like Jamey's. It took eight minutes for Dr. Jones himself to join her.

"Sorry, Detective St. James." An attractive middle-aged man with russet-brown skin and salt-and-pepper hair, Dr.

Jones was wringing his hands and shaking his head. "We're all juggling extra patients today."

"Because Dr. Camden isn't in?" Jamey prompted.

Dr. Jones nodded. "Not that I begrudge him."

"So you know the reason he and Cora took emergency leave?"

Dr. Jones hesitated. "I still don't understand why the police want to know that. What do John and Cora have to do with anything?"

"We know Senator Hathaway was here yesterday," she said. "We're following every lead we can." Not even a lie. Reece would like that.

He bit his lip. "I guess it can't hurt to tell you. They texted several of us around midnight. They eloped."

"Eloped?"

"Drove off to Vegas in the middle of the night."

Vegas was more than sixteen hours by car, and if they paid for everything with cash, they'd be untraceable. What a convenient explanation for suddenly being missing. "Is the elopement a surprise?"

"Huge surprise. They were planning a big wedding for June, long honeymoon, all of it," said Dr. Jones. "But then, I can't blame John for wanting to get Cora out of town with how nasty the press is turning on empaths."

"Because of Hathaway," said Jamey, hoping to prompt him again.

"Shocking business," he said, with a shake of his head. "I'm against the bill myself. It goes way too far, and I can't imagine losing Cora. But Hathaway's death is still a horrible tragedy."

Grayson's tip in mind, Jamey asked, "I understand some of the staff were trying to persuade the senator to withdraw the bill. Any luck?"

Dr. Jones made a helpless sort of shrug. "This probably

sounds impossible, but we actually thought we were convincing her. Yesterday was the third time she'd come back to talk to Cora this month."

"Did you talk to Hathaway at all during her visit yesterday?"

Dr. Jones shook his head. "I almost did, but Cora recovered in time."

Recovered? Jamey tried to keep her next question casual. "Was she sick?"

"Tough patient that morning," Dr. Jones said. "She passed out after the read. But she reassured us it was totally normal and no reason to worry."

Totally normal. Sure. Except Reece had never passed out after a read in his life.

She was tempted to ask for a patient name, but even if he knew, she needed a subpoena or a warrant first. "Thanks." She handed Dr. Jones her card. "I may be in touch."

Back in the lobby, she dialed up her most trusted officer. "Can you scope the neighborhood around an address?"

"Sure," Taylor said. "What for?"

"To see if the neighbors heard anyone leave the house in the middle of the night. But Josh," she added, "this is a big ask, it's off-the-books."

"I'll go alone," he promised. "Whose home?"

"Dr. John Camden and Cora Falcon."

"Oh, the other empath! You want to make sure she got out of town okay?"

"Something like that." Jamey recognized the footsteps behind her. "Gotta run. Be careful, all right?" she said, hanging up as she turned around to face the prick from the FBI, Agent Nolan. "You? Really?"

But Nolan just shook his head. He had an accordion folder in his hands. "I'm not here to fight."

"Then why are you here?"

"Same reason I bet you are. I wanted to talk to the staff about Hathaway's visit yesterday."

"You're still on this case?" Jamey said skeptically, because Grayson had made damn sure to lock out the SPD.

"Not on paper," Nolan said dryly. "But I'm supposed to just ignore a triple homicide and a murderer at large? Might as well throw my fucking badge away."

Jamey could grudgingly relate.

"I'm glad I ran into you, though, because I owe you an apology," he went on. "I was tired and stressed this morning, but I shouldn't have taken it out on your brother. It must have been so hard for a violence-averse empath to go to a homicide scene, but he still did and tried to help, and that's admirable. Is he doing okay?"

Jamey stilled. That was unexpected. "He's been better."

"I bet," said Nolan. "No hard feelings?"

"Sure." Feelings were Reece's territory. Jamey had bigger concerns than holding a grudge against an FBI agent also trying to solve a homicide.

Nolan held out the folder. "Here."

She took it. "What's this?" she said, as she thumbed through the folders inside, all labeled with names.

"Peace offering." When she glanced up, he added, "The schedules and reports of everyone who so much as saw Hathaway yesterday."

She looked up sharply. "You already got them?"

"I got a lucky tip," he said. "And these files weren't in records; they were in the mailroom, about to be picked up by courier to be taken to some nameless drop box in Bellevue. But it turns out minimum-wage couriers don't want to mess with the FBI. Or the Patriot Act."

Nolan pointed to the café across the street. "I'm going to

have to bring the files back before alarms get raised but I can share first. Let me buy you lunch and let you have a look."

Jamey didn't use tactics like that—but she also wasn't on this case with the SPD. She glanced in the folder again, gaze lingering on the label reading *Cora Falcon*. Stone Solutions was based in Bellevue, and a nameless drop box sounded suspiciously like something the Dead Man would have. Once these files shipped, she wouldn't see them unless Grayson decided to share.

And if something in the file on Cora could be related to all empaths—to Reece—

"I could eat," she said, and followed him out the doors.

Chapter Twelve

...but as the political climate grows more tense ahead of the vote on SB 1437, many are questioning why the Seattle Police Department continues to use taxpayer dollars to pay an empath consultant. Cedrick Stone, CEO of Stone Solutions and vocal supporter of SB 1437, has called it "inappropriate" while American Minds Intact president Beau Macy has expressed concern that the empath, Reece Davies, may have found his way to the force by exerting empathic influence on a relative within the department.

"I don't use empathy on my sister, that's ridiculous," Davies said, when asked to respond. "If I actually had mind-control powers, I'd make sure people only used the left lane for passing. Have you been on I-5 recently? I am obviously not in control of that."

The SPD has issued an apology for Davies' comments.

—the Seattle Daily,
"AMI raises concerns about SPD's empath consultant"

Jamey paged through Cora's file as Nolan stood in the café's line to order their food. Cora had seen six patients yesterday, four scheduled and two walk-ins, and kept meticulous notes on five of them.

It was number six that gave Jamey pause.

She was still looking at it when Nolan approached with two

porcelain cups of coffee. "Did you start with the empath's file? That's where I started too." He set one coffee by her hand. "What do you think about John Doe?"

All of Cora's other reports had real names and detailed paragraphs on the session. John Doe had been a walk-in with the fake name and a single word of explanation: *nightmares*. The appointment had been at ten a.m. the previous day.

"Seems like the odd one out," she said, setting down the file and picking up the coffee. Dr. Jones had said Cora passed out after a read that morning. Mysterious patient, no notes? She'd put her money on this John Doe.

Nolan took the seat across from her, shrugging off his coat. "I can't believe Camden and Falcon skipped town the day Hathaway was found dead."

Jamey tried to sound skeptical. "You're pegging a doctor and an empath for a multiple homicide?"

"Of course not, but I don't like their timing. I've got questions about Hathaway's visit with them yesterday and they're nowhere to be found." He picked up his own coffee. "Camden's car is gone from their house. We've put out an APB for it along the route to Vegas."

He tapped the paper on the table between them with his free hand. "And I wouldn't mind tracking down this John Doe either."

"You and me both," said Jamey.

"Could be a local crazy, maybe someone who followed Hathaway from the hospital?"

"Anything's possible."

"Ain't that the truth," Nolan muttered. "Detective St. James—"

"Jamey's fine."

"Jamey," he repeated. He looked around, then leaned forward in his chair and dropped his voice to a whisper. "Have you ever heard of an Agent Grayson?"

She eyed him over her cup. "I have an empath brother. Of course I've heard of the Dead Man."

"Have you met him?"

She considered the question. She wanted to keep the investigation quiet, but it wasn't like Grayson had been subtle when he'd made Reece puke on the steps of police HQ then catwalked his cheekbones through the station. "The whole force saw him today. Does the FBI have any good intel on him?"

"Jack shit." Nolan snorted. "He's above our jurisdiction. Above everyone's jurisdiction, apparently."

The waitress dropped off their food; for Nolan, a salad with grilled chicken and dressing on the side, and for her, a bacon double cheeseburger Reece never needed to know about.

Nolan picked up his fork, but didn't speak until the waitress had disappeared through the kitchen doors. "I heard Grayson left the police station with an empath. If this Falcon girl blew town for Vegas, that could only be your brother."

Jamey made a noncommittal noise.

"If I had an empath brother, I'd keep him far away from Agent Grayson," said Nolan. "The stories they whisper about Grayson at the Bureau—they make the Hathaway bloodbath look like a warm and fuzzy way to die."

Jamey had chased rumors too, of unspeakable actions covered up before any proof could be found—actions that would have been hard for even her to pull off, as strong and ironstomached as she was.

She'd assumed if she ever met the Dead Man, he'd be coming for Reece, and she'd be making that moniker more than a nickname. But now, faced with the truth behind the Hathaway murders, she was no longer sure she should be so quick to judge Grayson. "Their partnership is a temporary and necessary evil. It doesn't mean I trust him."

"I don't trust him either," Nolan said. "He took something from the murder scene."

She paused, burger in hand. "What?"

"I don't know. Something from the engine room. Small enough to fit in a paper bag."

Grayson hadn't told her he'd absconded with extra evidence. Trying to solve a case with the Dead Man was worse than playing poker with an empath. You still lost, but at least the empath gave back all your chips at the end.

Nolan cleared his throat. "There's more, but—" He glanced at the door again, like he was expecting someone to sneak up on him. "Agent Grayson probably wouldn't like it if I told you."

She furrowed her brow. "Why?"

"It's about your brother."

"Tell me," she said instantly, leaning forward.

Nolan glanced at the door again, then leaned forward too. "Agent Grayson asked about Reece. By name. Lots of questions, including about what happened in the ambulance with Braker."

Grayson hadn't told her that either. "What did you say?"

"Nothing. Even when he tried to make me." Nolan's jaw tightened. "I have bruises from where he slammed me against his truck, and the FBI told me to suck it up."

Grayson's truck, which he'd said was in the shop, getting detail work done on the passenger door. Fucking hell.

Jamey sat back in her seat. "Um, thank you," she finally said.

"You don't have to thank me. I'd never sell an empath out to the Dead Man," Nolan said. "I have some friends at the Bureau's Seattle division. I could get a couple agents to follow

Agent Grayson and Reece, off the record. They could keep an eye from a distance, then report back to us."

He met her eyes. "They wouldn't interfere, and Grayson never has to know. All I need to set it up is to know where Agent Grayson and Reece are going next."

Grayson had roughed up an FBI agent.

Reece was half Nolan's size.

"They're en route to Stone Solutions."

The corner of Nolan's mouth turned up. "I'll make the call."

STONE SOLUTIONS
Defending American Minds.

Reece glared at the enormous plaque dominating the entrance to the Stone Solutions campus in Bellevue. Beyond the sign were several buildings, the tallest a gaudy high-rise of sparkling glass that presided over a parking garage like an overdressed king.

His gloves prickled uncomfortably. "Welcoming."

"I'm told those afraid of empaths find it pretty comforting. You ever gonna turn in?"

Reece ignored him. "Big building," he said, as he idled at the entrance. "Guess there's big money in anti-empathy defenses."

"There is."

"How would you know?"

"I am an anti-empathy defense."

Reece sighed and turned into the complex.

"Straight ahead," said Grayson.

Reece side-eyed him. "You know where you're going?"

"I do. Park in that spot."

"That says reserved."

"Yes. Reserved for me."

"You have a *reserved spot* at this freak show?"

"And an office and a drop box. Hurry up."

With great reluctance, Reece parked in the reserved spot and climbed out of the car after Grayson. But as he looked up the side of the high-rise, he paused. "Those men are washing the windows," he said, pointing up.

"Windows don't generally wash themselves."

"They must be twenty stories up."

"Building's twenty-two stories, so that's about right." Grayson had stopped on the sidewalk. "You forget how to walk?"

Reece gestured at the window washers high above their heads. "Where are the nets?"

"Nets?"

"The safety nets! In case they fall."

"They've all got suspension systems," Grayson pointed out. "There're no laws mandating nets too."

Reece folded his arms. "It's the right thing to do."

"You know how you can tell I'm a specialist? Because I'm not even gonna try to make you let this go," Grayson said. "You can bring it up with management. Assuming we get to see them and don't expire on this sidewalk waiting on you to move your little feet."

"I *will* bring it up," Reece said. "And my feet aren't *little*."

Inside, the building's lobby was cavernous, everything bright white or made of glass. There were three flat-screen TVs, all tuned to the news, and modern furniture in the same white as the walls and floors. A large framed poster by one TV proclaimed, *We Support SB 1437: Protect American Minds*, while a coffee table offered several magazines for visitors, including AMI's monthly publication.

Four people were waiting on the sofas, all eight eyes on Reece. Then the whispers began.

"I am not welcome here," he muttered.

"You're really not," Grayson agreed, because of course he'd somehow been able to overhear that. "Don't wander off this time."

Oh right, because Reece wanted to stick close to *the Dead Man*. "So, Mr. Reserved Parking Spot, I assume you still know where to go?"

"I do. Just waiting to wrap up the confrontation with security."

"The what?"

But right on cue, a security guard was rushing at them, a middle-aged man with outrage on his face and his finger pointed at Reece. "You can't be in here."

Reece set his jaw. Definitely the last place an empath belonged. "Yes, I can. Legally—"

"This facility is exempt as a matter of national security." The guard made to grab him.

Reece drew back, hands flying up so the guard wouldn't make contact with anything but the gloves. But he needn't have bothered; Grayson was already between them. "Mr. Denton. He's with me."

"How the hell do you know my name?" the guard said hotly. "And who the hell do you think you are that you can bring an empath into Stone Solutions—"

"Evan Grayson."

Denton blanched. He covered his mouth with his hand and stumbled backward. "Agent Grayson."

He was rapidly losing even more color, and his obvious fear sent Reece's stomach tumbling. "Hey, are you all right?" he asked, starting toward him, but a woman's voice cut through the room.

"Security."

High heels clicked as a white woman with her hair in a

fancy twist crossed toward their group. Dressed in a lab coat over a fitted dress, she had a polished voice—and a strangely blank face, like a drop cloth hiding a painting. Even her voice gave none of her emotions away as she said to the guard, "What are you doing?"

"I'm sorry, Vanessa," said Denton. "I didn't know this man was—"

She interrupted. "You're fired."

"He's *what*?" said Reece, as the guard closed his eyes but didn't argue.

She ignored him. "Agent Grayson," she said, offering a ring-adorned hand. "Let me extend our welcome to you."

"Dr. Whitman." Grayson shook her hand. "You've been promoted."

"Would that it had been under better circumstances," Whitman said. "We were informed internally about Jason. I'm devastated."

Reece flinched. Her face might be a mystery, but he'd heard that lie loud and clear. "My sincerest apologies about this incident," she continued. "Cedrick will—"

Reece cut her off. "Why'd you fire your guard?"

Whitman finally turned to him, and her gaze zeroed in on his gloves. "And this is Mr. Davies?"

Sheesh. Everyone knew his name today. "Yes," he said curtly. "But what's important here is that this guy was just trying to do his job and you can't fire him for that."

"Fascinating." Her stare made Reece feel like a specimen in a petri dish. "Of course you're wrong. As the new director of Research and Development, I'm far and away this man's superior, and at-will employment allows for firing at any time for any reason." She turned back to Grayson. "As I was saying—"

Reece cut her off again. "You should give him back his job."

Denton stared at Reece in bewilderment.

Whitman laughed. "Marvelous. You could predict this one's reaction to the second." She looked up at Grayson. "What do you think?"

"I think you should do what the empath requested," Grayson said, to Reece's surprise.

"Then consider your position reinstated," she said to Denton, with a carelessness that gave Reece the unpleasant suspicion she'd been more interested in observing an empath's reaction to the firing than the guard and his livelihood.

"Mr. Davies also wants safety nets for your window washers," said Grayson.

Whitman laughed again, derisively. "Of *course* he does."

"And I think Stone Solutions should make that happen," Grayson said. "Today."

Her laughter vanished. "Of course, Evan. I'll arrange it."

She and Denton sure jumped quick to whatever *Evan* wanted.

Whitman shot Reece one of the fakest smiles he'd ever seen, then her gaze was back on Grayson. "I'm sure you've come to see Cedrick. I'm afraid he's abroad at the moment, but—"

"I'm well aware he took the company helicopter to Vancouver in the middle of the night. I came to talk to you."

Her expression flickered for the first time, the drop cloth shimmering for the briefest moment. "To me?"

"You *are* the new director of Research and Development."

"Ah." The fake smile was glued back on her lips. "Shall we find some privacy, then?"

"Dr. Owens' former office, if you'd be so kind."

Reece barely caught her tiny flinch. "As you like," she said, still pleasant. She turned and strode off to an elevator bank, high heels click-clicking across the floor.

Grayson looked at Reece and gestured toward her. "Go on, scoot."

"*You* scoot," Reece muttered, and took a step after Whitman when Denton spoke.

"I was going to throw you out." Reece turned to find Denton watching him, a lost look on his face. "Why would you stick up for me?"

Reece shrugged. "You were doing your job. Your company shouldn't fire you for that, even if I think your job sucks."

Denton stared at him until Reece squirmed.

"Best of luck with all your empath harassing," he said, then scrambled to catch up with Whitman and Grayson.

Chapter Thirteen

…the "phantom pain" phenomenon empaths undergo in response to imagined and/or anticipated pain to others is thought to be neurological, but the potential for dangerous physical impact on the empath experiencing it should not be underestimated. It results in measurable disruption to the empath's vital systems, and the impact on their other systems is not yet understood. Recommend measures be taken to ensure exposure to these type of stimuli is limited.

—excerpt from an early study funded by the Empath Initiative

The Stone Solutions elevator was so shiny Reece could see his own reflection. This was not a good thing.

"Fancy building," he said, trying to find somewhere else to look besides his image. His eyes landed on Grayson, who was also looking at Grayson in the mirrorlike elevator. That was probably a good view. Maybe there was something to his obsession with brushing hair. Or showering.

Whitman pressed the button for twenty-one. "We deserve to be well-funded."

The elevator began to rise and Reece tried not to squirm. Between the drop cloth hiding Whitman's emotions and Grayson's absolute blankness, the atmosphere in the elevator was stiflingly emotionless, like breathing your own exhaled air under a blanket.

Grayson cleared his throat. "Convenient that SB 1437 will triple that funding." Oh, look at that, he was paying attention to the conversation, not just admiring his own jawline.

"Hathaway's bill funds Stone Solutions?" Reece asked.

"As a rider," said Grayson.

Whitman smiled with no more depth than a drawing on a canvas. It gave Reece the creeps, the way her expressions were only on the surface without her real emotions obvious underneath. "It's business. You understand."

"I understand that the bill pays you and you pay him." Reece pointed at Grayson. "So I understand that all of you are making money off of stomping us down."

"He's prickly for an empath," Whitman said to Grayson.

"He's not a lab specimen who can't hear you," Reece muttered.

She turned back to Reece. "You should consider me an ally."

He furrowed his brow. It hadn't been a lie. She must have truly believed that trash. "In what nightmare?"

"I find you fascinating," she said. "You're better off with me than those who find you frightening."

What's frightening about pacifism? Reece was about to say.

Except that people were dead. And Grayson and Jamey thought an empath had done it. And that was one of the most frightening things Reece had ever heard.

He bit down on his tongue and didn't answer.

The elevator doors opened and Grayson held them for both Reece and Whitman. Another set of glass doors guarded R&D. Beyond the doors was a bullpen of people seated at white tables topped with black computers, faces fixed on glowing monitor screens.

Reece hung back, shoving his hands as deep in his hoodie pockets as he could.

Whitman was the one to scan her thumb in the security box, but Grayson still somehow managed to open the door for her, like he had lightning reflexes powered entirely by Southern manners. Reece trailed behind them through the lab. Eyes followed as they walked, but apparently a perk of tagging along behind the Dead Man was that the stares were on Grayson's face and shoulders and no one seemed particularly interested in looking at Reece.

He glanced at the walls and wished he hadn't. They were decorated with an assortment of framed Stone Solutions advertisements. *Our Minds, Our Business*, said one. *Autonomy, Not Empathy*, said another. And the biggest one at the hall's end, a brightly colored sign that simply read, *What Else Don't We Know About Empaths?*

He hunched his shoulders. "I don't like it here."

"That's about as surprising as the sun rising," said Grayson. "Although I suppose in this city, that would be a surprise."

"Oh great, you're a zombie and a comedian," Reece muttered.

They came to a stop at a door with a large nameplate reading *Vanessa Whitman, Director*. Whitman put a hand on the handle, but she didn't open the door, instead smiling politely but fakely up at Grayson. "I'm sure I don't know what you need with Jason's office."

Grayson leaned casually on the wall. "Dr. Owens was found dead this morning." He tapped her nameplate on the door. "Me wanting to see his office isn't surprising. You already moving in is. Some might be inclined to call that interference."

Her unnatural smile stayed unnaturally still. "You know I would never interfere with any investigation of yours, Agent Grayson."

Lie.

Well, that was interesting.

She finally pushed open the door and headed in. Grayson gestured for Reece to go in next, because of course he did. Reece squared his shoulders and tried to pretend he walked into lions' dens every day.

As he entered the enormous corner space, he was suddenly more sympathetic about Whitman's fast move. The view of Mount Rainier through the floor-to-ceiling windows was stunning.

The transition from Owen's office to Whitman's appeared half-finished. Two oversized mahogany bookshelves stood empty, boxes of books on the ground in front of them, and there was no art hanging, just a few framed paintings of beautiful Washington scenery propped against one wall. Reece didn't have any kind of eye for art, but he'd guess those were Whitman's.

Grayson shut the office door behind the three of them, and Reece was once again enclosed with their unsettling lack of emotions. He hadn't felt stifled like this in his tiny Smart car cabin when it was just him and Grayson.

He tried to ignore the claustrophobia and pointed to the imposing mahogany desk dominating the room. "At least Owens' desk is still in here."

Whitman jerked her head toward him. Her voice was tighter when she spoke. "How did you—"

"That wasn't empathy, it was stereotyping." When both Grayson and Whitman stared, Reece shrugged. "It's a manly desk and you smell like flowers."

Grayson raised his eyebrows, but moved to the desk and began to open drawers. Whitman steepled her fingers, pink nails contrasting with her white lab coat. "Fine, why not. I'm giving the office a *woman's touch*, as the saying goes."

Grayson opened one of the lower drawers. A moment later,

he held up a flat piece of wood. "Did you already add that touch to the false bottoms in the desk drawers?"

Whitman took a sharp breath.

Reece, who'd been crossing over to the bookshelves, glanced over his shoulder in time to catch the drop cloth lift for just an instant and her expression actually flutter with what looked like fear. It was gone an instant later as she tried to cover it with a small laugh. "Maybe Jason was paranoid."

"Maybe," Grayson said. "Though considering he's no longer with us, maybe he had a reason to be."

Reece furrowed his brow as he headed for the bookshelves. Grayson kept choosing softer ways to describe what happened to Jason Owens. He had to be doing it for Reece's benefit, but why? Professional courtesy? What did *professional courtesy* even mean if your alias was *the Dead Man*?

Behind Reece, Grayson asked, in a very casual tone, "Did you go out with Mr. Stone and the senator last night?"

Wait—what?

But Whitman snorted delicately. "I'm afraid I wasn't invited for sushi. Some of us have to work for a living."

"You got cages of empaths to check on?" Reece interjected, as he gave the first box of books a cursory glance and saw nothing but medical textbooks and Latin. "With little exercise wheels and water bottles and bars we can push for vegan pellets?"

"I see you think you're cute," she said, which Reece translated to mean that her blank face notwithstanding, he could, in fact, annoy her. "I'm an endocrinologist, same as Jason."

Whatever *that* was. Reece dropped to a crouch next to another box of books, lifting one cardboard flap. "Do endo-whatevers have any books with smaller words—"

"*No!*"

The unmasked panic in Whitman's shout split the dead air,

and hit Reece like a sucker punch as she leaped forward and yanked his hood. He was wrenched away from the box and toppled off balance, pain splitting his head as he smacked the hardwoods at her feet.

"Dr. Whitman."

Grayson's tone of voice hadn't changed. But Whitman dropped Reece's hood like it'd burned her.

"I was only trying to move him," she said, hands raised in a protest of innocence. "He fell too easily."

"Because he's not capable of a lick of self-defense," Grayson said, still neutrally. "He'll let you break his skull before he takes a chance of hurting you."

Reece slowly sat up, rubbing the sore spot on his head. He glanced between them. Grayson wasn't going through the desk anymore, just watching Whitman.

The fear flickered on Whitman's face again, and Reece frowned. Nothing about Grayson's words was threatening. What was she so afraid of?

Whitman said meaningfully, "The contents of that box are off-limits to an empath."

Grayson paused.

Reece hated this place that hated him so much. "It's just *books*." He lunged for the box before she could stop him again. "I do know how to read words, not just people—"

He saw inside the box and choked.

Grayson must have heard it, because he leaped over the desk with the ease of a hurdler and crossed the room in three long strides. He crouched in front of Reece and glanced in the box.

Next moment, he said over his shoulder, to Whitman, "We need the room."

"But—"

"I'm asking for privacy, Dr. Whitman."

The door slammed shut a second later.

Reece's breath was coming too fast, sweat beading on his brow. "Why did Owens have a whole box of books on—on—" He couldn't say it, couldn't bring his lips to form the word *torture*.

"It's not real." Grayson shifted closer. "It's just books."

"Pictures on the covers." Reece's chest was drawing up tight, phantom pain crawling over his skin, his back, the soles of his feet, and the palms of his hands. At least Grayson had moved between Reece and the box. He was blurry and edged by black dots, but he was all Reece could see. "It's real, those are real things—"

"They're books. Paper and ink. I know your brain is conjuring the real people those things happened to and you're feeling pain for them, but you're gonna give yourself an aneurism."

Grayson's emotionless voice sounded more unnatural to Reece's ears than ever and his face was still so *blank*. Reece screwed his eyes shut.

"Reece, you gotta breathe."

No, it was so much worse with his eyes closed, no distraction from pain, the images forcing themselves through his mind in an endless parade—

"Reece." Grayson repeating his name got Reece's eyes to open. "Stay with me. I'd try an old trick and say focus on me, but I don't make you feel better."

Reece shook his head, too fast. "Better than the books."

He immediately regretted the words. Why would Grayson bother to help him—

But Grayson was already leaning in. "Eyes on me, then. Come on. Deep breath."

Being face-to-face with the Dead Man should have sent Reece spiraling deeper. But Grayson had pitched his voice low enough to soften the lack of emotions, and this close, there were other things to notice besides the blankness of his face.

Like the scent of some stereotypically masculine cologne or aftershave, because of course that was what Grayson wore, or the way he was big enough to block out everything else.

"Breathe for me, Reece."

Grayson was close enough Reece could feel his body heat, not actually dead at all but as warm and alive as any other person. Close enough Reece could have touched him—if he was even more nuts than he already was.

"That's right. Keep breathing." As if reading his mind, Grayson reached out—but just to tap Reece's hand over the glove. "You staying with me, Care Bear?"

Reece sort of was. His chest still hurt, but the pain echoes were fading and Grayson was becoming more solid. Even the ridiculous nickname helped. He wiped at his sweaty forehead with the back of his glove. "Is all of Stone Solutions' security watching me have a panic attack?"

Grayson pulled back. "There are no cameras in here and it's soundproofed."

"Oh, good." Reece scrubbed the glove over his hot face. "I was wondering where we were going to have angry hate-sex."

Oh no, his stupid fucking *mouth*—

"What kind of man do you take me for," Grayson said, deadpan. "We only just met. I save hate-sex for second dates."

That startled a laugh out of Reece, maybe lowered his blood pressure a point or two. He leaned heavily against the bookshelf. "You're taking this well. Me falling to pieces over a box of books, I mean."

"You being your empath self is not gonna rattle me. Not ever."

Was that really true? Could Reece tell him about hearing lies, about his nightmares, and Grayson would know what to do?

Reece let his head rest against the shelf. He took a slow

breath, held it, then blew it out even slower. His heart rate was still too high, his skin clammy, and the books still lurking on the edge of his thoughts. Maybe he couldn't hear emotions in Grayson's voice, but the sound of that deep, rumbling drawl wasn't all bad. "You don't make me feel *worse*," he admitted. "And the accent's good."

"Well, there's no accounting for taste."

That got another surprised smile from Reece. He drew his knees to his chest. "You talk. About something distracting. Tell me what's wrong with Whitman."

It was a long shot, expecting the Dead Man to talk to him, but to Reece's surprise, Grayson obliged. "Dr. Whitman had put on fresh perfume," he said, moving to mirror Reece's position, his own back against the bookshelves, side by side with only about a foot between them. "I don't think she was going for a good impression, I think she was trying to hide her own sweat, 'cause I could smell that too. Office services should've been handling her move, but it seems like Dr. Whitman was doing her own physical labor, and my money's on scrambling to move books an empath has no business seeing."

He looked sideways at Reece, and together on the floor, their faces were much closer to level. "'Course, even if she should have been expecting a visit from me today, she shouldn't have known you were coming too. It's interesting."

"Very interesting," Reece said slowly, "but I was talking about her weird blank face."

"Oh." Grayson shrugged. "That's training."

"*Training?*"

"Meditation techniques, method acting, that sort of thing. It's mandatory for all high-level Stone Solutions employees."

"To hide their true emotions from empaths," Reece said, in realization. "It's another anti-empathy defense." He frowned. "I don't like it."

"Not so fun when the books close their covers?"

Reece wasn't going to answer that. "What's your problem, then? Are you the product of some kind of extra-extreme training?"

"Does it seem like it?"

Reece sighed. He was still closed into the office, but with only Grayson now, and the stifling sensation from earlier had vanished with Whitman. "No," he admitted grudgingly. "You're nothing like Whitman. If anything, you remind me of Jamey, except—" He clamped his teeth down on his tongue.

"Except what?"

Except Jamey has a heart, he'd been going to say. But he didn't. "Nothing," he said instead, firmly. Maybe he couldn't read any feelings from Grayson, but that didn't give him the right to throw it in his face as if Grayson didn't have them at all. "How did you know to ask Whitman about Stone and Hathaway going out together last night?"

"From you." When Reece furrowed his brow, Grayson added, "You said in the elevator that Mr. Adams had more loyalty to Mr. Stone than to Senator Hathaway. We're try-ing to find her killer and Mr. Adams wasn't talking; who else would he have been covering for?"

And despite the warmth still radiating from Grayson, a chill stole over Reece's skin. "Is this how you're planning to solve the case? Trigger the insight again—"

"No." Grayson said it without hesitation. "I thought you knew you had it and were in control of it. Triggering it the second time was an accident and I'll do my best to never do it again."

Reece pressed his lips together. "But maybe I should—if it helps—"

"If I was willing to throw empaths on the altar, I would've

Liar City

let you read the witness at the crime scene. This is not a way you can help."

"But why not?"

"Reasons."

"You could share them once in a while." Reece tightened his arms, bringing his knees closer to his chest. "That FBI agent wanted me to read that witness. If he or others knew I had this insight thing, that they could get what they wanted without worrying about the law, they might try—"

"I make sure they don't."

Grayson didn't say it as a brag, just stating a fact as calmly as he stated everything else. Reece scoffed. "The empath hunter protects the empaths? Yeah, right."

"You're the one who keeps saying hunter. I say specialist."

Reece rolled his eyes. He couldn't hear Grayson's lies, it was true, but that had to be bullshit, didn't it? As casually as he could, he said, "Why would it be such a big deal anyway, if an empath was hiding insight or—or something?"

"You don't need to know that either," Grayson said. "Just know my job needs me to be absolutely sure empaths aren't hiding any new powers from everyone else."

"Oh." Reece bit his lip. *You're not telling him about hearing lies, and you're not going to feel guilty about that,* he told his stupid empath conscience. *Maybe he talked you down, but he's still the Dead Man, and he didn't hesitate to use those cuffs on you. Give him a reason and he'll do it again.*

The shakiness hadn't fully left Reece's limbs, but he grabbed the bookshelf and forced his legs to stand anyway, also grabbing for the first subject change that came to mind. "Did you find whatever it is Whitman is supposed to be looking for?"

Grayson picked himself up off the floor too, a much more impressive action with his height. "That's a leap."

"Not really," said Reece. "Her mask cracked when you checked under the false bottoms of the desk drawers. You made her realize she should have searched the desk fully, but she's probably been too busy moving into the new office."

"Huh." Grayson eyed him. "You have a lot more going on under that hood than you let on."

Reece's stomach tightened. Yeah, he definitely wasn't coming clean. "You went straight for the desk drawers too. So what are you both looking for?"

"Nothing I'm gonna tell you about."

"But—"

"You can't keep your mouth shut for five entire minutes. You think I want you running around with both an endless supply of sarcasm and government secrets?"

"If the government secrets are about empaths, I deserve the truth."

"Sometimes you don't want the truth."

"More riddles." Reece sighed and leaned his head back against the bookshelf. "Can we go yet?"

He expected Grayson to tell him to suck it up, but instead heard, "Yes."

Reece blinked. "Really?"

"That was an awful big deduction about Whitman just now and your blood pressure is one more shock away from dangerous. I'd prefer your insight never kicks on again, but if it does while you're inside this building, I'll have to stop Dr. Whitman from squashing you between two sheets of glass and sticking you under a microscope herself."

There was a cheerful thought. "I thought you said insight was common."

"I said there was precedent." Grayson opened the office door and held it. "I never said common."

Reece swallowed and led the way out.

Agent Nolan shivered in the cold wind, watching through the café windows from the street outside as St. James put the files back into their accordion folder while a waitress bused their dishes.

He turned one shoulder, covering his mouth with one hand as he spoke into the phone. "I'm telling you, trying to get intel from St. James is like trying to get laid by a nun. It's a wonder I managed to find out Grayson and the empath were headed your way and in time to send you the text."

"Colorful analogies aside, I'm grateful for your assistance," Stone said smoothly. "But they're leaving our premises. Mr. Davies has destroyed yet another of our trackers—"

"You track the kid's car?" Nolan said in surprise.

"We track every empath in this country."

That sounded damn useful, if not exactly legal. "How'd you swing that?"

"My institution protects the American people, Agent Nolan, and we require a certain amount of leeway to do it. More than that, knowing where all of the empaths are helps me sleep at night."

Nolan snorted. "What are you scared of, that one's going to turn up in your house and ask how you're feeling?"

Stone ignored that. "Tracking Davies provides more of a challenge than most. I need to know where he and Evan are heading next, and they'll keep Detective St. James abreast of their plans."

Nolan sighed.

"I can offer you leverage," said Stone. "Mr. Davies had a panic attack while at our facility. Regrettable, but caused entirely by his own stubbornness and an inability to accept that others might know his limitations better than himself. Of course, I'm sure the good detective would prefer you didn't see it that way."

So Nolan would have to sugarcoat it for St. James and pretend to be concerned about Davies' delicate nerves. Why was everything about empaths so damn ridiculous?

"Beyond that," said Stone, "we're hearing rumors about a picture that might give you some excellent leverage."

Oh great. If there were empath selfies or nudes floating around, Nolan was fucking *done*. "What kind of picture?"

"I'll let you know when I have confirmation. And of course you have my gratitude, agent. I won't forget your services."

The call ended. Nolan palmed his phone for a moment. Was Cedrick Stone's gratitude worth getting mixed up in the empath circus? Then again, Stone Solutions apparently had fewer hoops to jump through than the FBI. Maybe Nolan could swing this into a career upgrade.

He put the phone away just as St. James came out from the café. "Thanks for the loan," she said, and she passed him the accordion file. "Any word from your agents?"

Nolan put on his best game face. "Sounds like Reece didn't have a very good time of it in Stone Solutions. Apparently he was looking pretty peaky as he and Agent Grayson left the building."

"What happened to him?"

Nolan spread his hands innocently. "Panic attack, maybe? It *is* an empathy defense facility; I can't imagine it was much fun for poor Reece to visit, especially with the Dead Man."

"Can your agents follow them?"

"Of course," he lied. "But it'd be helpful if I could tell them their next location."

"I'll let you know when I do."

Nolan glued a friendly smile to his lips and held out his card to her. "Call or text. Anytime, day or night."

St. James took the card just as her own phone rang. Her face brightened as she saw the caller ID and answered. "Liam? What's—"

Even at a distance, Nolan could hear a torrent of words burst through the phone's speaker, something about *Reece* and *handcuffs* and *Eyes on Empaths*.

"Liam," St. James said again. "Slow down, you're not making any sense. What—"

The voice came again in another flood, and Nolan thought he heard *tried to call* and *fucking auto-response*.

None of it made any sense to Nolan, but whatever this Liam person was saying was enough to make St. James' eyes narrow, and for some reason, chills broke out on Nolan's skin. Which, what the hell, she was just a hot chick with a badge, there was no reason for her to make a man like him nervous.

"Tell me everything," she said, and turned away, crossing the street back to the SVMC parking lot and her car.

Chapter Fourteen

What do I know about the Dead Man? Rumors, and that's it. I don't even know the full story of how he became the Dead Man; I'm not sure there's anyone left alive who does.
—internal note from FBI Assistant Director Jacobs

Reece was immensely grateful to be back in his own car and see Stone Solutions' gaudy office tower get smaller and smaller in his rearview mirror. He didn't even have a destination in mind as he drove, happy just to put some distance between him and that awful box.

"Pull into the first drive-thru or gas station you see."

Oh. Apparently, Grayson had a destination planned. "You eat? Something besides brains and the flesh of the living, I mean."

"I'm getting coffee." Grayson had pulled off his hat—and immediately checked his hair in the visor mirror, Reece hadn't missed that—but he still had his scarf around his neck.

Reece reached over and turned the heat up to full blast. "I knew it couldn't be real food. That would make you seem almost human."

Grayson's gaze flicked to the heater, then to the road. "So what happens when you run out of zombie jokes?"

"I will never run out of zombie jokes."

From its safely secured spot in the console, Reece's phone rang. Grayson cleared his throat. "Should I—"

"No, you should *not* answer my phone," Reece said. "Whoever it is will get my auto-response."

"*I* got your auto-response. I'm offering to spare them. To show them some *empathy*."

"Nice try," said Reece. "But no."

The car was silent for a moment, the city rolling past.

"I gotta ask," said Grayson, "do you even let the folks you're dating get that auto-response?"

"Maybe you didn't notice, but I'm a bit high-strung," Reece said. "Just a touch of anxiety. A dash of nerves. I can see how you missed it, I'm subtle, I know. So you may also be surprised to hear that people are not lining up to date a wildly annoying pacifist with biweekly breakdowns."

Reece's phone rang again. Grayson made an aborted move toward the console; Reece held up a finger in warning. "Don't you dare."

Grayson put his own hand back in his lap with something almost like reluctance. "Did someone call you that?"

"What?"

Grayson made air quotes. "Wildly annoying."

"Who *hasn't* called me that?" said Reece.

"I haven't."

Reece opened his mouth, then closed it.

"If someone's ever bothering you, you should tell me about it," Grayson said casually.

"Why? You're the *Dead Man*. What are you going to do about someone bullying an empath?"

"You just let me know if it happens," Grayson said, like that was any kind of answer.

A few minutes later, Reece pulled into a coffeehouse drive-thru. Grayson held up a credit card without looking up from his phone. "Your hands are still shaking. Get yourself some kind of sugar bomb too."

Wait. Had Grayson requested the stop for Reece's benefit, not his own? "But—"

"And don't be cheap because you feel guilty I'm paying. Remember that I make all my money off empaths."

Reece stared at him until a honk from behind made him jump. He eased the car forward. "Your knowledge of empaths is frankly freakish."

"Almost like I'm a specialist."

"Empath hunter."

"You're not locked up at the moment, are you?"

"*At the moment*, he says." Reece pulled up to the speaker. "Not the same thing as saying *don't worry, I'd never lock you up*."

They ordered drinks, and Grayson asked for some kind of complicated coffee with extra espresso shots and special-temperature milk. Reece drummed his fingers on the steering wheel as he waited. "I knew you'd have fancy taste."

"What if I told you I usually stir instant coffee into microwaved milk?"

Reece looked at him suspiciously. "Is that a thing in the place where that accent is from?"

"Not that I know of," said Grayson. "Accent is my dad's fault. The coffee is how my mom used to make it. I mean, I guess it can be hard to find the right brand in Texas; maybe you think that makes it fancy."

The Dead Man was from Texas. The Dead Man had *parents*. Of course he did, but still. "Hmm."

"What?"

"I just realized that you probably know everything there is to know about me," said Reece. "And I don't know shit about you."

"That's sort of the point of the Dead Man," Grayson said dryly. "No one knows me. I can't humanize myself; what would you do with your endless supply of zombie jokes?"

But you're not really dead. Don't you get lonely?

Reece bit it back. What was he planning to do, offer to keep the Dead Man company? Say *let's be lonely as fuck together*? Clearly his brain was still rattled from the latest meltdown.

After awkwardly maneuvering their drinks through his window and entrusting his to Grayson rather than the admittedly precarious cup holder, Reece pulled into a parking space, because an empath *specialist* ought to know better than to expect him to drink while driving.

"You finally gonna check your phone?" Grayson said, as he passed back the drink.

Grayson still held himself exceedingly carefully in the car's tiny space to avoid so much as their shoulders brushing. But when Reece took the drink and their fingers made contact over the gloves, Grayson didn't flinch. "Now that I'm safely parked, yes. And I will call whoever it is back—"

The phone went off again. Reece jerked, sending hot almond milk splashing out the top of the cup and onto his gloves.

"Crap." He scrambled for a napkin.

"That's my—" Reece realized his mistake just as Grayson said, "—hat."

There was a potent silence.

"Um." The fine wool of the hat was soaked in sticky syrup and almond milk. Reece tried not to squirm.

The chirpy ringtone went off again, and that was not helping.

"I'm, uh—I should get this," Reece said awkwardly, and picked up the phone and put it to his ear.

"Are you all right?" Liam demanded.

Reece blinked. "Yes?" he said, making it a question. He sheepishly held the dirty hat out to Grayson, who stared him down.

"Where are you?" Liam said in his ear.

Reece furrowed his brow. "Bellevue?"

"Bellevue?"

"Having a caramel almond milk steamer." Reece tossed the hat behind his chair, on top of Liam's blazer. "I'll buy you a new one," he promised Grayson, who just snorted.

"A caramel—are you under arrest?"

"To be honest, I'm never one-hundred-percent sure today." Reece moved the phone down from his mouth to address Grayson. "Am I under arrest?"

"Should you be?"

Reece rolled his eyes. "I'm not currently wearing hand-cuffs," he said into the phone. "Even after spilling vegan caramel syrup on the Dead Man's hat. So…maybe not?"

"You better not be," said Liam, "because I don't care how many times you've been handcuffed to some empath-curious pervert's bed—"

"Liking empaths does not make someone a pervert, jack-ass. And no one would ever *cuff* me to their bed. The hands are where the magic happens."

Grayson paused midsip and side-eyed Reece.

Liam groaned in his ear. "That's going straight to my file of *things Reece said that I can't unhear.* If you're not in hand-cuffs, why is the lead story on *Eyes on Empaths* about your arrest, complete with a picture of you cuffed over the hood of your car?"

Reece's stomach hit the floor. "What?"

Grayson was already taking the phone out of Reece's hand. "Explain," he said, as he put it to his own ear.

Reece couldn't hear Liam on the other side of the phone, and Grayson's expression never changed. After several moments, Grayson hung up without another word.

"Did you just hang up on Jamey's boyfriend?" Reece pointed

at Grayson. "Only *I* get to hang up on Liam. *You* have to be nice to him."

"I let you go before the reporters came." Grayson blinked, like the idea of something escaping his machinations was inconceivable.

"If there's a picture of me in handcuffs, that's all on you," said Reece.

"But I destroyed Ms. Macy's phone."

Reece's lips thinned. "You think Gretel Macy carries only one camera on her? What kind of amateur fringe blogger do you take her for?"

"Huh" was Grayson's less-than-reassuring response.

From the coffeehouse, Grayson directed Reece to drive south, all the way to Renton and a shady side street near the interstate.

"Fancy car," Reece observed, pointing at a black Maybach parked in front of a nondescript bar, a peacock among pigeons next to the mud-coated wagons and small pickups.

"It's Mr. Stone's," said Grayson. "His driver and I are gonna have a quick talk."

Reece wrinkled his nose. "Cedrick Stone keeps a chatty driver?"

"Nope."

"Riddle me this," Reece muttered, pulling in behind the Maybach.

When they entered the bar, Reece was momentarily unable to see as his eyes struggled with the dim interior. Squinting, he could make out a decent-sized crowd taking advantage of happy hour.

Several looks were directed their way as they walked in, most of them at Grayson. Reece was no expert on looks, but he was pretty sure that in this dive, a man as fit and good-looking as Grayson stood out even more than the Maybach.

But a few looks were on Reece—more specifically, on his gloves—and they weren't friendly. Maybe most people here didn't interact with empaths often. Or, he realized, as he took in the two TVs above the bar, they could be staring for another reason altogether. He hunched his shoulders and shoved his hands in his hoodie pockets.

Grayson, apparently oblivious to the stares, cut a path straight to a muscled man with a neat chinstrap goatee seated at the end of the bar. "Mr. Huang."

Huang turned, his expression cool. "Agent Grayson. A pleasure." He didn't stand from his barstool and he didn't flinch. Maybe anyone who could drive around Cedrick Stone needed to be hard to spook.

Huang's gaze went past Grayson to Reece with still no sign of unease. "Mr. Empath. Meeting any friend of Agent Grayson is of course also a pleasure."

"You sure he works for Stone?" Reece said to Grayson. "That might have been polite."

Huang shrugged. "It's a job. I'm looking for a new one."

"I like that decision." Reece pointed at Huang's hand, wrapped around a green bottle of sparkling water. "And this decision, especially for a driver. I hope no one else in here is planning to get behind the wheel sooner than *one hour after each drink*," he said, raising his voice enough to carry to the whole bar.

Huang's brows drew together. Grayson leaned against the bar counter. "Where did you take Mr. Stone and the senator last night?"

The man's face barely twitched. He must have already guessed what Grayson had come to talk to him about. "Where have you heard I took them?"

"To Mr. Stone's favorite restaurant. I'm a little sketchy on what came next."

Huang spread his hands. "Then I'm afraid I am too."

Grayson waited.

And waited.

The crowd around them seemed to grow very loud. Reece shifted on his feet. The bar giving him the evil eyes he could handle. The unspoken conversation happening between Grayson and Huang—that was a language he didn't speak. He wasn't used to not seeing straight through people, and it did bother him more than he wanted to admit.

The impasse stretched out uncomfortably long. Finally, Grayson pushed off the bar and said, in a relaxed drawl, "I'll come back without the empath."

"McFeely's!"

Reece jumped at Huang's outburst.

The color had drained from the man's face. "McFeely's," Huang said again. "I took them to McFeely's and then I went home. I didn't stay, and I didn't pick them up, and I don't know what happened to Senator Hathaway and I don't know anything else, I *swear*."

None of Huang's words were lies. "Why's he so scared?" Reece demanded from Grayson.

"You've been mighty helpful, Mr. Huang." Grayson turned away.

"What's McFeely's—" Reece threw up his hands as Grayson left without an explanation or a goodbye. He turned to Huang. "Thank—never mind," he said, since Huang wasn't listening anyway, just staring at his bottle like a man who'd barely escaped with his life.

Reece chased after Grayson and back out of the bar.

"John and Cora are a lovely couple. I think anyone who supports that awful bill has never met an empath themselves. You know how people just default to xenophobia. More coffee?"

Officer Josh Taylor did know and did want more coffee. He nodded at Ms. Dorothy Kirby, the seventy-five-year-old retiree who lived in the elegant bungalow next door to Cora

Falcon and John Camden on their tree-lined street in Mount Baker. "Yes, please."

She refilled his cup from her silver French press. Sometimes Detective St. James sent him into total shitholes. Today, Ms. Kirby's freshly ground coffee and quaint sunroom overlooking her backyard were a nice respite from blood-soaked yachts and anti-empathy conspiracists foaming at the mouth. "Did you see either of them yesterday?"

Ms. Kirby smiled. "Cora came by for a moment to drop off lentil soup for dinner; that angel knows how these cold snaps get into my bones. She was expecting John any minute." Ms. Kirby shook her head. "I was so looking forward to their wedding. But who can blame them for eloping? Next thing you know, someone will claim empaths mind-control their spouses and make it illegal to marry one."

Taylor wouldn't put it past the current Senate. There were rumors at the station that politicians were already fighting over who'd be the next to champion Hathaway's bill. "Did you hear them leave last night?"

She shook her head. "But I never hear their hybrids." She waved a finger. "That loud van, now, that I did hear."

Taylor sat up straighter. "Van?"

"Yes. It must have been around ten last night. What it was doing in this neighborhood that late, I'm sure I don't know. I peeked out the curtains when I heard the racket and saw it idling right in front of Cora and John's home."

"What kind of van?"

"Delivery van, not minivan. One of those European-looking things."

She could be describing the Ford Transit; they could have her come to the station and pick it out from pictures. "Did you see anyone get in or out of the van?"

"No, I could only see the back end. And anyway, it left a couple minutes later. Probably had the wrong address."

Not if Jamey had sent him here. Taylor sipped his coffee and tried to smile.

A few minutes of pleasant conversation later, Taylor went back out to his cruiser and called Jamey. He relayed everything Ms. Kirby had told him, then added, "You think it could be our van?"

"Could be," said Jamey. "Could also be coincidence."

"Oh, sure," Taylor openly scoffed. "Because you just happened to send me here after a coincidence."

She made a tiny huff. "It could happen."

"But it didn't," said Taylor. "Ms. Kirby is willing to come downtown and look at pictures."

"No." Jamey said it immediately. "Don't involve her and don't follow this any further."

But Taylor didn't want to let it go. It was the closest thing he'd seen to a lead all day. "Is there any chance a doctor and an empath could be connected to the murders?"

"Don't ask that question. And get going. I want you out of there *now*." She hung up.

Taylor frowned at his phone. He'd bet his badge that Jamey knew a lot more than she was sharing. She was no empath like her brother, but you didn't work with Detective St. James for two years and not figure out she wasn't exactly stock-model either.

He went to start his engine, looking out his windshield one last time at Falcon and Camden's home. Then he paused, key in the ignition.

A light was on in the upstairs window.

No one was supposed to be home, and he could have sworn no lights were on when he pulled up. He got out of his cruiser and studied the house, eyes narrowing when they landed on the garage. It was manually operated and had been closed when he arrived. But now, the crisp white door was a few inches above the ground, and he thought he saw wide black tires in the gap.

As he looked back at the house, the upstairs light went out.

He got out of the car and quickly headed up the walk. He ducked under the awning, out of the rain, and stood on the cheerful welcome mat as he rapped on the front door. The entry had been decorated with several pots of hardy flowers, their colors bright against the gray day.

He gave it two minutes, then rang the bell. Someone had turned that light off. He was here on a murder investigation and this was starting to look like exigent circumstances. He reached for his gun, ready to enter without a warrant.

But the door was suddenly flung open. In front of him was a pretty young woman, dark brown hair over one shoulder in a tangled braid, and her pink scrubs covered in blood. "Hi, officer," she said.

Then her hand was on his face.

Chapter Fifteen

From: Kapoor, Indira <i.kapoor@stonesolutionscorp.com>
To: Easterby, Aisha <a.easterby@stonesolutionscorp.com>
Subject: Re: Re: Soil samples

Running tests now, will call when done.

Ps. You've been at Stone Solutions awhile, right? Do you ever think it's weird that we get so much money to study the cutest, most harmless people on the planet? Like…do you ever get the feeling there's something that someone's not telling us?

Reece caught up with Grayson as they emerged outside the Renton dive bar into November's early twilight. The street was empty of people, just the beater cars parked along the curb in front of a locally owned hardware store and a weed shop. "What is with you and not saying goodbye? And do you know where we should go next? It seems like you know where we should go."

"I do." Grayson stuck out his hand. "Maybe I should drive."

"Not a chance." Reece clutched his keys possessively. "I'm only allowing you to sit in my passenger seat under duress, and I already know you don't drive like an empath."

"Worth a shot." Grayson dropped his hand. "Head for Pioneer Square, then."

They climbed into the car, and Reece turned the key. His car made a pathetic clicking and nothing more.

Oh no. "Not now," he muttered under his breath, uselessly twisting the key.

Grayson looked at the dashboard, then at Reece. "Why won't your car start?"

"You know your way around handcuffs but not the sound of a dead battery?" Reece climbed out of the car and went around to the passenger side.

When Grayson didn't move, Reece tapped impatiently on the window. Grayson lifted a hand, paused, then cracked the passenger door instead. Reece probably needed to fix that window. "You leave your lights on or something?"

Somethin'. Reece huffed. "Of course not. Sometimes batteries get old and they don't hold a charge very well."

"Oh," Grayson said, like this was news.

Reece gestured at him. "Any day now."

"Why am I going back out in the cold? We don't all have empath blood keeping us warm."

Reece pointed at the footwell. "That's where the battery is. You don't have to get out, just twist—"

Grayson swung the door open, forcing Reece back, and was out of the car a moment later without so much as brushing Reece's arm.

Not even chancing contact outside of the gloves, it seemed. Reece left the passenger door open and went to the hatch at the back.

Grayson followed and hovered behind him. "So do I buy you another battery?"

Reece grabbed his emergency jump starter, sending a plea

to the universe that it had enough juice left for a second jump. "No."

"What about another car?"

"Absolutely not."

"Your car can't cost a whole lot to replace," Grayson said. "I'm not sure I'm convinced it even is an actual car. How come your overprotective big sister hasn't bought you a new battery?"

"She has," Reece grudgingly admitted.

"But you still use the old one because…"

"Because I won't put the new one in until I've finished paying her back and she doesn't know how to install it herself and I hide my keys so she can't—you know, just because you don't have facial expressions doesn't mean I can't tell when you're judging me." He tried to slam the hatch, which only closed with an unsatisfying snick.

Grayson reached into his pocket where he kept his phone. "I can have a new car here in—"

"*No.* I have the emergency charger; it's my compromise with Jamey." And if ever there was an emergency reason to use it, it was to keep the Dead Man from buying him a freaking *car.*

Reece hooked up the cables and had the car running just a couple minutes later. Grayson watched the whole procedure with a curiosity that confirmed he'd never had to jump his own battery in his life.

As soon as Reece had the cover back in place, Grayson got right back in the passenger seat and firmly shut the door. Reece put the now-drained charger back in the hatch and then hesitated.

It had been hours now and Cora still hadn't called him back. Did she know she'd succeeded, that Hathaway had been going to withdraw the anti-empathy bill? Even if new senators took up the bill, even if it passed after all, Cora deserved to know.

But his gaze stole to Grayson sitting in his passenger seat.

Cora had tried to help him yesterday. It'd be poor thanks to put her on the Dead Man's radar, especially when the Dead Man thought an empath was responsible for Hathaway's death.

Reece did pull out his phone, but he called Jamey instead.

"Liam told me about the picture on the *Eyes on Empaths* blog," she said, without preamble. "He's drafting a statement calling it a *misunderstanding*."

Reece sighed. "He shouldn't waste his time," he said, as he slammed the hatch with more success this time. "I'm a menace who can't keep his mouth shut; I have it all coming." No lie in those words. Reece sighed again.

"But you're also my brother. He understands it's hard for an empath to hide their feelings, and he told me that no matter what your mouth says, your heart's in the right place."

Reece leaned heavily against the back of his car. They were both giving him more grace than he deserved, and Liam still hadn't run screaming from all the weird-ass things in Jamey's life. "And what does he understand about *you*, Jamey? And what's he going to do if he finds out?"

"I don't know," Jamey said, sounding very honest. "But he sure takes all your weird paranormal shit in stride. And speaking of you and the shit you get up to, put Grayson on the phone."

Grayson? With a shrug, Reece walked over to the passenger door. Grayson was already on the phone, but Reece knocked on the window anyway.

Grayson pulled the phone away from his mouth and cracked the door. "This conversation is not for empaths."

Reece held out his own phone. "For you."

Grayson looked from the phone to Reece, then took it.

"Grayson. Who—?" He promptly cut his sentence off. He listened for a moment, then said, "It was a—misunderstanding."

Reece snorted.

"He's—" began Grayson, then he paused. "But I—" He paused again. "Yes, ma'am. Yes, I—no, ma'am—yes. Understood."

He passed the phone back to Reece. "Consider this an apology for cuffing you over the hood of your car."

Reece blinked. "Um—okay?" He put the phone to his ear and took a few steps away from the car. "The Dead Man just said sorry to me. What did you threaten him with?"

"You literally don't want to know," said Jamey. "Where are you going now?"

"Some place called McFeely's."

"You're joking."

"You've heard of it?" Reece said in surprise. "You've never told me about it."

"I don't tell you lots of things. Grayson gets to break this one to you. Gotta go."

Reece made a face at the phone. He walked over to the passenger window, and when he knocked, Grayson opened the door all of an inch.

Reece folded his arms, phone still in hand. "I'm not going to like this McFeely's place, am I?"

"Your sister is making me tell you for a reason."

Of course he'd overheard. Reece was beginning to suspect Grayson's hearing was as good as Jamey's.

"Sooner you get behind the wheel, the sooner we get it over with," Grayson pointed out.

But Reece had a question. "Is Huang going to tell Stone he told you about McFeely's?"

"No."

Reece waited, but no further explanation came. He huffed. "How'd you get Huang to talk anyway?"

"You were there."

"Yeah, and I didn't see *anything*. One moment he's the Fort Knox of information, the next he can't confess to you fast enough. Is everyone with Stone Solutions scared of you?"

"It's smart to be scared of me." Grayson didn't say it like a threat. He said it simply, the way he might have said *it's smart to grab a hat if it's raining*.

But then, Reece never wore hats. He got in the car. "So you're totally okay going to this McFeely's place and digging up dirt on Stone?"

"Why wouldn't I be?"

"Because you and Stone have reached the *reserved parking spot* phase of your relationship. I'm expecting the engagement announcement any day."

"I hope I haven't given you the impression anyone can trust me."

That brought Reece up short. He looked over at the other man, but Grayson's eyes might as well have been a vault. "What's that supposed to mean?"

"Mr. Stone doesn't and shouldn't," Grayson said, in his inscrutable voice. "Nor should Detective St. James. And you most of all have got no business trusting me."

Reece quickly turned and stared out the windshield, needing to look anywhere but Grayson's blank eyes. "I don't understand."

"You don't need to understand. You just need to believe me." Grayson settled in his seat. "Pioneer Square. Best get going, it's gonna take us an hour to get there with an empath behind the wheel."

Jamey stood next to her car door and sent a quick text to Agent Nolan. Did she want the Feds following Reece? No. But had Grayson just shown he couldn't be trusted to keep his handcuffs to himself? Absolutely.

As she climbed into her Charger her phone rang, a number she didn't recognize on-screen. She answered. "St. James."

"It's Aisha Easterby. Grayson didn't want to tell you in front of your brother, but there's been another murder."

Shit. Jamey turned the engine over. "Just tell me where to go."

Not thirty minutes later, Jamey was pulling up to the customer parking area in front of a shady diner only a few miles from her own home. The blinds had been drawn, the neon *24 hours* sign turned off, and the windows papered with signs proclaiming the diner to be closed.

The door opened as she approached, bell jingling loudly. Easterby propped it open with her body, still dressed in the lab coat over jeans, this time with a messenger bag slung over her shoulder.

"Think we'll ever have a conversation that's not prompted by a corpse?" said Jamey.

"No," Easterby said. "I'm an ME. All my conversations happen because of corpses. Why do you think I have to ask other people for secondhand phone numbers?"

Inside the diner, Jamey recognized a few of the faces of those scurrying around, members of the team that had been at Jason Owens' home. The diner itself was instantly forgettable, the same cheap booths and barstool-lined counter as any other dive she'd been in. Although the bright red blood splattering the endless white Formica—that was admittedly different. "Where's the body?"

"Bodies. Chad Martin, the owner. Anton Webber, the cook. And Oliver Keith, a server." Easterby pitched her voice low enough no one would have been able to overhear. "Best we can reconstruct, Oliver Keith went out to tell the driver of a red i8 to move the car. Then he came back in and attacked his boss with a vegetable peeler."

"Well, shit," Jamey muttered.

"The cook tried to interfere." Easterby winced. "It didn't go well."

"Keith killed them both?" Jamey asked, and Easterby nodded. "And how did Keith himself die?"

"Heart failure. Probably caused by lethal levels of rage." Easterby gestured toward the back. "Bodies are in the kitchen. And this time, there's a witness."

After a quick look at the bloody mess in the kitchen, Jamey pushed out through the delivery door to the alley at the back. Easterby tagged just behind her as they approached a nondescript SUV parked in the alley next to the dumpster.

The witness, Penelope Morton, was younger than Jamey, with brown hair slipping out of its ponytail. She was slumped on the edge of the open hatch, a gray blanket around her shoulders and her nose and eyes bright red. Over the dumpster's unpleasant stench, Jamey could just make out the smell of tears and orange juice.

"No badge," Easterby muttered as they approached, again for Jamey's ears alone.

Jamey frowned. "But I have to—"

"You're not here with the police," Easterby whispered. "Like it or not, you're here on behalf of the Dead Man."

Jamey wrinkled her nose, but she didn't pull out her badge as she came up to the witness. "Miss Morton?"

"Penny." She sniffed loudly as her gaze swept over Jamey. "Who are you? Another cop?"

What cops? There was no one here but Stone Solutions lackeys. Easterby elbowed Jamey then, so she bit it back. "My name's Briony St. James. I just want to know what happened here."

Penny pulled the blanket more tightly closed and looked at the ground next to Jamey's feet. "Some fancy red sports car was parked in the customer parking for like half an hour without coming in. No one else was coming in either, so Ollie went out to tell them to leave. Then he came back in and went into the kitchen where Mr. Martin was chewing out Anton. And then—then—"

Her voice broke, and she squeezed her eyes shut. Jamey furrowed her brow. "Then what?"

Easterby cleared her throat. "Then Penny here was very smart. She hid under a booth and called 911."

Smart, yes—except Stone Solutions had showed up while the actual emergency responders heard nothing.

Penny took a shaky breath. "I don't understand why Ollie would do something like that."

Easterby answered. "I'm afraid Mr. Keith was under the influence of several powerful opiates."

"Drugs?" Penny repeated in shock. "But Ollie doesn't even drink."

"Addiction comes as a shock sometimes, I know," Easterby said, with what sounded like sincere sympathy even if the story had been a bald-faced Stone Solutions lie.

The story might keep Penny from learning the truth about empaths, but she still wasn't going to walk away from this easily. "Do you have someone you can stay with?" Jamey asked.

Penny sniffled. "My sister's coming for me."

Jamey made herself smile with a reassurance she absolutely did not feel. "I'm glad to hear that." Then she grabbed Easterby by the sleeve.

The other woman was a head shorter and Jamey had to slow her walk as she tugged her to the alley wall, out of earshot and far away from the dumpster. "Stone Solutions is intercepting our 911 calls now?" Jamey demanded.

"We've always monitored all emergency frequencies for any

cases that could be empathy-related," Easterby said. "How do you think Grayson knows where to go?"

Jamey shook her head. "That's not okay—"

"Barely a handful of people in the whole country know the true extent of what empaths can do," Easterby said, punctuating the words by pointing to the diner's back door. "And that truth cannot get out."

"I don't want it out," Jamey said. "But Stone Solutions should. If people knew empaths were capable of *this*, they'd throw every last dollar into anti-empathy defenses. There's an empath out there responsible for *seven* murders—"

"I know." Easterby ran a hand over her own neck, over the scar. "But no one can know that empaths are capable of this, and the empaths themselves aren't the true villains. We will get to the bottom of this and learn that the empath is also a victim, I promise you that."

Jamey frowned. "You're making it hard for me to paint all of Stone Solutions with the same brush."

"Was that—a *compliment*?"

"I said hard, not impossible."

Easterby grinned. "Still a compliment, Detective. And look, I've got something else for you." She reached into the messenger bag across her shoulder and withdrew a tablet. "These are the results from the tests you wanted done on the Ford Transit's tires."

Jamey straightened up.

"The mud from the van's tires had wood pulp mixed in, but it's old, and the lab thinks it's from a long-closed pulp mill. I got a location up in—" Easterby paused. "That's odd."

"What?"

Easterby traced a finger over the tablet's screen. "I talked to the lab over the phone and Indira named a spot near Everett. But this lists a mill to the south, in Tacoma. She must have updated the results and not called back." She wrinkled her nose. "Surprised me, that's all."

It took a lot more than evidence tampering to surprise Jamey. "Do you remember the location of the original place?"

Easterby looked up from the tablet. "Yes. But why—"

"Give me that one. In the meantime, let me know if you find that i8."

Chapter Sixteen

...the romance novel in question, Engaged to the Empath, *has been the subject of controversy since its publication. "We can't have books romanticizing empathy," American Minds Intact president Beau Macy said. "What's next, people seeking empaths out on purpose? Empath fetishists? Where would the depravity end?"*

—*excerpt from the* Emerald City Tribune, *"AMI calls for book's removal from libraries"*

Reece took the exit for James Street from I-5, then Grayson directed him through Pioneer Square to the Alastair Building, a four-story historic warehouse with arched windows and a brick facade in need of a power-wash. Sandwiched between an art gallery and a coffee shop at street level was a trim green awning, and beneath the awning was set of metal double doors with no markings or clue to what they held.

As Reece parked at the curb, Grayson cleared his throat. "Before we go in," he said, "how's that blood pressure?"

Reece side-eyed him. "Why?" he said suspiciously.

"Just want to make sure we're starting at a baseline somewhere near normal."

"And what, pray tell," Reece said, with biting sweetness, "is the reason you think it's about to rise?"

Grayson coughed. "Pretty sure it's going up as we speak."

"Well, *empath specialist*, maybe stop *setting it off*."

Grayson hesitated.

"What?" said Reece.

"Nothing."

"Oh no, that was not nothing, that was hesitation. Whatever it is you don't want to tell me, say it anyway."

"If you're sure you want to know," said Grayson. "I wasn't gonna say it, but you're a touch high-strung even by empath standards. When was the last time you read someone?"

Reece drew back. "Why would you ask that?"

"Most empaths have a lot of people in their life. Hard to *empathize* if it's just you. I don't meet a lot of empaths as alone as you seem to be."

Reece quickly looked forward, out the windshield. He didn't want to think about this, about any of this. "I haven't read someone myself since March," he said tightly.

"*March,*" Grayson repeated. "You know you've got all sorts of neurotransmitter and other issues, don't you? Because that empath brain would rather get its feelings from others than make its own? Just one more way y'all don't have the self-preservation instinct God gave a rock. Why so long ago?"

I felt so much pain I thought I was dying and now I have nightmares and hear everyone else lie what's wrong with me do you know?

Can you help?

"It—I—it wasn't a good experience," Reece managed to say.

"Oh." He could feel Grayson's gaze on him. "Someone I need to have a conversation with?"

Reece shook his head, the movement jerky. "No. That person isn't—" *alive* "—around. Not anymore."

"I can travel."

Reece huffed, not a laugh, not over this, but a tiny bit lighter. "Cute," he grudgingly admitted. "But why do you keep pretending that the Dead Man would stick up for an empath?"

"Have I *pretended* about anything since we met?"

Reece hesitated. No, Grayson hadn't—not when he'd cuffed Reece over the hood of his car, not when he'd talked him down in Stone Solutions until the phantom pain had stopped.

Reece shook his head to clear it of those thoughts. "Sorry, still not falling for it. Maybe that's how you fool other empaths, like, *hey baby, you just be your high-strung self and let me handle all that scary danger*, but respectfully, Agent *Dead Man*, I'm pretty sure you *are* the scary danger."

"Fair enough," Grayson muttered.

They climbed out of the car and approached the awning. "Are you ever going to tell me what this place is?" Reece asked.

"A club." Grayson pressed a tiny doorbell adjacent to the metal doors. "Of a sort."

After several moments, creaky bolts began to move, and then one of the metal doors swung open to reveal a mountain of a man in all black, even taller and thicker than Grayson but with a friendly face and relaxed shoulders. "Sorry, we don't open until—"

The giant paused midsentence as his gaze landed on Reece—more specifically, on his gloves. "Oh, you're here about the job! Pretty sure the boss will fall all over himself to hire you. You've nailed the look."

Reece blinked. "The look?"

"You know: snack-sized. Adorable. You've even got those big eyes that make you look all sympathetic and shit."

"What the *hell* are you—"

"We're here to see Mr. Frazier," Grayson interrupted.

Now the giant—bouncer, Reece was guessing—looked confused. "Frodo doesn't have any appointments."

"He'll see us," said Grayson.

To Reece's surprise, the bouncer took a step back and held the door wider. "Come on in, then."

Reece looked at Grayson in confusion. "I've seen two other guards today try to pick fights with you."

"They probably only see his pretty face," said the bouncer.

Reece gave the bouncer a narrow-eyed look. "And what do *you* see?"

"That Frodo doesn't pay me enough to lose that fight," the bouncer said easily.

"Riiight," Reece said, drawing it out skeptically. "So your muscles are—what? Made of marshmallows?"

"Mr. Lane was a marine," said Grayson, "and has black belts in three martial arts."

"Please, Diesel's fine," the bouncer said.

"Diesel," Reece repeated. "Is that your name or your engine?"

"I drive a Prius."

Reece scrunched his nose.

"Not too bright," Diesel said to Grayson. "That'll be another point in his favor. The clientele isn't looking for Einsteins."

Reece's mouth opened in outrage. "Did you just call me short and *stupid*?"

"Er—"

"And exactly what *clientele* wants that?"

"The freaks into—ah." Diesel squirmed under Reece's glare. "You know what? Boss doesn't pay me enough to handle you either. Follow me."

Diesel led them deeper into the warehouse, and up a narrow staircase with dark carpeting and what must have been an odd smell, because Grayson almost wrinkled his nose. The top of the stairs opened into a large, windowless space with standing tables along the exposed brick walls and a DJ stage at the far side.

To the left was a granite bar with fancy liquor on glass shelves that stretched to the high ceiling. A guy with complicated hair was stacking glasses behind the counter while the TVs overhead played some kind of sport. That was a nice change from the footage of Reece vomiting—

On-screen, four men in helmets piled onto a fifth man with a ball, smashing him painfully to the ground. The audience roared.

On second thought, not better at all. Reece quickly looked away.

Diesel took them to the right, past some bunched velvet ropes and poles pushed to the side, and into a short hall. He knocked twice on one of the unmarked doors, then opened it. "Boss, you got guests," he called, moving to let Reece and Grayson enter.

A short, hairy man—Frodo, Diesel had called him—was sitting behind a solid wood desk piled high with paper. When he looked up, his gaze zeroed in on Reece and he lit like Christmas had come early. "Yes."

Reece furrowed his brow. "Yes what?"

"You're hired."

"He already works for me," Grayson said.

"Excuse me?" said Reece. *"For* you? I'm barely working *with* you."

Frodo had excitedly gotten to his feet. "Come work for me instead." He gestured at a trophy on the desk, a huge novelty affair proclaiming him to be the *World's Greatest Boss*. "I'd be a better boss than Scary McAccent here."

Grayson shook his head. "He's not interested."

"He's not my boss and I can speak for myself," Reece snapped. "Maybe I *am* interested. I haven't even heard what the job is."

"Suit yourself," said Grayson. "But I hadn't pegged you as the type to get half-naked and take advantage of lonely fetishists for money."

Reece stared at him. Then he turned his stare on Frodo.

"McFeely's," he said slowly, as horrifying realization set in. "No. You can't possibly be—"

"The only club offering empath companionship in the whole country," Frodo said proudly. "We are a judgment-free zone of acceptance, open to all."

"He means he's a purveyor of feelings and bisexuality," said Grayson.

Frodo stuck his nose in the air. "I don't think I like your tone."

"I don't like this whole club!" Reece cut in. "And I don't understand. There are only two of us in Seattle and we sure as hell don't work here, so who are your empath companions?"

"Actors," said Grayson. "In fake gloves."

Reece's jaw dropped.

"Back this up to the important bit." Frodo pointed at Reece. "You said two of *us*. Does that mean you're—"

"One-hundred-percent genuine Care Bear," Grayson said for him, while Reece struggled to find words. "You should see him drive."

Frodo clapped his hands, looking more excited than ever. "Now I have to have you. Whatever he's paying, I'll pay you more."

"You could buy lots of car batteries," said Grayson.

Reece rolled his eyes. "He doesn't pay me. And he's not funny," he said to Frodo. *Lie.* Reece raised his eyes to the ceiling. "You know impersonating an empath is illegal?"

"We've had empaths for a whole generation," said Frodo. "Someone was eventually going to monetize empathy. Why shouldn't it be me?"

Reece rubbed his forehead. "I don't suppose you'd listen to the argument, *because it's wrong*?"

"Look how insightful you are." Frodo grinned. "You must be a real empath." He leaned forward. "It's an easy job. Nothing weird."

"Oh sure," Reece said, sarcasm tinged with hysteria, "because there's *nothing weird* about a *club* for *empath companionship*."

"Just look cute," Frodo continued cheerfully, right over Reece. "Listen to customers bitch, and pretend to care about their feelings—"

"Like hers?" Grayson held up his phone with a picture of Senator Hathaway on-screen.

Frodo glanced at it for less than a second. "Oh. The senator. Yeah, she was here last night."

Not a lie. "You're going to tell us she was here, just like that?" said Reece.

"I didn't vote for her." Frodo leaned back in his leather chair. "I always thought she had some nerve, trash-talking empaths all day, then sneaking into my club at night."

Reece threw up his hands. "But no one here is a real empath!"

"She didn't know that." Frodo gave a derisive sniff. "Not to disrespect the dead, but I can't stand hypocrites."

"I thought this was a judgment-free zone," Grayson said dryly.

"You had to have heard what happened to her," Reece said. "Why didn't you call the police?"

"Do the cops come in here to wash loads of booze-soaked gloves and listen to everyone whine about having to be sweet to assholes? If they don't do my job, why would I do theirs?"

Reece pinched the bridge of his nose.

"Now that someone's finally here, though, I'm happy to tell you whatever you want to know," said Frodo.

Grayson held up his phone again, a photo of Stone on-screen.

"Oh, Cedrick Stone." Frodo snorted. "What a bag of dicks."

Also not a lie. Reece hid his smile.

"Yeah, he was here. I don't know why, I don't believe for a second that he buys my actors as real empaths. Not the *great defender of American minds.*" Frodo layered the words with a thick sarcasm Reece could appreciate. "He and Hathaway were dropped off together. She drank up a huge bill on his tab."

Grayson held up another picture of a white man Reece didn't recognize. "He show up at all?"

Frodo's expression darkened. "Diesel?" he called, and the gigantic bouncer peeked into the still-open door. "Was Dr. Owens here last night?"

Grayson's eyes went to Diesel as the other man came into the room. "You know his name," said Grayson.

Diesel glanced at the picture then averted his gaze. "Yeah, he showed up just after Stone and the senator did and went into the VIP room too."

"Was he driving?" asked Grayson.

Diesel nodded once. "Red i8. He didn't valet."

"Did the senator leave with Owens?" Grayson asked.

"Not sure," said Diesel. "I didn't see anyone leave. I moved from the VIP's alley door to its inside door, to make sure Owens didn't wander out into the main club. They only had one waiter, and Cookie reported they'd all left before last call."

"That's a start," said Grayson, "but Jason Owens was found dead a few hours after the senator."

"*Dead?*" Diesel repeated.

Frodo looked equally shocked. Reece had some choice opinions about their business practices, but as far as he could tell, they hadn't known about Owens and weren't involved in whatever had happened to him and Senator Hathaway.

"How?" Frodo asked.

"We're not gonna talk about that part in present company," said Grayson. "But I'm gonna need any footage that may show any of them."

Frodo cleared his throat. "That might be tricky. You understand that I offer my patrons a safe refuge from the cold, cruel world—"

"It wasn't a request."

Frodo eyed him suspiciously. "Who did you say you were with again?"

"I didn't," said Grayson.

Frodo sighed.

"Why didn't either of you like Jason Owens?" Reece asked.

Frodo and Diesel exchanged another glance.

"Real empath," Reece reminded them. "And you two were not subtle."

"Dr. Owens would stop in every time I hired someone new," Frodo said, reluctantly. "Then give me grief about faking it and tell me to call if I ever get an actual empath on the floor."

"Like a hunter watching a pond of decoys, waiting for the real duck," said Diesel. "Or some kind of mad scientist tracking a unicorn."

A mad scientist with access to Stone's technology and books on tor—

No, Reece wasn't going think about the box; he'd already exceeded his breakdown quota for the day. He looked up at Grayson. "You've got a reserved parking spot at Cedrick Stone's company." He folded his arms over his chest. "Were you friends with Jason Owens too?"

It was stupid—so stupid—to be upset at the thought that Grayson might have been friendly with this unsettling Owens guy. Grayson had been honest that he was paid, at least in part, by Stone Solutions. Grayson was the Dead Man. He *should* have been firmly on Stone and Owens' side against empaths.

But Frodo was the one to say, "I'd guess Agent Grayson isn't *friendly* with anyone, and certainly not Dr. Owens."

"And why's that?" Reece said.

"Because Owens was a creep," Diesel said bluntly. "And I'm getting a vibe that if he'd known all this shit about Owens, Blondie here would have broken some bones."

Reece's knees buckled. Grayson grabbed him by the sweatshirt before he hit the floor. "Real empath," he drawled as he pulled Reece back upright by the hood. "Real aversion to violence."

"Oh, so sorry!" Diesel's eyes were wide. "I didn't—"

"You didn't mean to," Reece said, trying to steady his wobbly knees. Probably wasn't helping anything that he'd puked up what little he'd eaten. "Are they right?" he demanded of Grayson. "Not about the—you know—but about the not-friendly part? Why wouldn't you be best buds with everyone at Stone Solutions? You're an empath hunter."

Lie. Lie? Wait, what part of Reece now thought that wasn't true?

Oh no. Was it the same traitorous brain cell that had turned its back on Team A, the rational minds that were nervous around Grayson, and gleefully yee-hawed its way onto Team B, the *Wouldn't Kick Grayson Out of Bed* wackos?

"I keep saying specialist," said Grayson, and headed for the door, with Reece scrambling after him.

Chapter Seventeen

"If Stone's car drove away," Reece said, catching up to Grayson down the hall, "does that mean Huang's off the hook?"

Grayson glanced down at him. "Do I seem like I ever let anyone off the hook?"

"You seem like one big *specialist* sphinx full of riddles."

As they crossed the floor, a thin man with even thinner blond hair and glasses was coming up the stairs. He wore a

Stone Solutions polo shirt, and as his gaze landed on Reece, the man's eyes instantly narrowed.

"Mr. Egner." Grayson got between them before Reece could say a word. "The manager's gonna require your assistance recovering files."

Reece pointed at Egner. "You know him?" he said to Grayson.

"I sent for him," Grayson said. "He's head of IT at Stone Solutions."

Reece frowned. "But why—"

"You think Mr. Frazier is gonna find his files intact? Or you think someone deleted anything we might need to see?" Grayson jerked his head at Egner and pointed down the hall. "Office is that way. Or are you stalling for a reason, Mr. Egner?"

But Egner had gone still, cold eyes still on Reece. "That's a real empath."

Great, another Stone Solutions jerk who hated empaths. Reece opened his mouth but Grayson said, "Mr. Davies is not your concern."

"Dr. Whitman didn't say anything about having to deal with a real empath," Egner snapped. "She said I had to come to the fake empath club and fix whatever an Agent Grayson said—"

"I'm Agent Grayson."

Egner went white as a sheet.

"You done stalling?"

Egner scrambled down the hall without another word.

As Grayson turned into the main room, Reece scratched his head. "*Why* does everyone at Stone Solutions think you're so scary?" he asked, as he scurried after Grayson toward the granite-topped bar that ran along one of the brick walls. "Aren't you only dangerous to empaths? And isn't half of your attention reserved for your hair?"

"You implying hair care is scary? That would explain some things."

"No," Reece said. "I'm *implyin'* that the only thing that scares Stone Solutions more than empaths is *you.*"

The TVs above the bar were still tuned to sports—football maybe, but Reece wasn't going to look again. A tip jar plastered with AMI and Stone Solutions stickers was prominently displayed by the register and the guy with complicated hair was still rummaging around behind the bar.

"Benjamin Castillo?" At Reece's side eye, Grayson said, "You really think I walked in here without a list of employees and their schedules?"

Reece rubbed his temples as the bartender straightened.

"Just Ben's fine." Like Diesel, Ben had a sweet, friendly face, the kind that probably had people instantly spilling their guts over the bar; the kind people expected empaths like Reece to have. Ben had a glass in hand and was drying it with a small towel as his gaze darted over Grayson. "You said my last name right."

"I'd hope so," Grayson said dryly. "It was one of my grandmothers'."

"Oh, I love it when people surprise me." Ben pointed to his hair with the towel. "Love it when people don't fit everyone else's stereotypes and perfect little boxes. Granted, it's probably less that we're long-lost cousins and more that your ancestors helped themselves to the Philippines, but you don't look like you're here to colonize my bar."

"The less you know about me, the better off you'll be," Grayson said.

"Really," Ben said. "What scandalous thing do you do? Telenovela star?"

"Nothing that glamorous," said Grayson, which was a neat sidestep of *I'm an urban legend, but make it hot.*

Reece tapped the tip jar. "What's with the stickers?"

"Funny, right?" Ben's gaze had fallen on Reece's gloves. "Are you new? You're early. The companions don't start for a couple hours."

"I don't work here."

"So you've come for a drink?" Ben's expression turned cagey. "Ah, one moment."

He ducked behind the bar.

"You have grandparents?" Reece said to Grayson. "You didn't just crawl out of a grave somewhere?"

"We're gonna file the Dead Man's family under *things empaths don't want to hear about.*"

Reece frowned as Ben reappeared, pulling on black gloves. "Sorry," he said. "Took them off while washing dishes. We're not really open yet, but I can get you something. Empaths are super understanding like that."

Grayson coughed.

Ben gestured to Reece's gloves. "It's okay if you want to wear your costume in here. We empaths keep this club a judgment-free zone."

Reece pinched the bridge of his nose. "You're not an empath."

"Sure I am."

Reece held up his own gloved hands. "Government-issued, created from a patented, top secret weave including heavy metal threads to block me from reading anyone through an accidental touch." He pointed at Ben's. "Pretty sure those are polyester and from some dodgy costume shop. You know impersonating an empath is illegal?"

Ben shrank back. "I just work here, and Frodo wants everyone to—"

"Not today's concern," said Grayson. "Talk about Senator Hathaway."

The tension in Ben's shoulders relaxed. "Senator Hypocrite, we called her here." He bit his lip. "I feel bad about it now. Her death is awful."

Grayson held up the picture of Jason Owens. "You see him with her?"

Ben shook his head. "But Hathaway was in the VIP room all night, like she always is when she's here." He winced. "Maybe I should have called the cops when I saw the news, but we weren't supposed to tell anyone Hathaway came here. And I didn't see her myself at all, I just made drinks."

"Someone brought the drinks into the VIP room," said Grayson.

Ben nodded. "Cookie did. They wanted privacy, so Cookie's the only one who went in there all night."

"Then we're gonna need to talk to Ms. Cookie—"

"Mr. Cookie."

"Mr. Cookie," Grayson corrected, without blinking. "We're gonna need—"

"You can't," said Ben. "He's not coming back. He emailed and said he's moving to Australia today." He gestured at Reece. "That's why we're hiring."

"Australia." Grayson leaned on the bar, putting himself eye level with Ben. "And you didn't think you ought to call the cops when the only person who saw a US senator hours before her murder up and moved to Australia the same day?"

"I told you, we all promised not to tell anyone she came here," Ben said stubbornly. "Life is hard; people come here for a break. What kind of shit bartender would I be if I couldn't keep their secrets?" Then his expression faltered. "Cookie's okay, though, right? He really did go to Australia?"

Oh no.

Reece tensed, but Grayson said, "I don't know. But I'll find out, all right?"

If that was supposed to be reassuring, Reece couldn't tell, because it sounded the same as everything else Grayson said. But Ben nodded jerkily, and he did look like Grayson's promise had made him feel better.

Reece scrubbed a hand over his face. Maybe the video footage would show Hathaway leaving, or at least some clue as to how the night had gone so wrong. He looked to Grayson, but the other man's eyes were on the TVs above Ben's head again.

Ben noticed too. His gaze flicked over Grayson, like it had earlier. "You a football fan?"

Grayson continued to watch the screens. "Once upon a time," he said at last, then looked back down at Ben. "And if you want to pass for an empath, notice this one being careful not to watch the game because his little heart might stop if he sees another quarterback sacked."

Reece scowled. "Your *I know everything empath* shtick got old a long time ago," he said, as Frodo marched into the room, red-faced.

"When did I say Stone Solutions' director of IT could come look at my security footage?" Frodo demanded.

"When this became the last known stop of a murdered senator," said Grayson. "And you found all your files deleted, didn't you?"

"Not the point," snapped Frodo. "I have my own people to handle this sort of thing." He pointed up at Grayson, then down the hall. "My office, handsome."

"Excuse me?" said Grayson.

Frodo stuck his nose in the air. "We're about to fight and I don't fight in front of empaths."

"Ben's not an empath," said Reece.

"And we're not fighting," said Grayson. "Fighting implies reciprocation. I'm not gonna listen to a word you say."

Frodo drew himself up to his full height, which still left him shorter than Reece and somewhere below Grayson's shoulder. "Not in front of Ben and the empath. Come on."

"If that's what you want." Grayson followed him across the room to a spot along the wall, where Frodo began to gesture wildly while speaking in hushed whispers.

Not interested in joining, Reece perched on a barstool and pulled out his phone while he waited for Frodo to lose.

Ben leaned on the bar in front of Reece. "What can I get you?"

Reece reached around him to grab the tip jar. "I don't drink."

"Is there a biological reason for that?"

"You tell me, fellow empath."

Ben made a face. "Okay, fine. I can do all sorts of virgin drinks."

Reece turned the jar around in his hands, examining it. "I can't afford anything in this club."

"No problem, it's on the house."

"Pass. I don't want a faux drink from a faux empath as charity." Bingo: the Stone Solutions' phone number was on one of the stickers. He pecked it into his phone and balanced it in the crook of his neck.

Ben pursed his lips. Then, gamely, he said, "So. A real empath."

"No." Reece pushed the jar back into place as his phone began to ring.

"No, you're not a real empath?" Ben said in confusion.

"No, I'm not giving anyone in this club tips on pretending to be an empath so you can keep lying to the poor saps who come here."

Ben's mouth fell open. "Well, I got one thing about being an empath wrong. I've been being *nice*." He stomped off to the other end of the bar.

On Reece's phone, a receptionist picked up. "Stone Solutions, how can we defend your mind today?"

Reece pulled the phone away, gave it a look, then sighed and put it back to his ear. "Can I talk to the medical examiner, please?"

"Medical examiner?" she repeated. "We don't have any medical examiners."

Reece frowned. "What about a doctor, then?"

"We employ dozens of doctors in multiple practice areas." The receptionist paused. "What did you say your name was?"

Reece hung up. He was about to call Jamey when a glass of something red appeared on the bar in front of him.

He looked up in surprise.

"Shirley Temple," Ben said pointedly. "Because you need something sweet to offset being so bitter."

Not a lie. Reece would have been irritated, except—"This has cherries."

"*Extra* cherries," Ben confirmed. "And it's on me."

Reece territorially pulled the fizzy drink closer. He sipped, and his eyes fluttered shut at the rush of sugary syrup. Ben might have been a fake empath, but he was a real bartender. "It's good," he reluctantly admitted, through a second, longer sip.

"Oh, look at that, I got you to say something nice," said Ben. "That wasn't so bad, was it?"

It was admittedly hard to stay irritated when your mouth tasted like sugar and cherries. "I'm paying you for it."

"It's just a drink," said Ben. "Don't make it weird."

Reece cracked an eye. "Do you even like boys?"

"Do *you*? Or did Frodo make up the bisexuality thing too?"

Reece rolled his eyes. "I'm not going to speak for all empaths," he said, as he took another long sip. "But the list of people I like at all is short, and getting shorter by the day," he added pointedly.

"I bet you'd meet a lot of people you'd like here." Ben propped his chin on his hand. "Hell, every last person who walks through those doors would buy your drinks if you let them. It's a whole club for people into you."

"Please," Reece said. "People come here because they like *you*. You're all the nice things people want an empath to be. No one comes here because they like *me*. Even you assumed an empath would be sweet, not a grouchy jerk with a big mouth."

The corner of Ben's mouth turned up in a grudging smile. "At least you're self-aware." He glanced past Reece, his pupils dilating. "What kind of people does *he* like?"

"Now *you* made it weird," Reece said, as Grayson came up behind him. He glanced up at Grayson. "Is Frodo going to let that dick from Stone Solutions work on the computer?"

"Was that ever in doubt?" Grayson leaned on the bar. "Is that a Shirley Temple you're inhaling?"

"Shut up," Reece muttered, picking his drink up.

Grayson slid a credit card across the bar. "For the sugar rush."

Ben glanced expectantly at Reece, like he was prepared for the argument. When Reece just took another long sip, Ben's expression turned amused. "Oh, I see," he said slyly, picking up Grayson's card. "You only let *him* buy your drinks."

"Or maybe *you're* jumping to the wrong conclusion," Reece said testily. "Maybe I just work for him, did you think of that?"

Grayson raised an eyebrow. "I thought you were barely working *with* me."

"It's not—ugh." Reece huffed. "Part-time police consulting just doesn't pay as well as arresting empaths."

"I only handcuffed you that one time," said Grayson.

"That one time *so far.*"

Ben swiped the credit card and handed it back to Grayson. "Judgment-free zone or not, you two are a trip."

Grayson's gaze had gone suddenly to his phone. "TVs on local news, please."

Ben obligingly changed the station. A moment later, Reece was covering his mouth in horror. "Oh *no*."

There he was, on TV again. Only this wasn't the footage of him vomiting at HQ.

This was worse.

"If empaths had that kind of power we wouldn't waste it on pumpkins. We'd be hypnotizing Congress and brainwashing the President and—"

Reece stared helplessly at the TVs as screenshots of his social media popped up around an unflattering picture of him and the voiceover read his comments on *Eyes on Empaths*.

The picture flashed to live footage of Reece by his car near Hathaway's government building. *"Fine, yes, you caught me,"* he was saying. *"I was trying to get the First Amendment revoked with my crazy mind-control powers. Our forefathers were clearly high when they dreamed up freedom of press."*

Gretel Macy's video footage.

Oh no.

"Dude." Ben's eyes were glued to the TV. "Can you do that?"

Reece buried his head in his hands, watching the screen through his gloved fingers.

The anchor returned, his appropriately serious expression unable to hide the gleam in his eyes. *"That was empath Reece Davies, who was also filmed today vomiting on the steps of police headquarters downtown."*

The picture of Reece on hands and knees in front of HQ helpfully popped up on-screen, just in case he hadn't seen himself puke enough times today.

"Davies consults for the Seattle Police Department, where his own half sister is a detective."

The picture shifted again.

Ben's eyes popped wide. "*That's* your sister?"

Reece ignored Ben's open mouth as he sat up straight, hands falling to his lap, staring hard at the image of Jamey in uniform on-screen.

"*Detective Briony St. James has an exceptional record,*" continued the anchor, "*and some are now questioning whether it's a little too exceptional—and whether her empath brother could have anything do with that.*"

"Shit, I'd buy *her* drinks."

Ben's voice was distant over the high-pitched ringing that had started in Reece's ears. The camera panned over to a smarmy white man with a crisp suit and vaguely familiar face.

"*American Minds Intact president Beau Macy has once again consented to join us and share his speculation about Davies' influence on the SPD.*" The anchor shifted his serious expression to Macy. "*Where was such shocking footage of that empath captured?*"

"*It's AMI's footage, of course, but let's focus on what it shows,*" Macy said, without any credit to his daughter or her blog. "*It shows danger. It's obvious Detective St. James is under the influence of her empath brother. AMI has repeatedly called for this detective's suspension from the force—*"

The barstool toppled to the ground. Reece was walking, propelled by the anger licking at the base of his skull. How dare they drag Jamey into this—how dare they tie her name to this bullshit—how dare—

Grayson's flat voice managed to pierce the fog of Reece's fury. "Where're you heading?"

"To deal with the news," Reece snarled over his shoulder. Then he paused.

He was already halfway down the stairs to the front door of McFeely's.

Reece turned his head back toward the front door in confusion. Where *was* he going? He didn't know what station they'd just been watching. He didn't know where any of the news stations were.

He didn't even remember starting down the steps.

He looked up at Grayson, who was leaning against the railing at the top of the stairs, calm as ever.

"I…" Reece shook his head, as if he could shake his own thoughts straight again. Why were his ears still ringing? "I think…"

Beau Macy's voice echoed again in his head.

Repeatedly called for this detective's suspension—

No, not in a million years. Reece turned around.

"We got files to wait for," Grayson called.

Reece was already on his way down the stairs. "Screw the files."

"I need them."

Reece didn't slow. "Then you stay and wait."

"And watch you run off on a day when no empath ought to be alone—"

"They're trashing *Jamey*!" Reece shoved open the front door.

"Mr. Davies."

At the sound of his formal name, Reece stilled, hands on the open door. He clenched his jaw, then turned again to look over his shoulder, up to the top of the stairs.

Grayson held up the phone. "I make one call," he said, in that lazy drawl, "and I can have the press leashed."

Reece didn't move.

"We could quibble about the First Amendment and the press later." Grayson came down one step. "I can make Detective St. James untouchable now."

The offer hung between them, a heady temptation—or, maybe, a test.

But a test of what?

Reece closed his eyes. There was nothing to hear for a moment but the rushing of cars outside and the distant thumping of Ben's music.

Then he shook his head.

When he opened his eyes, he found Grayson studying him. Then he pocketed his phone and came down the stairs. "Come on," he said, as he gracefully maneuvered around Reece to get the door without any contact.

Reece watched his broad back for a second. And then he followed.

Agent Nolan sat in his Explorer, alone save for the occasional person braving the cold to scurry down the street past the Alastair Building.

Davies' ridiculous little car was still parked in front of the green awning where it'd been for the last hour. What was this McFeely's place anyway? St. James' text had just been a name and an address. Nolan had searched online but found nothing but vague phrases like *accepting* and *judgment-free*.

Nothing was making any sense today. They had one John Doe from hospital records to find, but somehow all the security footage from the hospital had been confiscated, and there were no decent witnesses because the hospital had been understaffed chaos and no one had had attention to spare. One nurse thought she might have seen someone go into Cora's office midmorning, a young man with dark hair and a hoodie, but that wasn't helpful—it described a good chunk of Seattle.

Hell, it described St. James' useless little brother.

The door beneath the green awning was suddenly opening. Nolan quickly slouched in his seat, peering over the steering wheel.

Nothing happened for a long moment, the door still cracked

but held in place. And then, finally, Agent Grayson emerged from the door, Davies at his heels.

They climbed into Davies' Smart car, and as the vehicle pulled away from the curb, Nolan sent a quick text message to Stone.

On the move.

He got his reply a moment later.

Follow, if you please.

Chapter Eighteen

For sale: limited-run first edition of Captain Feelings, *pristine condition. This collector's item includes the first issue of the short-lived graphic novel series, which starred the first empath superhero and was ended after protests by empaths, who argued that Captain Feelings didn't try hard enough to understand the point of view of his nemesis, Dr. Stoic.*

—internet auction site

"Park there."

"I see a fire hydrant."

"That's why the curb is free."

"No," Reece said. "Do you need me to drop you off so you don't have to walk in the cold?"

In the passenger seat, Grayson side-eyed him, but after a moment seemed to understand Reece was sincerely offering, not making fun of him. "What I need is for you to park sometime tonight," Grayson said. "We should just valet—"

"Valet? No way in—doesn't matter, there's a spot."

Reece passed a CR-V parked at the curb of the packed downtown street and pulled up alongside the Forrester just beyond.

Grayson snorted. "Even this toy won't fit there."

"Of course it will."

"No, it won't. But go ahead and try and give me another chance to say I told you so."

"It'll fit," Reece insisted.

"You think so?" Grayson leaned forward. "Tell me, which one of us is gonna be better at parallel parking, the specialist or the fussiest driver in the Pacific Northwest?"

Reece narrowed his eyes.

Then he threw the car into reverse, stabbed the gas, and, with two quick twists of the steering wheel, tucked it between the Forrester and the CR-V, straight as a ruler.

Grayson cracked the door to reveal the curb, less than an inch away.

Reece yanked up the e-brake with a satisfying screech. "Specialize that."

They walked a block through downtown to a restaurant tucked into the base of a corner high-rise, the windows emblazoned with the words *Yokota's Sushi House*. It was somehow familiar, except Reece was certain he'd never eaten there, and possibly never eaten anywhere this nice, period.

The hostess straightened as they walked in. "Are you Agent Grayson?" Her gaze darted over Reece, from his unwashed hair to his stained hoodie to his gloves, and her smile became strained. "Your table is ready," was all she said, though.

Reece kept his hands firmly in his pockets as she led them through the restaurant to a small booth at the back. "Please make sure Mr. Ohayashi is our server," Grayson said to her, and if he thought Reece hadn't noticed he was waiting for Reece to sit down first, he wasn't half the specialist he claimed to be.

But Reece had just realized he was starving, so he sat without poking at Grayson about his Southern chivalry. He picked up the menu, took one look, and tossed it straight back to the table. "Maybe you're here with a new admirer every night, but I can't afford any of this and I don't eat—"

"I need to be here for the investigation. I'm handling it." Grayson slid the menu back across the table to Reece. "Also, you got a real generous opinion of how much I date." He put his own menu to the side without cracking it.

Reece leaned back in the booth, eyes on Grayson suspiciously. "It doesn't seem like your style to care who the waiter is."

"It's not."

"So why would you ask for a particular server?"

"Better question is why I owe you any explanations."

Reece rolled his eyes.

Ohayashi came a couple moments later. Middle-aged, his bland waiter expression couldn't hide the smile lines around his mouth and eyes, and he didn't bat an eye when he saw Reece's gloves. Reece couldn't imagine why Grayson had specifically asked for this nice man.

Grayson ordered several things he didn't recognize. Ohayashi nodded, then pointed to Reece's menu. "I recommend the Bainbridge roll to all our vegans."

Reece blinked. "You know an empath?"

Ohayashi didn't seem surprised to be called out. "My daughter-in-law, in Portland." He offered Reece a commiserating smile laced with genuine sympathy. "Today must be hard for you."

The simple kindness from a stranger who cared about the empath in his family put a lump in Reece's throat, and despite the years that had passed, the loss of his mom abruptly stung like a fresh wound. He loved Jamey down to his bones. He could have loved a whole big family, if he'd ever had the chance. "I'll try that roll."

"Very good." Ohayashi disappeared.

Reece tried to push his feelings away. "You brought me to dinner at a restaurant with an empath-friendly waiter."

"That's not why we're here," said Grayson. "You saw the picture of this place just hours ago in Mr. Adams' office."

Reece finally realized why the restaurant looked familiar. "This was where Stone and Hathaway took Hathaway's assistant for his birthday. And Dr. Whitman made that comment about *not being invited for sushi*."

Grayson nodded once. "Turns out, Stone had a reservation here for two last night."

Reece pointed at him. "But that's not why you asked for Mr. Ohayashi as our waiter."

"No?" Grayson made it a question.

"Our waiter likes empaths. He has empath family." Reece leaned forward. "If Stone comes here regularly, I'm betting Mr. Ohayashi would recognize and avoid him. So you didn't ask for Mr. Ohayashi to question him. You asked for him for—" The words tripped on his lips as Reece realized what he was about to say. "For me? So I could be around someone nice to empaths?"

Grayson propped his chin in his hand. "You got to stop presuming to know me."

"Am I wrong?" Reece asked pointedly.

Ohayashi approached their table. Grayson was silent as he set a clear soda and a green-bottled beer on the table and vanished again.

"Can't hurt for you to be around someone who's not openly hostile," Grayson finally said, picking up the beer. "You've been a little less Cheer Bear, a little more Grumpy Bear, even for you."

Reece rolled his eyes, but he couldn't exactly deny that. The case *was* getting to him. His body hurt, not the phantom pain of a specific cruelty, but a low-level ache in his joints, upper back and shoulders, like he'd been carrying something too heavy all day. He'd lost his temper completely over Jamey on the news. If Grayson hadn't stopped him, he might have kept going.

He wasn't sure what exactly he'd been planning to say to the reporters if he found them. Or do to Beau Macy.

He wasn't sure he wanted to know. It was as if his emotions were slipping out of his control along with his empathy, and he was desperately grabbing for that fraying leash.

He pulled the soda close, and pointed to the beer in Grayson's hand. "If I'm grumpy it's because you're drinking on the job," he said, instead of admitting Grayson was right. "One of many reasons it's a good thing I'm driving."

Grayson took an unapologetic swallow. "It doesn't do anything for me." Another way he was like Jamey, then. She'd have to drink a liquor store to get a buzz. "And you're not driving much longer. My truck's on its way."

Of course he drove a truck. Reece should have seen that one coming. "You talk on the phone while driving. I'm not going to be your passenger."

"I can't give you a choice."

"But what am I supposed to do with my car?"

"Scrap metal, maybe?" Grayson said.

"My car works fine!"

"Except for the battery. And the passenger window. And the glove box. And—"

"Not my fault no one pays me piles of money to hunt rich dicks who probably jerk off to their own reflection." Reece immediately winced. "I didn't mean that."

An awkward silence hung as Grayson took a slow pull from his beer. "As I said: Grumpy Bear." He set the bottle down. "Relax, if you can. You're safe, for the moment."

Reece looked away, pressing his lips together so they

wouldn't tremble. He hadn't meant to lash out, and now the smallest kindness was enough to make his eyes damp. "Safe from *you*, you mean?" he said bitterly.

"No one should ever think they're safe from me," Grayson said, sounding brutally honest. "But I am trying to make sure you're safe from the rest of it. Even if your empath ass wouldn't know danger if it handcuffed you over the hood of your car."

Reece made a noncommittal sound. He didn't know what to do with that, the notion he wasn't safe *from* Grayson but was safe *with* him.

"I'm not gonna lecture you about empaths and stress, I'm sure you know all of it already," said Grayson. "But if I ask you to breathe for me again, will you?"

Across the table, Grayson's face was as unreadable as ever, but he didn't seem to be making fun of Reece. Even without discernable emotions behind it, the request felt genuine, somehow.

Reece took a deep breath. Held it. Let it out. He repeated the process, tracing his glove through the condensation on the outside of his glass so that water beaded on his fingertip. "I don't know why you bother to talk me down. Why would you even care what kind of bear I am?"

"I got my reasons."

"Don't you always."

"They went into a sushi joint." Nolan adjusted the volume on his headset as he pulled his SUV up to the curb in front of a fire hydrant.

On the other side of the phone, Stone asked, "Yokota's?"

Nolan's hackles went up. He wouldn't put it past Stone to be tracking an FBI agent too. "How'd you know?"

"Lucky guess." Stone sighed. "I'm afraid Agent Grayson is retracing my steps."

"Yours?"

"I brought Hannah to this very restaurant last night. If I'd had any idea it would be her last meal—well."

That sounded like real regret in the man's voice. But Stone was admitting he'd seen the senator only hours before her murder. "Why did you two have dinner?" Nolan asked carefully.

"We spent time together often. It's difficult to be a champion of a controversial cause," Stone said grandly. "You stand alone while smaller minds chip away at your faith, unable to understand the bigger picture you serve. I tried to offer Hannah support when I could."

Oh please. Nolan didn't like empaths, but pretending anti-empathy was a *controversial cause* was a ridiculous attempt at martyrdom. People were always eager to hate. Stone had shamelessly exploited fear and resentment to amass a personal fortune, and Senator Hathaway had done the same to keep herself in power.

Nolan could just make out the empath's little Smart car beater up ahead. Stone and Hathaway were not the underdogs.

"Look, I'm no fan of empath whining or their mind-raping trick," Nolan said. "But I'd be lying if I pretended to understand why we need Hathaway's anti-empathy bill. They all wear their gloves without complaint and I've yet to get called out on a case because some empath overstepped their bounds."

"So it must seem," Stone said lightly.

"And even if they did overstep, what exactly are they going to accomplish?" Nolan continued. "Telling us all how we *feel*? Harmless enough."

"Tell me, agent." There was something new in Stone's voice, something harder. "Do I strike you as the type of man who wastes his time?"

Nolan scoffed. "Of course not—"

"Then why do you believe I would make my life's work defending the American people against a harmless mutation?"

Nolan paused. He hadn't ever thought about it that way. "I suppose you wouldn't," he said slowly.

"And do you really believe that if empathy was harmless, Evan Grayson would be allowed to operate with his appalling impunity?"

Chills began to prickle over Nolan's skin. "I suppose I would hope not," he said tightly. "But if empaths aren't harmless, what are they?"

"Abominations."

Abominations. Nolan frowned, his stomach twisting with unease. That couldn't be right. Empaths were pint-sized whiners who couldn't tolerate others' pain, let alone cause it.

Weren't they?

"The most dangerous monsters are the ones that look like friends," said Stone. "I'm afraid I'm guilty of leading you astray this evening. I have not had you tailing Evan. I've had you tailing Mr. Davies."

Nolan looked to the dark glass of the sushi house windows, hiding the people within. "Davies? He's barely more than a kid—"

"He's a ticking bomb," Stone said, soft, menacing. "And the longer he stays with Evan, the greater the danger to the rest of us grows."

Nolan sat back in his seat. He couldn't be hearing this right. Maybe Stone was nuts. Maybe everyone involved with empaths was nuts. "What kind of danger?"

"Ask yourself if there could be a reason beyond politics that the Dead Man and I are involved in this case."

Nolan's stomach lurched—but no, that was insane. "With all due respect, Mr. Stone, you can't possibly think Detective

St. James' empath kid brother is somehow involved in a vicious triple homicide—"

He cut himself off.

That morning at the marina, Nolan had heard the screams of the witness, Vincent Braker. The sight of blood leaking from the man's eyes like tears was indelibly scorched into Nolan's brain.

But Davies had been in the ambulance too.

Had tiny, harmless Davies somehow done that to Braker?

"What I think," said Stone, drawing Nolan's attention back to his phone, "is that I ought to be allowed to protect those of us without the empaths' powers."

Nolan stared at the sushi house windows. "Do you really believe you might ever need to protect people from Davies?"

"Wouldn't you rather I don't wait until we all discover it's too late?"

Nolan's mind extrapolated a city of Brakers, people screaming, bleeding from their eyes. "If Davies could be dangerous, he should be locked up. He should be in custody, not out having fucking sushi."

"I have both the means to seize the world's most dangerous empaths and the facilities to hold them," said Stone. "But I'm afraid I can't."

"Why the hell—"

"He's with Evan. And it is Evan's condition for doing the work he does that he be exempt from all interference or reproach."

Nolan gritted his teeth. "You can't have some vigilante empath expert who's exempt from oversight! Agent Grayson's dangerous—"

"He's deadly," Stone said softly. "But he is absolutely necessary. So for as long as Evan desires it, Mr. Davies remains as untouchable as he is."

"No one is above the law."

"Dead men are, Agent Nolan."

Stone hung up, the line cutting out in Nolan's earpiece. Nolan continued to stare at the sushi house. Finally, he pulled out his phone, and thumbed through the personal pictures he'd taken of the murder scene, scrolling until he found one of Hathaway's face.

There'd been so much blood at the scene he hadn't noticed at the time, but it was there when you knew to look for it.

Blood tracks, down her cheeks, like tears.

Jamey parked her Charger by a small cove a few miles south of the city of Everett. The stacks of the abandoned pulp mill could be seen jutting above the dense tree line.

The property was protected by a metal fence topped with barbed wire and mottled with rust, but the chain and padlock securing the gate were shiny and rust-free. And beyond the gate, the muddy drive had fresh tire tracks.

She grabbed the padlock and, with one hard tug, snapped the chain. Not hiding her strength and other tricks was one nice perk to working alone.

She slipped through the gate and moved silently through the trees, following the drive until she came to the shell of the mill: tall silos standing along the water's edge, empty pipes crisscrossing between buildings, and a rickety boat ramp disappearing out into the cove. She listened intently with every step, but she heard nothing beyond the distant rumble of traffic on I-5 and the soft and endless rain dripping on the trees.

The sulfur smell of the chemicals used to treat the wood pulp still lingered beneath the scents of ocean air and wet cedar. But as she approached an old storage building, a new, sharp smell cut through the other scents: bleach.

The storage building's door wasn't locked. She listened for

a long moment and then quietly nudged it open, gun at the ready.

But her ears hadn't missed anything; there was no one here either. She glanced around the open space and her brow furrowed. Two metal gurneys were shoved up against one wall, the kind sturdy enough to transport handcuffed prisoners to the hospital.

She approached the gurneys, where the bleach smell was strongest—and beneath it, now, the lingering copper of blood.

She lowered her gun, swallowing hard.

What the hell had happened here?

"You ordered steak in front of an empath?" Reece said, as Ohayashi dropped off the food and left them to their meal. "Is it even cooked or did you order it the way it's practically still mooing?"

"Rare, and yes, I did." Grayson sliced through said steak with ease. "I can be a target or you can talk to me, whichever gets the feelings out."

If Reece were being fair, he'd acknowledge everything else Grayson had ordered was vegan. But *fair* was for rational, stable people, and Reece had long ago given up hope of ever being one of those. He swiped another sea-salted edamame pod, sucking the soybeans into his mouth. "I've been on or well over the edge of a nervous breakdown all day," he said. "Most people would be mocking me."

"They shouldn't," Grayson said simply. "The world would be a better place with more compassion."

"You sound like Jamey."

"I've met your sister. That's a compliment."

Reece let out a grudging huff. "And on what planet would I share my feelings with the Dead Man?"

"You're an empath getting dragged on a homicide investigation. I'm aware what it must be costing you."

Empathy from Grayson was going to undo Reece completely. He grabbed another edamame pod, like his hands weren't as shaky as his grip on his emotions. "And what is it *costin'* me?"

"Nothing hurts you as deep as someone else's pain," Grayson said, "and you're drowning in it today."

Jesus. A day with the Dead Man and Reece still wasn't ready to be seen through like this. He dropped the pod on his plate, jaw clenched too tight to eat. "I don't get to use that as an excuse. I'm not the one suffering—"

"But you're empathizing." Grayson shrugged. "Maybe humans aren't meant to hurt each other the way we do, and maybe that's why some hearts are too soft to stand it. Maybe there's nothing wrong with you for caring about other people's pain, and there's something wrong with everyone who doesn't."

Reece bit his lip.

"But if you keep taking in the city's anger and fear, you're gonna break," said Grayson. "So let me take some of it off your shoulders, Reece, because you can't hurt a dead man."

Nothing had changed in Grayson's face. He had the same blank expression, same unreadable eyes. He was still the Dead Man.

But he understood. And it had been so, so long since Reece had anyone but Jamey understand.

Reece grabbed his chopsticks before he looked at that thought any closer. "But you're not really dead," he said, because Grayson *wasn't*.

"Living dead, maybe." Grayson set his now-empty plate to the side. "Like those zombies of yours."

Reece toyed with the chopsticks for a moment. "I've never

actually seen a zombie movie," he confessed. "Because of the, you know. Brain-eating and stuff."

Grayson picked up his own chopsticks. "I know, Care Bear."

Reece snagged a soy sauce–soaked roll, welcoming the burn of wasabi in his nose. "If I talk to you—big *if*—how do I know what I say won't get me back in handcuffs?"

Grayson took a roll off the same plate, his arms long enough to easily reach Reece's side of the table even though their legs never seemed to bump. "You don't."

Reece rolled his eyes.

They ate for a few moments in silence, but it wasn't an uncomfortable one. The restaurant was quiet, the lights and music low. The tables and booths were far enough apart that only quiet murmurs could be heard from the others, and no one was paying attention to them. It was probably the calmest moment Reece had had all day.

He stole a look across the table. Maybe he couldn't read any emotions on Grayson's blank face, but like Grayson's voice, the sight didn't make him feel worse anymore. And maybe he couldn't talk about hearing lies, but maybe Grayson would explain the new horror Reece had discovered today.

Reece bit his lip, then said, "I don't like the thought that the kil—you know, the person behind what happened to Senator Hathaway. That it could be an empath. The thought of an empath without empathy, it's—it's terrible."

"Shattered your world to find out?" Grayson didn't say it with judgment, just patient as ever.

"Yeah," Reece admitted. "You and Jamey are telling me there's an empath out there with a jacked-up version of our abilities but not our pacifism, and they *hurt* somebody."

"I didn't want to tell you." There were no emotions Reece could read from Grayson's flat voice, but it didn't seem smug. If anything, he seemed apologetic. "I think it's better that empaths don't know. There's nothing you can do to help; it only hurts you to know it's possible."

Reece turned the chopsticks over in his hand. There were delicate flowers carved into the metal. He didn't want to tell Grayson he was right, that maybe blissful ignorance would have been better. "I don't understand how it could happen. Is it another mutation that makes an empath born that way?"

"You don't want that answer," Grayson said.

"Yeah, I fucking do," Reece said sharply.

"Are you glad you know what the killer is?"

"This is *different*."

"No, it isn't." Grayson said it like it was the final word. "I guard a lot of secrets for a lot of good reasons. And you're undoing all the work we just did bringing that blood pressure down."

"You drive me crazy," Reece said hotly, and oh hey, not even a lie. "You had me in cuffs but you let me go. You know I have insight but you wouldn't let a Stone Solutions scientist find out. You won't tell me anything but you'll talk me down. I can't tell if you're my friend or my enemy."

"The Dead Man doesn't have friends," Grayson said. "So maybe you got an answer out of me after all."

The fancy metal chopsticks clattered against the plate as Reece threw them down and stood.

Grayson lazily tilted his head. "Where do you think you're going?"

"Bathroom," Reece snapped. "Am I allowed to do that without the press reporting on it or the Dead Man creeping over my shoulder?"

Grayson picked up his beer. "You got three minutes."

"Whatever."

The restaurant's restroom was down the same short hall that ended in a swinging kitchen door. Inside, Reece rested heavily against the marble counter with the shiny sink faucets, putting his back to the mirror so he wouldn't have to look at his own wrecked face.

It had been a hard day. Hard week. Hard month after month, since March. Grayson was right, Reece didn't like being this isolated, but he was in no state to be around others and hadn't been since March. The thought of another read made his stomach roil.

And now, he wasn't just hearing lies. He'd seen the real-life version of the bloody tears that haunted his dreams, he'd discovered he could violate people with insight, and his empathy and emotions felt less stable than ever. And there was no end in sight; he couldn't tell Grayson, and even Cora hadn't been able to help. Had that really been only yesterday, when Reece had been at Cora's hospital, same as Senator Hathaway?

He ran a hand through his hair and sighed.

The door abruptly opened with a violent swing.

"Freeze, empath."

Reece looked up.

Agent Nolan was just feet away, gun raised and trained on Reece. His expression was furious. "Hands where I can see them," he snapped. "That means gloves in the air."

Reece gamely stuck his hands up. "What are *you* doing here?"

"What's it *look* like I'm doing?" Nolan bit out, keeping his gun on Reece.

"It looks like you're straining your blood pressure," said Reece, keeping his hands where Nolan could easily see them. "What's got you so worked up?"

Nolan stared at him. "Oh my God." The gun trembled slightly. "You care more about my *feelings* than my damn gun."

Wow, Nolan was really mad. Reece carefully kept his hands

raised. "It's not healthy to be this stressed. Trust me, I know a lot about it. Is there something I can do to help?"

"Shut up!" Nolan kept his gun on Reece. "How the hell are we supposed to keep empaths in line if even threats of weapons don't work?"

"I don't know why you're threatening me at all," Reece said honestly.

"Because unlike everybody else on this fucking case, I don't live in Crazy Town where I let the monsters run free."

Reece frowned. "I'm not a monster."

Lie.

He sucked in a breath.

That couldn't be a lie, he'd *meant* that, he *believed* that—

"Except we both know you are." Nolan moved closer, gun steady. "I figured out what kind of monster killed Senator Hathaway. The last one we'd ever suspect."

Reece flinched.

"Oh, don't worry about empaths' powers, everyone, because they could never hurt anyone," Nolan singsonged, bitterly mocking. "They always wear their gloves so everyone's safe. They're pacifists; biologically incapable of causing pain; all flight, no fight."

His expression turned flinty and cold.

"You're liars. All of you. You're killers."

Reece gritted his teeth. "I didn't kill Senator Hathaway."

"Maybe you did, maybe you didn't," Nolan said. "But there are only two empaths in Seattle, so I bring you in, I've got a fifty-fifty chance of having nabbed the killer."

Reece scoffed. "Cora didn't kill Hathaway either."

Lie.

His knees buckled. Reece grabbed for the sink counter before he could fall.

No. No, that was impossible—what part of him could possibly believe Cora had done it?

"I said don't move!"

Reece ignored Nolan. "Cora didn't kill Hathaway." *Lie.* "It was someone else." *Lie.* "It wasn't her!" *Lie.*

Reece clapped a hand over his mouth, breath coming hard and fast. He'd seen Cora *yesterday.* She'd listened to him talk about his nightmares. She'd read him and he'd go to his grave swearing she was pure kindness, pure sunshine.

He steeled his spine and whispered against his glove, "Empaths can't turn into murderers overnight."

Lie.

"You have the right to remain silent—"

Reece screwed his eyes shut.

Lies were intentional. He wouldn't hear his own words as lies unless some part of him *believed* he was telling a lie. But *what* part of him? What part of Reece believed Cora was a killer and he was a monster?

Chills broke out over his skin.

That morning, in the ambulance, he'd heard himself lie when he said *empathy can't hurt anyone.* But that was *before* he'd been at the police station—before Jamey and Grayson had told him how Senator Hathaway died.

Before he'd learned the killer was an empath, some part of Reece had already believed that empathy could hurt people.

Had he been lying to himself, hiding the truth, all the years he'd claimed to be harmless?

But how? How the hell could he keep a secret from *himself*?

Distantly, Nolan was starting up Miranda rights, but the ringing in Reece's ears was loud enough to drown it out. Pressure was building in his skull, like he was in a plane descending too fast—and suddenly Reece was in his memories of Stone Solutions, reliving his encounter with the doctor, Vanessa Whitman, and her surge of fear.

"No!" Whitman's shout is deeply panicked, cracking her mask—

Nolan's voice came from far away. "Anything you say can and will be used against you in a court of law—"

Her eyes are wide, wide enough to show the whites around the irises—

"You have the right to an attorney—"

She yanks Reece away from the box too hard, her movements fueled by her adrenaline—

She's scared of more than Reece having a panic attack.

She knows something Reece doesn't.

Nausea rushed him, turning his stomach inside out as Reece hit the ground in his memories and again in the present.

"—if you can't afford—fucking hell!"

Nolan's curse echoed off the bathroom walls. He was scrambling to the side and Reece numbly realized he'd just puked all over Nolan's shoes.

"Son of a bitch—" Nolan started.

Reece shot to his feet. He darted past Nolan, out the door of the bathroom, and staggered down the hall to burst through the swinging staff door into the kitchen.

The cooks and servers turned in shock and Reece froze, not knowing where to go—

"That way." Ohayashi pointed toward the back of the kitchen and what looked like a delivery door.

Reece ran for it, stomach still churning, putting his trust in every kind line on the man's face. He burst out into an empty alley, and his sneakers splashed in puddles of icy water as he sprinted for his car.

He'd just launched himself inside and slammed his driver's door shut when he heard the shout.

"Freeze!"

Reece looked up.

Nolan was standing in front of his hood, gun up again. "Out of the car."

Reece jammed his key in the ignition. The electric engine started with a soft whine.

Nolan's nostrils flared. "Last warning."

Reece almost wanted to laugh. *Hysteria*, his mind helpfully provided. He held Nolan's gaze and deliberately fastened his seat belt.

The vein in Nolan's neck pulsed. "Are you fucking kidding me?"

"Move out of the way," said Reece.

But Nolan stood his ground, a wall between Reece and the road. "Reece Davies, you're under arrest."

"You're stealing Grayson's lines."

And with a twist of the steering wheel and a stab of the gas, Reece took his car right up onto the sidewalk and sped away, leaving Nolan, the sushi house, and Grayson behind.

Chapter Nineteen

Subject behaved exactly as predicted in running toward potential trigger without gloves. Contact was made; however, no changes have been observed other than normal trauma response—withdrawal and isolation, depression, acute anxiety. A connection between subjects and triggers may be required; strongest connections are being identified for all subjects.

—unsigned case notes from March

The rain-slick pavement shone and the downtown lights glittered as Reece tore up the ramp onto I-5 under the silver-clouded night. He kept his eyes glued to the road as he did ten miles under the speed limit in the middle lane. The hand still wrapped around the steering wheel was trembling as he fumbled for his phone.

Jamey answered on the second ring. "I'm on my way to HQ. Is Grayson—"

"Cora might have killed Hathaway."

Jamey cursed. "Reece—listen—"

There was no surprise in her voice. "You *knew*," he said in shock. "You already *knew* it was her. Why didn't you *tell* me?"

"I was trying to protect you from exactly the nervous breakdown you're having!"

Oh no. Jamey believed it was Cora. Jamey must have had *reasons* to believe it was Cora. "How can it be her? I will swear on my empath grave that when I saw her yesterday, she wasn't capable of this."

"Yesterday?" Jamey's voice cracked. "You saw her *yesterday*?"

"Yeah," said Reece. "About my nightmares. She read me and passed out."

"Nightmares." There were so many emotions in Jamey's voice, Reece couldn't pick them apart over the phone. "You were at the same hospital as Hathaway yesterday and you didn't think you should tell me?"

"I didn't think it mattered! I didn't for one second think Cora was involved in the mur—in Hathaway's mur—"

"Don't try to say it."

He laughed, and yes, that was definitely hysteria in it. "At least now I know why Cora hasn't called me back."

"Reece, you've *got* to calm down," she said, and Reece tried to find his sister's steadiness somewhere in the phone's circuits, the voice he'd relied on all his life. "I don't think Grayson would have told you about Cora. Are you alone? Where is he?"

"Having sushi? Right behind me? Who the hell knows—"

Someone honked behind him, sending Reece's heart into his throat. A second later, a car darted out from behind him into the left lane and blew past him.

"Did I just hear a *honk*?" Jamey said in shock.

"I—"

"Are you *talking on the phone while driving*?"

Reece's words caught in his throat as his breath started to come faster.

"Oh my God." She sounded on her way to panicked, which wasn't helping him at all. "What happened to you?"

His voice broke as he said, "My insight kicked in and—"

"Your what—"

"—and I saw my memories of Whitman and I think she

knows, Jamey, she knows why Cora did this—*how* she could have done this—"

"Forget all that!" Jamey snapped. "You can't think about that now. You're going to pass out behind the wheel if you don't slow your breathing. Reece—"

He tried to focus on her voice, but it was too stripped by the phone, a shadow of the real thing. Another car swerved around him and the hand holding the phone began to shake. "Jamey, I have to hang up, I could kill someone—just like Cora—"

Not lies. Reece threw the phone down on the passenger seat.

Grayson and Jamey hadn't wanted to tell him the truth. They didn't want him to know, had wanted him to innocently believe that it was an empath who'd been born differently, not his friend, the sweetest person he knew.

How could Cora possibly be capable of this?

He tried to focus on the road, which blurred as he blinked back moisture in his eyes. Maybe this was how it started, being willing to use a phone while driving, taking that chance with human life, and then he'd become a killer overnight, able to use his empathy to—

No.

He tightened his jaw.

Not tonight. Tonight he was going to find out how it happened.

He drove past a speed limit sign, sixty-five miles per hour. Taking a deep breath, he gripped the steering wheel tightly with both hands and stepped on the gas until he was heading for Bellevue at sixty-six miles per hour.

Nolan was sprinting back to his Explorer when the door to Yokota's Sushi House flew off its hinges.

Literally.

Nolan ducked, covering his head with his arms as the door smashed into the sedan in front of him, sending a shower of glass raining over the pavement.

He looked up in time just in time to see Grayson crossing the street. Nolan raised the gun in one shaking hand. "Don't come any closer—"

But Grayson moved too fast, faster than Nolan could react. In a moment, he was in front of Nolan, grabbing his arm. The gun went off, the bullet flying harmlessly toward the sky as Nolan was lifted off the ground and the world turned on its head. A second later, his back slammed into the pavement, knocking the air out in a pained grunt.

Nolan looked up to see Grayson standing over him, his own gun in Grayson's hand. They were nearly the same size and Grayson had just flipped him like he weighed nothing.

"What *are* you?" Nolan wheezed out.

"Complicated." Grayson crouched and reached into Nolan's coat so fast he almost didn't feel it. When he straightened, he had Nolan's phone and car keys in hand. He turned the phone over in his palm. "Passcode."

Nolan gritted his teeth. "That's government property—"

Grayson cocked the gun.

"Seven two nine one nine," he blurted.

A moment later, Nolan's own phone was ringing on speaker, then a now-familiar voice answered. "Agent Nolan?"

Grayson nudged Nolan in the ribs with his boot, none-too-gently. "He *is* here."

"Evan." Over the speakerphone, Cedrick Stone sighed. "I'm afraid I'm a bit preoccupied at the moment; AMI is about to—"

"You're having me followed," Grayson observed, calmly as if he was commenting on the weather.

"I'm having Mr. Davies followed," Stone corrected. "I hardly think you can blame me."

Grayson nudged Nolan's ribs with his boot again. "I might surprise you there."

"You're exposing Davies to a murder investigation! A barely grown empath with the emotional stability of a house of cards, and now you're pressure-cooking him."

"I'll admit it's not ideal," said Grayson. "But I don't have a choice."

"You have *me*," said Stone, a new note of eagerness in his voice. "Give me the empath; let me take him off your hands."

"Not a chance," Grayson said flatly. "Stone Solutions has been compromised."

Nolan hunched into the pavement, trying to make himself as small as possible as Grayson and Stone had a conversation he didn't fully understand.

"Jason went rogue," said Stone. "You can't judge my whole enterprise by his actions. He was an isolated scientist, acting alone—"

"You saw Dr. Owens last night," Grayson cut in. "Handed over a senator who was drunk and blazed on prescription drugs."

"And why wouldn't I have?" said Stone. "We are not all Dead Men. The world's mere mortals have struggles you could never hope to understand and addiction is a terrible cross to bear. I had work that couldn't wait, but I wouldn't have left Hannah to face her demons alone. I had no reason not to trust Jason to see her home safely."

"Pretty speech," Grayson said dryly. "But I'm betting Dr. Owens knew Senator Hathaway's changing heart had just put his tens of millions in funding at risk."

Stone paused. "You know about her decision to withdraw the bill."

"I do," Grayson said. "So I'll say it again: Stone Solutions is compromised. Too many of you with too many motives; I'm not putting any trust in your organization now. We got seven bodies and a killer loose in Seattle thanks to Dr. Owens. And I'm getting the sense there may still be some of your staff who need a reminder that the empaths aren't their toys or lab rats."

"Jason Owens acted alone." Stone's voice had gone very high and sharp. "And now he's dead. Stone Solutions isn't *compromised*. Our organization's whole mission is to protect the American people—"

"Seems like that might be tricky from your hiding spot in Canada."

"Don't confuse strategy with cowardice," Stone said un-apologetically. "Consider who the dead are. You know full well the killer will target me next."

"I don't know anything *full well* right now." Grayson stared down at Nolan, who tried not to cringe. "And now I've got to deal with your latest lapdog. You shouldn't have brought him in; he's a liability to himself and the rest of us."

"He's an FBI agent," Stone said impatiently. "Helping me is his duty—"

Grayson hung up on Stone. He looked down at Nolan. "I'm afraid you've been lured into a situation far above your pay grade," he said, as he pocketed Nolan's phone. "This is the problem with trusting Mr. Stone. He'll say any slick words to get you on his side, but he'd blithely feed his own mother into a meat grinder to keep himself safe."

Nolan's own breaths were coming far too fast as Grayson crouched down by his head.

Grayson fixed him with eyes as dead as his moniker. "You ever hear any rumors about me?"

Nolan cringed but nodded. When Grayson continued to

wait, Nolan wet his lips and elaborated. "The rumors say don't mess with empaths."

"And why not?"

Nolan swallowed hard. "Because the Dead Man will show up, and he makes the punishment more unthinkable than the crime."

Grayson tilted his head. "Recap what happened tonight," he said, neither confirming nor denying Nolan's words.

Nolan didn't even try to lie. "I went into the restaurant through the kitchen's delivery door. Used my badge to get past the staff. I saw Davies go into the bathroom and went in after him."

"What for?"

Nolan's gun hung almost carelessly from Grayson's hand. "To arrest him," Nolan admitted.

"Were you planning to hurt him?"

There was no emotion in his voice and somehow that was more terrifying than if Grayson had screamed at him. "*No*," Nolan said hoarsely. "I might have used force if I'd caught him, for resisting arrest, but I didn't go in there planning to hurt him."

"And why do you smell like vomit?"

"Davies was telling me he and the other empath were innocent, getting upset, and then he suddenly fell and threw up all over me."

If that made sense to Grayson, it didn't show on that expressionless face. "You're twice his size and speed. How'd Mr. Davies get away?"

Nolan winced. "He bolted while I was still reeling from the puke. I chased him, but some waiter in the kitchen got in my way, and by the time I got past, Davies had made it to his car."

Nolan held his breath as Grayson seemed to consider everything he'd said.

Then Grayson tucked the gun away.

The air left Nolan's lungs in a rush. He slumped against the road—then realized it was vibrating under the deep rumbling of an approaching powerful engine.

Nolan followed Grayson's gaze down the street to see a black truck turn the corner. It stopped in the middle of the street, still idling. A woman jumped down from the driver's seat, dark brown hair in a ponytail and a pair of thick glasses on her nose.

"Dr. Easterby." Grayson held out Nolan's keys. "I'm afraid I'm going to ask to impose on you to make another delivery."

Easterby took the keys, glancing down at Nolan. The glint of streetlight caught her throat, illuminating a line of scarring. "What did he do?"

"Forgot the rules about empaths." Grayson knelt again, this time yanking Nolan's own handcuffs off his belt. "It seems several folks in this town forgot. I ought to make an example of someone."

Far from horrified or squeamish, Easterby's pretty face was hard as she stared at Nolan, and with dread, he got the sense she approved.

But then Grayson straightened up. "We can't let him go. He'll run straight to his FBI cronies and talk. But we can't take him to Stone Solutions either."

"Detective St. James is heading to police HQ right now," said Easterby. "I could take him there."

Grayson shook his head. "They'll ask too many questions. Agent Nolan here will be quick to spill what he knows about empaths and the heat's already too high. We can't let the truth get out. But there's one other place." He held up the handcuffs he'd swiped from Nolan. "There's a bouncer at McFeely's who's smart and tough enough to trust. We can hold Agent Nolan there until I've got a better option."

* * *

STONE SOLUTIONS
Defending American Minds.

Reece cursed under his breath as he looked past the sign toward Stone Solutions' building and grounds. This time of night, he had expected the campus to be dark.

He certainly hadn't expected a full parking lot and the building to be lit like Christmas.

He drove in anyway, heading straight for the front of the building. He stopped for a moment, idling his car. There was an A-frame marquee displayed before the front doors.

Welcome, American Minds Intact Members!

A piece of paper had been taped to the marquee: *AMI Emergency Strategy Meeting: 6pm–11pm, Conference Room A.*

Well, this made his plans more complicated. An empath couldn't exactly go sprinting up to R&D in the middle of an AMI meeting without causing a riot.

But there was a reason for what Cora had done, and Vanessa Whitman knew what it was. And Reece's bet was that there was a decent chance someone who *had to work for a living* was still at work—or at least, putting the finishing touch on her new office.

He scanned the parking lot again with more frustration. There were no spaces left—except the single free spot right by the front door, with its *Reserved* sign.

Grayson's spot.

No. He couldn't park in someone else's reserved spot, not even Grayson's. Reece would have to go back out of the campus and look for something on the street.

He idled for a moment longer.

Screw it.

Without letting himself think on it further, he whipped his car into Grayson's parking spot and killed the engine.

He took a breath.

This was fine. Everything was fine.

He could do this.

He sat for a long moment. Then he looked through his windshield at the *Reserved* sign again.

No, he couldn't.

He turned the key in the ignition, berating himself for being such a wreck, for being unable to even borrow the Dead Man's parking spot, for—

For not letting Jamey install the new battery.

A weak clicking sound filled the car as Reece thudded his forehead against the steering wheel. "Oh come *on*," he said, trying the key again, pumping the gas. "Just get me back out to the street."

Nothing. Nada. The engine wasn't going to start.

Reece sat up and let the back of his head fall against the headrest, heaving a loud sigh.

Okay. Fine. His car was staying here. He was already going to have to answer to Grayson for running from Yokota's; how much more trouble could he get in for stealing Grayson's parking spot?

But as he went to get out of the car, Reece paused. This was a gathering of the biggest empath opponents in Seattle. And he was an empath who'd been on TV all day in the same juice-and grease-stained hoodie. Even Reece had to acknowledge he couldn't just waltz in there and expect no one to notice.

He twisted to look at the floor behind his driver's seat, where Grayson's hat lay atop the navy blazer and glasses Liam had given him.

Trying not to think too much about what he was doing, he reached for the pile. He pulled off his hoodie and wiggled into the too-big blazer. With a silent promise to replace them, he popped the thick lenses out of the glasses and slid the empty frames on his face before grabbing Grayson's stained hat.

What am I doing? he thought wildly, as he pulled the hat down over his hair. As far as disguises went, this was about as effective as Superman passing as Clark Kent.

There was, of course, one more thing he could do to hide.

He looked at his hands.

Going out in public without his gloves was illegal. He hadn't done it since he was a child. But going into that building with his gloves on would light a match in a keg of gasoline.

He stared at his hands a moment more. Then, heart pounding, he pulled the gloves off and stuffed them into the glove box.

He finally climbed out of the car and, hat pulled to his eyebrows and bare hands where everyone could see, walked through the main doors of Stone Solutions.

Chapter Twenty

AMI likes to say that all monsters claim to be harmless and that's how they lure you under the bed. Of course, AMI members also think monsters only exist as foils to the heroes: that they are and have always been monsters, intrinsically evil, born not made.

No one learned anything from Frankenstein.

—A.G., untitled blog

Jamey considered her options as she sped toward HQ. Reece wasn't answering her calls and his location tracking was still off. He'd call when he got it together. She wouldn't let herself consider the possibility that he *wouldn't* get it together.

And in the meantime, there was someone else who had answers and was going to answer to her.

She reached for the police radio. "This is Detective St. James," she said into the scanner. "I know someone will make sure the Dead Man gets this message. He better call me. Now."

Two minutes passed.

Then her phone rang, the words *Unknown caller* flashing on the screen. She answered. "What happened to my brother?"

Grayson's deep voice filled her car through her speakers. "I'll find him."

"*How?* You made his phone untraceable and he finds and destroys every tracker you hapless spies try to stick on his car."

Grayson cleared his throat. "Detective—"

She cut him off. "Reece called me from behind the wheel."

There was sudden silence on the other end of the phone.

"You told me you were the best option to protect him, but this is what you've done," she said. "So when you talk, all I hear is *why yes, ma'am, I'd like you to kick my ass.*"

Grayson's engine revved in the background, a low, powerful rumble not unlike his drawl. "What'd he say?"

"Something about insight, whatever that is. Something about a Whitman, whoever that is."

Grayson's exhaust opened up with a roar and the turbos kicked in with a high-pitched whistle. "Then I know where he's going. And I'm gonna get him back."

She passed a station wagon merging onto I-5 at school-zone speeds. "He knows about Cora."

There was a loud honk in the background, as if Grayson had just swerved into someone's lane. "I know."

"He thinks this Whitman person knows something too."

"She does." There were more honks in the background. Grayson wasn't making any friends. "She knows things you don't want your brother to learn. But more than that, you don't want him discovering what he's willing to do to get that knowledge. *Seattle* doesn't want him discovering that. So I'm gonna get him back *fast.*"

Jamey felt a muscle tighten in her jaw. "You better."

She hung up on Grayson. She put on her lights and sirens, and the cars scattered before her as she sped down the highway back to police headquarters.

Reece's bare hands prickled in the cool air of the Stone Solutions lobby. He had to fight the urge to stuff them in the blazer's pockets, skulking past the strangers milling in the lobby as they made small talk and ate from tiny plates.

A voice was coming from a pair of open doors down the corridor, the electronic transmittal tinny and hollow.

"—*newest model will be created in Hannah's memory. She was an inspiration*—"

Head down, he moved toward the elevators as quietly as he could—

"What are you doing here?"

Reece stumbled and nearly fell.

A security guard loomed over him like a gargoyle. "Are you with AMI? Press?"

From this close, Reece could read the name *Wayne Smith* on the card hanging from a lanyard around the guard's neck. He seemed particularly tense.

"You obviously don't work here," Smith said. "You're like twelve."

Reece took a breath through his nose. "Press."

"What, like with a high school newspaper or yearbook or something?"

Whatever got him in the doors. Reece smiled tightly. "Go seniors."

"Ugh." Smith pointed to a table next to conference room's open doors, with a large *Registration* sign, manned by a middle-age woman whose xenophobia was so palpable Reece could almost taste it. "Go sign in."

Reece snapped his fingers. "Right."

Smith rolled his eyes dramatically and disappeared back down a hall.

Many of the eyes in the lobby were on him now. Not seeing much other choice, Reece went up to the table and the xenophobe. Just beyond the table, the doors of a huge conference room were open, and the face from Pitney Adams' framed picture projected onto a gigantic screen at the front of the full room.

Cedrick Stone.

"Hannah was a dear, personal friend," Stone's image was saying to crowd from on-screen. *"I know she'd want us to keep up the fight in her honor—"*

Stone was, of course, ignoring the pesky little snag about Hathaway planning to withdraw the bill. At least Reece hadn't had to hear Stone's lie in person.

People were packed into every chair and propped against the walls of the conference room. On the stage in front of the screen was a table with several panelists, Beau Macy in the middle.

Reece quickly looked away, turning to the woman behind the table, who smiled brightly at him. "Welcome, AMI Family member!"

AMI Family. Reece rubbed his temple. "Right."

Stone's voice drifted out from the conference room. *"—while sales of our product buoy the tireless fight against those who threaten the sanctity of all American minds—"*

"—and make me a billion dollars," Reece muttered.

The woman at the registration table blinked. "Excuse me?"

"Nothing." Reece tapped the table in between them and tried to act like a normal person whose bare fingers touched things all the time. "I'm press. Where do I sign in?"

She pointed to one of the many lists on the table. "This one. And I'll need to see some ID."

Reece carefully scratched out *Connor Kendrick* on the sign-up sheet and slid it toward the woman, along with his perfectly made fake driver's license. *Thank you, Jamey.*

The woman glanced at it, at Reece, then passed the license back. "I like your glasses, Mr. Kendrick."

Thank you, Liam. Reece shifted impatiently. "So can I—"

"I'll just need to see your credentials."

The world screeched to a halt. "My what?"

"Your press credentials. We don't have you on our list, and we wouldn't want just anyone to sneak in here and claim they were press!"

She smiled again with perfect sincerity. Reece just managed not to cringe. What really got him about xenophobes was their genuine warmth toward anyone they thought was part of their exclusive group.

"What station are you with?"

"Ah." Reece cast desperately for an explanation. "I have a blog, *Eyes on…Things.*"

"Oh." Her smile disappeared. She looked into the conference room, nose wrinkling. "Is there a convention of high school bloggers tonight?"

He followed her gaze to a man with blond-brown hair leaning against the back wall of the conference room, about Reece's size and maybe a couple years younger. "He and I make two."

"Well, that's two more than the AMI Family is going to appreciate," she said primly.

"What are you talking about?"

She gestured at him. "You're built like an empath. It makes people here uncomfortable."

Reece stared at her. "AMI has something against *short people*?"

She folded her arms. "Sir, you're raising your voice."

"People have no control over their height! That's the most ridiculous—"

The words were choked off as he was yanked backward by the hood.

"You're done," said Smith.

"But—"

"Keep making a scene and I'll call the cops."

Smith was dragging him toward the front doors. Reece

tried to dig in his heels and only succeed in tripping himself. "But—"

"I can handle him, Mr. Smith."

Oh *no.*

It was Denton, the security guard who'd tried to throw him out of the building that afternoon and had nearly been fired.

"I just clocked out," Denton said, staring Reece straight in the face with full recognition. "Harthan and Boone are still out on break and I'm sure you're needed in here. Don't waste your time on this kid. I'll take him out with me."

Smith snorted. "All yours," he said, tossing Reece toward Denton and immediately turning away.

Reece stumbled forward. Denton dodged, very careful not to let any contact occur as Reece tried to find his footing. "After you," Denton said, pointing at the front doors.

Reece slunk out the front doors with Denton right behind him, expecting to see the waiting police and worse, Grayson, this time with cuffs Reece wasn't getting out of.

But there was no one outside. Instead, Denton motioned to the side of the building. "This way." When Reece hesitated, he added, "I want to show you something."

Reece furrowed his brow but tentatively followed Denton around the side of the building to the back side, with its loading bays and dumpsters. There were two doors set into the back of the building, one marked *Staff* and the other labeled *No Admittance*, and wow, that did not make Reece feel better, a forbidden door in an anti-empathy facility.

"AMI of course doesn't know this, but we're having some issues with our security cameras tonight," Denton said, as he came to a stop in front of the *Staff* door. "They're out on several floors." He pointed up, over the door. "This particular camera is broken. I noticed it not long ago."

Reece shrank away. He hadn't pegged Denton as violent,

but Reece was shaken and upset and could have missed it. And he was nothing but a punching bag in a fight, not capable of swinging back—

But Denton just pointed at the staff door. "That's the back entrance to the building, the one for maintenance staff and security. There's a service elevator just inside, but you need a card to access it."

He held up his card. "Mine lets me go everywhere but the roof." He held it out toward Reece. "Shame I seem to have misplaced it."

Reece stared at him. Then, he reached out and took the card, exceedingly careful not to touch Denton's fingers with his own bare hand. "Why?"

"I put in my two weeks' notice today." Denton pointed at Reece. "You have a nice evening, sir."

And he strode off, hands in his pockets and whistling.

The guard's card worked like a dream in the service elevator. Reece took it up to the twenty-first floor, where the doors opened into a narrow hallway that led him to the same open bullpen space he'd been in just hours ago with Grayson and Whitman. The white floors, counters and walls nearly glowed under the low lighting, and the framed Stone Solutions advertisements on the wall seemed even bigger, and more ominous, in the night's strange shadows.

What Else Don't We Know About Empaths?

Reece ducked his head and kept walking.

There was nothing to hear but the hum of computers at the lab tables and the soft sound of his sneakers padding against the faux-wood floors as he made his way to Whitman's new corner office on the opposite side of the floor. And sure enough, bright light was spilling out through the half-open door.

But as he approached, he could see into the space, and it

was empty. Brow furrowed, he shouldered the office door all the way open.

The city lights of Bellevue glittered through the floor-to-ceiling windows, the view of Mount Rainier lost to the night. Owens' imposing furniture was gone too, the bookshelves replaced by a white divan and the desk replaced by a light and modern one, its surface bare save for a sleek laptop and a large white purse.

Despite the after-hours, deserted feel of the whole floor, which gave him the creeps, Whitman's stuff was here. She had to be around somewhere.

He perched on her chair to wait, some kind of ergonomic contraption with no back that teetered precariously as he struggled to balance. He glared at the laptop: he'd bet anything a ton of answers were right here in front of him, but he needed a flesh-and-blood person to talk to, not a phone and definitely not a machine.

After a moment, he leaned forward and ran a finger over the keyboard, the plastic smooth and cool against his bare skin. The screen automatically lit up, prompting him for a password to unlock it. Not much chance of that; Whitman was one of Seattle's top scientists while he could barely work a mouse. He could try to *guess* her password, but how could he? He'd only met her once. What did he even know about her?

He ran a finger over the keyboard again, as his gaze went to the walls. There was no trace of Owens left in the office. Even Whitman's art had already been hung up, every last one of beautiful Washington scenery—no. Every last one of mountains.

Her colleague had been dead only hours and Whitman had already moved into this office on the twenty-first floor. With its view.

Reece considered the computer screen.

And then he typed *mtrainier21* into the box.

The screen began to load.

Reece jerked back in surprise.

Don't ever try to use your insight on purpose.

He could practically hear Grayson's drawl echoing in his mind, like some kind of cowboy conscience. Maybe the Dead Man knew what he was talking about. Maybe insight could be dangerous.

Or maybe not. Because as Reece squinted at Whitman's monitor screen and the icons scattered over a picture of her crossing the finish line of a race, he realized he had no idea what to even look for. So maybe an empath could get into her laptop, but it would take a detective like Jamey to know what to—

Like Jamey. What would Jamey do?

Reecc chewed his lip, but that was easy. Jamey would first want to know what Whitman had just been doing. She'd go straight for recent documents.

It took a couple tries, but he finally managed to click on something that brought up a list of recent files. He clicked on the top one, a spreadsheet titled *Trigger Points*.

But it was just a spreadsheet of names, many of which even he recognized as other empaths he'd met or heard of. It was sorted by city, with Seattle at the top.

Cora Falcon: John Camden; Javier Falcon; Sarah Goldberg Falcon; Cristobal Falcon; Mia Falcon-Oakely; Demarco Jones...

The list of names tied to Cora went on and on. Her fiancé, her parents, her brothers and sisters and friends. All of the entries in the spreadsheets were full of names, every empath tied to a veritable village of people.

Except him. Because right under Cora's name was his, tied to only one other.

Reece Davies: Briony St. James.

★ ★ ★

The cameras were still down.

In the security room of Stone Solutions, Chief of Security Wayne Smith smashed a few buttons on the keyboard for the tenth time and cursed.

Pierce had sworn he was working as fast as he could, but the only useful tech rat, Egner, the head of IT, had been sent somewhere off-site by Dr. Whitman and he still wasn't back. It was going to be Smith's ass on the line if anyone figured out that the security cameras at the back of the building and every camera on the twenty-first floor were down during a meeting of all the AMI hotshots in the city. For crying out loud, *Beau Macy* was here.

And Harthan and Boone were *still* out on their break. They'd gone just minutes before the cameras went down and left him in this mess short-staffed by two guards. When they finally did decide to show their faces again, he'd tell them they could go ahead and show themselves right back out and not come back.

Smith was reaching for the phone to call Pierce again, to threaten to have his pay docked, when the door opened. Smith turned, snarl on his lips—

But it was a young woman, vaguely familiar-looking, with shiny hair, red lips, and a perfectly tailored little skirt suit. Probably rich and probably with AMI; he better find some manners.

"I'm sorry, miss, but this room is off-limits." Smith turned, trying to block the monitors with his body. "If you're looking for the bathroom—"

"Are you the head of security?"

Smith gave a single nod. He tried to keep his voice polite. "No visitors in here."

But she slipped into the room, shutting the door behind her. "I have to talk to you."

Who the hell did she think she was? "I just told you we can't—oh!" He straightened as he finally recognized her. "You're Beau Macy's daughter!"

Her lips pursed. "Gretel Macy. Yes. But I also have a blog, *Eyes on Empaths*—"

Smith snapped his fingers. "Oh yeah yeah yeah, I read it. Everyone here does. I liked the story about the empath who mind-controls pumpkins."

"He wasn't using empathy on the *pumpkins*—"

"Your dad is a good man, keeping your little project going on top of everything else." Smith shook his head in amazement. "He must work so hard to do it all."

Gretel's lips pressed flat. Her gaze stole behind him. "Are those monitors supposed to be blank?"

Shit. "Did you need something, Ms. Macy?" Smith said, through gritted teeth.

"The empath police consultant, the one from the pumpkin story." She lowered her voice. "I saw him tonight. He's here."

Smith scoffed. He didn't have time for some entitled daddy's girl desperate for attention. "I'm sure you think that would be very exciting," he said, because she was probably too spoiled to keep danger and excitement straight. "But there are no empaths here. I promise everyone is safe. This is Stone Solutions; we have the best security in the city."

"He's wearing a disguise—a hat and glasses."

Smith paused. That did describe the kid who'd started yelling at Margaret at the registration booth, the one Denton had escorted out.

Then he shook his head. "I've seen the news today. I would have seen that empath trying to sneak in."

"Really?" She smiled thinly. "Because he wasn't wearing his gloves."

Smith froze. Then he grabbed the phone up off the desk. "Pierce," he barked into the phone, "tell me you've fixed those cameras on twenty-one."

Gretel gasped. "The security cameras are out in R&D?"

Pierce was babbling some excuse into the phone, but Smith wasn't listening. "Then set off the alarms and lock down the whole lab! Most of AMI is here tonight—we can't take any chances. I'll take a team up to twenty-one. If anyone's up there, they're a rat in a cage."

Chapter Twenty-One

Ignore Rule 1; no one understands why that's in there. We're here to defend people against empathy, not to care what happens to the empaths.

—note taped to a Stone Solutions security training manual

Reece sat frozen in Whitman's chair, staring at the screen.

Trigger Points.

He planted his elbows on the desk and chewed on his thumb. Jamey was his trigger point? Trigger for what? And Cora's fiancé, John Camden, was one of hers? As far as he knew, there was still no trace of Cora or Dr. Camden. What did that—

He hissed at a sudden sharp pain in his hand and yanked his thumb from his mouth. A flash of red caught his eye, and he realized that, without the protection of his glove, his teeth had drawn blood.

Shaking his hand out with another hiss, he glanced around to see if Whitman had tissues anywhere. Maybe in the purse on the desk…

A shrill siren rent the air, and Reece toppled off the chair, smacking the ground.

"Attention," a recorded female voice said, far too calmly, as emergency lights began to flash. *"Lockdown mode has been initiated for floors eighteen through twenty-one. There is a suspected se-*

curity breach and no one is allowed to exit the floor at this time. You will be evacuated by security when it becomes possible. Repeat. Lockdown mode initiated for floors eighteen through twenty-one. There is a suspected security breach—"

Reece swore. Then he swore again, more vehemently, and scrambled up to his feet. He darted out of Whitman's office, footfalls echoing as he ran to the short hall and the security elevator he'd ridden up in.

He stabbed the call button repeatedly but the elevator doors remained firmly shut. Swearing, he turned to the emergency stairs and yanked on the door. It wouldn't budge. He grasped the handle, braced a foot on the wall and pulled with all his strength. It still wouldn't move.

Reece buried his hands in his hair and began to back up. Maybe—maybe he could—

The security elevator began to whir. Relief coursed through him; he still had the guard's card; he could ride the elevator down, maybe find a place to hide—

The doors opened and, too late, he realized the elevator wasn't coming up to rescue him.

"Freeze!"

It was Smith the Gargoyle and two other security guards. All three of them had nightsticks in hand.

Reece put his hands up automatically. "I can explain!" *Lie.* He raised his eyes skyward.

"Take off the glasses," Smith ordered. "And the hat. Slowly."

Reece's stomach plummeted. Moving carefully, he pulled off the hat and tossed it to the ground, then dropped Liam's glasses to the floor on top of the hat.

Fear crossed Smith's face. "It *is* you." He pointed at Reece with the baton. "I threw you out. How did you get back in?"

"My magical mind control," Reece's mouth decided to say. He instantly regretted it as the solid end of Smith's baton slammed into his stomach. Reece doubled over, his breath knocked out, pain surging at the spot of impact and radiating through his core.

"Did you hear him admit he used his powers?" Smith said.

Reece tried to draw in enough air to speak, to explain in small words what sarcasm was. "I was—"

Smith jabbed him again, just as hard, this time in the shoulder. Reece went down, arm momentarily numb and unable to cushion or slow his fall. He winced as the same shoulder hit the ground, followed by the side of his face.

Before he could stand, Smith put the baton on Reece's cheek. "I barely have to tap you. What are you made of, glass?"

"Don't you wish," Reece bit out. "You'd hate to face someone who could fight back."

Smith's face darkened. "Are you reading me?"

"You couldn't *pay* me to read that cocktail of hate."

Smith's nostrils flared and he raised the baton. But one of the other guards put a hand on his arm. "He's baiting you. He needs touch for the mind-raping thing, remember?"

Smith seemed to consider this. Then he crouched, pressing the baton into Reece's cheekbone again, this time hard enough to make pain blossom across his face.

"I could shatter your whole mouth with one easy swing," Smith said lowly. "So how about you shut up?" He pointed at the emergency stairs with the baton. "Down the stairs. Hands where we can see them, the whole time. You make one funny move and I'll see how many of those fragile empath bones I can break."

None of Smith's threats were lies. He took a step back, and Reece managed to get to his feet.

He stepped toward the stairs, but Smith jabbed him in the back with the nightstick and it sent him stumbling. Reece bit back a noise of pain and looked over his shoulder. "You want me to walk or not?"

"I want you to *shut up*." Smith was still brandishing the nightstick. "We've got lots of things that don't require touch. I would love an excuse to use a Taser on you."

Also not a lie. Reece opened his mouth, but the sight of the three faces arrested him. They were all angry, yes, but they were also afraid.

Of him.

Shame, hot and sour, flooded Reece's stomach. He clamped his teeth into his lip to keep in his words and went to the stairs without fighting.

The twenty-one flights down were endless, and anytime he slowed, Smith's baton jabbed him again. He was panting by the fifteenth floor, sweating by ten, and ready to drop by the time they reached the ground floor.

One of the guards held open the door. Stone's projected voice was still droning on, somewhere beyond the open door, filling all of the first floor.

Reece hesitated, trying to make out Stone's words, when a hard jab of the baton between his shoulder blades sent him flying forward through the doorway.

He stumbled across the narrow hall and smashed into the opposite wall, barely managing to catch himself before he fell again.

"Hey!"

Chest heaving, he rested his sweaty temple on the wall as he turned his head at the sound of Gretel Macy's familiar voice. And there she was, at the end of the hall, phone in hand but eyes on him.

He groaned. "Of *course* you're filming this."

Through his half-lidded eyes, he saw her look at Smith. "Did you *hit* him?"

"Don't worry, Ms. Macy," said Smith. "We're handling the threat. You're perfectly safe."

But Gretel didn't move. "He's not a *physical* threat. He can't even hit back."

Smith's mouth thinned. "Let us do our job, miss. We're Stone Solutions' trained security. We know how to handle an empath."

Lie. Reece almost wanted to laugh. Then the baton hit the wall in front of his face, too close for comfort. "Keep moving, empath."

The jabs of the baton corralled him down the hall, in the opposite direction from Gretel, to a narrow door at the end. One guard unlocked it, opening the door to reveal a storage closet full of discarded office odds and ends.

Another hard jab of the baton between his shoulder blades sent him flying forward, stumbling over a broken rolling desk chair and crashing to the floor of the claustrophobic space.

He rolled onto his back with a grunt. Smith and the guards filled the doorway. "You've already been reported," said Smith. "Enjoy this room while you can; you'll be moved somewhere a lot less pleasant as soon as the authorities arrive."

Authorities. The police? Jamey? *Grayson?* "Wait—"

Smith slammed the door, and the bolt slid shut.

Jamey had just dropped into her seat at her desk to check police intel for signs of Reece when her phone buzzed with a message from Aisha Easterby.

Reece found. Grayson handling.

Her relief lasted all of a moment. Grayson couldn't handle Reece's driving, let alone Reece himself. She'd get back on the scanner, tell Grayson to grow a pair and call her himself.

But as she started to stand, she heard Lieutenant Parson making his way to her.

"My office." His voice was more clipped than normal, and the few other officers in the bullpen turned their heads in Jamey's direction.

Nonplussed, she followed Parson. As she shut the door behind her, he took a seat at his desk and didn't waste any time. "Your empath half brother was caught breaking and entering into the R&D labs at Stone Solutions during an AMI meeting." He leaned forward, folding his hands on the desk. "Without gloves."

Jamey blinked. She'd heard that right. She just didn't believe what she'd heard. "Is he—"

"I don't know what his condition is," Parson interrupted. "I was ordered not to send any officers. The Dead Man is handling everything."

Not a chance. "I'm going."

"You can't," he said testily. "Federal jurisdiction preempts state in matters of empathy, you know that. And the Dead Man preempts *everything*. Grayson is handling Reece personally."

"Parson—"

"This is not a suggestion, Detective," he said. "It's an order. The press was covering the AMI meeting. They know he consults for us, they know he's your brother, and it doesn't look good for the department."

"I don't care how it looks," she said honestly. "I care about Reece."

She turned to leave.

"There's one more thing."

She stopped, hand on the door.

Parson cleared his throat again. "You're on suspension."

She turned back to him in shock. "Excuse me?"

"The press was already questioning Reece's involvement

in your record. Now he's likely to be brought up on a B&E at the country's biggest empath defense facility." Parson's tone was sharp. "Everyone from AMI to the mayor is calling for your head. I've got to do something."

She didn't say anything. The silence stretched out between them.

Finally, Parson tapped his desk. "I need your badge. And your gun. You can drive the car until you get a replacement."

She blinked. Then she stepped forward. She drew her Glock, unloaded the chamber, and dropped the gun and her badge on the desk. She put her hands on the desk and leaned forward, looking him straight in the eyes. "Keep them. Forever."

Parson drew back. "Jamey—"

But she turned her back on him and stepped out the door.

Wayne Smith strode back to the security office, chest puffed and mood high. He'd caught the empath, and left a good bruise or ten. That had to be worth a raise and a promotion.

But as he opened the door to his security room, he stopped short. A tall man in a fancy coat was standing in the middle of the room, studying the security monitors.

Didn't anyone with AMI respect rules? "Hey," Smith snapped. "You can't be in here."

The stranger turned just enough that Smith could see his profile; unexpectedly young, younger than the Macy girl, with the kind of perfectly styled hair you saw on magazine covers. In a ridiculous Southern drawl, the man said, "I was told you're head of what passes for security."

Smith bristled. He didn't have to take that shit from another entitled brat. In an exaggerated imitation of the awful accent, he drawled, "Well, I wasn't told the rodeo was missing a clown."

The man didn't react to the jibe, just went back to the monitors and all twenty-two floors of Stone Solutions. "Where's the empath?" he said, not looking at Smith.

"The empath's not for sale," Smith said, in a nasty tone. "I'm turning him over to the authorities."

"Yup. Me."

Smith snorted openly. "The only thing I'd believe you're an authority on is looking pretty."

Again, the man didn't react to being insulted. Instead, he pointed to one of the monitors, which was paused on an image of the empath in front of the security elevator on the twenty-first floor. "Mr. Pierce fixed the cameras."

"How did you know they were down?" Smith demanded.

The stranger ignored the question. He pressed a button on the keyboard and the footage began to play. Smith saw himself, Hank and Warren emerge from the elevator and corner the empath. Then he watched himself on-screen as he jabbed the empath with the baton.

The empath bent double, clutching his stomach. The stranger tapped the screen. "Not very sporting of you, roughing him up. He's a lot smaller than you."

Sportin'. Roughin'. Smith was already tired of listening to him. "He broke into a protected empathy defense facility. *Gloveless.*"

The footage was still rolling, the empath on the ground now, Smith's baton on his face. He could see his lips moving as he threatened to break the empath's teeth, his bones.

The stranger tilted his head. "An empath can't hit back."

"That's the little mind-raper's problem, not mine."

The stranger was still staring at him with flat hazel eyes. "That's against company policy."

"Policy? You mean that joke of a rule book?" Smith scoffed. How dare this pretty boy walk in here and judge him? "Nothing about this concerns you. You better be either the president or the pope, because otherwise you're getting locked up with the empath where you can wait for the police."

He grabbed for the man's arm.

The stranger moved faster than Smith expected. Before Smith could make contact, a boot was planted in his chest, hard enough to send him crashing backward into a table of wide-screen monitors.

Thousands of dollars of security equipment shattered against the floor as Smith scrambled to stay upright, swearing loudly. "Who the hell—"

"Evan Grayson."

The Dead Man.

Smith barely caught himself on the edge of the table. "Sir," he said, as fear flooded his stomach, "sir, I swear, I had no idea—"

"Obviously." Grayson leaned down. "That company policy exists for a reason."

"We thought it was a joke!" Smith blurted out. "We're an *anti*-empathy facility—how could we have a rule that says never hurt empaths?"

"Because I wrote it." Grayson glanced at the closed office door. "Where's the empath?"

"Supply closet," Smith stammered. "Locked in."

"Guarded?"

"Y-yes, three guards, I—" Smith licked his dry lips and tried to find words. "Sir," he tried again, trying to straighten and finding his legs shaky. "I promise we won't let that empath hurt anyone—"

"Not my concern."

"No?"

"No." Grayson was gracefully sliding the heavy coat off

his shoulders. "He's got a way of poking his nose where he shouldn't and this office is about to be off-limits."

Chills broke out across Smith's skin. "Why?"

Grayson calmly tossed the coat to the side. "Some parts of my job I don't share with empaths."

Chapter Twenty-Two

Empaths Don't Come with Terms of Service (Even If No One Reads Them): Why empathy is more dangerous than letting your phone, tablet, smart watch, computer, internet browsers, apps, chats, virtual assistants, location sharing, GPS, and social media record your life. Read our five-part series, live on the blog this week!

—*Gretel Macy, blogging for* Eyes on Empaths

Jamey was alone in the locker room, out of her suit and into her jeans, when Aisha Easterby called. Jamey balanced the phone in the crook of neck and her foot on the bench as she laced her boot. "You better be calling to tell me Reece is okay."

"I am. And he is. Grayson's handling everything."

A rush of air left Jamey. She dropped down to sit on the bench. "Is Reece hurt?"

"Bruised and scraped. Security was rough with him. But Grayson will handle that too."

Jamey scoffed. "How? Give them gold stars?"

Easterby coughed. "Not exactly." On the other side of the phone, she cut her engine. "He's not the enemy, Detective."

"I'm not a detective anymore."

"You want Grayson to fix that?"

Jamey huffed. "I don't want any favors from any of you. You lost Reece."

"He's—" Easterby took a moment. "—tricky to keep eyes on."

Jamey stiffened. That wasn't an apology. That was a warning. "You want to lock Reece up."

"No!" Easterby paused. "Well…yes. Sort of. Grayson wants to move him to a safe house."

A safe house. Away from the violence, the press, from all the things that would hurt him. But how many strings would be attached? And would Reece ever come back?

"No," Jamey said shortly. "I don't trust anything related to Stone Solutions."

"It's not part of Stone Solutions. It's not on any records—it's just Grayson's."

"Nice try," said Jamey. "But I don't believe Evan Grayson has a safe house. He's a one-man battalion; he doesn't need one."

"You're right. He closed on it thirty minutes ago."

Jamey paused.

"It's what I'm trying to tell you," Easterby said, more quietly. "Grayson takes down empaths when he has to, but when he can save them—that's what he does."

It wasn't enough, and Jamey was tired of being kept in the dark. "You're going to have to spell out exactly what he's trying to save Reece from."

Easterby sighed. "You know it's classified, I can't—"

"You can't take Reece anywhere without convincing us first."

Easterby was quiet for a moment. "Okay," she finally said. "I'll show you."

Jamey's phone beeped. She pulled it away from her ear to see a series of images: handcuffs, busted open; a straightened-out bobby pin; smashed bits of something electronic. "What are these?"

"What Grayson took from the engine room of Stone's yacht."

Jamey shook her head slowly. "I don't understand."

"Cora Falcon kept bobby pins for her hair in the back pockets of her scrubs."

Jamey nearly choked. "And used them to break out of a pair of *handcuffs*? She's a therapist. You don't learn that in college, that's the kind of skill you learn if you're—"

"A highly trained soldier? The type who might be forced into terrible situations, who might come home with PTSD and work with a therapist?"

Jamey stared at the picture.

"We call it insight," said Easterby. "Empaths absorb someone's strong emotions, and their empathy connects the dots about that person in ways that other minds never could."

Insight. Reece had used that word too.

"We tell everyone empathy needs touch," Easterby admitted. "But insight only needs the right empath and the right moment of powerful emotion. There are several empathic abilities that work without touch, and the stronger the empath, the less they need it."

Like detecting the sound of lies. Jamey thumbed to the next close-up. "And the smashed electronics? No chance that's Owens' missing phone?"

"No. It's a webcam."

Webcam? Jamey put the phone back to her ear, angry now. "Someone was watching? Watching what? What the hell was done to her?"

"She was forced to break out of handcuffs in a yacht engine room, and the rest of her night was probably much, much worse." Easterby's voice was heavy. "She's also a victim in all this. The real perp may still be out there, ready to do the same to Reece. Let us take him somewhere safe. For his sake. For *Seattle's* sake."

The silence stretched out between them for several moments. "Reece will never agree to go with you," Jamey finally said. "He doesn't care about protecting himself."

"Grayson can convince him." Easterby paused. "Have I convinced you?"

Jamey's jaw tightened. She hung up without answering.

"Come on, come on." Reece balanced precariously on the broken chair and stretched his arm and phone even closer to the ceiling. Ugh, *useless*. No matter how he strained, he couldn't pick up a signal.

The door cracked open.

Reece nearly toppled off the chair, grabbing onto the back just in time. "I should get a phone call," he demanded, hopefully with dignity and not like he'd nearly fallen flat on his face.

But it was a new set of eyes peeking in through an inch-wide gap. "Did you mind-control someone into being your guardian angel?"

Reece blinked. "What?"

"You're being released without charges. I'm supposed to move you somewhere nicer. Hurry up."

The eyes disappeared, leaving the door cracked open.

Reece stared for a moment. Then he scrambled off the chair.

"Who?" he asked, as he stepped through the door and found the guard already halfway down the hall.

"Someone higher than me." The guard was walking so fast Reece nearly had to run to catch up. "And keep your distance. No touching."

Reece huffed, the aches and bruises protesting as he scrambled forward. "Why do people keep thinking I *want* to read them? You can all keep your prejudice and paranoia to yourselves."

The guard gasped and moved even faster.

Oh, great. Reece broke into a jog. "I wasn't reading you!"

"Stay out of my head!"

"If I could get in your head, don't you think I'd make you *slow down?*"

Two minutes later, Reece found himself in a small, side conference room with a large mahogany table surrounded by black leather chairs and a flat-screen TV soundlessly playing commercials on the wall. The room also had glass walls, meaning all Reece needed was a sign reading *Stupid Empath* and the monkey-at-the-zoo feeling would be complete.

With a sigh, he dropped into the chair that was farthest away from the TV, wincing as his bruised ribs protested. The guard took a position outside the room.

Reece was just pulling up Jamey's number on his phone when the conference door was gingerly opened.

He looked up automatically and then slapped his palm over his face. "There's no way you're the one who sprung me."

Gretel Macy was standing in the doorway. "Of course not." Her phone was in hand but not raised. Maybe she wasn't recording. For once. "You're out because someone ordered it, and the rumor is it's someone even Stone Solutions can't fight."

He frowned. "So why do you get a visit?"

She came all the way inside, pulling the door shut behind her. Outside the glass walls, the guard had stepped to the end of the hall, scanning like a lookout. "Your current guard is a fan of the blog." Her lips thinned. "And my dad."

"Lucky me," Reece said, with extra sarcasm. He put an elbow on the table and leaned heavily on his palm. His bare fingers sank into his hair, and he quickly straightened, tucking his gloveless hands out of sight under the table before he freaked her out. "What do you want?"

But her gaze wasn't on his bare hands. It was on his face, on his cheek where Smith's baton had been. "Why'd you break in?"

"Does it matter?" he said heavily.

She shrugged, eyes still on his face. "Maybe."

He sighed. "I thought someone had information that could help a friend."

"And you thought that justified using your empathy to commit a crime?"

"I didn't use empathy to get in here! Just a disguise."

She looked extremely unimpressed by that. "You actually tried to sneak into the nation's foremost facility for anti-empathy defense by throwing on a pair of glasses?"

Ah. "You saw me." Reece sat back in the chair. "You must be the one who reported me. So you actually recognized me?"

"Taking off your gloves doesn't make you invisible," she said.

"It did to the rest of the building."

"Well, I'm capable of looking past a pair of gloves," she said shortly. "I know your face. Which, by the way, you've got—" She brushed her own cheek.

He wiped at his cheek, wincing as something stung. He looked down, and saw his fingers had come away bloody. "The guards weren't happy to see me."

"About that." She shifted on her feet. "I didn't—uh." She bit her lip. "I did report you. But I didn't know they were going to get so rough."

Reece scoffed. "What did you think would happen? That I'd get a medal for my B&E?"

"No, of course not, but you can't even hit back and I just— never mind, I don't know why I'm trying to talk to you."

Lie. She started to raise the phone, then dropped it right back down. "No, I do know why I'm talking to you. How did you know I do all the work on the blog myself?"

Reece rubbed his cheek. Now that he was aware of the bruise, he couldn't stop poking it. "You never bring anyone with you to stalk me."

"That's not it," she said impatiently.

"Why are you surprised I know the truth? You think I can do all sorts of crazy things, like mind-control pumpkins."

"I don't think you mind-control the—ugh." She huffed. "This is different."

Oh. "Because it's about *you*." He rolled his eyes. "Why does no one care until things are about them?"

"Everyone in this city thinks I'm nothing but an ornament while my dad does the work. Everyone except you." Her mouth was pinched. "Did you use empathy on me?"

"No," he said, drawing the word out. "I'm just not a dick." *Lie.* Reece pinched the bridge of his nose. "Look. Your problem isn't that some empath you hate believes how smart you are and how hard you work. It's that everyone you care about doesn't."

She pursed her lips. The conference room was silent for a long moment, and then she said, "Do you want to give your side of the story?"

"Not if you were the last blogger on earth," said Reece. "I ran my stupid mouth and you put it all over the news."

"I didn't—"

The guard tapped on the glass window and made a frantic gesture. She muttered a curse. "I didn't release my footage to the news," she said hurriedly, and it wasn't a lie. "My dad did that, without asking me first. Your sister is amazing. I want her looking for Hathaway's killer, not suspended."

Reece froze. "What?"

"You don't know?" She glanced out the glass at the pan-icking guard, then darted forward and hit something on the remote. "You better watch," she said, over the suddenly un-muted TV. "And if you change your mind about giving your story, call me."

"But what did you say about Jamey?" he demanded, over a loud commercial for a mattress. But she'd already slipped through the conference room door and was hurrying away down the hallway.

"*—Reece Davies, an empath, is in custody tonight after allegedly breaking and entering into Stone Solutions, makers of anti-empathy defenses—*"

Reece looked over at the TV in horror.

The local news was back, and rolling grainy security camera footage of Reece from tonight, as he entered the front doors of Stone Solutions in Grayson's hat, Liam's glasses and blazer, and with his bare hands where everyone could see.

"*Davies is the half brother of Detective Briony St. James of our own Seattle Police Department. An investigation has already been opened into Detective St. James' record, with the public and now the mayor calling for her job as Davies' crime tonight opens up new alle-gations of his unnatural influence on his sister and the SPD.*"

Reece covered his mouth with his hands.

The footage switched back to a reporter in a plastic pon-cho, dotted with rain as they stood just outside the building Reece himself was in, in front of the Stone Solutions sign at the campus's entrance. "*The SPD has yet to release a statement, but sources tell us Detective St. James has been indefinitely suspended from the force. Stay tuned for more on this story.*"

Diesel watched as the black SUV pulled up to the yellow curb directly in front of McFeely's. The driver's door opened, and a woman with a ponytail and glasses came around the back, rocking the brainy look. Very cute.

"Dominique Lane?" she asked, eyeing his shoulders and arms.

He nodded. "Are you Dr. Easterby?"

"Yup." The neon lights of the café next door caught her throat, which was mapped with a twisting scar. Brainy, *tough* chick. But who didn't have scars of their own? She reached for the tailgate of her SUV as she added, "Agent Grayson said you'd be expecting me."

He was. Grayson had sent him a polite but unchallengeable text, and Diesel wasn't going to ask how he'd got his number. This wasn't Diesel's first rodeo with tough guys, but Grayson obviously wasn't a typical cowboy.

"The club's got a break room we can secure, ground floor, behind the stairs. It's all his." Diesel reached in his pocket for a set of keys and held them up. "Can I help?"

"If you don't mind." Easterby opened the hatch of the SUV, revealing an unconscious man in a suit, handcuffed with duct tape over his mouth.

Diesel glanced back at her. "I'm better off not knowing the details, arcn't I?"

She gave him an approving look, not just for his shoulders this time. "You really are."

The night was busy but more or less back to routine when a police cruiser pulled up in front of the club, just as Easterby had. A thirtysomething white man in uniform climbed out of the driver's seat and fixed Diesel with a strangely blank stare.

"Is Detective Briony St. James here?" he asked, his voice as devoid of emotion as his expression.

Nice to know the night could always get weirder. "I don't think there any detectives here right now," Diesel said honestly.

The officer didn't ask for more information. He simply turned and got back in the car.

But he didn't drive off, and a few moments later, he got back out of the cruiser, and this time two men in private security guard uniforms also got out. The group left the cruiser illegally parked and strode right up to the club.

As the officer reached for the door, Diesel cleared his throat. "All of you like empaths, officer?"

Empaths were a federal, not state or municipal affair, and the Seattle cops had always left McFeely's alone. If that was going to change—

But the officer's expression shifted for the first time, his eyes lighting with the fervor of a cultist. "Devoted to them," he said rapturously.

All right, then. Even cops could be fetishists. Diesel opened the door to let the three of them inside, then went back to manning his post.

Chapter Twenty-Three

...that year also saw the hit single "Into Your Emotions," the first song by an all-empath boy band to chart in the US. Their follow-up songs, "Don't Hurt Me Baby (I'm a Pacifist)" and "Inner Beauty Is Hot," also charted overseas.

—*excerpt from* Grungy Feelings: A Memoir of a 1990s Subculture

Reece was still at the oversized wooden table, face buried in his folded arms, when the conference room door was flung open, not with a fearful nudge but with the confident shove of a man who had nothing to fear.

Gretel's words rushed back to Reece: *You're out because someone ordered it, and the rumor is it's someone even Stone Solutions can't fight.*

Reece didn't look up. "So is it Mr. Dead Man? Agent Dead Man? Pretty Soldier Sailor Dead Man? We've never really settled on what I should call you."

The lazy drawl filled the room. "You find Dr. Whitman?"

Reece winced. Of course Grayson somehow knew why he had come to Stone Solutions. "Feel like pretending I didn't commit a misdemeanor trying to talk to someone who's nowhere to be found?"

"Sure. Because technically your stunt was a felony."

Reece groaned and buried his head farther into his arms. "Is Jamey really suspended because of me?"

"I could fix that," Grayson said, which was a yes. "But she doesn't want my help."

Reece winced again. "I'm the worst brother in the world." *Lie.* No comfort; he deserved that to be the truth.

"All little brothers are pains in the ass," said Grayson. "I've known at least one who's got you beat. Come on, let's go."

Reece raised his head.

Grayson was holding open the conference room door.

Reece exhaled in a rush and got to his feet. He walked the few steps toward the door and then paused, barely a foot of space between them. He tipped his head back—way back—to look up at Grayson. He searched Grayson's face, but there were no emotions, no hints, nothing Reece could interpret as a feeling.

"So am I under arrest?" he finally asked.

Grayson looked down at Reece without moving away. "Don't you think I would've left you to the guards' tender care in that case?"

He could have. Or Grayson could have cuffed Reece again himself, subdued him without so much as a grunt of effort. But he hadn't done either of those things—he'd come to rescue Reece, and now they were again close enough to touch. And without his gloves to block that touch, Reece would have felt Grayson's warmth against his fingertips.

Not dead, no matter what people called him.

"I don't know," Reece said honestly. "I don't think I know anything anymore when it comes to you."

Grayson's gaze darted over Reece, lingering on his cheek. "They got rough with you."

Reece looked away. "I'm fine." He tried not to cringe at the sound of the lie, ducking out through the door Grayson was holding open for him and hurrying down the hall.

Grayson followed, one step behind, Reece's fast pace just a leisurely stroll with his long legs. "You want revenge?"

Reece furrowed his brow in confusion. "Revenge?"

"I can make it happen. Locked room, no records, complete freedom from consequences—"

"Stop," Reece said sharply, his stomach protesting even the implications of Grayson's words. "The guards were just doing their jobs." *Lie.* His ears heard the sour notes as the twinges of his bruised muscles confirmed them. But Reece stubbornly said, "I'm the one who broke the law. No one should take that out on them."

Grayson continued to watch him for a long moment, giving Reece the unsettling feeling he'd just taken another test. But then Grayson shrugged and kept walking, like nothing had happened, and Reece had no idea if he'd passed or failed.

As they emerged into the lobby, an unfamiliar security guard rushed up to them. "Agent Grayson, sir," he said breathlessly. "Our apologies for the oversight. We're having the car towed right now."

Towed? Reece's eyes widened. "Wait—no—"

He broke into a run.

A moment later, he skidded out through the building's automatic front doors just in time to see the back of his car, attached to the lift of a tow truck and disappearing into the night.

"No, no, *no*—" He sprinted after his car, but it was too late; in seconds, even the truck's taillights were swallowed up by the dark.

He stuttered to a stop in the middle of the Stone Solutions drive as his already-spent lungs seized up. He bent at the waist, soft rain falling on his hair as he tried to catch his breath.

"Problem?"

Chest heaving, Reece glanced back to see Grayson, standing on the front curb tucked safely under the roofline, hands in his coat pockets, apparently without a care in the world. Reece tried for the dirtiest look he could muster.

"My car just got towed." He dropped his head, still panting. "It's going to cost a million dollars and they'll take it all the way to California."

"More like four hundred dollars and Tacoma. That's what happens when you park in a reserved spot."

"So *you* called for the tow?"

Grayson raised one eyebrow. "No."

Reece sighed. The accusation had been unfair of him; Grayson wouldn't bother with something as petty as calling in Reece's parking violation. He'd even gotten a straight answer out of Grayson this time.

Grayson cocked his head. "You make any more bad decisions tonight I ought to know about?"

Reece screwed his eyes shut, but the night's humiliation might as well be complete. "I left my gloves in my car."

There was a weighty, *judgy* silence.

Reece winced. "What am I going to do?"

"Me arresting you is still on the table."

Reece stiffened.

"Fact is," Grayson said casually, "losing your gloves is about the least of what I could arrest you for."

It didn't matter that he couldn't hear Grayson's lies. Both of them knew that was the truth. Reece looked up at Grayson, squinting as raindrops got in his eyes.

Grayson withdrew a hand from his pocket to point to the souped-up black F-150 illegally parked just to the side of Stone Solutions' front door. "Or I could give you a ride."

Reece didn't move. He stood for a moment, cold rain dripping from his hair down his neck as Grayson opened the passenger door and held it like a perfect Southern gentleman.

"If I get in your truck," Reece said, "will you let me back out?"

"Count up all the laws you just broke and ask yourself if this is really a choice."

Point.

Jamey made one last stop at her desk to grab the three things she wanted to take with her before she left HQ: her research on Grayson, a framed picture of her and Reece as kids, and the Wonder Woman figurine Liam had given her after their second date.

But as she grabbed the items, she heard familiar footsteps coming down the hall.

"Jamey!"

She looked up to see Liam. He'd shed the tie and undone the top buttons of his shirt, the closest to casual she'd ever seen him get at work.

"Jamey," he said again, and he sounded pissed. "I just heard the news. I'm so sorry, are you okay?"

"I—" But to her surprise, the words stuck in her throat, unable to get past the sudden lump. *I don't have a job, my brother's in danger, the Dead Man wants to hide him, and I might never see him again—*

Something must have shown on her face, though, because Liam grabbed her hand. "My office."

The few people milling around the station this late were staring at them. They were always careful not to reveal their relationship at work—

But they weren't coworkers anymore.

She let him tow her down the hall. "You shouldn't talk to me here," she said as he shut the door to his office, trying to focus on words she could say. "No one nice or normal should be hurt by this, I'm toxic to your reputation now."

"Fuck your suspension. After all you've done for this city, the cowards are selling you out to save their own image." He let go of her hand, which immediately felt colder without his. "I heard what Reece did tonight. And I heard they sent that guy after him, the Dead Man."

She leaned against the wall, next to a framed picture of Juneau's Mendenhall Glacier Liam had taken himself. "Grayson wants to put Reece in a safe house."

Liam frowned. "Are you going to let him?"

She let out a breath. "I don't know," she admitted. "When I think about it, my ears start to ring, but I don't know if I can protect Reece by myself—and I'm having all these, these *feelings* about it, and Liam, I am *no good* at feelings—"

"You don't have to have all the feelings by yourself," Liam said. "You know I'm here."

He was here. Reece had broken the law, she was off the force, they were dealing with a hostile press and inexplicable empathy and a guy called the Dead Man, but Liam was still here.

"You're working late," she noticed out loud, because she didn't know how to say all the emotions jumbled in her heart.

"The SPD needed to issue a statement about this mess," Liam said. "I didn't trust anyone else to get this one right."

She furrowed her brow and stepped across the room to his desk. He let her, watching as she moved his mouse to brighten his screen and the document he'd been working on. "What do you—*oh*."

Her eyes read the last line of the press release.

The SPD stands behind Detective St. James and her brother as valued members of our team.

She took in the rest of the screen, his email sent box. "You released this already." She stared at the statement. "You told all the press in Seattle that the SPD stands behind us. *Both of us.*" She looked up in shock. "Parson's going to fire you."

"Then he can fire me," said Liam. "You're the bravest, most selfless person I've ever met. I'm not writing some cowardly shit against you, not tonight, not ever—"

Jamey threw her arms around Liam's neck and hugged him tight. "Thank you," she whispered, turning her mouth toward his ear, their cheeks brushing. "I—thanks."

"You're—*oof*—welcome."

Oops. "Sorry," she said, as she quickly loosened her hold.

Except he tightened his. His arms had gone around her waist, under her coat, and she could feel the warmth of his hands against the small of her back through her T-shirt. She could still smell the last trace of the morning's cologne on his neck.

"You've got to show me your weight-lifting routine sometime," he said lightly. "I swear you might also be the strongest person I've ever met."

"Am I?" she said weakly.

"Yeah." He grinned. "It's hot."

She made a small half laugh of surprise. And then they were kissing, and she was off the force anyway, what was anyone going to do if she and Liam swept everything off the desk—

Her phone buzzed. She had to pull back, out of Liam's arms to get it out of her pocket. She made a face and held it up. "Text from Grayson."

Liam sighed as his arms fell to his sides. "I suppose there are other things happening tonight."

She scanned the message. "He says he's got Reece, but Stone Solutions' IT is taking too long recovering the security footage at McFeely's." She frowned. "If Grayson is tied up moving Reece somewhere safer, I should check on the club."

"I can come with you," Liam started.

She reluctantly shook her head.

"But—"

"Something terrible is going on, so much worse than I ever imagined." Jamey wanted to wrap her arms around his neck again and tell him all of the truth. She wrapped her arms around herself instead. "Just—lock your door. I'm going to let the Dead Man take my brother to a safe house, so maybe be ready for me to show up at your place in the middle of the night and get—" she waved a hand awkwardly "—*feelings* all over you."

"Oh," Liam said weakly. "Yeah, okay, you can do that. You can definitely do that." As she turned away, he caught her hand. "You promise you'll check in tonight, no matter what happens?"

He looked very serious. Maybe she wasn't the only one who got to worry about danger. "I promise."

"I'm holding you to that," he said, as he let go. He added, wryly, "So is this the part where I say *go get 'em, tiger*?"

That made her smile. "What, am I Spider-Man now?"

"You tell me."

Liam still had his wry smile, his deep brown eyes meeting hers. She reluctantly turned away, blowing him a kiss over her shoulder on her way out of his office.

She was going to get through tonight, and then she was going to tell him everything.

Chapter Twenty-Four

What role do emotions play in attraction? Can it ever be purely feelings—or purely biology? Join us tonight for a virtual panel discussion with a special empath guest from Portland!
          —flyer in the psychology building at Rainier University

Reece bit his bare thumb as he perched on the passenger seat of Grayson's truck, Liam's damp blazer crumpled in a ball next to him. It wasn't like he was going to be able to relax, no matter how plush the cab was.

Grayson climbed into the driver's seat in one graceful move, completely unlike the awkward way Reece had struggled up into the giant truck's passenger side. He snagged the blazer with a finger, and a moment later it was draped over the headrest behind Reece. "Not everything is a stained hoodie."

"I already owe Liam new glasses. Might as well rack up that tab." He sighed. "Yours too. Sorry about the hat."

"The real shame is nothing's covering that unwashed hair anymore."

Reece snorted. A moment later, the engine woke to life with a deep rumble that shook his bones. "Aggressive."

"It's got some upgrades." Grayson fiddled with the buttons on the steering wheel. "That means it's fast, if you need a translation."

"Raptor edition with aftermarket tuning? Upgraded twin turbos, cat-back exhaust, cold air intake?"

Grayson did a full head turn in Reece's direction.

"You think I drive my 1,600-pound death machine around without knowing a few things? Cars are dangerous." Reece cleared his throat. "You need me to *translate* what your fancy upgrades do? I bet you don't even know, you just threw money at mechanics and told them to make your truck fast."

Grayson drew his head back. "I know how they work." He paused, and Reece heard him mutter, "Basically."

Grayson reached into the crew cab's back seat, and a moment later, something soft landed in Reece's lap. "If you're taking off the blazer, at least put that on."

Reece picked it up. A hooded, zip-up sweatshirt with a University of Texas logo, way too big for him. "Is this *yours*?"

"I'm cold just looking at you in that T-shirt." Grayson turned back to the wheel. "I'm sure I don't have to tell you, but put your seat belt on. I don't drive like an empath."

"You didn't have to tell me that either."

Twenty-four hours ago, Reece didn't believe in the Dead Man, and now he had his hoodie. He pulled it over his shoulders, threading his arms into sleeves that were long enough they came down over his hands. The fleece inside was still so soft it was almost silky, not scratchy from a million wears and washings like his own collection. Probably didn't see much use in the warm places accents like Grayson's came from.

Grayson pulled away from the curb, and Reece craned his neck to watch out the window as the building disappeared behind them. He'd rather have been in the Dead Man's truck than in Stone Solutions ever again, but in fairness, some of that sentiment might have been the seat warmers. "I expected you to have some kind of crazy anti-empathy defenses in here."

"I'm enough."

Reece snorted. "So where are we going?"

Grayson glanced at him, then his gaze went back to the road. "For a drive."

Oh *no.*

Reece lunged from his seat for the passenger door, clawing at the handle.

Grayson calmly adjusted the rearview mirror, like Reece wasn't fighting with the locked door. "I'm not gonna let you jump out of a moving vehicle. I know empaths have no sense of self-preservation, but I do draw the line somewhere."

This had to be it, Grayson was actually going to—

"I'm not gonna arrest you either."

"You should." Oh great, that wasn't a lie.

But Grayson shook his head. "Running after Whitman was stupid, but I know why you did it. And I know you're not trying to use insight on purpose."

Reece slumped, letting his head fall back against the seat. "But we're going for a drive?"

"We're gonna talk." Grayson headed toward the interstate. "How much do you know?"

Reece ran a hand over his face, his bare palm hot. "I know Cora killed Senator Hathaway."

"I see." Grayson's drawl of course revealed none of his feelings about that. "Have I got Agent Nolan to thank for sharing that knowledge with you?"

Not exactly. Reece shook his head. "Nolan sped it up, but I would have got there on my own eventually. There are only two of us in Seattle, and it wasn't me, so that leaves her. But I don't understand why—no," he corrected himself, "I don't understand *how.* How could it be her? She is pure kindness. I'm telling you that as an empath."

"I believe you," Grayson said quietly.

"Then how? How could she—could she have—"

"Corruption."

The hairs on Reece's neck stood on end. "What does that mean?"

"It means an empath can wake up the sweetest soul in Seattle," Grayson said, still quiet, as he took the truck up onto I-5, "and then, by midnight, become a serial killer."

"But *how*? What could possibly—passing on the right is *illegal*!"

"Gloveless empaths in glass houses shouldn't throw stones."

"I'd never throw a stone in a glass house. Someone could cut themselves on broken glass. In fact, I don't think I'd throw the stone in the first place; that doesn't sound safe."

"I do believe you're missing the point."

"No, I see your point. I also see you think a turn signal is a suggestion." Reece watched Grayson's profile for a moment, shadowed in the darkness of the truck's cab. "What's corruption?" The word tasted wrong in his mouth, like milk gone sour.

"It's what we call it when an empath changes," said Grayson. "They get stronger powers. Brand-new powers."

Despite the seat warmer, Reece was suddenly cold. "New powers?"

Grayson nodded. "But at a terrible cost. All that empath pacifism twisted to sadism. Empaths don't just become capable of killing; they enjoy it."

Reece bit his knuckle, his teeth sharp against his bare skin. "And how does an empath become corrupted?"

"I'm not gonna tell you that part."

"*Seriously?* Agent Grayson—"

"It's classified for good reason, Reece. No one should know how to corrupt an empath. For the empath's sake; for the world's sake."

Reece sat back with a huff, mouth thinning as Grayson drove past a sixty-five-mile-per-hour speed limit sign without slowing in the slightest. "You said we were going for a drive, not a spot of your reckless endangerment."

"All these opinions about my driving might give me a new opinion on your arrest."

Reece scoffed. "You can't arrest me for pointing out you drive like crap."

"Try me."

"Please. You'd have to stop the truck, and then who'd violate the three-second rule and ride all these bumpers? That Civic isn't going to tailgate itself."

Grayson took a breath. Let it out. "I don't have to stop this truck to get you in cuffs—or a gag."

"Don't threaten me with a good time," Reece sniped. "And on the subject of your wretched driving, how about we stop pretending this is an aimless trip and you tell me where you're really taking me at unsafe speeds?"

"You've got to stop trying to read me."

"You've got to stop thinking you're completely unknowable."

Grayson's gaze stayed on the road. Thankfully. Then he said, "We're going to a private airstrip. And then you're going somewhere safe."

Reece clenched his jaw. "You're locking me up—"

"No," Grayson said, surprising Reece with the straight answer. "Not prison. Protection."

"*Protection.*"

"Yes."

Reece scrubbed a hand over his face, and found his palm clammy with sweat. "I'm not going."

"Reece—"

"Cora's my friend! I'm not getting stashed somewhere safe to hide until all the bad stuff is over. I'm going to help her."

"Help her." Grayson gave Reece a searching look. And a

heart attack, as it meant his eyes were off the road as he passed an eighteen-wheeler at ninety miles per hour. "You gonna help her murder her way through Seattle?"

Reece drew a sharp breath.

"Corruption can happen to you too," said Grayson. "With every passing moment, there's a chance you're closer to it. I'm not protecting you from the world; I'm protecting the world from *you*. So I think you're gonna go where I take you, and stay where I put you, because you're not gonna put the world in danger, are you?"

Reece's righteous fire fled. He slumped, eyes squeezing shut. "I just—"

But the words stuck in his throat. Because what could he say?

He had new powers. He had violent nightmares. And some buried part of him had known all along that when Reece said *empathy can't hurt anyone*, he was telling a lie.

And now he had the word for it—*corruption*.

Grayson just didn't know Reece was at least partway corrupted already.

So he swallowed all his words, and rested his temple against the window. Grayson looked back at the road, and they rode without speaking, their silence filled by the quiet swish of windshield wipers and the soft Latin pop layered over the engine's rumble.

Despite everything, after a few miles, Reece's eyelids were closing on their own. The truck's cab was warm and comfortable, and he was sleep-deprived, wrung out from too much adrenaline, his body tired and bruised. Grayson's hoodie was butter-soft against his skin, the sleeves long enough that Reece could tuck his bare hands inside.

But as he felt himself start to drift into sleep, something tickled his mind, some terrible thought trying to take shape like glowing eyes in a dark room slowly showing claws and teeth.

Was corruption contagious?

Because if he was corrupted—and Cora had read him yesterday—

He bolted upright, hands covering his mouth.

"Care Bear?"

She'd read him yesterday and passed out after the read. And then she'd become a serial killer.

Had she become corrupted—because of him?

"Reece." Grayson's drawl was the most clipped Reece had ever heard it. "What's going on?"

"I—" *I'm a monster and I've made another monster what have I done Cora—*

"Reece—"

But the truck disappeared as Reece was reliving the moments in McFeely's passing the IT guy on the stairs.

Cold eyes, too cold for compassion about Hathaway's death—

Pinched mouth, annoyed at having to help—

Tight jaw, angry that he's seen a real empath, looking for ways to get small revenge—

"Pull over!"

Grayson swerved across three lanes of traffic. With a screech of tires, he pulled the truck into the forested shoulder. Reece fumbled for the door latch and this time it worked. He toppled from the truck into the cold night air, falling to his knees in the mud and wet grass before heaving up what little was left in his stomach.

"*Ugh.*" He managed to flop onto his back before his arms gave out. He let his head fall back against the ground and stared up at the clouded night sky, welcoming the biting cold of the icy rain dotting his face. "I am having a very bad day."

Grayson leaned over him, broad shoulders and unreadable face filling his line of sight. "You all right?"

"I've been better," Reece said weakly.

"Fair enough," Grayson muttered. He crouched at Reece's side and wrapped his arms around himself. "You were nearly asleep. I wouldn't have expected insight to kick in. Something you want to tell me?"

Reece hesitated.

Grayson hadn't said it with menace. It sounded like a genuine offer to listen. For all his talk of arrest, Grayson's actions had been on Reece's side all day, even after Reece had broken several laws and into Stone Solutions.

And most of all, at that moment, Grayson looked so *harmless*. Not the bogeyman at all, just a person, like everyone else, a Southern boy in Seattle trying to keep warm while he'd left his coat in the truck. Maybe he really was a specialist, not a hunter. Maybe he knew what was going on with Reece. Maybe Reece could tell him the truth.

But Grayson's drawl still echoed in Reece's mind.

You, most of all, have got no business trusting me.

Reece blew out a very long breath. Maybe Grayson could help. Or maybe he'd just lock Reece up next to Cora and throw away the key.

"No, nothing to tell you," Reece said, not meeting Grayson's eyes. He made himself ask a question he didn't actually want an answer to. "You said insight wasn't a good thing. Is that because corrupted empaths have it?"

Grayson nodded. "And they can wield it like a weapon."

Reece screwed his eyes shut.

"But," said Grayson, making Reece crack an eye, "on occasion, it can manifest in an uncorrupted empath, if you put them under enough stress."

Reece let out a breath. "Me, stressed? *Today?* No way."

"Sarcasm is not an actual art. Practice doesn't make perfect."

Reece turned his gaze back to the clouds, gray against the night sky, trying not to see Egner's unpleasant face. He thought instead of his earlier insights: Adams' secret; Whitman's password. Of a power that Grayson had warned him never to use on purpose, that could be wielded like a weapon. "Does insight let me see what I want to know?"

"I don't think you need the answer to that question."

So yes.

Grayson was studying his face. Reece didn't want to know what he might be looking for. "What'd you see?" Grayson asked.

"*Egner.* That bigoted computer guy back at the McFeely's club." Reece shook his head. "I don't want to know anything about him. I want to know about *Cora.*"

Grayson stilled. Then he was upright again. "We have to go."

Reece groaned. "Give me two minutes—"

"I can't."

He thudded his head against the grass. His legs felt like jelly. "No gloves means no hand up from you, I suppose."

"You wouldn't want it."

Whatever that meant. He watched through heavy lids as Grayson strode toward the truck, phone out. Reece made a face. "Do we really have to get to the safe house right this second?"

"Not the safe house. McFeely's." Grayson opened the truck door. "And yes: we have to go *now.*"

The street outside the fake empath club, McFeely's, was a study in contrasts: a full line of cars jammed in along every inch of curb, but no people to be seen. Jamey parked along a stretch of yellow curb a block away. She'd been by the club before, of course; she kept an eye on the place, in case anyone ever got any funny ideas that might ripple out to Reece.

But no one ever caused trouble and she'd yet to see a real empath within one hundred yards of the club, so until now she'd never had a reason to go in.

As she walked up the street toward the green awning, she could pick up distant thumping bass coming from the warehouse's second story. Under the awning, she rang a bell next to the metal double doors.

A moment later, one of the doors opened, the music suddenly louder. A good-looking brother stepped out, even taller than Grayson with muscles filling out his T-shirt. Without question, the *smoking hot bouncer* Easterby had told her to look for.

"Agent Grayson said Stone Solutions tech is still here, working on the security footage," she said, without preamble. "He was supposed to tell you to expect me."

The bouncer blinked. "You're Detective St. James?"

"I was," she said. "I'm just Jamey now."

"Jamey, then." He didn't press, just pointed at himself, causing his enormous bicep to flex. "Diesel." He gave her another look, assessing, like she was a puzzle and he couldn't quite see how the pieces fit. "So the little empath who came by here earlier—he's your brother?"

"Why?" she said pointedly.

Diesel held up his hands. "Just wondering how he's holding up," he said. "Everyone's hard on empaths today. Well," he amended, with a wry smile. "Not here, obviously."

"Obviously," she said dryly. "Let's get this over with. I don't actually need to linger in a club that caters to people with a kink for my brother."

"Oh, it's not really about that," Diesel said, ridiculously earnest. "Most folks are here because they crave empathy, you know? A place to be accepted and listened to and..." He trailed off. "Wow, you and Reece have the exact same glare."

She folded her arms.

He smiled apologetically. "I'll just take you to see Frodo."

He led her inside and up a flight of stairs, deeper into warehouse, until the stairs opened into a large space pulsing with music and flashing lights. A tiny girl in a short dress, tall boots, fake gloves, and bunny ears was perched on a barstool, doing shots with a young man in a dress shirt and loosened tie, like he'd come straight from a late night at the office. Cute, but not an empath any more than Jamey was.

"People buy these kids as real empaths?" she said, nearly having to shout over the music.

"Why wouldn't they?" Diesel called back.

Because the real empath she knew wouldn't be doing shots with rich workaholics; he'd be lecturing everyone on the evils of drinking and driving and hiding their car keys.

Diesel took her in the opposite direction of the bar and tables, down a roped-off hall into an office with a solid wood desk and beautiful floor-to-ceiling windows, probably the building's originals. The office was clean save for the two laundry baskets on the floor, one full of white tablecloths and one full of black gloves.

"I'll get Frodo." But Diesel had paused, glancing at her again. She wasn't being checked out, though—not like that, at least. This was something else.

"What?" she said.

"I'm obviously the bigger of the two of us, by a lot," he said. "But I never, ever, ever want to get in a fight with you, do I?"

Her eyebrows went up. "You're observant."

He gave a modest shrug. "One boss, coming up."

He disappeared, leaving the door open. As she looked out the window at the empty street a story below, her phone went off.

En route to McFeely's. Be careful.

They were coming here? Grayson had said he was taking Reece to the safe house. Why the change of plans? And there was no way the Dead Man telling her to *be careful* meant anything good.

Before she could text Easterby for an explanation, under the music she could just hear small feet and short legs coming down the hall. A moment later a short, hairy man appeared in the doorway—Frodo, undoubtedly.

"I can't believe I'm missing Ben and Bunny wrapping half the financial district around their pinkies," he muttered as he shut the door, and that probably wasn't meant for Jamey's ears. More loudly, he said, "Look, Detective St. James—" He turned around and blinked. "You're the empath's sister?"

"It's just Jamey," she said. "And I want to talk to the Stone Solutions' IT guy."

"Yes, yes, of course," Frodo said. "But you have a very impressive air, and now I'm wondering—how much sway do you have with Reece? Because we have a job opening right now and I think—"

"How about you just be grateful no one's shutting down your touchy-feely hive of faux-paths and take me to the server room?"

Frodo sighed. "I see tact runs in the family. Follow me."

He took her to the door at the end of the hall and knocked, for all the good it would do anyone with average hearing inside over the sound of the bass. Frodo went for the door, but Jamey got there first, shielding him with her body. She slowly opened the door, muscles tensed—

But the opened door revealed nothing dangerous, just a pale man lounging on a computer chair and thumbing through his phone. He looked up with a loud grunt. "Did you bring my dri—whoa," he said, as his gaze landed on Jamey. "Do I know you?"

"No." She glanced around the small space brimming with computer equipment, but he appeared to be alone in the room and unharmed.

The man scratched his head. "I swear you look familiar, and there's no way in hell you're one of those fake mind-rapers."

Frodo bristled like an angry cat and stepped forward. "Now, see here—"

Jamey put a hand on Frodo's chest and gently pushed him out of the server room into the hall. "I got this."

"But—"

"Go watch Ben and Bunny with those traders." She pulled the door shut on Frodo's protests.

The IT guy sat up straighter, phone discarded on the desk next to the keyboard. He had a grin on his rattish face. "So we're alone now." He pointed to himself. "I'm Derek Egner, director of—"

"I don't care," she said, cutting him off. "Don't call empaths mind-rapers."

A nasty expression twisted his face. "I can call them whatever I—oooh." He snapped his fingers. "Now I know why you look familiar. I've seen your face on the news. You're that hot detective, the one with the brother who's a mind—"

She grabbed him by the front of his Stone Solutions polo and lifted him bodily out of the computer chair. "Don't call empaths mind-rapers," she said again, just as flatly.

He squealed. "How the hell are you this strong—"

"I don't have time or patience for you to waste, *Derek.*" Their eyes were level as she gripped the collar of his shirt. "So how about you don't call my brother that again?"

He nodded resentfully.

"Good," she said. "Why are you messing on your phone instead of recovering the security footage?"

He squirmed like a worm on a hook. "I uh, I had some time while the, uh, the hard drive was defragging—"

"Nice try," she said. "But that's bullshit."

He grimaced. "Fine. The footage fixed itself."

"Fixed *itself*?"

"I restarted the system, and when it rebooted, the security feed was intact."

"And you didn't tell anyone you'd recovered footage relevant to a murder investigation because…"

He winced. "Agent Grayson had already left with that mind—ah, left with the empath." She waited. He winced again. "And the sucker who runs this place let me have free drinks."

"Christ," she muttered. She let go of Egner's shirt and he stumbled onto his feet. "Show me," she said, as he steadied himself on the wall.

He ducked his head and scrambled over to his chair. She stood behind his shoulders as he clattered away at the keys for a moment, then the screen promptly filled with security footage of the alley next to the warehouse.

"There are no cameras in the VIP room itself," Egner said. "This is the best we got, the private entrance in the alley."

He pressed something on the keyboard and the footage began to play at enhanced speed. "Mr. Stone and the senator show up around ten in his Maybach," he said, pointing as on-screen, a fancy car pulled into the alley and Cedrick Stone and Senator Hathaway got out of the back seat. Hathaway was already unsteady on her feet, leaning heavily on Stone's arm as they climbed the stairs up to where Diesel was holding open the door.

Egner zoomed the footage forward even faster, slowing

when a BMW i8 drove into the alley. "Jason Owens shows up not long after that. He parks in the alley and goes into the room. The bouncer disappears. A town car pulls up two minutes later and Stone gets in and leaves. Owens and Hathaway are in there until last call, then they get in his i8 and drive away."

She watched the footage for a minute as all that played out, then bent and looked more closely at the screen. "Back it up to when Owens arrives."

He gave her a look but did as asked. She watched as Diesel opened the door for Owens, who went in. Diesel jumped down the stairs and disappeared from the footage. "We've got security footage of the VIP room's inside door too. The bouncer goes in the club and spends most of his time keeping an eye on it. Owens and Hathaway never went into the main club," Egner said, as on-screen Stone came out the alley door. "Meanwhile Stone takes off right after Owens arrived. Looks like he and Owens didn't even take the time to talk to each other."

"To you. To me it looks like someone spliced this footage."

"What?" He leaned forward, staring at the screen. "I don't—"

"The puddles." She pointed to the pockmarked streets of the alley, at the very edge of the screen. "The rain had just started up when Owens arrives and this pothole is still mostly empty. When Stone comes out, the time stamp reads two minutes later but the pothole is full."

She tapped the screen. "Someone took out a chunk of footage and put in this doctored version for you to find. So maybe Stone was in there with Owens longer than it appears—or maybe someone else showed up too." Jamey cleared her throat. "You might have seen that if you hadn't been dicking around on your phone."

Egner paled. "Oh no." He began pulling up files, his hands unsteady on the keyboard. He glanced at her, then back to the screen. "Please don't tell Agent Grayson. *Please.*"

But deep beneath the music, out on the street, she heard the rumble of a big engine and upgraded exhaust. She straightened. "You might get to tell him yourself," she said, and left the sweating Egner frantically typing, closing the door behind her as she went to meet Grayson and Reece.

Chapter Twenty-Five

Privacy concerns, sanctity of the mind, blah blah blah. My smart watch knows my heart rate but will it listen to me? Tell me it understands my problems? Give me the empaths any day.
—online review of McFeely's

They were pulling up to a curb in Pioneer Square an appallingly short time after Reece had vomited onto the shoulder of I-5, far sooner than they would have been if Grayson had an ounce of respect for traffic laws.

As Grayson stopped the truck and shifted gears into park, Reece glanced down automatically. He narrowed his eyes. "Move the truck."

"We're just—"

"Now."

"But—"

"You know what you did."

There was a moment of silence. Then, eyes fixed forward, Grayson put the truck in reverse and backed up until his front bumper no longer infringed three inches into the yellow curb in front of the fire hydrant.

Next moment, Grayson had opened his own door and elegantly slid down from the truck. He'd already pulled his winter coat back on by the time Reece had leaped down and met him at the front of the truck.

Reece gestured at the coat. "Why do you need that? We're only walking half a block."

"Half a block in half-frozen rain. Maybe I wouldn't need the coat if I still had a *hat*."

Oh. Right. Oops.

Grayson didn't ring the bell this time, just opened the door himself. Diesel was just inside, chatting with a pair of women.

"You're back," Diesel said to Reece, as they passed on their way toward the stairs. "Change your mind about the job?"

"Not likely," Reece said.

"Shame," said Diesel. "I like your sister too."

Reece lit up. "Jamey's here?"

He darted around Grayson and tore up the stairs, and as he cleared the top he saw Jamey heading their way.

Reece reached for her, but she was faster, her arms already closing around him. He buried his forehead against her shoulder and hugged her back. "Grayson wants—" he started.

"I know."

Her grip was so tight he could barely breathe. "I have to go," he said, knowing she'd hear him even over the music. "I have to let them take me; I'm dangerous."

She put her cheek to the top of his head, her body tense as a bowstring. "They told me it's not a prison, it's a safe house," she said. "If that's a lie, I'll come for you."

"You will, I know you will," he said. "And *that* is the truth. You can take it from me."

With one last, desperate-edged squeeze, she let him go. As he lifted his head, for a split second he caught Grayson's gaze lingering on them, unreadable as ever.

But then the moment was gone as Jamey said, "Where are your gloves?"

Reece winced. "Tacoma?"

She opened her mouth, then shook her head. "I don't want

to know." Her gaze lingered on him, or at least on the University of Texas logo emblazoned across his chest. Her lips quirked up. "Nice hoodie."

Reece folded his arms, the sleeves covering his hands.

"Status?" asked Grayson, as he shed his heavy coat in the warm club.

"Egner's an incompetent jack-off. Fake empaths are mesmerizing Seattle's bankers. Most of this club wants the bouncer. I assume that's business as usual for everyone."

"Grayson said we had to come back right away," said Reece. "What's going on with the tech guy?"

"That useless ass completely missed that the security footage was doctored." Jamey was watching Grayson, whose eyes hadn't stopped darting around the club. "You don't seem like that's your biggest concern, though," she said to Grayson. "You seem like you're looking for something. Do you know something you're not sharing?"

Grayson shook his head. "Only maybe." He glanced down at Reece. "But *maybe* still means there might be danger, especially for you. So if you try to wander off this time, I really might cuff you and stick you back in my truck."

Reece gave him a dirty look. "Why would I wander off in a club for fake empaths?"

"I don't know, why can't you get through dinner without a near-arrest and a felony?"

Reece made a face.

Grayson started toward the hall with the server room, and Jamey and Reece followed. But right before they reached the server room door a familiar little man popped up, blocking the path.

"Detective St. James, Agent Grayson!" Frodo clasped his hands. "How good I've caught you. The three of us need to have an extremely important conversation."

Jamey and Grayson exchanged a look. "We do?" said Jamey.

"Of course, of course! Follow me." Frodo led them to his office, where a half-full laundry basket sat on the floor, several tablecloths folded into a crisp stack on the heavy desk.

Grayson tossed his overcoat on a visitor's chair as Jamey leaned on the wall.

"Now," Frodo said pleasantly, "I've been nothing but helpful today. And in return, I need assurances that whatever you find in that recovered security footage won't be used against me or my establishment."

"No," said Jamey and Grayson together.

But Frodo raised his chin. "Not everyone looks like you two," he said. "I know better than most that the world is a hard, unfeeling place. This club is a haven of kindness and acceptance. If it gets out that my patrons are being investigated by the police and—" He gestured helplessly at Grayson. "—whatever Handsome here is, McFeely's will be ruined."

"Buy some horses and fake horns and start a unicorn ranch," said Jamey.

"A bisexual unicorn ranch," said Grayson. "You'll make another fortune."

They both turned and walked back out the office door and into the hall.

"Oh, come on," Reece said, as he chased after them, Frodo right behind him. "I don't like that this place exists, but Frodo's here in the middle of the night, doing the laundry, even though he's the boss. The club obviously means a lot to him, even if it makes him a liar and a dirty swindler."

"Thanks," said Frodo. "Sort of."

Grayson and Jamey ignored them, heading for the server room. Jamey reached it first, opening the door without knocking. Reece huffed and reached for her arm. "All I'm saying is it can't hurt to hear Frodo out—"

Jamey jammed her shoulder against the server room door, slamming it shut in front of her, while Grayson grabbed Reece by the hood, yanking him backward. Reece nearly fell but Grayson caught his sleeve, keeping him on his feet just long enough to swing him through the still-open door of Frodo's office.

Reece stumbled into the room, only just managing to straighten up. "What the—"

Without a word of explanation, Grayson shut the door in his face.

Jamey shoved Frodo behind her as the man began to sputter.

"You're just going to let him manhandle your brother?"

She didn't respond, just blocked his body with her own. With Reece safely out of sight, she cracked the server room door again.

Her eyes darted from the body on the floor to the blood splattered on the walls. It couldn't be coincidence that Grayson had rushed here because of Egner—and now Egner was dead. And here she was with a body, no gun, no badge—and a club packed with people, a killer possibly still loose among them.

She grabbed the chair resting against the server room wall and pulled it into the hall, firmly shutting the server room door.

"What's going on?" Frodo demanded. "What happened in that room?"

Grayson was leaning on the door of Frodo's office. The knob was rattling, and she could hear Reece's indignant yelps coming from within. "Let me out! Agent Grayson! *Jamey!*"

She slid the chair across the hall to Grayson. "It's been eleven minutes since I talked to Egner. He was fine."

"This wasn't emotionally induced suicide like Owens," said Grayson under his breath. "This was done by someone else."

He jammed the chair under the doorknob of Frodo's office, barricading Reece in. The doorknob was still shaking, and Reece was still yelling, but empath strength wasn't breaking through that chair.

Grayson bent to his ankle holster and then tossed something her way. "Here."

She caught it. A .44 Magnum. They didn't carry these on the force.

Grayson moved away from the door, another gun in hand. Jamey stepped next to him, heart racing. There had been two huge men found dead on the yacht with Hathaway: one with deep bruises on his throat, the other with a shrimp fork embedded in bone. And now, whoever had stabbed Egner had done it with enough strength to splatter his blood up the walls. "I can still call the department."

"No backup. Just us." Grayson glanced at her. "Can you evacuate?"

She nodded once.

"Evacuate?" Frodo's voice hit a new level of shrill as Grayson disappeared into the crowd. "Will one of you please explain what on earth—"

"Blondie looks like he's on a mission." Diesel appeared behind Frodo, holding a glass of something red and fizzy. "Is some unlucky bastard about to get their ass kicked?"

"I'm sure I don't know!" said Frodo, high and panicked. "I don't know anything tonight. Why do you have a Shirley Temple?"

"I told Ben that Reece was back." Diesel looked around. "Where *is* Reece?"

The pounding came again from Frodo's office door. "Frodo! Jamey! What's going on?"

Diesel blinked.

Jamey nodded at Diesel's arms. "Are those muscles just for show or do they work?"

"They work?" Diesel said slowly, making it a question.

"Great." She pushed him in front of Frodo's office door, drawing a breath of surprise from Diesel, who probably wasn't used to other people being able to move him. "You guard this door."

There was pounding intensified. "*Jamey!* Let me out!"

Diesel looked at the door, and his eyebrows drew together. "Is that—Reece?"

"Guard it with your *life*," said Jamey.

"But why is Reece *barricaded* in the boss's office?"

"No one in or out," Jamey ordered. "Don't open that door, no matter what you hear Reece try." She grabbed Frodo by the arm. "With me."

"But what's happened?" Frodo protested, as she dragged him a few steps down the hall. "I don't understand what you and Agent Grayson are—"

Jamey bent down to speak quietly in his ear. "Egner's dead."

Frodo gasped.

"Murdered," she clarified. "Violently. And the killer may still be in this club." *And have the ability to change emotions like a radio dial.* She left that out.

Frodo had gone very pale. "But I just spoke to Mr. Egner thirty minutes ago," he stammered. "How could he be dead?"

Grayson or Stone Solutions could come up with an explanation for this one. "We need to prioritize the living," she said. "We need to evacuate before anyone else gets hurt. I don't care if you have to promise everyone free shots in the street, just get them out of the club. You understand?"

Frodo wiped at his brow with one hand. He shot a glance down the hall, at Diesel leaning on his office door. "What about Reece?"

Diesel was guarding the door, and there was no other way in or out of Frodo's office besides the second-story window. Reece would be safe while they evacuated. Pissed, but safe.

"He makes too good of a target. He can't defend himself, and he'll get distracted trying to help people and forget to be careful." *And whoever was watching Cora on that webcam might be after Reece as an encore.* Jamey left that out too. She bent to look Frodo in the eyes. "Hey. You with me?"

He wiped his brow again but nodded.

The club's main room was wall-to-wall packed in what was certainly a fire code violation. Frodo went to the DJ, and Jamey kept her eyes peeled around the room as the two of them conferred with tense hand gestures. Grayson was nowhere in sight.

The music cut off. All of the patrons turned toward the DJ's booth, murmuring in confusion.

Frodo stepped forward and the room fell eerily silent. He cleared his throat and raised the microphone, which was shaking in his hand.

"We have a surprise for all of our guests tonight." His voice was shaking too. "We're taking the party to the streets where—"

A panicked cry rebounded off the nineteenth century bricks. "There's a dead body in the server room!"

The crowd erupted into chaos, surging for the stairs en masse, pushing and shoving for the exit.

Jamey cursed and leaped into the fray.

"Frodo! Agent Grayson! *Jamey!*" Reece kept rattling the door-knob even though he knew it was useless. Something on the other side was door blocking him in.

The thumping bass suddenly cut out. Distantly, Reece

thought he could hear Frodo over a microphone. He took advantage of the quiet to pound on the door. "What's going on?"

"Sorry, kiddo," came Diesel's voice through the door. "But your sister said to guard this door, and no disrespect, but she's both hotter and scarier than you."

"Diesel?" Reece put his mouth against the crack between the door and the frame. "Diesel, come on, just let me—"

"There's a dead body in the server room!"

Reece froze. "Ben?"

That was real terror in Ben's voice. And that hadn't been a lie.

Reece smacked the door with his fist, so hard the sleeve of the hoodie came down over his hand. "*Ben!* Are you okay?"

A dead body. But who—how—

The server room.

Egner.

Reece's knees buckled, sending him to the floor as the screams started in the club. He squeezed his eyes shut, forehead on the door as scared people began to run, fancy shoes scrambling over wood floors.

How could Egner be *dead*? Jamey had just talked to him. Had someone killed him while they'd been only feet away, in Frodo's office?

Against the door, Reece's hands began to shake.

But he couldn't fall apart; he had to keep it together. There was a whole club out there of people who could be in danger.

"Jamey!" He slammed his palm against the door, hard enough to cause another bruise. "Agent Grayson!"

Then, in Reece's pocket, his phone buzzed with an incoming text.

Only four people in Seattle had his phone number. Grayson and Jamey wouldn't call in the middle of that mess, which meant it had to be Liam.

Liam.

Reece grabbed his phone like a lifeline. If Liam knew Jamey was in trouble—Liam would help—

But the text wasn't from Liam. It was from the one remaining person who had Reece's number.

Reece stared at his phone in shock. A picture of Vanessa Whitman was on-screen, her wide eyes shot through with far too much red.

Cora's message was below.

Orca's Gate Marina dry dock. 30 minutes. Come alone.

The crowd stampeded down the stairs like spooked cattle. Jamey pushed in the opposite direction of the flow, her eyes on the far end of the room.

There was no sign of Grayson—or Cora, and when did an empath become a worse thought than the Dead Man?—but at the back of the room, where ropes and a curtain marked off the VIP area, the door to the VIP room was cracked.

With Grayson's Magnum at the ready, Jamey shouldered it open.

A gasp of surprise escaped her. Officer Josh Taylor stood in the center of the room, flanked by two men in security guard uniforms. All three of them were holding their bodies unnaturally still, their dead gazes fixed forward—on Jamey.

On the floor were the tiny fake empath in bunny ears and the man in office attire, their bodies crumpled in poses too broken to be alive.

"Josh." Jamey's gaze darted from the bodies back to her officer. "What's going on?"

Taylor didn't answer. He only blinked, too slowly. And then he moved.

Jamey and Taylor had worked together for three years. Taylor was formidable for most crooks, keeping himself in great shape. He'd been brave enough to spar with her once at the gym, and she knew exactly what the man was physically capable of.

So she was completely unprepared when his boot connected with the gun in her hand faster and harder than he'd ever been able to move.

The gun careened to the wall, and then she had to duck as his fist came flying at her face. She grabbed his arm and used his momentum to spin him toward the bricks, but he turned it into a dive, and when he rolled back up to his feet, the Magnum was in his hands.

He wiped at his eye in an automatic sort of way, gaze never leaving her. And when his hand came away, his cheek was bloody.

And he lunged for Jamey again, just as the two security guards did the same.

Reece stared at the picture of Whitman on his phone's screen.

Outside the door of Frodo's office, he could still hear the panicked crowd tearing through the warehouse. Was Cora responsible for Egner's dead body in the server room too? Based on the terror on Whitman's face, it seemed possible.

If Reece had the chance to find Cora and stop her—*save* her—he had to try.

He looked up and around the office, from the heavy desk in the middle of the room with its stacked tablecloths, to the floor-to-ceiling windows, to Grayson's coat resting on a nearby chair.

His mind offered a truly terrible plan.

But it wasn't like he had another choice.

Reece grabbed the coat and dashed to the desk. As fast as he could, he tied tablecloths together with weaver's knots, then secured one end of the makeshift rope to one of the legs of the desk.

He glanced out the window to the street below. Everyone running away from the building, nobody milling in front of it. It was as safe as he was going to get.

He picked up Frodo's *World's Greatest Boss* trophy. It was heavier than it looked, maybe actual bronze. He hefted it in both hands and, with a silent apology to Seattle's historians, swung it through the air and let go.

The original window of the nineteenth century warehouse shattered on impact, the trophy smashing on the ground a story below, thankfully without hitting anyone. Reece kicked out persistent shards with his sneaker, then fished Grayson's keys out of his coat pocket and grabbed the end of his table-cloth rope.

He paused at the window frame, looked back at the heavy desk, and held his breath as he climbed through the window.

It held his weight. He let out the breath, braced his feet against the old brick wall, and began to climb down.

No one paid any attention to him as he picked his way down the bricks as fast as he could. He jumped the last couple feet down and was instantly lost to the crowd, just another escapee.

He sprinted down the block, keys clutched tightly in one sweaty fist, weaving and dodging to avoid touching anyone until he made it to Grayson's truck.

Reece unlocked the truck and clambered up into the driver's seat. "Come on, *come on*," he said through clenched teeth as he had to move the slow electronic seat forward to reach the pedals. He shoved the paltry MPGs from his thoughts; getting all the way to the marina in his remaining minutes would mean speeding anyway.

The truck's engine came to life with a roar. He threw it into reverse and punched the gas, and the tires screeched as the truck spun in a tight one-eighty just as fast as he could have hoped.

"Atta girl," he said aloud. "Now show me how you behave for a boy who can drive."

He switched terrain modes for a more responsive throttle map and longer rev range, applied throttle until he'd built up the revs, then released the brake and took off.

Chapter Twenty-Six

The Empath Initiative just restricted empath research to approved facilities ONLY. There are THREE approved facilities in the ENTIRE country.
National security, they say. Such bullshit. I've spent the last two years studying empaths' siblings. I was on the cusp of a break-through, and now I have to throw it all away.

—twenty-year-old note from the medical school at Rainier University

A shot rang over her head as Jamey dove through the open VIP room door. She grabbed the legs of a barstool and swung it just as one of the security guards rushed her, sending him flying into the brick wall.

She leaped to her feet, eyes on Taylor as he raised the Magnum. She launched the barstool at him, buying herself a second as he dodged.

The second guard got arms around her neck with an inhuman growl, but she reached back and grabbed his shoulders, flipping him over and across the bar into the shelves. Dozens of stacked glasses and liquor bottles shattered.

Taylor aimed the gun again and she went for his legs. The two of them hit the floor, and she rolled them. She grabbed for the gun in his hand, but his grip was too strong, and his knee connected with her stomach hard enough to wind her.

She barely had time to gasp as a barstool was coming down

at her head. She rolled, away from Taylor, away from the first security guard, smacking into the base of the bar. The guard slammed the barstool down, not at her but over her, and then he held it, pinning her to the ground like a butterfly in a net.

Jamey shoved at the barstool, but the guard was as unnaturally strong as Taylor had been. "Josh, *stop.*"

But Taylor was getting up, Magnum in hand, the other guards at his side. All three of them oblivious to their injuries, to the blood now running freely from their eyes down their cheeks.

Taylor raised the gun and Jamey had nowhere to go—

Three rapid gunshots split the air. Two for the security guards, who dropped lifeless to the floor—and one in the center of Taylor's forehead.

Jamey drew as sharp breath as Taylor fell back against the wooden floor, eyes wide open, body still as stone. She looked up to see Grayson, who didn't holster the gun as he said, "I heard glass break. That was the bar?"

"You just *shot* three people." Taylor was on the floor and the grief was already coming. "You shot *Josh.*"

"He was about to shoot you." Grayson was moving through the room, tensed. His gaze flicked to the broken bodies on the floor. "Your officer was enthralled by an empath. He didn't know who he was anymore. If he had, do you think he would've wanted us to let him keep slaughtering folks in this club?"

She took a breath through her nose. "We could have—"

"There's no help. There's no coming back." Grayson dropped a cursory glance behind the couch. "You saw them bleeding. Their bodies were destroying themselves. They probably had minutes left, but they would have killed you and as many as they could before they died their own agonizing death. And there was nothing we could have done to stop it."

Jamey shoved the barstool off her, and it clattered to the floor. "They deserved better."

"They did." Grayson was looking over the bar, examining broken glass. He nodded toward the other bodies, the girl in bunny ears, the man with the loosened tie. "So did their victims. This is the world of the Dead Man, Detective. There's a reason I never bring anyone into it."

Jamey got to her feet, staring at Taylor's unmoving body, the burn in her chest searing her throat, her eyes. She crouched at his side and took the Magnum back, but adjusted him to a more peaceful position. Closed his eyelids before she stood.

"I'm not a detective anymore," she said, and pushed past Grayson back into the main club.

He followed at her heels without comment.

She kept the Magnum up as she scanned the now-empty room, littered with broken tables, broken glasses, the DJ tables abandoned. "They were too fast. Too strong." *Too much like me*, she didn't say. "Is this what Cora does? Creates devotion, then jacks up the hormones that fuel emotions to make thralls with super-strength? Is that how a tiny sixty-five-year-old senator killed two men your size?"

Grayson nodded. "But they've got a time limit, because all that rage will kill them, if nothing else does first." He was walking toward the bar. "And it's not the only thing she can do. She can twist emotions all sorts of ways, or send people into catatonia, like you saw with the witness at the marina."

She hadn't gotten any news about the witness since that morning. "What's Braker's condition now?"

Grayson picked his way over the shattered glass. "He didn't make it."

Jesus. Braker was dead, just like Egner, and Taylor, and the businessman and the fake empath from the bar, and all the rest. A giant stack of empathy-connected deaths in a span of hours. This was the nightmare the Dead Man was up against.

Grayson leaned over enough to see behind the bar, then shook his head. "I don't understand why there were only three."

"*Only* three?" said Jamey.

"Ms. Falcon is an empath who's been reading veterans for years. She wouldn't march to battle with only three soldiers."

That was a good point. "So where are the others?"

Grayson's gaze darted around the club. "Hiding?" he said slowly, then his eyes snapped to hers. "Or—"

"Or this wasn't a real battle," she realized in the same moment. "They were never meant to stop us. They were meant to distract us."

But as she spoke, she heard the roar of a souped-up engine out on the street beneath the chaos. And then the screech of tires.

A second later, Grayson and Jamey were both sprinting for Frodo's office.

Diesel was still there, leaning on the wall next to the door. He held up his hands, the Shirley Temple glass now empty on the floor. "No one's been in or out. And I promise I didn't open it, just like you asked, even when I heard the crash—"

Jamey pulled him aside as Grayson kicked the chair away and yanked open the door.

The office was empty, one giant window broken and a rope made of tablecloths still dangling through it. Grayson's coat was tossed on the floor nearby.

Jamey and Grayson were shoulder to shoulder at the window a second later, staring down at the last of the fleeing clubgoers and a street now devoid of cars except her Charger.

"Your brother stole my truck," said Grayson.

Escape? Sure. But *stealing*? "He wouldn't," she protested, even though Reece obviously had.

"He's in big trouble."

"Oh, come on," she said. "He's a great driver, he won't even ding it."

"Not that," said Grayson. "He stole my truck to run *away* from a crowd of terrified people in danger. I can only think of two reasons an empath might've done that, and I'm betting it's because he found a bigger danger to run to." He shook his head. "But what?"

Reece's words suddenly came back to Jamey, too high and too breathy as he fought a panic attack behind the wheel.

At least now I know why Cora hasn't called me back.

Oh no. "I have to go." She turned away.

Grayson got in front of her, blocking her path. "Do you have some idea?"

"I'm not sharing it with you, empath hunter." She twisted around him.

But he was back in her way.

"I'm not hunting your brother. I'm trying to save Seattle. And I'm trying to save *him*." Grayson held her eyes. "It's like standing at a cliff's edge and wrangling a lemming in a hoodie. But I'm trying. So please: tell me what bigger danger could have found him while he was locked in Mr. Frazier's office."

She hesitated. Thought of handcuffs and bobby pins. Of safe houses bought that day. Of Aisha Easterby's words, *Grayson's not your enemy.*

She pressed her lips together, then said, "Reece tried to call Cora this morning. They're friends. She has his phone number."

Grayson's gaze went past her, back to the broken window. Then he darted around her, ducked under the window frame, and jumped.

Jamey blinked. She stuck her head out the window frame and saw Grayson unhurt on the sidewalk below.

He looked up at her. "You coming?" he called.

What was one more secret in the Dead Man's hands? Jamey ducked beneath the frame herself and leaped down after him, catching herself in a crouch. The impact wasn't pleasant, but she straightened, unharmed. "So you know about me too."

Broken glass crunched under their feet as they started toward Jamey's Charger. "It's rare," said Grayson, "but it happens every now and then to an empath's sibling. You turned out stronger and faster than everyone else, because growing up with an empath changed how *you* grew up."

"Wait, what?" Jamey said. "How?"

"Theory is they use empathy to change their sibling, same as they change their thralls, just slow enough not to kill you," Grayson said, as they strode across the street, perfectly matching each other's fast pace. "And the sibling ends up with some natural immunity to empathy, like you've been inoculated."

"But *why?*"

Grayson shrugged, the gesture caught in the yellow glow of the streetlamp. "Could be because the little empath loves their sibling so much but isn't able to control their empathy yet. So that love has a tangible impact, on accident. But most researchers take a different view."

Jamey eyed him. "Which is?"

"That it's a manipulation by the part of an empath that controls corruption. To make sure they have someone to protect them when they're a vulnerable pacifist, until they get old enough and strong enough that corruption can happen."

"Oh, that theory is *fucked up*," Jamey said.

"The animal kingdom is full of parasites. Nature's kinda fucked up," Grayson said dryly.

"But the squishy pacifist *is* an empath's real nature," said

Jamey, as they reached her car. "They're not just a—a *host* for
the corrupted empath."

"Scientists are divided on that one too."

"Then that's also fucked up." Jamey narrowed her eyes.
"And what about the Dead Man? Which one do you think
an empath really is?"

"I think it doesn't matter." Grayson was pulling his phone
out as he went around to the passenger side. "We want them
to stay pacifists either way."

Jamey put her hand on the car door. "I can't help but notice that I'm not stronger and faster than *you*."

"Well," said Grayson, "even by snowflake standards, I'm
special now." He held up his phone, a map on-screen. "I've
got a tracker on my truck. We can follow."

Jamey nodded. "I'll call for backup."

But Grayson immediately shook his head. "No backup.
You just saw what Ms. Falcon can do. We're not gonna give
her more weapons."

Jamey paused. "How does that not go double for us? We'd
be even more dangerous than everyone else."

"We would. But how much can your brother read from
you?"

Not much. But Reece could still hear her lie. Jamey hesitated, then said, "I don't think I'm going to be immune to all
of Cora's empathy."

"You won't be," Grayson agreed. "But you've got more resistance than most folks."

"Most," she repeated, a thought occurring to her. "But not
the special snowflake. You're completely immune to anything an empath can do, aren't you? Any power, no matter
how strong?"

Grayson met her eyes over the top of the Charger. "How'd
you guess?"

"Because no one calls me the Dead Woman."

"You should probably be grateful for that."

Jamey wished for Reece's abilities in that moment, because the words seemed laced with a meaning she couldn't interpret. She opened the car door. "How screwed are we?"

"Screwed?"

"How big a head start does Reece have?"

"You're stressing catching up to your empath brother? You got lights, sirens, enhanced senses and reflexes—"

"Look at the map," Jamey said impatiently.

Grayson raised his eyebrows, but looked down. "He's going north, and he's made it—" He stared at his phone. "Far."

"Don't let his bitching fool you." Jamey ducked into the driver's seat as Grayson dropped into the passenger seat. "He decided at sixteen that safe driving required good driving. He can drift off-road without crushing a single flower."

She turned the engine over. She wasn't a detective anymore; using the lights and siren was a crime. She turned them on without hesitation.

"Huh," said Grayson. "So *drive like an empath*—"

"Doesn't mean what he lets people think."

And she hit the gas to chase after Reece.

Nolan could hear a crowd stampeding down the stairs above him, terrified shouts layered over the pounding of feet. Grayson had said he was sending him back to the McFeely's place, then Easterby had slipped him something. Nolan had woken up handcuffed to a rolling chair in a small, windowless room with a cheerful rug, a couch, and a pair of old armchairs. A poster on the wall had a list of ideas for self-care.

He tried to yell through the duct tape covering his mouth, but there was no way he'd be heard over that ruckus.

Then the doorknob to his room began to rattle. It rattled

again, and again, and then the door was thrown open, revealing not Grayson, or St. James, or even the giant bouncer who'd checked on him once, but a shorter guy with complicated hair and keys held in his empath-gloved hands.

He saw Nolan and drew up in surprise. "Who the hell are you?"

"FBI," Nolan tried to say, but it didn't escape the tape.

The new guy huffed and stepped forward, ripping off the tape.

Nolan yelped at the sudden pain. *"Fuck."* He licked his sore lips. "FBI."

"Yeah, and I'm a real empath. Get out."

"My badge is—"

"I don't want to see your fake badge! I was trying to be a good friend and cheer up a grumpy empath and instead I found a *dead body.*"

"A *body*? What—"

But he'd grabbed Nolan's rolling chair. "This is the staff's wellness room," he said, as he yanked the chair along the wood floor and into a tiny hall, "and I'm not sharing it with some creepy lying stranger in handcuffs!"

He left Nolan in the hall and slammed the door.

Nolan blinked. People were still coming down the stairs like water down a waterfall. "FBI," he tried. Nobody seemed to hear. He took a deep breath. "FBI!"

He thought he might have heard a pause in the crowd's steps. Then a short, hairy man poked his head around the stairs.

"Oh my goodness," said the man. "Who are you?"

"FBI," Nolan grit out. "Badge is in my pocket."

The little man pursed his lips. "This is a judgment-free zone of acceptance and we allow fantasies of all sorts. But we've been ordered to evacuate and now is really not the time—"

"Get me the hell out of this chair," Nolan gritted out, "before I have you locked up for obstruction and kidnapping and anything else I can think of."

The little man bristled. "There's no need to be rude." But he left the stairs and came over to Nolan. *Finally.* "How do I—"

"The keys are on my belt."

The little man had Nolan out of the chair just a few minutes later. He stood, shaking out the pins and needles in his arms as the blood returned. He pulled his badge out and shoved it in the man's face. "Why are you evacuating?"

The man's face crumpled. "The dead man, the computer one." He put a hand over his mouth but not in time to hide his trembling lip. "So shocking."

A *murder*? While Nolan had been locked in a closet? Ugh, he'd be a laughingstock. "I'm going to need your phone. And your car."

The man didn't look happy, but handed over a cell phone and a set of keys. Nolan pocketed both and went for the door. But as he opened it, he froze.

Grayson and St. James were tearing toward her Charger.

Nolan stayed in the doorway and watched as they spoke for a moment, then climbed into the car. St. James hit her lights and siren and then sped off.

There was no way St. James was willingly working with the man that hunted empaths.

Unless she thought she had a really good reason.

Like catching a murderer.

He was done trusting Cedrick Stone and Grayson and St. James and the rest of the circus. They needed *real* muscle to deal with empaths.

He began dialing on the borrowed phone. St. James' car was property of the SPD and they'd be able to track it. Wherever

St. James and Grayson were going, Nolan was going too—
along with a SWAT team.

Or three.

"You said you could only think of two reasons Reece would
run," Jamey said, as she blew north on I-5 as fast as she could
push her car. "What was the second one?"

"The obvious one," said Grayson. "That he ran from people in danger to save his own skin."

Jamey huffed. "I wish."

"No," said Grayson. "You don't." She glanced at him, and
he added, "Because when an empath's become capable of that,
that's when I step in."

Her hackles rose. "That's when you hunt them down, you
mean."

"When I have to."

"I knew it." She weaved around a sedan doing fifty-five in
the far-left lane. "And you keep trying to tell me you're just
a specialist."

"I do the things the world needs me to do."

"The world doesn't need to you to save it from Reece."

"Not today, maybe."

"Not *ever*." Jamey dropped the car to third, sped past an
SUV.

"I can't promise you that," said Grayson. "You've seen the
carnage a single corrupted empath can cause in the space of
hours. You've seen why I have to stop them, why the Dead
Man has to exist. I can't take chances, I can't be soft, or innocent people pay the price. So I'm trying to save your brother
from corruption, but if I can't, I'll take him down, and I won't
hesitate."

Her tires hit mud as she used the shoulder to pass an eighteen-
wheeler. "Over my dead body."

"If that's what it takes."

They rode without speaking for another minute, the siren loud and jarring.

Jamey cleared her throat. "I think you're just pissed he stole your fancy truck."

"It didn't help," said Grayson.

Chapter Twenty-Seven

We all go a little bad sometimes.
—*tagline for the 1987 horror B movie* My Psycho Empath Girlfriend

The dry dock at the Orca's Gate Marina was as big as an airplane hangar, boats tucked into cubbies made by metal shelves like a giant version of Jamey's shoe rack. The dry dock's main overhead lights were off and the yellow night-lights shone on the boats, which cast strange, oversized shadows across the concrete floor.

Reece walked straight up the center of the dry dock, past a giant forklift big enough to lift boats. The soft padding of his sneakers was achingly loud in the silence, but there was no point in hiding. Cora knew he was coming.

At the middle of the dry dock, he heard a soft whimper. He was running before he knew it. "Dr. Whitman!"

Just ahead, huddled on the bow of a small skiff, was Vanessa Whitman. Her vacant eyes stared into space, and while she wasn't bound, she wasn't moving to escape.

He dropped to his knees at the side of the boat. "Dr. Whitman?"

She didn't react.

"Vanessa, it's Reece." He was reaching for her before he could stop himself. Maybe he wasn't useless, maybe his empathy could reach her, maybe he could help—

"Hands to yourself, Reece."

He froze with hands outstretched.

That *voice*—

Reece had been so intent on Whitman that he hadn't noticed, but he saw Cora now in the shadows, leaning on the next boat. Her hair was in a long braid over one shoulder, and she was still in the pink scrubs she'd been wearing when he saw her yesterday.

"Back up," said Cora. "Hands where I can see them. Make one funny move, I'll take it out on Vanessa."

Reece bit his lip. Hands up, he stood, and took several steps backward, his gaze on Cora. He didn't know what he'd expected to see. Bleeding nose, bleeding eyes? But there was none of that. The changes were so much more subtle; the once-kind eyes now shuttered at the edges, mouth hard instead of smiling. And her voice, all wrong, the sweetness gone and replaced with something cruel.

This wasn't the Cora he'd seen yesterday.

Corruption, his mind supplied.

Maybe, but how? Never in a million years would Cora have willingly corrupted herself.

Back on the boat, Whitman made a choked cry. Reece flinched. Cora huffed, almost a laugh, and held up one bare hand. "If you don't like her crying, I can change the channel."

He swallowed, angry and sick at once. "That's horrible."

"Don't knock it 'til you try it." She pushed off the boat. "I knew you'd come."

"You would have done the same once." The lights caught the stains on Cora's scrubs. Was that—blood? Hathaway's, maybe, or others'? "What happened to you?"

The corner of Cora's mouth curled up in a mockery of a smile. "They call it corruption." She gestured in Whitman's direction. "But that's a word dreamed up by frightened scientists. I'm not corrupted, I'm *evolved*." Cora cocked her head. "Do you know how it happens? Or are you still sheltered from your real nature?"

"You think this is your real nature?" Reece demanded. "Scaring people, hurting them, mur—" Despite everything, the word still stuck in his throat.

Cora laughed. *"Murder,"* she said, drawing it out. "The word is *murder*, as in, I didn't murder anyone, I made them murder themselves and each other."

"That's not what empathy is for!"

"What's it for then, Reece?" she baited. "Nightmares?"

Reece flushed. "I told you about those as your patient. I came to you for help."

"And now you're back for more," she said, and he flinched. "Oh, I bet you told yourself you were rushing here to help Vanessa here, or maybe even to help me. But you're here for yourself. You want the truth. You want to know how this happens, because you want to know if it's going to happen to you."

"That's not true." He winced at the sour sound of his lie. Cora was a far more intuitive empath than he'd ever been.

Cora grinned like he'd told her a secret. "Whatever you say." She hopped up to sit on the deck of the boat, within arm's reach of Whitman.

"What are you doing to her?" he said warily.

"I've got all these new powers," Cora said, almost thoughtfully, "and I got to wondering which ones might work without touch."

Reece tried as hard as he could to keep his emotions off his face.

"A scientist like Dr. Whitman appreciates that I need more information." Cora looked at Whitman. "And of course, a *test subject*."

Whitman whimpered.

"You're trying to control her emotions without touch?" Reece said, in horror. "You're practicing your new abilities on innocent people?"

"Innocent," Cora repeated, voice dripping with scorn. "Who's innocent here? Jason Owens, Hathaway, those men on the boat—none of them were innocent and neither is Dr. Whitman."

Not a lie. Reece furrowed his brow. "I don't understand."

"Don't you? Places like Stone Solutions, and the people who run them, don't think twice about hurting someone else if it leads to their own gain. I was a path to profit; they *wanted* this." Cora gave a delicate little shrug. "I just wasn't supposed to fight back."

She still wasn't lying. Reece looked at Whitman again. Blood was welling in the corner of one glassy eye, a scene straight out of Reece's nightmares.

This had to be his fault. He'd become corrupted first, and he'd spread his corruption to Cora. "You wanted me here," he said. "So here I am. And you can have whatever you want from me, just don't hurt anyone else."

"Oh, I don't think I should promise that," Cora said sweetly. "Especially considering who we're waiting for."

Reece stilled. "We're waiting for someone?"

"The next piece of the plan." The glint in her eyes intensified. "Your sister."

"Park here," said Grayson.

Jamey hit the brakes, bringing the Charger to a halt on the street, just before the main entrance to the marina. Squinting into the dark, she could see the red i8 and big black pickup truck about fifty feet away, parked in front of the marina's dry dock. "Why so far?"

"You might have some natural defenses, but once you get

close, Ms. Falcon will sense your emotions. Some corrupted empaths can even project their own emotions, spreading them to anyone nearby. I don't know if Ms. Falcon is able to do that yet, and I don't know if it will work on you, but let's not test it."

Great. Jamey killed the engine and looked down into the marina's parking lot. It was a ghost town, the SPD tent and yellow tape still up, but as props on a stage, just for show. Everyone had been pulled off the scene hours ago in the sweep of orders from the Dead Man. Grayson had probably saved a lot of lives.

"So Cora can sense when people get close." Jamey kept her eyes on the truck Reece had stolen. "She can thrall people's emotions and fuck up their limbic and endocrine systems, and she might be able to project her own feelings. *Please* tell me that's the fucking limit?"

"Not quite," said Grayson. "She can hear you lie."

Jamey's heart stuttered. She snapped her head in Grayson's direction. "She can what?"

"She can hear it when someone decides to lie." Grayson was looking at the dry dock, not at her. "All corrupted empaths can. It's usually the first new power they get."

Oh hell. "Can an empath get only certain new powers? A new ability like hearing lies but not the sadism?"

"No."

Jamey tightened her jaw. "*No*, because you're positive it can't happen, or *no*, because you've never seen it?"

Grayson paused. He turned hazel eyes on her. "Because I've never seen it," he said slowly. "But I've seen most everything there is to see involving empaths."

Jamey faced forward again. Fine. *Most everything* wasn't everything, and unless she saw Reece murder someone with her own eyes, she'd keep faith.

There was one other question she needed to make herself ask, because Reece had admitted Cora had read him yesterday. "Is it contagious? Can empaths spread the corruption to each other with a read?"

"I don't believe you'd want Ms. Falcon to get her hands on your brother, regardless."

Jamey scrubbed a hand over her face. That hadn't been why she'd asked, but now she had a new tension crawling up her spine. "What does she want with Reece?"

"Hostage, if we're lucky," Grayson said. "The other option's worse."

"I don't think either of us count on luck." She reached for the glovebox and the .44 Magnum Grayson had given her.

But his hand wrapped around her wrist. His grip was gentle, but Jamey could feel his hidden strength, unnatural as her own, like he might be the first person she'd ever met who could match her in a fight.

"You can't." His skin was cool as his eyes bored into hers. "Not in front of your brother."

And a piece of the puzzle finally fell into place. "Because it might trigger the corruption in Reece." She didn't make it a question, but Grayson gave a curt nod anyway. Her breath left her in a rush. "What causes it? The gun? The violence? Death?"

"We don't know all the ways, and I'm not about to let people run tests on empaths to figure them out. But we do know one way." He let her wrist go. "Dr. Easterby showed you the handcuffs in the engine room. And you said you found gurneys at the pulp mill. Did you smell blood?"

Jamey recoiled from the implication. "You think Cora was taken there?"

"Maybe. Maybe not just Cora."

"By who?" Jamey demanded. "Jason Owens?"

"I'm gonna find out," he said, low and gravelly. "That's another part of my job."

Jesus. "But why would anyone ever *want* to corrupt an empath?"

"Sometimes people just want to see if they can make a monster," Grayson said quietly. "But in this case, there was tens of millions of dollars in anti-empathy funding at stake. I'd guess Dr. Owens was looking for a surefire way to convince Senator Hathaway not to withdraw her bill. He thought he'd take the sweet, sunshiny therapist, the very therapist whose kindness and empathy was weakening support for the bill, and use her to show Senator Hathaway what Stone Solutions is really defending against."

Corrupting an empath on purpose for money. Pure evil. It sounded like motive to her, but not Owens' motive alone. "He was far from the only person who'd lose if that bill doesn't pass."

"I know. And the webcam in the engine room makes me think he wasn't working alone."

Easterby's words came back to her: *Grayson's not a villain. He takes down empaths, when he has to. But when he can save them, that's what he does.* "How does Reece fit into this?"

"I sent your brother to you because I thought you'd hide him, and I thought that'd be enough to keep him safe. But then Dr. Easterby's team found Owens' body, and I found the smashed camera on the boat, and I realized that Owens probably had a partner, someone out there who might still decide to target another empath."

She glanced at him. "Could it be the Whitman person Reece went after?"

"Could be," said Grayson. "Or it could be someone else. I'm not scratching any suspects off the list, and I'm not gonna quit until everyone behind this has been found and stopped."

She considered him. "So you really have been trying to protect Reece?"

"Protecting the world from empaths means protecting empaths from the people who want to corrupt them." Grayson's features were just visible in the dark car. "All day I've been trying to make sure the most insidious thing your brother can do is backseat drive. Even if he's perfected it to an almost superhuman level."

Jamey snorted. "I bet Jason Owens' missing phone would tell us who he's been working with." She opened the driver's door. "Any leads?"

"I would have told you if there were," Grayson said, as he opened his own door.

"You have to think about it like Reece," she said. "You've got a high-level Stone Solutions guy with evidence incriminating someone else. What does Reece think about the people at Stone Solutions?"

Grayson hesitated, his hand on the passenger door. "He thinks the only thing that scares them more than empaths is *me*."

Jamey snorted. "Well, maybe you're the answer then. Most crooks don't want to take the fall for their cronies. Maybe Owens knew he was going to be killed by an empath, and he wanted something even scarier to go after his partners. And maybe he thought that was you."

Grayson appeared to be thinking that over as they came around to the front of the car.

"So what's our plan?" she asked.

"I could use some bait."

"Not a problem." She took a step forward.

"Detective."

She looked over her shoulder at Grayson.

"It's risky," he said. "You're resistant to empathy but not

immune, especially not to a corrupted empath, and if Ms. Falcon gets her hands on you—"

"I'm not a detective anymore." Jamey looked back to the dry dock that held her brother. "And it's not a problem."

Grayson stepped to her side. "Then you draw Ms. Falcon's attention. And I'll do the rest."

He turned to leave. She cleared her throat. "Agent Grayson."

He stilled expectantly, handsome face fixed on her.

Jamey cocked her head. "Are they a brother or sister?"

"Who?"

"The empath in your family tree."

He paused, and for a long moment she thought he wasn't going to answer. But then he finally spoke. "Brother."

"And what's his opinion on your career choice?"

"I doubt he has one." Grayson's drawl was flat as ever. "He's dead."

Sudden sympathy flooded her stomach. "I'm sorry for your loss," she muttered, knowing the words weren't enough.

"I've moved on," was all Grayson said.

And then he was gone.

Chapter Twenty-Eight

I still don't get why they insist we both need to be here. I just have a weird feeling about this.

*—final text message on an empath's phone,
recovered at a San Francisco crime scene*

We're waiting for someone?

The next piece of the plan. Your sister.

Something in Reece flared with dark heat, like black lightning. "No," he said sharply to Cora. "Me you can have. My sister's off-limits."

Cora laughed. "Jason Owens gouged his own eyes out because I made him *want* to. You think I've still got limits?"

Despite her graphic words, his knees held steady, buoyed by his anger. "Leave my sister alone."

"We all have our trigger points. Our loved ones, our heroes." Her eyes flashed and she jerked her head toward Whitman. "Vanessa here keeps a list of them. One of mine was John."

Was John. As far as Reece knew, there was still no trace of her fiancé, alive or otherwise. "Where is he?"

"I could tell you," said Cora. "But it would make your nightmares worse."

Not a lie. Shit. "What did you do to him?"

"Oh, Reece." She leaned forward. "I loved him with all

my heart. I would never have hurt a hair on his head. So what makes you think it was me?"

Also not lies. Reece felt his nails bite into his bare palms, and looked down to find he was clenching his hands into fists. Something dark was building at the back of his mind, like the low rumble of thunder before a summer storm.

"I'm so glad you came to see me yesterday," Cora said conversationally, as if they were back in her office at the hospital. "After I escaped the engine room on the yacht, I knew I was different but not exactly how. But when I got my hands on Senator Hathaway, I discovered I could change her emotions as easily as changing a channel. And when she started bleeding from the eyes, I thought of your nightmares. And I wondered."

She tilted her head. "You're not a normal empath anymore either, are you? I bet you haven't been since March."

Reece gritted his teeth. He wasn't going to think about March right now. "It was a bad read."

"And you walked away with nightmares you can't shake," Cora said. "Did you get any new powers too?"

Reece went cold. "No."

But Cora grinned. "Liar."

Reece stilled. "What did you say?"

"You're lying." She tapped her ear. "I can hear it now. It was the first new thing I could do, and how I knew there was no going back to who I was."

No going back? No—no, she had to be wrong.

"So what can you do now, Reece?" she asked. "What are you hiding?"

Reece took deep breaths and didn't answer.

"That's all right," she said patiently. "I'll find out."

He watched her swing her feet, knocking the side of the boat like blood wasn't starting to trickle down Whitman's cheeks only inches from her hands. "What do you want with Jamey?" he bit out.

"I could tear this city apart on my own," she said thoughtfully. "But I've always been more of a team player."

Chills erupted over Reece's skin.

"Of course, in your current state, you're worse than useless," she went on. "But I feel certain your sister's coming, and she's going to help me evolve you too."

"No," Reece said, and stepped forward. "I can help you."

As the words left him, he blinked.

That hadn't been a lie.

Before he could think on it further, the door at the far end of the dry dock creaked.

"Reece?" Jamey's voice echoed off the warehouse walls.

"Get out of here, Jamey!"

"Reece!" He heard relief and concern in his sister's voice, heard her break into a run, light steps that echoed so quickly they could only be hers.

As she came up on their boats, Cora held up a hand. "That's close enough."

Jamey stopped. Her gaze flicked from Reece to Cora to Whitman.

"Briony St. James." Cora's once-sweet voice now twisted Jamey's name into something chilling. "Just the girl I want to see." She cocked her head again. "What's wrong with you?"

"Really?" Jamey gestured at Whitman's bloody face. "What's wrong with *me*?"

Cora laughed. "You're different. Everyone else I can feel, like hot little suns of emotions burning around me. You, though—you're cold. Barely there. Like a ghost."

"A ghost can't throw your tiny ass clear through the wall of this dry dock," Jamey said flatly. "Your murder spree stops now."

Cora only smiled. "Stop this." She put a hand on Whitman's face—and Whitman screamed.

The pain and terror in Whitman's voice drove like an ice pick into Reece's heart. He was stumbling forward without thought. "Don't don't *don't*—"

"Enough!" Jamey's shout rang off the boats. She put both hands in the air. "Not in front of Reece."

Cora casually took her hand off Whitman's face. The screams stopped, replaced by soft moans as Whitman slumped to the deck. "As long as we understand each other."

Reece took a shuddery breath. *You're worse than useless*, Cora had said. And she was right; he was nothing but a liability, a puppet with strings everyone could use to yank Jamey around.

"Between us girls, I don't think Vanessa here is going to last much longer," said Cora. "I've been swinging her moods around like a carnival ride. It's not good for the heart." She looked Jamey over openly. "You, though—I think you're going to be a challenge. But I've got some ideas."

Reece's eyes narrowed.

Jamey straightened, ready for a fight, but it was Reece who stepped forward, rage building—

There was a small *snick*, the soft sound loud in the cavernous warehouse. Whitman made another sudden cry of pain.

Reece gasped, gaze locked on the dart in her arm—

"Tranquilizer," came the familiar drawl.

Cora hit the ground on hands and knees, retching hard, as Grayson jumped down from the highest row of boats and landed easily on his feet.

"You already got used to being queen of the chessboard." Grayson approached her, and Reece was pretty sure he'd expected that *Cora* would throw up the first time she heard his voice. "Didn't account for a pawn off your radar."

Cora gagged again, and despite everything she'd done,

Reece's stomach lurched in sympathy. But her eyes were narrowed in understanding as she looked up at Grayson and said hoarsely, "You're the one they call the Dead Man."

"I keep saying it's not just a nickname," said Grayson.

Cora couldn't fight Grayson. It was over.

Reece let out a shaky breath, his knees weak as the adrenaline left him in a rush. But Jamey was there, her steady arm around his waist to keep him upright.

Cora still knelt on the ground, coughing. On the deck of the boat, Whitman's eyes had closed—tranquilized, Grayson had said. Not dead.

Grayson's gaze darted to Jamey. "Reece needs to leave."

"Could not agree more." Jamey began to pull Reece away, down past the boats.

Reece dug in his heels.

"Reece," Jamey said, with urgency in her voice, like she was considering carrying him out of there. "Come on."

But Reece couldn't move. He could *feel* it in a way he'd never felt an emotion without touch before, prickling like static against his skin, rolling off Cora like the incoming tide.

Fury.

"Can you feel that?" he whispered.

"Feel what?"

"She's angry."

Jamey shook her head no, but they both looked over their shoulders, where Cora and Grayson were facing off.

"You don't want an uncorrupted empath to see us fight?" Cora's voice was mild, but Reece could hear the rage under it, like a pressure cooker building. And he could see it in her face, a cornered animal, claws unsheathing.

"There won't be a fight," said Grayson. "There's not a single empathic ability that works on me. There's nothing you can do."

Cora's face was flushed, her jaw tight. But then, suddenly, her face smoothed out, triumph flashing in her eyes as she calmly said, "Then I surrender."

Lie.

"*Evan!*" Reece lunged against Jamey's grasp. "Evan, she's lying, get *down*!"

Grayson dove into a skiff just as the dry dock doors burst open in a hail of gunfire and thundering boots.

Reece was bodily lifted off the ground as Jamey threw him into the closet boat and jumped in alongside him. "Shut your eyes," she ordered.

"But—"

She shoved his head to the floor of the boat. "*Don't. Look.*"

Gunshots echoed off the fiberglass sides of nearby boats. Had someone been hit? Reece tried to lift his head. "Is everyone okay—"

She shoved his face back down. "I said don't look." This time, her hand stayed on his neck, keeping him in the boat. "It's a SWAT team. Maybe more than one."

Reece's stomach plummeted. "*SWAT teams?*"

Gunfire and shouts surrounded the boat, fury in every hard voice.

Jamey ducked down next to him. "Jesus, there's at least fifteen of them."

Fifteen. Shit. "But *how*?" Reece whispered. "Where did they come from? How did they find us?"

Jamey shook her head helplessly. "No idea. Stone Solutions wouldn't have sent them—although they'll probably show up *now*, since the fuckers spy on everyone."

Another round of gunfire echoed through the dry dock. Someone cried out. Reece felt the ricochet like the echo had left cracks in his bones, phantom pain breaking out over his skin like burns.

Jamey peeked over the skiff's edge, then ducked down again. "What a fucking mess—they're fighting Grayson and each other. *Why?* How can Cora control this many? She didn't touch anyone."

"It's not control, it's p-projection." His voice broke, and he realized he was shaking, the only steady point Jamey's strong hand on his neck. "She's projecting her own anger, that's why I felt it. Officers already tense before battle—they can't resist, she lit them up like a match to gasoline."

"And if she does manage to touch them, she can thrall them." Jamey's tension was palpable. "And Grayson's going to be holding back, trying to spare their lives."

More shouts came, louder, closer. "She's got other plans for us," Reece whispered. "She'll enrage them and thrall them and send them all after Evan."

"Fifteen SWAT officers, armed and devoted and furious—he can't fight all of them." Jamey pulled their foreheads together. "I need to help him."

"Jamey—"

"I can help Grayson stop all of the SWAT officers without killing anyone, but only if I know you're safe."

"But—"

"Listen to me." Reece had never heard Jamey so serious. "You can't watch. The violence, maybe the death—that might be one of the triggers that could start the corruption in you."

And Reece understood. "Like in March." Their eyes met. His lower lip trembled. "Corrupt me further, you mean."

"I meant it the way I said it." She lifted her hand off his neck. "Keep your head down. If you want me to protect you, to help Grayson, to make sure no one else dies, you *have* to stay down. *Promise me.*"

He swallowed. Then he nodded.

She leaped from the boat. Reece curled into a tight ball on

the floor of the boat and pulled the hood of the sweatshirt over his head. A second later came the sickening crack of bone against bone; some unfortunate SWAT soldier on the receiving end of her fists.

He screwed his eyes shut, trying to ignore the gunshots, the shouts, bones breaking. But did it matter if he heard it? If he saw it? He was corrupted already.

And he'd spread it to Cora when she read him. Jamey didn't know that part, didn't know all of this was his fault.

I can help you, he'd said to Cora, right before Jamey appeared.

And it hadn't been a lie.

Maybe, if Reece could just get to Cora, he could stop this.

He lifted his head. He could still feel Cora's battle fury against his skin. He could keep his eyes down, follow the emotion like a thread and find the source without ever watching the violence around him.

He scrambled out from the boat. He moved down the row, darting from boat to boat, eyes fixed on the ground. Cora would feel him coming, but if he could just get close enough for touch—

Suddenly, there she was, not hiding at all but openly coming his way, flanked by two SWAT officers. Their expressions were blank save for devotion, and he could hazard a guess who they were now devoted to.

Cora grinned. "You're coming for me." She spread her arms in welcome. "Come get me then."

I can save you.

It hadn't been a lie. Reece broke into a run. He had to try— Jamey was faster.

She leaped over a boat and crashed into Cora before she and

Reece could touch. A second later, the two women smashed down onto the concrete.

"Jamey!" Reece's shout of horror echoed around the dry dock.

No, no, no—Cora's words hadn't been for him, they'd been for Jamey.

Reece found new speed in his body, lunging for his sister.

But Cora's two thralled SWAT officers grabbed him, holding him back. "No, let me go!" Reece yanked uselessly against their hold. *"Jamey!"*

Cora and Jamey rolled over and over on the concrete, Cora finally coming out on top with both of her hands on Jamey's face. Jamey's eyes were wide with shock.

But then Cora gasped, her hands clutching her head. Her face contorted and she fell off Jamey, and Jamey turned on her side and retched.

Reece gasped and Jamey looked up.

Reece's heart stopped in his chest. Something was creeping into Jamey's eyes, something that wasn't his sister.

Jamey made a noise that wasn't at all like herself either. She shut her eyes, shaking her head like she was trying to clear it.

Cora curled in a fetal position. She groaned in pain before her eyes rolled back and she passed out. The SWAT officers holding Reece slackened their grips and he broke free, sprinting toward Jamey.

"Stay back!" Jamey's ragged order stopped him in his tracks. She was still on the ground, one hand up to stop him. Her face was screwed up, her body shaking. "Reece—"

She blinked, and he saw it—red in the corner of her eyes.

And then she was on her feet, sprinting for the dry dock doors.

"Come back!"

Reece lunged after her, too fast, his stupid legs a trembling mess that buckled under him. He tumbled to the ground, a burn searing his palms as they slid out in front of him on the concrete.

He pushed up, ignoring the pain in his hands, planning to shove himself to his feet—

But giant boots were in his way, and the gun in his face wasn't a tranquilizer.

"*Now* you're under arrest," said the Dead Man.

Chapter Twenty-Nine

*Do not make the mistake of thinking an empath can be reha-
bilitated. When they reach that point, they can only be stopped.*
—*classified training manual, Stone Solutions' internal enforcement team*

Reece stared up at Grayson, palms stinging, arms shaking.
"What are you doing?"

Grayson didn't lower the gun. "My job."

"Jamey needs our help," Reece snarled, "and you're wasting time with your *riddles*—"

"This is no riddle. My job is keeping the world safe from
corrupted empaths." He gestured at Reece with the gun. "Like
this one."

Oh no. No no *no*—

"Nice trick," said Grayson. "Hearing lies. How long've you
been able to do that?"

Reece stared pleadingly at him. "Evan, my sister—*please*—"

"Don't waste your breath begging. It doesn't work on me."
Grayson said it in the same flat tone he'd said everything since
they met.

"But Jamey—"

"The longer you stall, the longer it'll be before I can go
after her—"

"Since March," Reece blurted.

Grayson stilled. Reece got the sense that wasn't the answer he expected. "Keep talking," said Grayson.

"The bad read—the worst." Reece's voice cracked. He didn't want to talk about this, didn't want to relive it, but Jamey needed help.

"Crime scene with the SPD?"

Reece shook his head. "I used to have my own place, a basement studio near downtown." Because Jamey liked the quiet, with her sensitive ears, but Grayson was right, Reece hated isolation. He'd wanted to live in a busy area where there were always other people about. "The family upstairs was on vacation. I was home alone when I heard it."

"Heard what?"

Reece swallowed. "Pain," he said hoarsely.

The memory surfaced, seared into his mind in terrible clarity. "There was a man in the backyard. Cops called him a meth-head, in the report, said he was breaking into the main house upstairs. But I didn't see him trying to get inside. I saw him lost in the grass, foam on his lips, convulsing."

"You ran to him," Grayson said, "and forgot you'd come straight out of your house and weren't wearing gloves?"

Reece winced again. "Yes. Now please—"

"What happened next?"

Reece shook his head helplessly. "Report said he'd overdosed on a bad combo, but when I touched him, all I felt was agony. And I couldn't pull away."

Grayson's expression hadn't changed once. "Then what?"

"Jamey." Reece blew out a breath. "She was supposed to be camping with Liam, but he'd gotten sick, so they came back early." His throat was tight. "A neighbor had heard the man in the yard and called it in, and Jamey heard my address on the police scanner. She got there first—kicked the fence down trying to find me. But she was too late."

"You felt the man die?"

Reece had felt the man's emotions vanish like someone had just—turned him off. Reece distantly realized he was shaking. "I don't know what happened next. I blacked out, and woke up three days later at Jamey's place. And when she said everything was fine, I could hear her lie."

"What do you remember from those three days?"

Reece looked up at the roof, anywhere but Grayson's dead eyes. "Her begging me to hold on."

If Grayson found that interesting, it didn't show on his face. "Any other side effects?"

"Nightmares. Insomnia. Fun stuff like that."

"You hurt anyone?"

"What? *No.*"

"You want to?"

"No!" *Lie.* Reece flinched. Was it the corruption, twisting his truth? Did the corrupted part of him want to hurt people, and that made Reece a liar?

Regardless, Grayson didn't seem remotely convinced. "Hearing lies starts the corruption," said Grayson. "Maybe you really managed to stall it for months or maybe you're the best actor I ever met, but either way, you're dangerous."

"Then *help me*," Reece snapped. "You think I *want* to hear myself lie about hurting people? You think I want to be a monster? You say you're an empath specialist, not a hunter, so *help me.*"

Grayson only cocked his gun as calmly as he'd pushed the sushi menu across the table. "You wanted my help, you should've asked for it in March."

"I didn't think you were *real* in March—"

"You know how real I am now. And you've had chance after chance to tell me the truth today."

"And why would I have," Reece said, through clenched teeth, "when you told me all day not to trust you?"

"Because I also told you corrupted empaths get new powers," said Grayson. "You had to wonder if it was happening to you."

Reece flinched. "If I had told you," he said hoarsely, "would you have bothered to listen? Or would we just have ended up like this sooner?"

"I guess we'll never know," said Grayson. "Because you're the biggest liar in this city, and I'm not gonna start believing you now."

"But—"

"And what I would or wouldn't have done doesn't matter," Grayson said. "There is no help."

The words hit like a sucker punch.

No help? No way to stop the nightmares and lies? No way to make sure he could never hurt anyone?

"That can't be," Reece whispered.

"I've been trying all day to protect you from this fate, I just didn't know I was too late. Corruption's a one-way street. Once it starts, there's no coming back."

"Don't tell me that," Reece said desperately. "Don't tell me I'm doomed."

But Grayson shook his head. "Your powers will only get stronger, and you'll become willing to use them for pain and worse as the sadism sets in. You say you aren't a murderer yet, but you will be."

A murderer.

Not just any murderer, but one with abilities other people didn't have. This was why Grayson was above the law, why he could operate however he chose. He was the last fortress that stood between sadistic superhuman killers and innocent people.

And now Reece was on his way to becoming the monster of other people's nightmares, and there was nothing he could do to stop it.

He closed his eyes. He couldn't bear it. "Then why haven't you already killed me?"

"Have I ever said I kill empaths?" Grayson gestured with the gun. "Get up."

Reece didn't move. "But I thought—"

"Thought what?" said Grayson. "I'm not your partner. I'm not your ally. And I'm not your friend. Now get up." He took a single step backward but didn't lower the gun. "Slow."

Reece still didn't move, just stared up at Grayson, chest heaving. "If I cooperate," he said, trying to keep his voice steady, "will you promise to save Jamey?"

Grayson stared at him for a moment. Then he said, "Yes."

Reece let out a shaky breath but slowly got to his feet. All around the dry dock, the SWAT team members were on the ground, chests rising and falling.

Alive.

And Whitman and Cora were alive too, Whitman on the boat across the dry dock, Cora on the concrete where she'd fallen off Jamey.

"Phone and wallet on the ground," Grayson said. "My truck keys too. Kick it all my way."

Jaw tight, Reece did as he was ordered.

Grayson lifted the phone, the battered wallet and then the keys up into his hands with neat flicks of his boot that let him keep his eyes, and his gun, on Reece.

Reece's gaze went back to Cora, his chest aching. "What did Cora do to Jamey?"

"You're well aware I'm not in the answer business."

"Evan, *please*."

Grayson's gaze went to Reece's eyes as he tucked Reece's

things away. Finally, he said, "An unstoppable force met an unmovable object."

"I don't—"

"A corrupted empath versus your sister's innate resistance to empathy; they were too evenly matched."

"You've seen it before?"

Grayson nodded once. "Ms. Falcon was knocked out, but it won't hurt or change her."

"And Jamey?"

Grayson's gaze flicked to Reece's eyes again. "She'll teeter between sanity and madness until one state of mind wins."

"Which one?"

Grayson pocketed his own keys. "We'll find out."

Reece's throat tightened. Grayson pointed at the closest boat, a small but pristine skiff with a blue canopy. "I need to deal with Dr. Whitman and Ms. Falcon first."

Reece clenched his jaw but went where Grayson was pointing.

"What was it you promised me earlier? Your empathy doesn't work without touch? Not at all, never has, today was the first time?" Grayson had pulled out his handcuffs. "I had it right the first time I cuffed you."

"At least you bought me dinner this time," Reece muttered.

"More the fool me, then," Grayson said. "I needed a reminder that the Dead Man can't be trusted—or trust anyone else. I'll remember this. Up against the boat."

"You don't have to cuff me. I'll stay put."

"You haven't *stayed put* even once today. You think I'm gonna take chances now?"

With a huff, Reece held out his arm, and Grayson snapped a cuff around his wrist, over the hoodie he'd given Reece, without ever making contact with his bare skin.

"You never touch me anywhere but the gloves," Reece said, before he could help it.

Grayson snapped the other cuff around one of the canopy poles on the skiff. "Should've realized you're so touch-starved you'd notice that."

That stung. "Yeah, I noticed," Reece bit out. "You need the protection that blocks my empathy? Is the big, bad Dead Man really that afraid to touch an empath?"

"Maybe," Grayson said, in his lazy drawl. "Or maybe you should remember my voice made you and Ms. Falcon vomit and ask yourself just what my touch is gonna do."

Reece's eyes widened.

"But if you're so interested in finding out—" Grayson leaned toward him.

Reece shrank away and shook his head rapidly.

"Good choice," Grayson said dryly, pulling back.

Reece's gaze went past Grayson. Cora hadn't moved from where she'd passed out on the dry dock floor. She looked like she was sleeping, like the same old Cora, small, harmless, sweet as sunshine.

Reece's throat tightened. She'd tried so hard to help him yesterday and look how he'd repaid her. "What are you going to do with Cora?"

"I gave you enough answers already."

"Maybe I could—"

"No." Grayson started to walk away.

"But I think her corruption is my fault," Reece blurted.

Grayson paused, turning back toward Reece, and tilted his head like that didn't make sense to him. "How do you figure?"

Reece might as well tell him; his truths were all out and he had no reason to keep secrets now. It would be a relief to confess. "I saw Cora yesterday, at the hospital, as her patient.

She was trying to help me with my nightmares. She read me and passed out."

"John Doe," Grayson said, almost to himself.

"I think that read spread my corruption to her," Reece said. "Please, let me try to help her, let me try to take the corruption back—"

But Grayson shook his head. "It wasn't you."

"What are you talking about?" Reece snapped. "Of course it was me. It had to be me; how else would she have—"

"It wasn't caused by you on accident," Grayson said. "It was caused on purpose, by bad people doing very bad things. And I'm gonna deal with them, just like I'm gonna deal with you, and with Ms. Falcon, and with Dr. Whitman, and with your sister. I'm gonna deal with everything. It's what I do."

"But—"

Grayson cut him off. "You didn't corrupt Ms. Falcon."

And despite everything, Reece found himself believing Grayson. Maybe later, he'd even be relieved. "But I could still try to help her."

"No," Grayson said. "If she gets her hands on you, she *will* try to make you a murderer."

"And why would you care?" said Reece. "You just said corruption's a one-way street. You said I'm already a monster and beyond hope. What have you got to lose by letting me try?"

Grayson hesitated, his gaze lingering on Reece. And then he turned away without a response.

"You could give an answer once in a while!" Reece glared at Grayson's back. "Hey," he snapped. "You made me a promise."

"A team is already looking for Detective St. James," Grayson said, not turning around, "and has been since the moment she ran."

"A *Stone Solutions* team?" Reece said, in horror. "No. I want you to do it."

Grayson gestured around the dry dock. "I got two empaths keeping me busy."

"You. Only you," Reece repeated stubbornly. "And I want Jamey unharmed."

Grayson did pause at that, turning to look over his shoulder. "She's strong as a bear and out of her mind."

"But you can still save her," said Reece.

Grayson gaze darted to the cuff. "No flinch that time. That's not a lie, then—you really believe that." He shook his head. "Bad idea, believing in me. Look where it got you."

Reece curled his hands, nails biting his palms.

Grayson's face gave nothing away as he said, "Any final words? It's you, I know you've got them."

Reece stubbornly looked away.

"Suit yourself. I've got some."

Reece couldn't stop himself from looking up at him, the blank hazel eyes and expressionless face that had somehow grown familiar in a short time.

"I'd be dead without your warning," said Grayson. "You gave yourself away to save my life. And I ought to say thanks."

"Manners? *Now?*" Reece rattled the handcuff. "Don't bother. I don't want your thanks."

Grayson shrugged. "I cost you your freedom. Can't blame you for regretting it."

Reece watched him walk away, toward Cora. He wished he could say something biting about how he should have just let Grayson die.

But he was tired of lies.

"I don't regret it," he whispered to himself, as he slumped against the boat. "Your life was worth the price."

Grayson stilled, and too late Reece remembered he had the same too-good hearing as Jamey.

Then a new voice cut through the dry dock. "Hands up, Agent Grayson."

Shit.

Agent Nolan emerged from behind the forklift, his gun up. "Didn't hear me come in, did you?" he said bitingly. "Too busy fighting the SWAT team? Or is the great Dead Man in too much pain to pay attention?"

Reece's gaze shot to Grayson. Reece hadn't seen any pain on his face, but he should have remembered he never saw *anything* on Grayson's face. And it was so obvious now that Reece looked for it, how Grayson was favoring one leg, hunching around his ribs.

"I'll heal," Grayson said flatly. "How about you put that gun down, Agent Nolan? You don't look well."

Nolan laughed, a mad edge to it. His eyes were suspiciously red-tinged. "On the contrary. I can finally see my path to revenge. You're a dead man, Dead Man." And he laughed again, unsteadily.

A sickening shiver went down Reece's spine. Like the SWAT team, this was rage too, but colder, a vengeful and calculated fury. "Did Cora get to you?" Reece said in horror. "Or is this what her projection did—"

"Shut up!" Nolan's snarl echoed off the dry dock. "I'm going to kill you too, empath." He gestured with his gun at Grayson. "I'm just taking down the biggest monster first."

"Wait—" Reece automatically moved forward, only to jerk against his handcuff.

"Not the time, Care Bear," Grayson said, his eyes on Nolan.

"I'm going to help—you said I'm corrupted, maybe I can project too—"

"Reece, *stop*." Grayson's drawl was quiet but unmistakably an order. More loudly, he said, "Agent Nolan, put the gun down."

Nolan laughed again. "Make me."

Reece squinted as something new flashed on Nolan's chest, a small red dot, like a laser pointer—

Oh *no*.

"Evan," he whispered, body freezing up. "Evan, his chest—"

"I see it." Grayson glanced up at the boats, then back at Nolan. "Agent Nolan, we have been surrounded by a Stone Solutions team. If you make a move against me, they'll kill you."

Nolan furrowed his brow. He glanced down at his chest. "Oh, a sniper," he said, with an eerie calmness. "I should have seen that coming."

"Agent Nolan has been thralled." Grayson's voice was louder, loud enough to be heard around the dry dock as he called, "Do not shoot him in front of the empath, do you copy?"

"Negative, Agent Grayson," came an answer from somewhere in the rows of boats. "Our orders are to prioritize the Dead Man's life over everything else, empaths included."

The red dot was still on Nolan's chest. Reece tried to get air into his lungs, phantom pain flaring along his sternum, across his ribs. Distantly he realized he was shaking. *"Evan."*

"It's gonna be okay, Reece," Grayson said, never taking his eyes off Nolan.

Nolan laughed his crazed laugh. "Looks like it's going to be a race then."

It happened in slow motion.

Nolan aimed his gun at Grayson.

Grayson leaped toward Reece.

And as Grayson's hand touched his, Reece's knees gave out, darkness rushing him as he fell backward, seeing rows of boats and the distant ceiling above, feeling the cuff bite his wrist as gunshots echoed through the dry dock.

And then everything was black.

Chapter Thirty

Unforgivably shortsighted, to talk about extermination where there is still use to be extracted from the empaths. We've barely started to mine their potential.

—unsigned note at [redacted]

"Ouch."

With a wince, Jamey lifted her head off dirt. *Dirt?* Oh. She'd fallen.

She rolled over to her back, sharp rocks jabbing at her ribs. A creek was babbling nearby while above her head, pine trees and naked branches stretched toward the dark sky and hazy milk clouds that hid the stars.

All she remembered was running east, away from the marina and city, away from people, then everything had been red. How far had she run with Cora's empathy in her system?

She exhaled, her frozen breath ghostlike in the dark. Her face was uncomfortably sticky. Maybe she'd hit her head on the rocks? *Because blood on your face from a head wound is better than the alternative explanation*, she thought grimly, as she wiped roughly at her cheeks with her sleeve.

Fumbling awkwardly for her hip, she managed to extract her phone from her jeans pocket and turn it on. The call was answered on the first ring.

"Jamey!" Aisha Easterby was shocked enough Jamey could hear it through the haze. "Are you all right? We heard—"

"Send Grayson."

"But—"

"Only Grayson to get me. It's too dangerous for anyone else. *I'm* too dangerous."

"I *can't*." Easterby lowered her voice, quiet but strained. "Grayson's out of commission. There was a confrontation, he got hurt, he needs more time."

"I don't think I have more time." Something warm was trickling down Jamey's cheek. She was going to pretend it was sweat. "Can Stone Solutions handle me?"

"We've got the resources to handle Grayson if he ever turns against us. But—"

"Send Stone Solutions, then."

"Jamey—"

"The biggest and baddest you've got."

"You don't want Stone Solutions to come for you," Easterby whispered tightly. "I can send the police—"

"*No.*" Faces flashed in Jamey's mind, people she would never want to hurt.

"Who's Liam?" Easterby said, and Jamey realized she must have said his name out loud. "Never mind, I've got a lock on your phone." Easterby's voice was warped, like she was balancing the phone against her shoulder. Computer keys clicked in the background. "You're pretty far from any cities. Maybe it's safe to wait for Grayson—"

"It's not." Far above the trees, the night was finally giving way to the thin dawn. Jamey blinked and saw flecks of red in pale gray light. "You know what empaths can do to their thralls?"

"Yes, but—"

"I'm already faster and stronger than most people." Jamey blinked again, and more red spotted her vision. "Cora's empathy is still in my blood. Think what I could do to innocent people."

Easterby's voice dropped to the barest whisper. "The people who will come from Stone Solutions are not innocents. They're going to come armed—guns, Tasers, chains."

"If Stone Solutions doesn't come for me," Jamey said, "someone else could find me. And Aisha, I don't want to hurt anyone." She raked her sleeve over her eyes again. "Send a team or I'll call 911. I know Stone Solutions will intercept the call anyway."

Easterby swore. "All right," she whispered tightly. The computer keys were clacking again, even faster. "All right. But you owe me an empath's phone number after this. Doesn't have to be your brother's, but you do have to get it for me, because I don't get out much and my coworkers are corpses."

Jamey snorted. There was a thundering in her ears, like a stampede, and it was getting louder.

"Hang in there." Easterby sounded very far away. "It's going to be okay, stay with me—"

But the words were swallowed up by the roaring in Jamey's ears as the dawn drowned in red.

"Ouch."

The pain was the first thing Reece became aware of again, his head pounding like a bass drum as he cracked open one eye. There was a gray cloth roof-liner above his head, faintly matched by the thin gray light of morning. His hands were cuffed on his stomach and there was cushioning underneath him.

He let his head fall back to the fabric beneath him. "This isn't the Dead Man's truck."

"Empath's awake."

Reece leaned his head to the side, seeing two men he didn't recognize in the front of what seemed to be an SUV. "Did you drive with me on your back seat?"

The men ignored him. The one in the passenger seat touched his earpiece. "We're parking now—"

"You didn't even buckle my *seat belt*?"

"Shut up," said the driver.

"You could have had to slam the brakes," Reece protested, as the two men climbed out of the front, leaving the doors open. "And I would have flown forward and hit the windshield and put both your lives in danger, and then you might have swerved and then hit someone else—"

The door at Reece's feet opened. "Let's go," said Passenger.

He reached in, grabbed Reece, and yanked. Reece went flying out of the SUV, cuffed hands too clumsy to catch himself, and hit the pavement hard enough to hurt. The next moment, the man had Reece on his feet again, clutching his arm in a bruising grip with a hand covered in thick black material that was too familiar.

"Are you two wearing *empath* gloves? There's no way you're empaths."

"You're right," Passenger snapped. "But you are, and we're not stupid enough to touch you without protection."

"There's a sex joke in there somewhere," Reece muttered.

They frog-marched him toward the building, and Reece recognized where they were: the back of the Stone Solutions high-rise, where he'd snuck in through the service elevator. Had that really only been hours ago?

Driver had a gun out and on Reece. Reece ignored him. "Where's my sister?" he demanded, as Passenger pulled him toward the other door, the one labeled *No Admittance*.

"We told you to shut up," said Driver.

Reece ignored him. "Where's Agent Grayson?"

Driver and Passenger exchanged a look. "The Dead Man's down for the count," Passenger said.

"What?" Reece stumbled. They were moving too fast for him to keep up. "What happened at the dry dock?"

"Didn't you know?" said Passenger. "The Dead Man's touch knocks empaths out. He did our team a favor, leaping for you, but he took the FBI thrall's bullet doing it."

Reece's heart stuttered. "Evan was shot?"

"Don't get your hopes up that it's more than a nickname now," Passenger said curtly. "The Dead Man's not like the rest of us. If anyone can beat a bullet, it's him."

Driver unlocked the *No Admittance* door, which led to an upscale waiting area for another elevator. In the elevator, Driver scanned his thumb, and then pressed the button for the roof.

The elevator began to rise, and Reece's stomach plummeted.

Less than a minute later, the elevator doors opened into a glass room. The roof stretched out before them, a helipad at the far end. And in the middle of the roof was the man from Adams' picture, from the AMI meeting, from TV.

Cedrick Stone.

The glass room's doors opened automatically. The two men pulled Reece down the roof toward Stone, whose face was set in a blandly pleasant expression, characterless as an unadorned white wall. "Mr. Davies," he said, hair and long coat blowing in the wind. "We finally meet."

Reece cringed. The timbre of Stone's voice was all wrong, worse than Whitman's had been, straitjacketed into an unnatural flatness that revealed no emotions. Stone was ringed by half a dozen men and women in uniforms, all of them wearing empathy-blocking gloves like his handlers.

"Gloves all around, huh," Reece said sarcastically.

Stone smiled like an actor onstage. "Some people believe a good offense is the best defense."

"I don't care about your offense or defense for me," Reece said. "Where's my sister?"

Stone gestured to the sky. Reece looked up, and saw the helicopter approaching. "On her way," said Stone.

He said it easily, but something about it still put chills on Reece's skin. "Is she hurt?"

Stone smiled again, and this time, Reece caught something under the mask, like the edge of a rock barely hiding the decay beneath. "She matters a great deal to you, doesn't she?"

Cora's voice echoed in Reece's head, and too late, he heard it for what it was: a warning, from one empath to another.

We all have our trigger points.

"We have a very pleasant campus in British Columbia," Stone said. "Cora Falcon is on her way there right now. We can secure corrupted empaths there, true, but it's also a research facility, looking for ways to prevent and even reverse corruption. Between us, I think it's pointless, but Evan insists we try. The pleasantness is also on Evan's insistence, because he seems to think the empaths are also victims in this. Neither would be my choice, you understand, but as you may have noticed, he has quite a lot of sway on account of what he is."

"Is he alive?" Reece demanded.

"Such a typical empath," Stone said, with a sigh. "I'm trying to explain what's going to happen and all you can do is worry about others." Stone bent, so their faces were level. "Really, Mr. Davies, you should be wondering what's going to happen to *you*."

The helicopter was touching down, the wind from the blades sweeping across the roof.

"So we're going to this place in BC, then?" Reece said. "Me and Jamey both?"

Stone nodded. "And don't worry; we're going to take good care of you."

Lie.

Chapter Thirty-One

Sugar and spice and everything vice, that's what little empaths are made of. Some folks have to learn that the hard way.

—unsigned note found in the ashes of a laboratory

Reece's eyes darted over Stone's face, the polite smile, the perfect mask. No one else would ever have guessed. "Liar," he whispered.

Stone went very still. "What did you just say?"

"You're a *liar*," said Reece. "What are you planning to do to Jamey?"

"You heard me lie." Stone straightened up. "Well. Now, that is interesting."

Reece looked across the roof, at the just-landed helicopter. Most of the goons on the roof were rushing toward it. Stone held up a hand, and they stopped just shy of the helicopter. Then Stone beckoned to Passenger and Driver, who forced Reece closer to Stone.

"You can hear lies." Stone was studying Reece's face, his eyes, intently. "But I don't think you're fully corrupted, because a corrupted empath wouldn't reveal himself out of fear for someone else. Could it have resulted in partial corruption, then? Fascinating. I didn't know that was possible."

"What are you talking about?" Reece demanded.

"The dying man in your yard," said Stone, like it was obvious. "We thought you hadn't been turned at all, and we chalked that up to the two of you being strangers. Added a nice little data point to our research. But we were wrong, because you're a liar too, Mr. Davies. A corrupted empath walking around my city as if you're not a danger to everyone in it."

Reece stared at Stone. "How do you know what happened in March?"

"Not much point in hiding if you can hear my lies, is there?" Stone said, in his horrible mockery of pleasantry. "Jason and I set it up."

"What?"

"That's right," Stone said, without remorse. "Waited until you would be alone, found a junkie, offered him some very potent drugs, and stuck him in the yard where you'd hear him and come running. Empaths are so tiresomely predictable, but it does come in useful."

"He was in agony," Reece said hoarsely.

"He had to be, didn't he?" Stone said, without remorse. "We had to see what would happen to *you*."

Reece was going to be sick.

"Of course, we weren't expecting your sister to arrive, or to see her kick down a ten-foot fence like it was made of toothpicks. That's also how we learned you had changed your sister, same as Evan was changed. And good thing we discovered that too—we knew to use the stronger chains today."

Chains. All of Reece's questions caught in his throat.

Stone bent to put his eyes level with Reece's again. "If you're already at least partially corrupted, however, that does save me some steps, because you should already have strong enough empathy to figure this out. So tell me—if you were a director of Research and Development at an anti-empathy facility, and you were fleeing an empath who was undoubtedly going to kill you, what would you do with your phone?"

"What?" Reece said, nonplussed.

"Do I need to use smaller words? Write it in crayon?" Stone said. "What did Dr. Jason Owens do with his cell phone?"

"I don't know what you're talking about," Reece snapped.

"Very well. We'll do this the hard way."

Stone nodded at the helicopter and a moment later, the doors opened.

"No."

Four guards were yanking Jamey out. She was wrapped in chains and her face was streaked with blood beneath her eyes and nose. But her eyes were open and clear, and when her gaze lit on Reece, she began to fight.

"I wouldn't bother, Ms. St. James," Stone said, as they brought Jamey closer. "Those aren't run-of-the-mill chains any more than you were a run-of-the-mill detective. They were designed to hold Evan, should it become necessary." He spread his hands. "You see?" he said to Reece. "A good offense comes in handy."

The guards shoved her to her knees, and Reece flinched as bone cracked against the concrete. "Jamey—"

"I'm okay." Reece flinched again at her lie. She wiped her bloody face on her shoulder. "Speaking of Grayson, where is he?"

Reece glared at Stone. "Hurt."

"There was an altercation at the dry dock. Evan chose not to get himself to safety, but to leap into the path of Agent Nolan's gun to knock your brother out," said Stone. "A pointless sacrifice, like so much of what he does, and he paid the price."

"It was brave," Reece said, voice shaking only a little. "Braver than anything you've done in your life, I bet."

"You're coming to his defense; how sweet," Stone said dryly. "Have you already forgotten he arrested you? He must know you're corrupted. If he was here with us, why wouldn't he side with me?"

"He wouldn't," said Reece.

Stone scoffed. "Oh, this should be good. Tell me why I'm wrong, empath, as if you could possibly understand the Dead Man."

"Because corruption is supposed to be a one-way street, but he took that bullet so I wouldn't see Agent Nolan die," Reece said tightly. "Which means there's a part of Evan that doesn't believe I'm a lost cause—some part of him believes I'm still worth saving."

Reece caught the uncertainty that flashed in Stone's eyes. "And that scares you," he realized, "so much you can't hide it. Because if Evan thinks I'm worth saving, he's going to look for me, and you're terrified of him—"

"Enough!" A muscle in Stone's jaw twitched. He turned to Jamey. "Official records will show you both are being transferred to BC. The record will also show that the helicopter had an unfortunate accident on the way. Evan will believe you died in transit and never know the truth."

Reece didn't like the sound of that. "What truth?"

Stone smiled horribly. "I bet your sister can guess. You just focus on my questions, Mr. Davies."

"Or," said Jamey, "how about you don't tell him shit, Reece."

Stone looked at one of the men holding Jamey and nodded once. The man curled his fingers, brass knuckles flashing, and then he cracked his fist against her jaw hard enough to snap her head back.

"No!" Reece lunged against his captors like a dog against a choke collar. "Don't—"

"It's okay." Jamey slowly straightened her head, tilting it side to side like she was simply stretching her neck. "He's going to have to hit harder than that."

There was a new cut on her lip. She was *bleeding.* "I don't care—"

"He doesn't," Stone agreed. "Your brother will answer any questions because he can't bear the slightest act of violence against you."

"Don't hurt her," Reece said desperately. "Please. Just ask your questions—"

"I already did," said Stone. "Where is Jason Owens' phone?"

"I don't understand—"

But Jamey snorted. "Of course." She spit a mouthful of blood, whether from the blow she'd taken or from her nose, Reece didn't know. "I wondered why we were doing this dance up here instead of already on our way, but here it is."

"Here *what* is?" Reece said helplessly.

"You were part of the whole plan, weren't you?" Jamey said to Stone. "The broken webcam Grayson found in the yacht engine room—I bet that was for you. I bet you saw it when Cora broke out of the engine room, and you didn't warn anyone, just bolted for Canada on your helicopter. Did Jason Owens call you as he was speeding back to his house, expecting you to protect him? But you left him to his fate to save your own skin, realizing too late that he had proof of your involvement?"

Stone's expression had grown ugly. "That's enough." He bent to look Reece straight in the eyes. "Use your empathy to figure out where Jason Owens would have hidden his phone."

"Don't tell him anything," said Jamey. "He's planning to kill us either way."

Stone only smiled. "She's almost as charming as you." He held Reece's gaze. "Maybe we don't know everything about empathy, but we know one guaranteed, no-fail way to corrupt an empath. Has anyone told you what it is?"

Reece swallowed.

"You torture the empath?" Jamey guessed.

"Please." Stone scoffed. "Empaths don't care what happens to them. No, if you want to corrupt an empath, you need *someone else's* pain."

Reece went cold to his core.

"You find a trigger point," said Stone. "A person they love unconditionally with their big empath heart—and then you apply *pressure*."

Stone looked pointedly at Jamey, then back at Reece. "So make yourself useful, Mr. Davies, because the moment you cease, you and your beloved sister are going to become useful in another way."

Reece thought he might vomit. There was a ringing in his ears, growing louder. "That's what you did to Cora."

"We'd learned from our failure to change you—or what we thought was failure. We knew we needed someone Ms. Falcon loved. We used her fiancé to induce a corruption in her more impressive than we could have even hoped. I've never known another empath who's picked up new abilities with her speed." Stone's expression shifted, actual regret lighting his eyes for a moment. "Hannah's death wasn't part of the plan, a tragic and regrettable accident. Jason misjudged how quickly Cora would adapt, and he paid the price for that. Rest assured I won't make those mistakes with you."

Stone gestured at Jamey. "Your sister, of course, brings something special to the table too. With her strength, how much pain do you think she'll be able to take? How long will she fight death? I'd be lying if I pretended I didn't want to see just how far we can take your corruption, to see what you'll become."

Reece yanked at his captors' arms again. "Why the hell would you do something like that? Why not just kill us?"

"And waste such a valuable research opportunity?" Stone said incredulously. "Your sister has natural defenses against empathy, and I assure you I don't take losing that research lightly. But we're not the only country with empaths. Imagine: spread across the planet is a field of daisies we barely understand, all ready to become nukes if someone presses the right button. We need to know exactly what those buttons are. And then we need to raze the field."

Reece was suddenly shoved to his knees, inches away from Jamey.

"Take a good look at her, Mr. Davies, and think very carefully about how difficult you want to be. The fate of the two of you is sealed, but you can decide when it comes."

Reece looked into his sister's eyes, streaked below with blood. When he spoke, he tried not to move his lips, and kept his voice softer than a whisper. "Is Cora's empathy out of your system?"

She briefly shook her head no.

Reece's heart sank, and with it, the darkness pushed forward a little further. "I'm not letting them do this—"

"Don't you dare," she hissed. "We did not get through three days of madness for you to go dark side now."

"Break them up," Stone snapped.

Reece was yanked backward, away from Jamey. He could feel something in his blood, like simmering water about to break into a boil. Could he do what Cora had done in the dry dock, project his own feelings, set off every minion on this roof, and give the two of them time to escape?

"He corrupted Cora," he said, loud enough for Stone to hear.

"That makes *him* the monster," said Jamey. "Not Cora. *Not you*."

Stone scoffed openly. "Sticks and stones, Detective."

Jamey's eyes darted to the side, past Stone, so quickly Reece almost missed it. Then she lifted her chin. "If you think I'm just here to be broken to break my brother, you're in for a surprise."

She blinked, and to Reece's horror a bloody tear escaped her eye. "You've seen what happens to an empath's minions, how an empath can turn up their strength and speed to my level. But I can still feel Cora's empathy in my blood; she's jacked up all my senses. How strong do you think she made me? How much faith have you got that these chains are going to hold?"

Stone's expression flicked with sudden fear.

Then Jamey swept her leg out toward one of the men holding her, so fast and hard Reece heard bone snap. She dove backward as the man's shriek of pain was accompanied by the sound of guns drawn all over the roof.

But Jamey wasn't running for the elevator. She'd jumped to her feet and backward, to the half wall surrounding the building's edge, not flinching from the twenty-two-story drop behind her to the ground below.

Reece's heart leaped to his throat.

"Hold your fire," Stone said sharply.

All across the roof, his lackeys hesitated.

Reece tried to lunge for his sister, tried to fight the men holding him. "Jamey—"

"Get down," said Stone.

Jamey took a step back, closer to the edge. "You don't have me, you don't have a way to corrupt Reece."

Stone drew his own gun and put it to Reece's temple. "Get. Down."

But Jamey didn't flinch. "You won't kill him."

"Why wouldn't I?"

"Because you need me to figure out where Owens' phone

is before Evan finds it," Reece said, the answer tumbling from his lips. "You'll do anything to stop the Dead Man from finding out what you've done."

Jamey made a sad face. "What a shame you're too late."

Stone froze. "What?"

Something small and black sliced the air in front of Reece like a bullet. It struck Stone's hand and he shrieked in pain, dropping the gun and leaping back. The gun clattered uselessly to the roof on top of the shattered remains of a—cell phone?

"Appreciate the distraction once again, Detective."

Grayson.

He was next to the glass room with the elevator, the door to the emergency stairs closing behind him. He was listing slightly to the side, and his coat was covered in blood.

But he was here.

"Evan," Reece whispered.

"Evan." Stone's mask was gone, nothing hiding that fear. He looked at Jamey. "But how did you—"

"Heard feet running up the stairs." She smiled with narrowed eyes. "Fast ones."

Grayson took a step forward. "Woke up in a hospital," he said. "And funny thing was, no one seemed real keen to let me leave. But I had to insist, because I remembered it's been an awful long time since I checked my drop box here at Stone Solutions."

Stone took a step back. "I can explain—"

"And good thing I did." Grayson nodded at the ground and the smashed remains of the cell phone. "'Cause I had a package waiting."

Stone had gone pale as a ghost. "Evan—"

"Did you know Dr. Owens was recording y'all's phone calls? You, in particular, had a lot of interesting things to say about empaths. And speaking of empaths—" Grayson slid the coat from his shoulders and tossed it to the side. "Care Bear, be a peach and close your eyes so your sister and I can kick some ass."

Reece barely had time to screw his eyes shut as chaos broke out around him. The helicopter took off, rising passengerless into the sky. The men holding him let go as they shouted and chased after it. Reece hit the roof on hands and knees and awkwardly scrambled forward, trying to get to Jamey.

Boots were suddenly in front of him, blocking his path. He looked up at one of Stone's lackeys, into an angry face and outstretched gloves—

Jamey slammed into the man with her shoulder, sending him stumbling into another man Reece hadn't even seen coming so they both toppled to the ground. She jerked her head at the elevator. "You shouldn't see this."

Reece scrambled up to his feet. "It's ten against three—"

"It's about to be ten against two once I get you the hell out of here, and Grayson and I are not going to hold back."

Reece choked on a hysterical noise. He was trying so hard not to watch the fight, but he could hear gunshots and blow after blow hitting home. "Jamey—"

"Move your feet, Reece, let's go."

Together, they stumbled across the roof, Reece still in hand-cuffs, Jamey with the chain around her arms. Another man popped up in front of them, but Jamey kicked him in the chest, sending him flying across the roof and into the industrial HVAC system hard enough to dent it.

Reece cringed, an echo of pain flaring along his own back and spine.

"Sorry." Jamey wiped her face on her shoulder. "I'm still a little more *me* than normal."

Reece looked at her in alarm. "Jamey?"

These red tears were new.

She blinked hard. "I told you Cora's empathy wasn't out of my system yet. But I'll beat it. Am I lying?"

He bit his lip and shook his head no.

"I believe I can beat it," she said. "But I need to know you're safe. Come on."

They stumbled another few steps and then—

"Get down!" Jamey slammed into Reece, sending him stumbling behind a planter.

He gasped as he saw the bullet hole just feet from where he'd been.

"Cover your eyes." And she was gone.

Reece drew his knees to his chest and buried his face between them. This time he wouldn't look. This time he would stay put and let Grayson and Jamey handle it, let them turn Stone and the evidence on Owens' phone over to the police.

Except Grayson had—

No.

Reece scrambled up to his feet. "Evan!"

He sprinted forward, trying not to look at the unmoving bodies that littered the rooftop, focusing on Grayson's tall figure across the roof.

Grayson was standing over Stone, who had a gun raised in one shaking hand. With unnerving calm, Grayson planted his foot down on that arm, and Stone screamed.

Reece pushed himself faster. "Evan—"

"Reece." Grayson was holding Stone's gun hand down under his foot. "You've got to learn to run away."

"Please don't kill him," Reece begged.

"What makes you think—"

"You destroyed Owens' phone. You only would have done that if you didn't plan to need the evidence against Stone."

"You really think you got me figured out," Grayson said. "What you got is sixty seconds to get yourself in the elevator and out of here."

"Don't." Reece bit his fist. "Please."

"You hear that?" Grayson said to Stone. "You were gonna make him a monster, and now he's begging me to show you mercy."

Stone spit blood. "We all know you're the biggest monster here."

"You're the monster," Reece said angrily. "Not Evan."

Stone laughed hysterically. "Oh, naive little empath. I've got nothing on Evan Grayson." Stone spit again, and Reece realized in horror that he'd lost some of his teeth. "Has Evan told you his secret? Why he can stomach any act of violence without a flinch? Why his voice makes you vomit, why his touch knocks you out? Why they *really* call him the Dead Man?"

Stone looked up at Grayson, no mask now, just bitter hate. "Because he's as dead inside as a corpse. His feelings aren't hidden from you. He doesn't have feelings at all."

Stone wasn't lying.

"But that's impossible," said Reece. "No one would be born—"

"Oh, he wasn't born that way," Stone said hatefully. "An empath changed him."

Reece drew back. He looked up at Grayson, but the man's face was as unreadable—as dead—as ever.

"Was it really necessary to make him hear that?" Grayson said, as calmly as if he were remarking on the weather.

"He thinks you're his knight in shining armor," said Stone. "He's already forgotten you turn on your allies faster than the wind can change."

"You're not an ally." Grayson stepped closer to Stone. "You think you're gonna corrupt empaths on purpose? Twist them into killers for your scientists to study, so you keep swimming in profit? I don't need feelings to have an opinion on that."

"I bet you don't," Stone said viciously, like his words had a deeper meaning Reece didn't understand.

Grayson only tilted his head. "The folks in this city have forgotten why empaths are off-limits." He pressed harder with his boot on Stone's arm. The gun fell from Stone's hand, clattering to the rooftop. "Ms. Falcon took care of Dr. Owens. Your death needs to be worse."

"No!" And before Grayson could pick up the gun, Reece flung himself to his knees, a shield between Stone and Grayson.

"Care Bear—"

Reece moved his cuffed hands so his fingers were only inches from Stone's face. "If I touch him, I'll feel all that pain."

Stone froze. Grayson's gaze darted from Reece to Stone, then back to Reece. "Move, Reece."

Reece stretched his hand even closer, close enough he could feel the heat radiating from Stone's skin. "I'll do it. I'll touch him. You won't kill him if I'm reading him because of what I might turn into."

Grayson held still as a stone. "You got to stop presuming to know me."

Reece lifted his chin. "He's the monster. Not us."

Grayson might have hesitated.

But it was too quick to tell, because at that moment, an inhuman roar cut across the roof.

Jamey.

There was nothing of his sister in that sound. Reece looked over in horror to see her sprinting right toward Reece and Grayson, blood on her cheeks again, no hint of sanity or recognition in her face.

"Jamey, stop!"

The words had barely left Reece's throat when Grayson stepped forward and grabbed her.

And then pivoted and threw her off the roof.

"NO!"

Reece lunged forward. But the handcuffs caught on Stone's coat, and Reece's hand landed on Stone's face.

Only instead of reading anything from Stone, Reece's rage and grief burst out from him and into Stone, ensnaring him completely.

Reece's vision narrowed to just Grayson's dead face. "How could you?"

"Reece—"

"Shut up." The black lightning had rocketed to full charge, ready to strike. Stone was wholly his, the man's face slack, his emotions locked tight in Reece's mental fist. "That was my sister."

"I—"

"I said *shut up.*"

Grayson's eyes darted to Stone's face. Reece was distantly aware Stone's fingers had closed around the gun again, blood already welling in the man's eyes, trickling from his nose.

But Reece didn't let Stone's emotions go. "Maybe you're immune to empathy," Reece said, shoulders heaving, "but how about a bullet?"

And full of Reece's heartbreak and fury, Stone lifted his gun in broken fingers and aimed straight between Grayson's eyes.

Grayson didn't flinch.

And Reece knew now it was because he couldn't feel fear. Or regret. Or joy, or love, or anything at all.

Because an empath had stolen his heart and made him a living dead man.

For a long moment, neither of them moved.

Then Reece slumped. He pulled his hand away from Stone, and the man dropped the gun, his head lolling back against the roof. His bloody eyes closed, his chest rising and falling as if in sleep.

Reece slowly put his shaking hands on his head.

Grayson didn't speak for several moments. Then he finally said, "I don't understand."

Numbness was swallowing up the black lightning, sending it back to whatever cave in Reece's mind it hid in. He heard shouts as police officers began pouring onto the roof through the elevator room and the fire stairs.

But he kept his gaze on Grayson's boots. "Don't you remember what my surrender looks like?"

Grayson's eyes never left Reece as he held up a hand to the approaching SPD. The officers stopped a few feet away from them, weapons raised, confusion on all of their faces.

Then Grayson said quietly, for Reece's ears alone, "You could have killed me."

Reece closed his eyes. "I know."

"But you didn't."

"I didn't."

Grayson, for once, didn't seem to know what to say.

Chapter Thirty-Two

The world needs the Dead Man. What the Dead Man needs can never matter.

—crumpled note in Evan Grayson's handwriting

Down in the reserved parking space in the parking lot of Stone Solutions, Reece sat on the open tailgate of Grayson's truck, still in Grayson's too-big hoodie, his cuffed hands in his lap. SPD officers bustled around him, giving him a wide berth.

He should already be in prison by now. No doubt Grayson had warned everyone that Reece couldn't be taken to a normal prison. Maybe they'd take him to an empath prison, or that place in British Columbia. Maybe they'd lock him away in the basement of Stone Solutions.

Maybe none of it mattered anymore.

He heard the echo of big boots on the pavement, the sound of someone perfectly capable of moving with silence who wanted their approach to be heard.

Reece swallowed. "Did I kill Stone?"

Grayson stopped only a foot away. "No."

A straight answer for once. Reece tried to feel relieved but found he couldn't feel much of anything. Or maybe he felt too much of everything. Shock, for now.

The grief would come.

"Reece."

Reece took a slow breath and reluctantly looked up.

Grayson's blood-stained coat was gone, replaced by a navy blue SPD sweatshirt that was stretched too tight across his shoulders. His arms were crossed around his body for warmth, the sleeves at least three inches above his wrists. "I have to show you something."

His face was, as always, a vault. Reece didn't think he could bear the sight, especially now that he knew why.

He looked away. "I realize you might not be the most emotionally sensitive person in the world," he said, through a tight throat, "but even you can't think I want to see you right now."

"I'm sure you don't. I have to show you something anyway." Grayson pointed up the side of the building. "Look."

If he looked, maybe Grayson would go away and leave Reece to his numbness alone, so he grudgingly tipped his head back and squinted into the gray skies.

And then he stilled.

Ringing the high-rise around the twentieth story were the safety nets Reece had wanted yesterday, the ones Grayson had told Whitman to install to protect the window washers. Only now, SPD officers were riding up the side of the building on the washers' lifts—and that wasn't a window washer caught in one of the nets.

Reece's heart leaped.

It couldn't be—

Grayson leaned against the open tailgate. "I didn't kill your sister."

Jamey. Reece covered his mouth. "Is she—"

"Alive. Some bruising, but this is your sister; she's just gonna walk that off. She kicked the last of the madness too. She's gonna be fine."

Jamey was alive. Reece couldn't stop staring at the scene in the sky, his heart pounding and fit to burst in his chest.

Then he realized what Grayson had done. "You knew the net was there." He tore his eyes off Jamey and stared at Grayson. "You threw her into the net on purpose."

Grayson shrugged.

Reece thought he might cry. "Why didn't you *tell* me? On the roof?"

"You weren't really in a place to listen."

"But I could have *killed you*!"

"You didn't."

A laugh escaped Reece, half sob, half hysterical. "You're impossible." He blinked back the hot wetness stinging his eyes. Jamey was *alive*. "I'd hug you right now if it wouldn't knock me out," he said, wiping at his eyes as an officer walking by began whistling a happy little tune.

Grayson glanced at the officer. After a beat, he looked back at Reece as he lifted up a set of keys. "Ready to get out of the cuffs?"

Reece blinked. "I'm not under arrest?"

"I was under the impression you didn't care for it the first time. Or the second. But if the third time's the charm—"

"No, of course not, but—" Reece looked around, then lowered his voice. "I tried to kill you."

Grayson shrugged. "Nobody's perfect."

"Even you can't just blow that off!"

"It's not like it makes you special. More than a dozen folks have already tried and it's not even noon."

"But Evan—"

"Mind the hands."

Grayson bent, the movement shifting the sweatshirt's crewneck to show the edge of white bandages beneath. Reece held very still as Grayson unlocked the cuffs, careful not to let their bare skin touch. "Will I ever be able to touch you without getting knocked out?"

Grayson raised an eyebrow.

"Hypothetically," Reece hastily added, rubbing his wrists.

"You do remember I'm the one who put these cuffs on you?" Grayson said, as he tucked the handcuffs back onto his belt.

"Nobody's perfect," Reece echoed lightly, and don't think he hadn't noticed that wasn't a straight-up *no*. "I'm surprised the cops got here so fast."

"Mr. Lee called them."

Reece furrowed his brow. He squinted at the group of officers at the base of the high-rise and realized that yes, there was Liam's camel-colored coat in the sea of navy. Liam was wringing his hands, and his head was tipped far enough back to put a crick in his neck as he stared up at the officers bringing the lift to Jamey in the nets.

"Your sister never checked in with him last night like she promised," said Grayson. "He paged me through the police scanner."

"Paged *you*?" Wow. Liam had sought out the Dead Man for Jamey. "And you told him to come to Stone Solutions and bring the whole department with him?"

"It didn't take any convincing. He's a brave one, and I get the sense he's all the way in with Detective St. James."

Reece watched Liam watch Jamey. "Yeah," he said, with a tiny smile. "Yeah, I think he is."

"Well, now you've got each other, and you've got Mr. Lee." Grayson pushed off the truck. "And I better—"

"Don't move," Reece snapped, gratified when Grayson actually stilled. "You got hurt for me. You came to *save* me. How can you claim to be some kind of dangerous empath hunter—how can you be called the *Dead Man*—when you did something like that?"

Grayson leaned back on the truck. After a moment, he said, "You know what I really am now."

Reece bit his lip. "Stone said an empath changed you."

Grayson nodded once. It almost seemed like he wasn't going to say anything more, but then he said, "My brother."

Reece's heart stilled.

"Alex became corrupted. I tried to get him help. I asked the wrong people."

"Evan—"

"It's not a story an empath would ever want to hear." Grayson's eyes were fixed on the scene in the sky. "Just know there are worse people than even Mr. Stone out there, and I try to make sure they stay in the shadows."

Reece swallowed around the lump in his throat. "I thought you didn't have feelings."

"I don't. But I have memories. And I see Alex's ghost in every empath I meet." Grayson finally looked at Reece. "So now you know the truth about the Dead Man. He's not really a hunter *or* a specialist. He's vengeance."

Vengeance. Maybe, but not only. "Protection," Reece murmured. "For the world, and for us."

"That's a very empath way to put it," Grayson said. "But if you like."

Reece met his eyes, and this time, the blankness didn't make him want to look away. "Then who's Evan Grayson?"

"Gone," Grayson said simply. "Evan Grayson is the real dead man. I have my memories, but the man I once was might as well be six feet under, because there's nothing of him left."

Grayson said it with no hint of sadness or regret.

Because of course he did.

Reece's heart twisted. He leaned in closer. "You know I can't hear it when you lie," he said quietly, "but I think you might have just tried to tell one."

Grayson was the one to break eye contact that time.

They stayed in silence for a several moments, watching the platform with Jamey get closer to the ground and Liam moving in to meet her.

"We've leaked some select details to the press," Grayson finally said. "Hathaway's murder is being pinned on Stone. Your sister's getting the credit for catching him. She'll be off suspension before lunch." He held a business card out to Reece. "But if she's done with the force and ever looking for another job, tell her to get in touch."

"You want her to be the Dead Woman?"

"Never."

Reece accepted the card, plain white with only a phone number and a single word: *Vanguards*. "This wouldn't happen to be for some kind of new, Dead Man–led super-secret spy team?"

"Wouldn't be a secret if I answered that." Grayson pushed off the truck again. "So here we are. A whole day's gone by, the real perps found, but I've still got the same problem I've had since we met."

"What's that?"

"What do I do with you?"

The question sounded completely genuine, like even Grayson didn't know. Their eyes met again.

"You have to do something with me," said Reece. "I don't ever want to become—well. You know."

"I do."

Reece looked at the card in his hand again. "Can this team help?"

"That's why I formed it. One of the reasons, at least." Grayson nodded at the card. "Call that number. They'll help you get new gloves, get you on a check-in schedule, all of it." He cleared his throat. "And if you need more incentive, they already got your car back. Kind of a shame; I was gonna re-place it."

Reece snorted. His gaze stayed on the card. "And if they ever suspect I'm slipping, will they call you in so you can stop me?"

"Yeah," Grayson said quietly. "They will."

Reece blew out a breath. "Good."

"*And* they'll call me in if they think you're a target." Grayson added dryly, "I know you forgot that part because you're only thinking of the danger to other people, but I didn't."

Reece glanced up, and no, absolutely nothing about Grayson made him want to look away anymore. He waved the card. "So this is like a hotline, then?"

"Someone'll answer, no matter what time you call."

"But it's not your number?"

"No."

"Oh."

Grayson tilted his head. "I'm no expert on feelings, but that sounded like disappointment. And I gotta be honest, I don't know why you'd be disappointed to hear that."

Reece tried to shrug. "It'd just be nice to know I could call you. Just—you know. If I ever needed to."

But then, Grayson had said it himself: they weren't friends.

But maybe they weren't enemies, and maybe that was enough.

Grayson eyed him for another moment, then nodded in Jamey's direction. "She'll want to see you."

Reece hopped from the tailgate to the ground, eager to confirm for himself that Jamey had made it. But he looked back at Grayson, standing by his truck in the sweatshirt that didn't fit.

Alone.

Reece wrapped his arms around himself. "What about you?"

"I have business waiting on me," said Grayson, all mysterious like he thought he was.

"What kind of business?"

"The kind I wouldn't tell an empath about."

"I hate your riddles." *Lie.* Huh. Reece had so many words fighting for space, but what came out was, "You, um. You probably want your hoodie back."

Grayson didn't answer that, instead pointing over Reece's head. "Go see your sister."

Reece turned to see the lift reaching eye level, heard the cheer rising through the waiting officers like a rolling beat on a kettledrum.

He sprinted forward, a couple officers catching sight of him and clearing a path through just as the lift touched ground. "Jamey!"

He reached for her, but she was faster, jumping down from the lift and wrapping him up in a hug so tight his ribs protested. His eyes felt hot again as he pressed his face to her shoulder. "Are you okay?" he asked.

"Yes." Not a lie. "You?"

He blinked hard and nodded, then hugged her as tight as he could before pulling back.

Then her eyes darted to someone behind him. He glanced over his shoulder and saw Liam standing apart from the crowd. He was watching the two of them and shifting from foot to foot, hands jammed in his pockets.

Reece opened his mouth to say something, maybe *there's another hero* or maybe just *thanks*. But then Liam said, *"Jamey,"* and Jamey was past Reece in a blur of motion, throwing her arms around Liam's neck. He hugged her back, so tight he lifted her off the ground.

And maybe Liam didn't know yet that Jamey could have lifted *him*, along with some of the officers, without breaking a sweat. But based on the way they were so clearly trying not to make out in front of half of Seattle's police force, Jamey was going to tell him soon, and Liam was going to handle it just fine.

Reece turned, thinking he'd go back to Grayson—

But the black truck was gone.

Reece's smile disappeared. The reserved space looked too big now, too empty. He found himself walking to it anyway.

He reached the *Reserved* sign, leaned against it, and sighed. That was it, then. Grayson was only coming back if his team decided there was danger, and Reece didn't want danger, so no more Grayson.

And that should have been fine. Good, even. Grayson was the Dead Man; Reece should want him to stay gone.

He looked at the too-empty parking space, and sighed again.

He'd call the number on the card Grayson had given him, but he would need a new phone first. And to get that, he'd have to beg a ride from someone, figure out how to scrounge up for it—

"Reece Davies?" A man in a courier uniform was coming his way down the sidewalk.

Reece scratched his head. "Yeah?"

The courier held out a padded envelope. "For you."

Reece furrowed his brow but took the envelope and tore it open. He reached inside, and his hand closed around something soft. He withdrew a new pair of gloves, not stiff like his old ones but flexible and nice to the touch, and pinned to one of them was a note in neat handwriting.

New model. Needs beta testing.

Interesting. But there was something else still in the envelope. The hoodie sleeve slid down over his hand as Reece reached in and pulled out—

His cell phone?

On the screen was a text, not from an unknown number but from an area code he didn't recognize. He opened the message.

THIS is my number

Reece let out a surprised laugh. The phone in his hand beeped again.

If you need me, call me

Reece bit his lip, still smiling as he texted back.

Any reason?

Any reason

He still had Grayson. Reece's heart felt lighter as he sent another text.

What I need is for you to stop texting while driving

Should have seen that coming. Never change, Care Bear

Reece's fingers tightened on the phone.

Above his head, the clouds had cleared for once. He took in the morning sun, bright in the sky, and exhaled.

★ ★ ★ ★ ★

Author's Note

Liar City's alternate Seattle takes inspiration from the real Seattle, but apart from the setting, all people, corporations, organizations, and abilities described herein are intended as entirely fictional.

Acknowledgments

So much gratitude to those who helped this book become reality:

To C, always, for believing in me;

To LP & JW, for their support and encouragement, and to my family and friends;

To Victoria, who met Reece and Grayson in their early days;

To Arianna, who's been there through sunshine and rain, who cheered for this book when I really, really needed it;

To my author crew, who console for the lows and celebrate with the highs;

To my readers—I am endlessly humbled by your enthusiasm and love;

To my editor, Mackenzie Walton, whose keen eye and skills have helped me find the path forward from the 1920s to an alternate Seattle;

To the Carina Press team who make our books shine—Kerri, Stephanie, and the art, marketing, and production teams;

And to T, who brings me more joy than I knew could exist.

Julien Doran does not believe in monsters.
But he's going looking for one.
Read on for an excerpt from
Pack of Lies *by Charlie Adhara.*

Chapter One

It was exactly the sort of place you'd expect to see a monster. A lonely mountain road, a forest so old it creaked. Hell, it was even a dark and stormy night. Or dark and snowy, anyway. But the way the wind was hurling restless flurries against the windshield as the trees swayed vengefully overhead was enough to put even the most assured traveler on edge.

Julien Doran had never felt less sure of anything in his life, and he'd hit that edge at a running jump about two weeks and two thousand miles ago. Right around the time he'd turned his back on everything—the shambled remains of his family, career and common sense—at the suggestion of a dead man.

He might still get lucky. He might never make it to the elusive Maudit Falls and instead spend the rest of eternity driving up and down these mountain roads until, eventually, he'd become just another one of the dozens of urban legends the area seemed to collect like burs.

They could call him Old Doran. The Fallen Star. Forty-four years of carefully toeing the line distilled down to this one inarguably absurd decision, and told at bedtime to frighten children into obedience. Don't you know better than to throw your life away on a lie, little one? Do you want to end up like Old Doran? A man who turned down the first role he'd been offered in four years to instead take a secret flight across the country. A man who thought he could open a wound so recently closed, it still wept at the edges. A man who went looking for a monster.

Listen, they'd say. If you listen really closely, you can still hear his voice echoing through the mountains, calling out, *What am I doing here? What did I think I could change? Did I miss my turn?*

Julien glanced at the GPS on his phone, but it was still caught in an endless limbo of loading, the service having cut out about fifteen minutes ago.

"The town proper is on the other side of the mountain," the clerk at the last rest stop had told him. A woman with metallic-rose eyeshadow, a name tag that said Chloe and the unmoving smile of someone sick of delivering the same canned dialogue to every wide-eyed, monster-hunting tourist who passed through. "You'll see plenty of signs for Blue Tail Lodge as long as you stay on the main road. But whatever you do, don't get out of your car after dark. That's when Sweet Pea is his most dangerous."

Chloe had gestured with rote unenthusiasm to the huge display by the counter. A rack covered in souvenirs, and a six-foot-tall cardboard cutout of an ominous, pitch-black figure with glowing green eyes. It had hooves for feet, long, delicate claws instead of hands and the flat face of a primate, obscured by shadow. The figure was standing up on two legs but sort of stooped over, arms held awkwardly as if caught midway through dancing the monster mash.

"Mr. Pea, I presume," Julien had said, reaching out to touch one long cardboard claw. Then he pretended to shake its hand and added in a deep, formal voice, "Mr. Pea's my father. Please, call me Sweet."

Chloe's smile hadn't flickered, which was very fair. Rocky would have known what to say. He would have known the right questions to ask, the right words to use, the best attitude to strike to get Chloe on his side, talking and spilling secrets that couldn't be sold on a souvenir rack.

"Have you ever seen it?"

"Me? No." Chloe shook her head. "But my sister's ex was out hunting and swears it passed right through the campsite. Tore into his cooler and stole all his coyote traps."

"Wow. That's…" The way it always was. *No, I've never seen anything. But my dentist's kid's teacher's nephew woke up in the woods with less beer than he'd remembered packing and a missing ham sandwich. Alert the media—they walk among us.* "That's something."

"Are you in Maudit for—"

"The skiing," Julien cut her off quickly, and launched into his own canned dialogue, taking the opposite approach to Chloe, his voice a little *too* bright, smile *too* mobile, overselling his story. "I would never have thought of North Carolina for it, but a friend recommended the slopes here. He said it's snow without having to freeze your, ah, nose off."

"We get our fair share. And plenty more than that up the mountain," she said, watching him closely, the beginnings of the same frustration in her eyes he'd seen in dozens of people trying to place the face behind the glasses, the fading stubble, the lines that grief and age had carved in unequal measure around his eyes like permanent tear tracks. "I'd pack an extra pair of thermals if you're skiing Blue Tail this weekend, though. For your, *ah, nose?* There's a cold front coming." She tapped the box of single-use heat packs by the register pointedly and Julien dutifully placed a handful on the counter.

He attempted a casual nod at the looming cutout. "Why 'Sweet Pea'? Not exactly the most intimidating name."

"Well, he doesn't need it, does he? Anyone around here knows you don't want to be caught out at night with a monster like that, whatever you want to call it." She plucked a deck of novelty playing cards off the display and placed them on the counter next to the heat packs. "Everything you need to know about Maudit Falls and its most infamous residents is in here. Only $21.99. You know, something to do when you're not *skiing*." That's when her eyes had widened in genuine excitement. "Hey, aren't you..."

Of course he'd bought them. How could he not? Sweet Pea wasn't the monster he was hunting. But it was why Rocky had first come to Maudit Falls, and Julien was here because of him. Why else would he book a vacation in a town whose idea of a fun roadside souvenir was fifty-two spooky local legends? Why else had he done anything at all this last waking nightmare of a year?

Now, as he took a particularly sharp curve up the narrow mountain road, Julien wished he'd left the cards behind and bought a map instead. One a little easier to follow than what Rocky had left for him. This simply could not be the way into town. It wasn't even plowed, for goodness' sake. Just sort of tamped down, which gave the road a colorless, unfinished look. Like nature itself had been peeled back to expose a slippery layer of quilt batting. On the other hand, it wasn't like he'd passed any paths more traveled. There'd been one unmarked turnoff that couldn't have been anything but a service road. That or the perfect set for the first ten minutes of a horror film, which might still be the case considering the seriously questionable choices that had led him to—

An animal leapt in front of the car. Julien had a split second to register the huge, dark shape darting out of the woods, the twin reflection of headlights bouncing off inhuman eyes, staring directly at him, before he jerked the wheel instinctively to the right at the same time a thud rang in his ears.

Weightless slipping. The feeling of suddenly being airborne without getting out of your seat. And then the car dropped down with tooth-cracking finality, directly into the snowy ditch.

For a long moment the world felt impossibly still and silent. Empty. He couldn't hear himself breathing. He couldn't hear himself think. Julien lay against the steering wheel, dazed, pain-free and peaceful for the first time in over a year. Then, like a lever giving way, his body sucked in an agonizing gasp of air. With it, the gears of his brain began to grind once more, and it all came flooding back.

"No, no, no," Julien whispered. He disentangled himself from the locked-up seat belt and opened the door, barely thinking, and then had to catch it when the gravity of the tilted car sent it hurtling back into his shin. Julien climbed quickly out of the ditch and stumbled down the road, unusually clumsy. "Please no. Please, please, please." His hands were shaking, a low, constant tremble, and his arms felt so light, so flimsy that he had the nonsensical urge to let them float above his head, like untying two trapped balloons.

Julien squeezed his fists tight at his sides. Enough. *Do something. No one else will.* He scanned the road, walking back to where he'd swerved, looking for the animal. Not wanting to see it—needing to find it.

But there was nothing there.

Julien found the gouged snow, dark with dirt where he'd first slammed on the brakes and skidded off the road, but that was the only sign of the violence he'd braced himself for. No body or blood. No fur or feathers. No sign that he'd hit anything at all. Except he had.

Hadn't he? That awful soft thud. Not soft in volume but in texture, if sound could have such a thing. Body-soft. Maybe it hadn't been hurt. He hadn't been going fast. Not at all. Even slower than the limit, with all this snow. Maybe the animal had been able to roll over the car and just keep running?

Julien stalked from one side of the road to the other as if he'd find some clue as to what to do now. As if the animal might have left a note with a sad face and its insurance information. He'd never hit anything before in his life. If it had been there in the road, he could call…animal control? Some sort of wildlife rehab, maybe? But would they send someone to hike into the woods at nine at night to track down a wild animal that may be injured or may be fine?

Julien blew out a long breath that clouded in the air and reluctantly walked back to the car. With no cell service it was a moot point. He'd need to hike down the road until he could get bars, anyway. He'd need a tow truck, too. The very top of the windshield was shattered and long cracks ran like roots over the rest of the glass. The rental company wouldn't be pleased.

The right front corner of the car was flattened, as well. A pool of headlight glass was sprinkled like multicolored confetti in the snow. *Congratulations! You fucked up big-time!* Oddly, there wasn't any other sign of damage in the front. Not that Julien could tell. Nothing on the hood either. Almost as if the only point of impact was the windshield. Was that even possible? If so, maybe the animal really was less injured than he'd feared.

Julien got closer to examine the roof. Even with the car at this awkward angle he was tall enough to see two distinct dents, right in the center. "What the hell?"

Julien ran his hand over one. It was about the size of his palm but distinct. More than a mere ding. As if something heavy had…what? Landed on its feet, then launched itself into the air and kept running? The paint was scratched, too. Four short contrails behind each dent.

Carefully he dragged his own four fingers down the white marks, and the back of his neck prickled as if someone was watching him.

Julien turned, scanning the road and the dark forest beyond. "Hello?"

Barely more than a whisper, his voice still sounded disrespectfully loud. It was only then he realized just how quiet the surrounding woods were. *Unnaturally quiet.* Like every living thing was collectively holding its breath.

Julien took a couple steps into the road, and his boots made a soft creaking sound on the tightly packed snow. "Hello? Is someone there?"

No one answered. Nothing made a sound. Well, of course not. What had he expected? Sweet Pea to waltz out of the trees doing his best Lurch impression? *You rang?*

Julien snorted at his own uneasiness. What did he know about the *natural* amount of noise wild animals were supposed to make, anyway? The closest he ever got to nature in L.A. was when his ex-wife Frankie sent weekly photos of Wilbur the mountain lion sneaking over her fence at night to drink out of the pool. He'd gotten one early that morning in the airport getting ready to board.

Call me back. I'm worried about you. And so is Wilbur!

He'd call her eventually. When he had good news. Or at least something better than this. If he told her he was in Maudit, he'd have to explain why, and right now he couldn't even explain it to himself. He couldn't even *think* it without wondering if the whispers were true. That maybe after years of being wound so tight, something in him really had just snapped.

Julien hauled his bag out of the car, ignoring the subsequent ache in his chest where the seat belt had bit into muscle and skin. There wasn't any sense second-guessing it now. He was either going to find what he was looking for in Maudit Falls or he wasn't. If the latter was true, he'd have proof that Rocky had been wrong, and there was nothing hidden on this mountain but superstition and perilous infrastructure. And if the former…well. He'd cross that bridge when he came to it. Hopefully in a working car.

Either way, he wasn't going to find anything sitting around alone in the dark. He'd done plenty of that these last four-teen months already. Julien began the long trek back down the road, phone in hand.

Ten minutes later, the cold air killed his battery.

"Dammit," Julien whispered. Then, wondering why he was bothering to whisper, yelled it again as loud as he could, followed by a string of every curse he knew. Considering his upbringing on the back lots of Hollywood, that occupied a significant amount of walking time.

It took another fifteen minutes of swearing before Julien finally came across the lone turnoff he'd passed before. *Maudit Falls Retreat*, claimed a very discreet wooden sign tucked back into the woods. It wasn't abandoned or a service road at all—it was some sort of place of lodging. Julien felt a wave of relief. Here there'd be people, power, maybe even a bed for the night, if he couldn't get a ride on to Blue Tail Lodge. Julien took the turn.

Even less effort had been made to clear the snow, and soon the legs of his jeans were soaked with frigid water. He began to shiver and his fingers felt thick and clumsy with cold. Despite the urge to break into a jog and get the hell out of the dark already, Julien stuck his hands under his armpits and kept his steady, careful pace. He'd hardly be able to tell people he was here for the skiing with a broken ankle. When researching the area, there hadn't been anything online about a Maudit Falls Retreat. No mention of it in Rocky's notes either. Hopefully that meant it was a small, word-of-mouth bed-and-breakfast as opposed to shut down entirely.

Five minutes later, he realized neither was true as the road spilled into a clearing in front of a large, gorgeous building.

"What are you doing hiding all the way out here?" Julien murmured, impressed despite himself. Two stories, expansive and surrounded by a wraparound porch, the retreat was a mass of polished wood, stone and glass. Most of the front seemed to be windows, and past the reflected moonlight, Julien could make out a low light inside. He tried the heavy wooden double doors, and to his relief they opened.

The lobby was even prettier than the outside—soothing in juxtaposition to the intimidating exterior. The back of the room was mostly taken up by a large wooden reception desk while to the side a couple of comfortable-looking chairs and a couch were centered around an enormous stone fireplace. Wide pine plank floors were polished to a soft gleam that reflected the light of the fire burning low. That and an old-fashioned green glass desk lamp were the only sources of light. The room was completely empty.

"Hello?" Julien called out. His voice echoed and seemed to get lost up in the high rafters. "Is anyone here?"

Julien walked up to the desk. A large painting of a waterfall hung behind it. The titular Maudit Falls, perhaps? The canvas was a violent mess of blues and purples and a lone figure stood on a cliff's edge with their arms extended, as if begging with the water, as if this very scene was where the falls had got its cursed name.

Vaguely unsettled, Julien called out again. "I've had some car trouble!"

Silence. A bed was starting to look unlikely. He walked toward the open door at the back of the lobby and peered into the darkness. He opened his mouth to call out again, but something stopped him.

Julien took a few steps into the hall, squinting into the

gloom. There was an open door on the right, and he peered around the corner. "Is someone there?"

A pair of reflective inhuman eyes stared back at him and Julien yelled out, stumbling backward. The eyes jumped to the ground with a soft thud and a cat darted between his ankles and scurried into the lobby.

"Fuck." Julien exhaled and laughed at himself.

He felt a little ridiculous, but also reluctant to wander farther into the building. Because it'd be rude, and not because his heart had thus far only sunk back down to the general vicinity of his throat, of course. All he needed was a working phone, anyway. Or power. Surely no one would mind that. Julien walked quickly back into the lobby and, with only a second's hesitation, helped himself behind the reception desk. The sooner he could make a call, the sooner he'd be out of here.

There was no landline. But, crouching, he found the outlet the desk lamp was plugged into, deep at the back of a low shelf, and quickly got his charger out of his duffel and his cell hooked up. As he stood, the Sweet Pea card deck fell from his pocket and bounced out of sight. Julien knelt to retrieve it, and yelled a second time when a furry little paw darted out from under the desk and snagged the back of his hand.

"Fuck's sake," Julien sighed. "You know, so far I'm not too impressed by Southern hospitality." He got even lower to peer under the bottom shelf and sure enough found the same cat staring back at him smugly, card deck half tucked under its chest.

"If you're down there looking for a bed that's just right, Goldilocks, mine's upstairs."

A man's voice. Behind him. Julien shot up to his knees so quickly he would have smashed his head into the desk's top ledge if not for the warm, soft hand suddenly cupping his crown just long enough to act as a buffer between his skull and the wood, then gone. The only proof it had been there at all was a faint tingle where he'd been touched and the distinct absence of a painful head.

"Thanks. Hell, you sca-scared me," Julien stuttered. For half a second it looked like the man standing over him had blank, colorless eyes, as flat as the cat's. But then he shifted his weight and Julien could see it was just a trick of the light. They were a perfectly conventional gray. Nice-looking, even, though perhaps a little washed out in a pale face framed by black hair. Slightly less conventional was the dangerously short, peacock blue silk dressing gown he wore over, Christ, nothing at all, if the cling of that fabric wasn't lying.

"My apologies." The man cleared his throat politely and Julien tore his gaze back up, embarrassed. "I'm not up to date on the proper etiquette for interrupting a thief. It seems an invitation to bed only terrifies one half to death. How disappointing for the ego." He squinted at Julien critically. "To be fair, a keen-eyed observer might argue you looked about three-quarters of the way there on your own. To death, that is, not to bed."

Julien gaped, unsure what to feel more offended by first. At least the critics had the heart to call him names behind his back. "I'm not a thief," he said finally, because it wasn't a crime to look old and worn-out quite yet.

"A housebreaker, then," the man said, inspecting one of his own fingernails with a bored expression. "An interloper. Persona non grata, though admittedly you look very *grata* indeed from this angle."

Julien felt warmth spread down his defrosting body and he quickly pulled himself to standing. The bruise across his chest throbbed and he had to bite back a grunt of pain— unsuccessfully it seemed, from the way the man's eyes narrowed with curiosity.

"You're bleeding." It was a statement, not a question, and Julien glanced down at the back of his hand, surprised the man had noticed.

"Your cat scratched me."

"If you're hoping to sue, I should tell you her owner is on his honeymoon and would react poorly to being interrupted."

"Of course I'm not going to sue."

"In that case it's nothing less than you deserve, you trespassing fiend."

"I'm sorry," Julien said haltingly. "I was under the impression that this was a hotel."

The man ran his hand over the wood of the desk with a thoughtful expression. "Is this the *impression* you were under? See, I would have called it a desk, myself, but then I'm a simple, straightforward sort of soul. What you see is what you get."

"Well, I can see quite a bit," Julien muttered under his breath, and to his surprise the man grinned and just leaned back against the wall, causing the robe to slip even higher up his legs.

"And what exactly were you hoping to get all the way down there?" He seemed totally untroubled to be practically naked in front of a stranger. Maybe soaking wet, half-frozen and *three-quarters of the way* to death, Julien didn't look very intimidating. Maybe the man felt physically secure with his younger body and thick, powerful-looking thighs.

The tingling on Julien's scalp where the man had touched him intensified and he dragged an impatient hand through his hair. "I was looking for an outlet to charge my phone."

"But of course you were. I've been known to get on my hands and knees for the sake of an outlet myself. Carry on, Raffles." The man tilted his head to the side, studying Julien in a lazy, knowing sort of way. "Unless you need someone to play Bunny?"

It was the sort of over-the-top flirting men did when they were utterly certain it wouldn't go anywhere. Teasing and unserious with no genuine interest. Meant to fluster and nothing else.

"I said I'm not a thief," Julien said tightly, suddenly feeling as weary and washed-up as he apparently looked. The crash must be catching up with him. "I'm sorry; it's been a hell of a long day."

He thrust his hand out, then quickly retreated when the man simply regarded it with a single raised eyebrow. Fair enough.

"My name's Julien. I'm on my way to the ski lodge, but had an accident a little ways up the road. My phone's dead, so I hiked down this way and saw the sign and, well, yes, I came in and helped myself to the power. I'm sorry if I surprised you or made you uncomfortable at all." He could hardly say it with a straight face. The man didn't look like he knew the meaning of the word *discomfort*. "Are you a, uh, guest here? Owner?"

"No." The man smiled sharply. He had a small heart-shaped mouth that gave his whole face a sort of pointy, foxy look. "I'm a thief." His gaze flickered toward the door with a distinct frown and Julien instinctively did, too, just as a loud banging sounded.

"What's that?"

"Some cultures call it knocking. You wouldn't be familiar," the man murmured, slipping past him with a sway in his hips that did interesting things to the silk.

Julien looked purposefully away and followed him into the lobby just as the man opened the door. On the stoop stood a woman, dripping with blood.

Julien swore and hurried closer. "What the hell!"

The woman took one wide-eyed look at him and sagged forward, forcing Julien to reach out and catch her. Her body felt cold and fragile against his and she let out a long shuddering sob and began murmuring something frantically into his chest. Julien looked over her head for help, but the man in the robe had backed away, expression closed, almost wary, and Julien felt a corresponding prickle of unease.

"Are you hurt? What happened?" he asked.

"Sweet Pea," she cried. "I saw the monster!"

Don't miss Pack of Lies *by Charlie Adhara,*
available wherever books are sold.
www.Harlequin.com